The Fall of the Wizards

Book 1

Bildungsroman

By Paul Calhoun

Beware of
haystacks

Paul Calhoun (signature)

Cover designed by Paul Calhoun

Cover art by Daria Bashutkina

This is a work of fiction. Names, characters, businesses, places, events, locales, and incidents are either the products of the author's imagination or used in a fictitious manner. Any resemblance to actual persons, living or dead, or actual events is purely coincidental.

First printing: September 2019

ISBN 978-1-7330613-1-5

Zunvect's Note, foreword to The Life of the Founder and an Account of the Foundation of Modern Spellcraft pt. 1, an autobiography by Wizard-Lord Zunvect the Sunlord:

This account is inaccurate. It is impossible for me to remember everything that ever happened in my entire life verbatim, especially after the unfortunate events immediately preceding my own death. I recall a great deal in the abstract, but since many of my personal journals were lost millennia before I reawakened, I can only give a partial account from my own perspective. As such, other sources have been inserted occasionally in order to aid completeness, especially in cases where I was either not present or not conscious. My old master, Xetic-Nal - may he one day rest in peace - has been anal to a fault for as long as I've known him and his journals record every important event of his post-vitality. They are not impartial, however, nor are they the complete truth since he would never release documentation that might suggest he'd done many of the evil things I knew he did. Nor would he have made note of many facts which are important to me and to the reader but were of no interest to him at the time. My last major source of recollection comes from the writings of my one-time employee, evangelist, and lab monkey Lorn. Though written from the perspective of a layman who is in the service of a great lord, his accounts have the advantage of being absolutely faithful to events as they occurred. He didn't have the imagination to invent, nor the judgment to abridge. Every word I said in his presence was taken down. I miss that monkey-gnome-thing. He really knew how to do the job.

In any case between my recollections, the writings of my master and my servant, and the odd excerpt from a relevant book of the period, this version will be much more accurate than those of any history book you've likely read about me. You're welcome.

Idalia 1:

A Familiar Setting for a New God

Idalia Periscalitin, Mage of the First Order, knelt before her god. This was Zunvect the Mighty, the Sunlord, Patron of the Magi, and the last Wizard-Lord to die. He was the earthshaker and ultimate thaumaturgical musician. Floating above the stone floor as if gravity was a habit he'd given up long ago, his enormous frame dominated the small chamber she had summoned him into. The room was illuminated only by a few dimly charged crystals, and yet it seemed as if he stood in a summer sun, bright and harsh as the light which leaked from his eyes and spilled from his mouth when he spoke. "Isn't that a little much?"

Idalia, a demonologist, finished the fourth containment circle and began on the fifth. "You're not escaping again." She told him, making her painstaking way around the captured deity. The lightweight navy blue and midnight black outer robe did little to cushion her knees, nor did the sturdy trousers beneath. The robe signified her affiliation as an expert in alien life forms both local and foreign.

"I don't intend to. Actually, I was more interested in the fact that this room is rectangular."

"So?" Idalia snapped, looking up. Her knees were starting to bother her.

Zunvect contrived to look innocent. "Only that geometry suggests that your sixth circle will intersect with the wall. I am a god; it would look very bad for my mistress to ward herself into a corner. Unless you mean to cross the circle afterwards and make this whole exercise pointless."

Idalia threw the conductive pen to the floor and rose, eyes smoldering. She spared a quick glance down to make sure that none of her five gold medals in the shape of whirlpools had fallen to the floor. She normally didn't wear her awards, and was beginning to think that trying to impress Zunvect with her unprecedented number of First Contacts had been a mistake. "I wouldn't be doing this if you weren't intent on destroying yourself. Why did you provoke the most powerful magician in the known universe?"

"He started it." Zunvect whined, quailing before her ire but unable to move because she'd locked him in place. While he looked impressive floating six inches above the ground, it was not by choice. Her wards were perfectly spherical and had nailed him in place with arcane force.

"You stood in the middle of a street and shouted, 'hey boney, let's see how you do this time!' At which point, Lord Xetic-Nal appeared, waved his hand, dissipated you, and told you that you were a colossal ass. Then he vanished again." She pinched her nose. "You're barely four days manifested, Zunvect. How did you expect that to go?"

"I – I don't know." Zunvect said. A staff made of black metal chased with silver flashed into his hand. Glowing spheres orbited each other in complicated patterns above it, and runes glowed in sequence up the length. He gripped it, looking lost as he regarded the spheres. "I don't remember why I even did that. It was stupid and yet … I know it was necessary. I don't remember every aspect of my death anymore, but something about it made me sure I needed to provoke him." He gripped it like he might a lover who was dangling from a precipice. It was his life, and he had given it life in turn.

Idalia looked pointedly at the staff. "That wasn't so easy to get either. Do you know what President Chronomarien said when I offered to trade?"

"Yes." Zunvect said, regaining some of his aloof air. "I *can* perceive the minds of the magi no matter how recent my rematerialization."

Idalia glared at Zunvect. "Don't show off. The staff you made to trade with was better than the one I was trading for, so what did you know that we don't? The President is going to have to answer a lot of questions for letting me take an eight-thousand-year-old artifact offworld. As far as I can tell, it's all been so you can have your favorite phallic replacement back."

"None of that matters."

"The hell it doesn't! The Board of Governors will roast her alive for this, and the Senate will be laughing behind her back if they don't throw her out on the spot. It was bad enough being forced to run offworld and seek refuge here in the Emerald Citadel, but I doubt after this that either of us will be welcome on our homeworld ever again."

Zunvect caressed the length of the staff fondly. "I can't access the minds of the magi like I ought to. Seeing the contents of Silveria's mind to find out what she wanted most took all the mental focus I could achieve. It's infuriating. I am the god of organized magic and the magi *are* organized magic. Your knowledge should be..." Zunvect's gaze cleared and his knuckles whitened again. "This staff belongs to me. That's all you need to know."

"I'm –"

"All right, you also *should* know that it's the repository of my memories up until shortly before I died. That's why I went after Xetic. It said that doing so would be important." His eyes focused for a second. "He didn't kill me. He could have. I mean, he didn't kill me this time. All he had to do was remove all knowledge of me from the memories and records of the magi. A trivial thing for him, if somewhat time consuming." Zunvect's eyes went misty again.

"The memories … they take time to reintegrate. I lost a lot when I ascended."

"Everything."

"Everything but my purpose." Zunvect agreed.

"The Senators are losing their minds themselves right now. When I retrieved you, I…" she looked embarrassed, "I seem to have also freed the entire pantheon from stasis. The Long Silence is over. I imagine the priests must have fallen off their chairs in surprise when their gods started talking to them again after eight thousand years without a word. Imagine praying for generations only to be nodding off after your cup of tea and have God tap you on the shoulder and ask you what the time was. The balance of power is going to shift severely. It'll take centuries to clear up. Still," Idalia added brightly, "at least I have one god in my corner, even if I forced you into it. That ought to count for something when I decide it's time for us to go back. Why *were* you attacking the gates of heaven?"

"It's a long story."

"I bet." Idalia stretched and sat down. "You may as well start then. The Loopies – "

"You shouldn't call them that in their own stronghold. It's very impolite."

Idalia waved her hand impatiently. "They can't hear me and we're about eighty centuries out from your quaint notions of propriety. But excuse me, the Lupines. Our dear brothers in the art from the Order of the Emerald. The Emerald is a scholastic order like our own magi, and their 'first-to-publish' culture is even worse than our own. I agreed to give them first access rights to whatever you tell me, so we'd better give them a good story. I was hoping you could tell me about some of the events of your life that we don't already know about."

Idalia's First Contact awards had been earned as part of ambassadorial work, and she knew how to keep a straight face. What she'd really traded the Lupine Brotherhood was herself and Zunvect as bargaining chips in a future negotiation with the magi, and the stories were a personal project that just happened to help her argue that the Loopies shouldn't trade her away immediately. This was her chance to revitalize a career that had stagnated in the last decade. Summoning a god, binding him to tell her his past, and publishing a tell-all book about the secret life of one of the most revered humans in history would make her a household name.

"There's more than a few stories missing from the official accounts." Zunvect said darkly. "You only know a small portion of what really happened. I know; I have seen the minds of the magi. It might take months just to set the record straight."

"What's to know?" Idalia said. "You were a great and powerful Wizard-Lord of the old order; the strongest ever and trained by Lord Xetic-Nal, himself already four thousand years old by then. You decided that the Wizard-Lords were corrupt and overthrew them. At some point you devised the spell which you put on Lorn the first Node and began the mutation that has provided us with our most powerful magical talents ever since. Died in an accident, and Lorn took over the cause. That just about covers it."

"Xetic was seven thousand years old, it didn't just occur to me to crash a four-millennium old culture on a whim, and I didn't die by accident. Oh, and your assumption about Lorn's mutation, while correct in some ways, is obviously based more on ignorance and rumor than on contemporary accounts." Zunvect said acidly. "So now what do you know?"

"Don't be silly. We have Lorn's diaries –"

"The ravings of an idiot who grew up to be a lunatic."

"- and Xetic's writings -"

"Yes, and of course *he* wouldn't leave out crucial details to make sure nobody traced the whole thing back to him."

" – and contemporary opinions!" Idalia shouted over him.

"Do you have Larirem's take?" Zunvect asked, in a voice that told Idalia he knew the answer.

"No, his writings were lost."

"Vektar?"

"His too."

Zunvect laughed, though Idalia couldn't understand why. "Did you know I was married?"

"Of course I didn't! You weren't!"

"I was." Zunvect said quietly. "And anyway, none of those people were there at the beginning. None of them could tell you why I became who I became. The first person on your list to meet me was Xetic, and I was already seventeen by then. Early enough for most, but not for me when I died at the age of thirty. Lorn wasn't there until I was twenty-two, and the others – the origins of your contemporary opinions – met me at about the same time." Zunvect levered himself against the solid walls of the wards around him to approximate sitting cross legged. "Do you want the story now? Grab your pencil and get good at shorthand because there's a lot to cover." When Idalia just looked annoyed, he smiled softly and continued.

Zunvect 1:

Sorcerer

My birth and upbringing were a bit of a cliché. The usual sort of thing out on the frontier. Mother died in childbirth, older brother, father who was distant but loving in his own way. Forgive me if everyone, even then, refers to me as Zunvect. One thing that seems to have been jarred entirely from my memory is my real name. This narrative is therapeutic, but there are some things that will probably be lost forever – unless old boney decides to cough up. I go to the trouble of making this quite clear because I don't want anyone to think I fear onomancy. It's a load of nonsense and even in those days we knew it. As if someone's name could have power over them.

We were farmers. Big surprise. In a village like ours you were a farmer, a blacksmith, a baker, or if you were very lucky you owned the tavern. Of course there were odd jobs and Ivan Solinsky the all-around doctor – we'll get to him later. In fact, we were even more the typical "young man becomes something great" story. We didn't even have a pasture or much in the way of livestock. We farmed the way you see in picture books. There were crops and all the things you had to do to make sure you had crops again, like irrigation and planting. There were a couple of pigs out back every year which we raised and butchered ourselves, but for the most part we grew grain and wheat. Very boring, a lot of hard work. In fact, it was boring, hard work that started it all off.

We lived in the shadow of the mountain. It was a high mountain as mountains go, and rocky. The rocks often spilled down and so our land was rocky too. As the sun rose, it silhouetted the tower on the top of the mountain, a spire that seemed to us to be as tall again as the mountain itself. The Wizard-Lord Vectreon lived there, our ruler though we never saw him. Though his shadow fell over us every day we learned to forget about him. Wizard-Lords were far away, and there was work to do.

My dad – Boris Stetza since you're writing all this down – told me to dig the well. I was twelve. I didn't want to dig a well. "It's not fair!" I said petulantly.

"Of course it's fair." My father said in that insufferably calm and wise way of his. "I dug it last time and your brother Mikel did it the time before. So, you do it this time." He picked up his hoe and that was that. He and Mikel were going off to weed and I was going to dig a well. I was angry in the way a twelve-year-old gets when they don't want to do something, but can't think of a good reason to give when their fathers come back and find out they've not done it. Half an hour later, I regarded the puny hole I'd managed to dig so far, knowing that it would be all day and perhaps the rest of the week before I finished. I was already broad shouldered and strong for my age, but digging a well was hard work for a grown man and I was hardly that. I grew angrier and angrier at the idea of missing out on seeing my friends in the village, going into the woods, perhaps sharing a glance with the innkeeper's daughter who was a year older than I was and stirred me up in ways I wasn't ready to handle. All that outrage filled me and then sort of *left* all at once. I could feel it draining, feel it exiting my body in a strange way that left a me-shaped hole in the world. For the tiniest moment before everything vanished, I thought I saw something flit from me to the hole, but it was all over too quickly and in the immediate aftermath I had bigger things to worry about.

I woke up to see my father kneeling over me. "Zunvect? Zunvect!" He cradled my head.

"Wha…" I could barely even begin to ask what happened. I turned my head and the world spun, but not before I saw the hole.

It was big, but not in the direction a well ought to go. Dirt clods were scattered all around us. Mikel ran up, breathing heavily. I guessed I hadn't been asleep or knocked out or whatever it was for very long. In the back of my mind, a rational voice that seemed quite far away tartly pointed out that instead of a well I had a pond. A louder voice was asking where it had come from. Most of me felt like the time I'd fallen off of a small cliff while playing up on the mountain to the east. Before my father told me that it was a bad idea to go up there and glanced at the tower at the top as if expecting fireballs and bolts of lightning to fall on us as punishment.

"Zunvect, are you all right?" My father asked, starting to help me to my feet.

"No, he is not!" A sharp voice called. "And let him lie down again before he falls down. You ought to know better than have a person stand up when they've been clobbered over the head, Boris." It was Ivan Solinsky - see, I told you I'd get to him – coming down the road, puffing and as agitated as I had ever seen him, which was saying a lot. I'd seen him face down an ogre without breaking that slightly knowing smile of his. He sat next to me and held out four fingers. "How many?"

"Four." I ground out.

"Where does it hurt?"

"My head. I feel like I've been – "

"Like you've been struck with a mallet. I imagine." Ivan said. He dusted his hands on his long robe and leant over my face. "Eyes are a little too wide." He poked me in a few places and when I didn't yelp he looked pleased. Healing me would have been exhausting work. "Probably gave yourself a good hard knock when you went down. Lucky that your father's so good about clearing rocks off your land." He let my father help him up. "Nice pond."

"Zunvect was supposed to be digging a well."

"The widow Mochoff told me once that he was hopeless at geometry when he was doing his lessons."

"Can you please go back to where you started that thought?" My father asked respectfully. Ivan was the smartest man in town, but he did have a habit of acting like people knew what he was thinking.

"Zunvect's a sorcerer. It's a classical first manifestation." Ivan told my father. "A young man gets mad he has to dig the well, or make post holes, or maybe clear out last year's growth from a field left fallow. Then suddenly the entire farm is up in smoke. Don't worry," Ivan said, seeing my father's distress. "It's not going to happen again. He's been building up inside probably for a year or two and now it's all come out at once. Like a dam bursting and now the river is flowing at its proper height. An impressive show – I saw the clods flying from the Androsky farm – but a unique event in a sorcerer's life." Ivan looked over at me. "Do you feel like you can stand?"

"I don't know." I said. My head didn't feel like it was surrounded by wool, but now I was dizzy for a different reason. I got up. "I'm – I'm a sorcerer?"

"Yes. Which means that you're going to need a lot of education." The amused smile returned when he saw my expression. "Yes. You don't get to know magic until you know the right way and reason to use it." My face fell even more, and he clapped me on the shoulder. "Don't feel too bad. You used to love my stories. Now you get to learn them in extraordinary detail." He turned and started to go. "Send him up tomorrow morning. I'll have everything ready by then."

"Wait a minute!" My father called back. "He has to finish this well."

Ivan turned around, eyebrow raised. "Your son is learning to be a magician and you complain that the well isn't dug?"

"My son the magician will not become a magician if he has no water to drink nor food to eat." My father countered.

Ivan nodded. "Ah, the wisdom of necessity. Fine. Send him up the following day, but no later. I know his hands will be missed but what must be must be. When he can earn his keep with magic, I am sure your loss will be repaid."

I haven't mentioned it yet, but Ivan was a magician himself. In fact, much better. Ivan was a veterinary sorcerer. Master of the Regional College of Veterinary Sorcery up north. We were very lucky to have him, and all the more because he didn't make a fuss about the fact that he was immensely overqualified to be the attending sorcerer for a village of less than two hundred people along with their various livestock and pets. In return, parents gave their children an extra hard smack if they called him a cow mage, and then made them apologize to him even if he wasn't in earshot when they said it. He was gracious about it – or as gracious as someone like him could be – and after having *me* tagging along for awhile, I think even the smallest child appreciated how skilled he was, but I'm getting ahead of myself.

The two days weren't long, but neither were they short. I guess I wasn't really sure what to feel about being told that I could do magic. As best as I can remember, I alternated between trying to think of it as just another day on the farm and being unable to think of anything. I was a magician and perhaps more. Thoughts of going to a big city or advising merchants flashed through my imagination. I knew I couldn't be a veterinary sorcerer. Ivan's job was way too hard and he knew more than I ever would about everything.

Maybe I could be a street magician – doing little lights and fireballs for coins. That sounded more manageable. I fretted about how it would affect dad and Mikel, but Mikel was older and would have inherited the farm one day in any case. I was better off finding my fortune elsewhere. If I worked hard, maybe I could become a traveling entertainer and send a few coins back to help the town. It was with these thoughts swirling through me that I made the first of hundreds of trips to Ivan Solinsky's cottage. It was a long way for a boy used to a village of around two hundred – all the way at the edge of the north woods. The cottage of the cow mage – or for our lucky generation Master Ivan, MRCVS – had been built centuries ago when the town had first been settled. It was originally a trapper's hut before being slowly expanded by successive magicians who kept the town's livestock and residents in general good health. Now it was the second largest residence in town, second only to the inn-tavern-mayoral mansion-town hall that Mayor Bowbringer owned, lived in, and ran the town from. We had a Mayor because someone had to be Mayor. It made sense that the only person with a room big enough for a gathering of the whole town would also preside. His job, when he wasn't being the innkeeper and barman, was settling the myriad small squabbles of a farming community, talking to the tax collector, and presiding over marriages. On the excessively rare times when there was a real crime like a sheep rustling or a murder – not for two hundred years in the latter case – the entire adult population took care of it.

Anyway, politics of a small town nobody has heard of aside, the point is that Ivan's place was - by my standards - imposing, remote, and mysterious. No doubt Ivan, a man who had traveled more than ten miles and seen a wizard, considered it a cozy private dwelling with just enough space for himself, his surgery, and the result of a thousand years of magicians doing their best to obtain any book that somehow made its way to our community. To a twelve-year-old to whom reading was a mystical art, it seemed more books than could be read in a lifetime. Naturally, I ended up reading almost all of them in a couple of years.

Ivan saw my mixture of awe, shock, and ruminatory haze at once. "It comes as a hell of a shock to most of us, Zunvect." He observed, stroking his tobbacco stained beard. It was strange, he despised smoking and never had a puff in his life and yet he somehow managed to look like he had just finished a pipe. "Your da raised you to be punctual. Good. Come along in and we'll get started."

"I heard there'd be a lot of meditating and making little rocks fly around. I don't know as I'd be very good at sitting in one place and being all peaceful like that." I gabbled.

"Then it's a good thing we're not doing that." Ivan replied with a twinkle. "You don't learn to *do* magic afore you learn *why* you're doing it." He saw my face fall. "That's right. History, mathematics, geography, politics. All that comes first, *then* comes the meditation and little rocks. By then you'll be begging for it." He grinned.

"But what if I pop off again?" I asked, nervous and feeling cheated. "I could hurt someone next time."

"That was a spasmodic twitch." Ivan said dismissively. "Like waking up one day with an extra finger; first thing'll happen is it'll move like crazy because you're not used to it. You know what it feels like, so you won't do it again. Besides," he said with a knowing smile, "no one can refill their internal resevoir of magic that quickly. Like I told your father, it's probably been building for months, maybe even a year. If you lose control, the worst you can do is rattle some cups in the cupboard. By the time you can control some real power, you'll be *able* to."

"I feel pretty full right now." I said defiantly.

Ivan sighed, knowing he'd have to play along. It's the best thing to do when a young magician insists they know better. "All right, Zunvect, how does it feel?"

"Like – like a hot – no kind of tingly – I'm not sure how to put it, but it's everywhere!" I insisted. "Just like I felt right before I saw it go out and make that hole."

Ivan's tolerant expression faltered. "Saw? What did you see?"

"It's sort of like the … whatever it is that comes out of you when you heal our pig." I said, on shaky ground now. Dad had told me I was just imagining it. After he got all nervous when I told him I could see him, and the pigs, and anyone walking around in what was – I guess – pitch dark to them I'd stopped mentioning it.

I told this to Ivan and he hurried inside and came back out with a crumbling leatherbound tome. "What does it look like?" He asked.

"People and animals are bright, and so is anything hot. It sort of fades away at the edges. When you use magic, something like that but wavy moves through you and into whatever you're healing."

Ivan paged through the book rapidly, then closed it decisively. "One problem at a time, I think. If you insist that you're still dangerous, then we need to take that seriously. One of the most important things I can teach you about magic, Zunvect, is that a small risk with a big hazard is still worth investigating. It never does to be dismissive just because you don't think something will happen. I've had hundreds of people mistake a deer or a strong wind for an errant troll, but I always look because one out of a thousand times, it *is* a troll." He ran in and put the book back. "And just in case you're right, we'll go into the forest. I know a clearing not far from here where it won't do any harm if you churn up the ground a bit. Come on."

It was shading towards midmorning when we emerged from the trees into a long, narrow place where the soil had worn away to expose bare rock. Some scrub brush and grasses poked out from cracks, and a goat looked up from its browsing. I remember thinking that it must have wandered down from the mountainside for the day. Nothing within walking distance was far from the slopes of the mountain, as the older folk said, and no one left the view of the tower. I looked up at the cloud-piercing home of Lord Vectreon and then reflexively away, warding off the feeling that at any moment the Wizard-Lord might be watching me. "What are you going to do?" I asked, realizing I had no idea and that the kindly vet was also a ruthless pragmatist. For the first time since I'd learned I was a magician, I was afraid of what the lessons might require.

"Nothing except observe and advise." Ivan told me. "What *you* will do is prove your hypothesis true or false." He picked up a rather large stone and balanced it on a narrow rock. "This feels about one kilogram, so it should be easy enough to figure out how much power you've stored up by seeing how far you can push it." He stepped behind me, leaning down so I felt his beard on my ear. "Close your eyes and reach for where you feel magic inside you. Try to concentrate it all in one place and then send it out to strike the stone. Make it *move*."

This wasn't a lot to go on, and I felt a bit cheated since there seemed to be so many books about it and people spent years learning. Still, I could only do as he asked, and my breath came raggedly to me when I felt the magic squirm and slip around inside me. It was a feeling that was both ticklish and extraordinarily uncomfortable. Like something alive had stirred and slid against the inside of my skin. I pushed at it, forced what felt like ten sacks of stuff towards my hand, which I pushed reflexively in the direction of the stone. My eyes may have been closed, but I could still see with that strange half vision that showed me a ball of bright light directly in front of me. It was ragged like my breathing was, pulsing, and swirling, trying to escape. Strands of the stuff trailed from it to my hand and up my arm. I pushed and it swelled, but I still couldn't quite force everything out. The strands were attached somehow, refusing to part from me. I was afraid that if I pushed any harder, I might end up tearing my skeleton from my flesh, so instead of pushing the magic within, I hurled the magic that had gathered outside of me towards the stone, imagining it was a solid ball that would hit the stone like the wooden balls we sometimes played games with. My eyes flew open as I did so, and my power was invisible to my normal sight. The stone wasn't at first, but then it too disappeared.

"Where did it go?" I gasped, mostly out of breath but also surprised.

Ivan had been watching more closely since he wasn't taking his first steps into an ethereal world. His eyes tracked something farther and further up than the stone I'd been working to move. His gaze moved slowly downward. "Good question." There was a crack like an avalanche, and I saw a tree on the other side of the clearing shudder. "There's the answer. Zunvect, a quick calculation as an exercise while I think. How far is it to that tree?"

"I'd say about a kilometer."

"Good. So, in meters per second, how fast would you have to go to reach it in, say, five seconds?"

"Two hundred." I replied, after thinking for a few seconds. Pardon me if I wasn't quite as quick on arithmetic as I am now.

"And if that tree is the same elevation as we are now, what's the free fall distance that stone would have had to travel in order to return to the same height after five seconds?"

"I don't know."

"It's half the gravitational acceleration multiplied by the square of the time."

"Is gravity about ten?"

"Something like that. Remember that it must first travel up before it comes back down. That is, to fall *back* to our current height, it has to go to a certain maximum height."

"That's about halfway." I replied. "So … thirty meters about?" The response really took a strong five minutes as I found a stick and tried to write things out in the dirt. I'm sure that helped Ivan do a bit of thinking in between.

"Good. We establish an arc one kilometer by thirty meters. That's very squashed, so let's just call it a traversal of about one and a half to two kilometers. So just to keep it a very low estimate, three hundred meters per second to hit that tree. What's that in kinetic energy?"

This one took me a very long time just to remember. "One half mass times the square of the velocity. So, if it's one kilogram then that's half of three hundred squared which is … forty-five thousand joules?"

"Not a lot of energy by itself, Zunvect." Ivan told me, chewing the words as they came out, and speaking in a tone I'd never heard before. "A human being for instance eats about two hundred times that." I felt crestfallen at the news that what had felt enormous was in fact the equal of a morsel of food. "The problem is that I watched that stone *accelerate* to get that kinetic energy. And it did so in less than a tenth of a second, I'd wager. So for a very brief instant there, your *power* output was something above half a megawatt." He looked out at the sky as if searching for an answer. "Your hypothesis is supported, Zunvect. I will have to teach you magic alongside your other lessons. Come, I must redraw my lesson plan, and you can do some reinforcement exercises while I do so." He swept off, for the first time that day seeming more like a sorcerer than a scholar as he strode purposefully back towards his cottage. I trotted to keep up and the few times I succeeded in getting alongside of him, I saw something very sorcerous in his expression. Concern, deep thought, mysterious power. Almost like a Wizard-Lord.

The exercise turned out to be more prosaic than I thought it would be. The word I used at the time was 'boring.' However, one thing I learned quickly from Ivan was pragmatism, and there was no point in arguing with his logic.

"If you don't need to refresh your memory on the topic, then it should be easy." He said of the monumental chore of transferring more than half his books from the floor to the shelves. "And if you find alphabetizing and re-shelving a simple thing, then feel free to skip to the next step of doing so while also sorting them in terms of their topics. The sooner you get to know every book in this house and its location, the better."

His tactics worked and while he hummed and scribbled away, I moved all the books in his house either to a shelf or from one shelf to another. The goal being to put them in both alphabetical order by author and in alphabetical order by topic – as best I could. There were a lot of books that seemed to just be about nature. When I was done, he groused that I needed to understand the differences between physics, geology, and zoology, but that for the time being it would do well enough. Now that the cottage's floors were clear of books, I realized just how large a space Ivan had. His house was at least four times bigger than mine, and I got to have my own room with Mikel! The wood of the floor was shiny and smooth once I'd swept it clean – on my own initiative in hopes of putting Ivan in a better mood – and the bookshelves which lined almost every wall were of the same wood. I'd thought Ivan had a lot of books, but the cottage seemed to be made for a lot more since all the books he owned weren't enough to take up more than two long walls' worth of space. The walls themselves were irregularly shaped stones held together with … I looked more closely, and Ivan noticed me poking the walls.

"That's right, no mortar. What most people don't know, and I don't intend to tell them, is that this cottage was built by the very first Wizard-Lord who ruled our territory. The reason the town's tried to sell it only to sorcerers is that any enchantment is best left to the experts. In my expert opinion you'd better not prod it too hard or the whole thing might fall down on our heads."

Ivan laughed as I backed away. "Construction magic was never my interest, but I know enough to reckon that if it's been here this long, it probably isn't going away anytime soon. I'd wager a pick-axe or a hammer would bounce right off. Doesn't mean you shouldn't be cautious, though. You've shown you can do some real damage if you aren't careful, so best you don't extend any feelers until you know how to control them. Any road, that's why there are so many bookshelves built right into the walls. Wizard-Lords prize their libraries above all other things, so I imagine that even when he lived in this temporary dwelling, he brought his whole collection with him. That's also why there are so many empty shelves now. The Wizard-Lord on the Reclamation crew who got our territory came here with a fully stocked library, and all I've got is what little makes its way here on the trade routes. It's getting on towards afternoon now, so there's no point in starting in on learning any magic. That's best done in the morning when you've got your whole mind to think about it. That said, now that you've had a browse through my own collection, mayhap you have a notion as to what you'd like to start on?"

He asked knowing the answer and I answered knowing he already knew. "Weeerrl." I grinned. "I remember you saying that there was a lot more to know about Wizard-Lords when I asked in Missus Mochoff's class. You said that there wasn't time to tell everything about them because it would take days to say it all. Most people only need to know that they pay taxes and sometimes join the army, and that Wizard-Lords are best respected when they showed up, and otherwise left alone."

"I also recollect that you came to visit me several times to hear more." Ivan replied drily. He took down the very book I'd been looking at when he asked the question. "To understand the Wizard-Lords, you have to know why we have them and the history of their rule. Best to start at the beginning then, a place not many people go when telling stories because of superstition." He handed me the book, which was leather bound and felt like it might come apart despite the rigor with which Ivan cared for his books. "Take this home and mind that you don't mishandle it. Tell your pa I let you out early but told you that you had to read the first two chapters by tomorrow. You can tell him that because it's true and I'm telling you to do it now. Don't let your brother have it; he's a good lad but has fingers like sausages."

"I will!" I said, excited. "But why are people superstitious about the beginning?"

"When you reach the first name, you'll know." Ivan told me. "Now get going or you won't have any light to read by, seeing as how you'll be keeping my book away from candles and the fire."

Introduction to *A History and Analysis of the Rule of the Wizard-Lords*, 6th ed, vol. 1 (3492 [X.R.[1]])

While this history is concerned with the events and people involved in the period after the Reorganization, and so the Wizard-Lords, their actions, and those who helped and hindered them, a mention must be made of the Xetic's Reorganization itself. It is the purview of another book (we recommend *Xetic-Nal: The Reorganization Period*) to explore the influences that led to the Reorganization – and since most of

---

[1] XR added to clarify which era this volume belongs to, Ed.

the primary sources are no longer extant, this is mostly speculation in any case – but the Reorganization did not occur overnight, and much of it was ongoing as the Wizard-Lords began their rule. Xetic-Nal himself is, of course, the chief architect of the radical changes that spanned the world, though the disappearance of the Uidrana and the subsequent weakening of the Intendant Races left the gap he acted within. The most important factor, however, in the successful transition from local, secular rule to an almost universal Thaumocracy was the vision Xetic-Nal brought to the task. No one else would have had not just a five, ten, or even hundred-year plan, but a thousand-year mission in which he kicked off, executed, *and* performed the post-implementation review at the end of the process, leading to the next thousand-year plan.

Though he has retired to a more academic position now, the fact that there is an undying, unsleeping, and significantly more magically talented individual providing oversight to the Wizard-Lords as a whole has been the true source of their continued success and the reason that all but two major polities are ruled by Wizard-Lords, with over 95% of the human population submitting to the ultimate authority of the only human ever to transcend mortality. Xetic-Nal's reorganization of humanity into a hierarchy with him at the apex may not have been the beginning of human civilization, but it did make civilization civilized.

Zunvect 2:

First Test

Dad told me I had to be back early the following day to help him with the hogs, but I was bursting with a question that couldn't wait, so my first words to Ivan that morning were, "What happened to the other five hundred years?"

"Good morning to you, too." Ivan said as I burst in. "I'm glad to see you so full of energy." He took the book from my hand and put it aside so I wouldn't damage it in my enthusiasm. I'm ashamed to say I might have been waving it a little for emphasis. "Why don't you get through the *first* three thousand five hundred years of history before worrying about the more recent events."

"But – but –" I protested. "It's not complete. I wanted to learn about our Wizard-Lords, but they won't show up until the end and there were only two of them by the time this book was written."

"True, but out here books aren't easy to come by. Besides, you'll learn plenty from the actions of the Wizard-Lords in the east that apply just as much to those who rule us. Lord Vectreon wouldn't show up in *any* book, I'd wager, seeing as how he's only been around two hundred years or so. It's hardly worth putting out a new edition every single time a new Wizard-Lord takes over. Did you read the first two chapters like I told you? Good, then you know that there were only seventy-eight territories when that book was written. As you probably also know from my lessons when you were a boy, there are now eighty-six, with eighty-four Wizard-Lords at any given time."

"No, I don't know why there are that many territories," he told me, anticipating my next question. "There are two fewer Wizard-Lords than towers because Lord Xetic has three of them. Now!" He clapped his hands. "The floor is clear, so let's sit down and work on keeping you from giving your da more holes to fill."

We sat opposite each other, cross legged. "Regular breaths, eyes closed – I know that doesn't help you as much as other people, but it still does *something*. Feel the magic? It's inside you but also flowing around us. Out of the ground and into us to fill us full of magic. It feels like it's suffusing your entire body, but that is an illusion of the mind, a way to process thaumic instinct into a somatic feeling. Breathe deeply, in and out... Feel at peace with the world around you and dive deep into the magic and your self. Surround it with your consciousness and divide magic from self. Feel only what *you* feel, not what the magic makes you. When you are angry, the ground must stay still. When you are in love, let it be your love. Pure and human. Magic intensifies emotion, feeds on it to try to give you what you want. That path is unpredictable; magic must answer only to your intellect in order to be used in spellcraft. Breathe in ... out."

I didn't want to tell him that I knew he was wrong. There was magic around us, yes, and the strongest came from the earth, but it was also coming down from the sun and even the stars had a little. I didn't want to argue, to say that a candle had magic, that a river in motion had it. I sat there and absorbed the true lesson, that magic served the mind. That my magical self could only be mental, and that emotion and spirit should be cut off from the power within me. It was the ethos of all magicians of our time, that which limited us, but also kept us safe. The magi of your time understand this a bit better than we did, though I like to think that the calm of my self-reflection that morning was at least as good as any technique taught now. It's a memory I cherish as a time before magic became a burning passion and the center of my soul. Before I was obsessed with its use and expansion. It was a moment of purity and peace that came to me far too few times in my life.

Ivan has been dead for over eight thousand years, and I regret not thanking him more now that I look back across that gulf of time. He was wiser than most magicians I have met. Or maybe he was just untroubled by the knowledge that burdened me later; the information that was a responsibility to control and protect. Either way, I am very happy to have had him as my first teacher, ignorant as he was.

We were wading through a geometry lesson – even now I'm really bad at anything related to angles and planes and that – when I remembered to tell him what my father had said.

"Fair enough. Boris has been more than generous with your time so far. He's probably worried about you. You can tell him that you're not going to burn the house down, so you need only do your lessons mornings four days a week, but three days for the whole day. Again, what is the rotation and translation needed to …"

Of course, Ivan wasn't at his cottage every day I went to see him. Sometimes he was on call, and quite often I ended up going with him. The benefit of living on the opposite side of town was that few of his early morning calls were close enough that he could send a farmhand to fetch me out of bed to assist him, and our farm was not on his route anywhere else. I still got used to being roused before dawn and in the middle of the night, though, and quickly found that applied anatomy was Ivan's most in depth lesson plan. It wasn't his fault; he was trained in veterinary sorcery, so he saw no reason not to teach me. At first.

It was less than a week after our first instruction in magical control that I arrived at the cottage to find it dark and Ivan nowhere in sight. I wandered around, and then realized where he must be. It took an hour of asking around, but I finally found out that one of

Nyatrusha's cows was off her feed and Ivan had gone to find out why. It wasn't the first time I found him almost shoulder deep in a cow's rectum, but it was the first time he pointed to a bucket of water and soap and told me to lather up. It was my first time really getting to grips with animal work. Despite all the muck I'd shoveled with the pigs, it was very different having my arm inside where the muck comes from. I was tall for my age, so it wasn't a physical problem for me to reach wherever Ivan wanted me to, but I wasn't sure I knew why he was having me do a rectal examination when I had no experience of what to look for.

"Where do you think that experience comes from?" He asked. "Of course, ideally, I'd have taught you more bovine anatomy beforehand, but there's a lot you can work out just by trying it." Nyatrusha looked as dubious as I did, and for much the same reason.

"All right, so now that I'm in here, what am I supposed to be doing?"

"First off, does the cow feel like she has a fever?"

"Ivan, I have *never* done a rectal examination before. She feels very hot. I have no baseline to compare that to." I said, measuring my words carefully. I think I said 'baseline.' It's hard, sometimes, to remember my younger self's limited vocabulary.

"Fair point. Wash up and we'll try you on a healthy cow to see if you can tell the difference." Ivan said. "Come on! We haven't got all day. I'm sure Mr. Nyatrusha has a lot of work to do."

"Hang on!" Nyatrusha said. "He can't just stick his hand into every one of my good cows. It'll put them off their milk. And what's wrong with that one?" He demanded, pointing at the cow I was gingerly extracting myself from."

"She has nephritis, and I'll cure her in good time. She isn't going to keel over just because I take a few minutes to get my assistant some education. As for the discomfort to the other animal, I'm sure Zunvect will be very gentle."

"Not with them big hands, I bet he won't." Nyatrusha grumbled. "Have it your way, Ivan. You always do. But next time I send you milk, it'll be from the cow he put his hand up, so you just mind that." He bustled off, but was back in time to see me start on the next cow.

"So, can you feel it?"

"Not really, Ivan, but I can see it just fine." I grated, tired of his apparent assumption that my hand could register tiny differences in temperature. It couldn't, but my *eyes* certainly had the ability to note that the one sick cow was somewhat hotter than the others."

"Eh, what's he's seeing?" Nyatrusha asked.

"Magic things." Ivan said shortly. "All right, Zunvect, that's good. It would be a waste of a spell for most of us, but there's no point in me keeping you from using that for diagnosis. Right, in that case can you tell me *where* the infection is?"

"You already said nephritis, but it does appear to be around here." I put my hand on the cow's back, in about the spot I saw the brightest spot – one that didn't belong.

"Wonderful. Now, one of the best ways of spotting it is a vaginal examination. Get washed again."

With a sore arm and a disgruntled dairy farmer looking on, I continued in our lesson. At the end, I watched eagerly as Ivan performed the curative spell. It was long, but nephritis was common and so Ivan had it memorized. The arm motions and words blended together, but in a way that tugged at me as if I ought to know them already and had just forgotten. "It's just a highly targeted antibacterial, really." Ivan told me on the way back. "Most of the spell is giving a precise location so that I don't end up damaging more than I have to."

"Can't you fix the location just with your mind?"

"Of course, but that's harder. Magic is enough effort without adding further complication. Another reason to make it so narrowly targeted is that, while the spell itself is a mental effort, calling up magic is a physical drain in direct proportion to how much you use. Any time you use a spell, it's best to be economical. Unless it's an emergency, of course." He looked sidelong at me. "You want to prove that, don't you?"

"Of course."

"All right, but don't blame me if you feel like hells when you have to dig, or water, or shovel tomorrow. It's probably for the best anyway. It's like a muscle that way and it's never too early to exercise."

"I thought you didn't want me using magic this early." I grinned.

"I'm coming around to your way of thinking."

"Ivan, what does Xetic-Nal look like?"

"Why do you ask?"

I shrugged. "People always talk like he's a god or a monster. I've never even met Lord Vectreon, and everyone in town acts like he's a god as well. The only people I've met who seemed unafraid of them are you and the priests, and the priests are always on the move, so they're never around long enough for a Wizard-Lord to notice. We can *talk* about Lord Vectreon. Everyone just shushes folk who bring up Xetic. Or they look around in fright like they expect him to appear out of nowhere and take them away. They wouldn't even know him if they saw him, now would they?"

"That would depend on if he wanted to be known."

Ivan talked while taking a small wheel of cheese out of his pocket and popping it in his mouth. Ivan said sorcery was hard and hungry work and that it always helped to have a snack handy. I took him at his word on that. "From what little is said about his appearance in my books, I'd say he usually looks like a walking skeleton in fine robes but is otherwise a rather nondescript person."

"Really?" I said, rising to his bait with a dry tone.

"Yes. Short too, from what they say. Truthfully, I have no idea if that's right or wrong. I've met Vectreon once or twice, but as far as I understand it, not many people get to have a word with Lord Xetic-Nal. The more time you have, the more precious it gets, I suppose. Now, you go in and do a bit of reading up on what the inside of a cow looks like so you can do a bit more helping next time. I need to get the spell ready."

"What spell?" I asked eagerly.

"The one to see just how much you can actually *sustain*, young man. It's a long and tiring piece of work, but I'm looking forward to it." He beamed. "I never really expected to be on the other end of this one. First, though, we need to clean the muck off or else your father's going to have some words for me. I think I'd better find you a leather apron like mine if you're going to be my assistant."

Of course, I wasn't paying attention to the detailed diagrams and descriptions while Ivan worked, and he knew it. I was watching real magic. Not the pinches of stuff he used in routine mastitis cures but the broad motions, long intonations, and flow of power of proper spellcasting. He seemed to be working on a smooth stone cylinder about twenty centimeters tall and ten wide. It had a hole in one end and a misting of power surrounding it, emanating from Ivan and being slowly swallowed up. The incantation lasted for at least twenty minutes and when he was finished, Ivan's eyes were sunken, and he was breathing heavily. His first act after finishing was to dump a bucket of well water over himself and then eat a plate of bread, cheese, ham, and potatoes.

"We'd better hope that there isn't anything worse than a rash for the rest of the day because that took as much out of me to prepare as it will from you to complete." He said through an overstuffed mouthful of almost solid beer.

"What is it?" I asked, looking out the window at the stump where he'd left the object.

"Old." He said through a huge bite of ham. "I was lucky to get it when I was at the College. It's a sort of magicians' testing device in truth, but when properly primed it's also a very effective way of safely practicing your channeling. That is, exercising your magical strength. The hole draws your power in as you send it toward the device, converting whatever spell or energy you project into heat. There's an array of tightly packed cells into which the heat diffuses. The higher the setting on it, the more power it takes to heat the device. Just to be safe, I've used the 'testing' version of the enchantment, which is the highest degree it can be set to. I've never had to cast that spell before. It takes a lot because it wraps the arrays in a very dense layer of diffusion and protection. When I was first tested this way, I could barely get it to warm up at all. When I left, I was still only able to get a dull red glow. The dean of the College once showed off for us and got it as far as yellow. I won't lie, Zunvect. What you did in that field last week is yellow territory if you can keep it up for more than a couple seconds. When I've had my pie, we'll go and find out."

I was on the edge of my seat, foot thumping the floor with energy as he ate. It seemed like he was drawing his meal out – and he probably was, resting as well as eating. I rushed out the door the moment he started putting his plates in the basin to soak, and my elation grew to the point where I thought my stomach would spill out of my mouth when he reverently opened a book full of diagrams that meant absolutely nothing to me. The diagram he did show me was a bit easier to work out.

"Move your arms like this, and then say these words just as its labeled. I'll write out the phonetic for you just to make sure, and that reminds me that if you're going to be so blasted advanced that I'd better put phonetic reading on the curriculum for the very near future."

He told me to fetch a small table, and he propped the book up on it. It was to my right and the training device was about a hundred meters in front of me, still resting on the stump. The clear, cool day seemed at odds with the hot blood surging through me. The device almost mocked me with how peacefully it sat, waiting to show whether I was even a color at all. I started to hurry through the spell, but Ivan stopped me after the first line.

"Slower, more purposeful. If you slur, you might just do nothing, or you might accidentally transliterate something that means something, and I'll find myself having to reattach your hands."

I stopped, took a calming breath, and started on the spell again, enunciating carefully and making sure every motion was as written. Ivan made a small note which I later found out was a reminder to himself to also add some arcane exercises to the phonetic lessons, so that I would be able to handle the motions of spellcasting with greater fluidity in future. I think I remember the spell. It goes like this ...

What? It sounds like a dire curse? Lady, that's how real spells sound. Gutterals, sibilants, hard consonants. Good strong verbal components. Spells these days are all rolling the tongue and long strings of vowels. You sound like a gargling Elf.

Now don't interrupt. I was coming to a turning point in my early life. What the spell did was complete the conduit between me and the device. I could choose how much of my power I let flow through it, but it was almost impossible for me to force it to flow anywhere else. I could feel the magic seething, trying to be used. I remembered Ivan's warnings about overtaxing myself at first and only let what felt like the tiniest trickle of it out. The device remained solid and unchanged, and then grudgingly turned an extremely dark shade of red.

"How do you feel?" Ivan asked.

"A little disappointed," I replied. Once the spell was in place, I could just about converse comfortably without losing the conduit.

"If you mean 'not tired' then put some more into it!" He urged. I eagerly increased the flow and kept increasing it, the conduit filling and then having to grow wider to accommodate the surge of magic.

"Red ... good! Orange! Yellow! I thought you had it in you!" Ivan crowed. "Wait, are you sure you feel all right?" He sounded worried.

"Sure. I could do even more." I assured him.

"Well, if you feel up to it. Green... blue ... *purple*." He whispered. "Zunvect, are you *sure* you're not tired?"

"Well, I am getting a little bit sore holding my hands up like this." I said, knowing it would tweak him. "And concentrating this long is giving me a headache."

"You can stop now." I let my arms fall to my sides as the now white-hot device cooled with a dull plinking sound. Now that I'd seen it in action, I thought it might have been some kind of ceramic. "You don't need to practice channeling, Zunvect. You're as powerful now as you'll ever need to be. I ... I need to do some studying. Go back home and tell your dad I let you out early." I'd never seen him look so ... haggard. Like all the years of care had suddenly appeared on his face all at once. He moved with a leaden step.

"But – but what – "

"Go home!" He said sharply, the fire in him rekindling for a moment. "I *need* to think about this. Purple means – and then white…" The color was draining from his face. "It means I need to think." He repeated, as if he were holding on to that sentiment for his life.

He stopped at the doorstep. "Zunvect, can you just … whistle a tune for me?" I did so without question, his tone telling me it was vitally important I comply. "I see. No, I really don't." He grasped the door frame, his knuckles going white. "It makes no *sense*." Ivan kept on mumbling to himself as he closed the door, leaving me outside with a rapidly cooling testing device and no idea whether I ought to be ashamed or ecstatic.

I didn't see Ivan again for a week and when I did, he looked tired but resolute. "I'm here to see Boris." He told me. When he saw my expression, he softened. "I'll be teaching you again soon, but there's something that needs to be discussed."

"If it's about me, I ought to know." I said mulishly. I was angry. Forgive my pettiness but I still think I had a right to be. I'd been working harder than ever on the farm every day, glancing up the road every time I rested for a moment, waiting for Ivan to come and tell me what had happened. Now here he was, but instead of an explanation, I was being told that it needed to be 'discussed' and not with me.

"By rights, I ought to." Ivan sighed. "This is bigger than me, Zunvect. I *need* to talk it over with your father and the rest of the village."

"The rest – what's going on?" I demanded, and my dad came out to see what the commotion was.

"Softly, Zunvect." Ivan warned. I only noticed then that there was a fine mist of dust rising around us. The earth was shaking. "It serves your intellect."

"Then," I said, fighting the magic down and trying to regain my reason, "I think it only right that I be present for any discussion."

"Zunvect." Ivan held my shoulders. I think it was the first time I'd ever felt his hand when I wasn't sick or hurt. "Yes. It is right. But I can't. Think about that. We're facing something that is very, very dangerous. It becomes more dangerous if you know what it is. I can't expose you to that. Boris, I've already told Bowbringer and he's got most of the village coming along. I'm sorry to surprise you like this, but you can take some comfort in knowing that *no one* knows why I'm calling a meeting. Only that it must be closed, and it must be now."

"Hasn't been a closed meeting in over a hundred years." My dad said, as if commenting on a snowstorm in summer.

"No. Not for a very long time indeed." Ivan agreed. "We're having one now. I'll say to you what I said to Bowbringer and everyone else who asked: trust me. This is a matter of sorcery, but it's also a matter that concerns us all."

"It's about Zunvect."

"Yes."

"You can't tell him what it is."

"Not even after the meeting, no. If he knows, it will make things incomparably worse."

"Sounds a mess of sorcery to me." My father said. "Zunvect, see to the watering."

"But dad-"

"If you can't trust me and you can't trust Master Solinsky, who can you trust?" He handed me his watering can. "You're twelve, and it's a hard time, but if it helps you to know, I agree with you. It isn't fair, but if Ivan says it keeps you safer, it's best if you follow his advice. I've never heard of anyone who went foul following Ivan's advice."

"I wish I shared your confidence." Ivan said, and then winced as if the words hurt him somehow.

It was indeed the first closed meeting of the village adults in over *four* hundred years. Nothing so important had happened since Lord Avactur had called up the militia and we'd had to figure out who went and who stayed. Not every adult attended, either. Mikel was technically old enough, but barred. As were quite a few loose tongued members of our community. It was not the only secret Ivan kept from me, but it was the biggest and it was about me. That stung doubly. It lasted well into the night and when my father came back with Ivan, all he told me was that Ivan would come tomorrow to start teaching me again, and that I'd better listen to everything he said. "What happened?" I pleaded.

"We had a very long discussion." My father said. "That's all I can say." It really was all anyone who had been there could say. 'It was a very long discussion.' That seemed to be the agreed upon statement to be made about the most momentous event in generations. It angers me to this day that they kept it from me, and the worst part is that, with all that I know now about the situation, I'd have probably done the same as they did.

Excerpt from *Testimonies of Zunvect*, a manuscript of collected interviews and personal writings released in 8126 MR by Xetic-Nal[2]

---

[2] Xetic's explanation for over 8000 years' gap between collection and release: "I didn't think it was all that important. I mean, nobody asked."

Proceedings of village meeting regarding disposition of the Wizard-Lord one day known as Zunvect, approximate reconstruction based on interviews with attendees

BOWBRINGER: Ivan's called us all here on a matter of the greatest import. Master Solinsky.

SOLINSKY: Yes, Mayor. Everyone. Hello, Eva. Mikhail. Oh, good. I'd hoped you'd make it, Mrs. Androski. It's about Zunvect. You know I recently took him on as my apprentice.

ANDROSKI: I hear he's been a very diligent young man. Put his hand right up a cow's arse because you told him to. That's what I like in a boy; does what his elders tell him to.

SOLINSKY: Yes, Mrs. Androski.

NYTRUSHA: Yeah, but that cow's been looking a bit cross-eyed since he did it. I reckon he had cold hands.

SOLINSKY: I recently did a routine test to see how powerful he was. *The testimonies indicate a very long pause* The tests came out ... ambiguous.

ISKANDUR: Eh, that does that mean? Enough of the big words. Speak plain!

BOWBRINGER: Show more respect for the sorcerer.

ISKANDUR: Magic ... in my time we-

SOLINSKY: I think he's a wizard.

Testimonies indicate another pause, even longer than the first, and then pandemonium. Bowbringer is unable to restore order. Analysis of the wood of the tavern indicates sorcerer grade 2 (veterinary) threw a class 1B lightning bolt at the chandelier and missed, requiring several attendees to find water buckets. Records indicate this depleted metabolic capability of s.g.2(v) by 47%. Meeting continues after the fire is extinguished.

SOLINSKY: I *think*. There's one problem. He can whistle.

ANDROSKI: What in the hells has that got to do with anything, you daft firebug?

NYATRUSHA: Are you totally ignorant of everything but how to plant wheat, Androski? Wizards can't hear music. Everyone knows that.

SOLINSKY: Not quite. They can hear it, but they have no idea if it's good or bad. They can't carry a tune. Whatever part of them makes them a wizard also makes them solidly and completely incapable of telling one note from another. They can tell they're different, but not how, if you see the distinction. The point is that Zunvect is both musically inclined and as powerful as a wizard. And yes, before anyone asks, I am absolutely sure that my test was accurate.

BOWBRINGER: So that's the question before us, isn't it? Do we turn him over to Lord Vectreon?

STETZA: If it's the law.

SOLINSKY: It is, Boris. But that's the problem, isn't it? The law says we have to turn over suspected *wizards* to Lord Vectreon. I've told you flat out he can't be.

STETZA: I won't say I'm not relieved to hear that, but I won't have you sticking your neck out and putting the village at risk for my son unless you're sure. It's not right.

BOWBRINGER: You said he's as powerful as one.

SOLINSKY: Yes, but he failed the deciding test. He can appreciate music. If Lord Vectreon ever asks, I'll tell him just that. I might be disbarred.

ISKANDUR: You'll be executed if he disagrees!

NYATRUSHA: We can't go on without someone who knows medicine, Ivan. Is it worth that risk?

BOWBRINGER: Does anyone have any further factual statement? Any argument that hasn't been made? No? Then we put it to a vote. Ivan was right that it concerns us all.

No one was willing to say how anyone voted, save that sorcerer Solinsky voted to shield Zunvect. It is known from their subsequent actions that this is what they did.

SOLINSKY: I asked that this be confidential for a reason. Zunvect cannot know. He's already sensed that he's unusually powerful and my tests have confirmed that, so I will train him as I would a particularly powerful sorcerer. I'll try to edge around just how powerful he is for as long as I can. He'll find out – I'll tell him when he's older – but a twelve-year-old can't be trusted, no matter how mature he seems. Not with this. Were he to know, he might try to act on it and that's the worst thing that could happen. I'll keep him doing animal work – he can't raise any flags with those spells – and try to keep him from stretching out too far. If he *does* use a powerful spell, the Wizard-Lords will know of it in seconds. They may not realize its source immediately, so we'll have some wiggle room, but that's the fear we must all be aware of. Every spell above the threshold will be seen, and if he casts too many in a certain period of time, they'll be able to find him. A big one here or there doesn't hurt, I hope. I'll do my best. We'll have to agree on what we tell people when they ask about this meeting. Let's figure out what our explanation is.

Zunvect 3:

Buried Evil

So that was that. I was very happy to go back to Ivan's cottage and learn from him, but there was a bit more distance between us now than there was before. I knew that something had happened, something big, and something to do with me. Trying to pry it out of Ivan was as fruitless as trying to get my father to talk, and I was too scared of Ivan to make an attempt with anyone else. Not of him, I suppose, but afraid he'd stop teaching me again if I pried. I need not have worried. Prying would have only made him more determined.

Months passed, and I finally got sick of work and tore through Ivan's few books on humans until I found a passage saying that social interaction was key to development and so please can I go to the midsummer dance.

"You don't need to work so hard at it, Zunvect. All you needed to do was ask." He said in a huff. This wasn't true and we both knew it. He'd been pushing me hard on enunciation, meditation, and the slow dance-like exercises which grew faster every day until I could make what had seemed, at the start, to be a hideously complex series of gestures as fluidly and quickly as if I were waving hello. The fact that he was spending far less time than he'd promised on learning about the world would have made me suspicious if I weren't so happy to be learning magic. Not that I'd used any magic, but at least I was learning how!

"You know what I'm going to tell you." He said before letting me embark on my day off. He was solemn, grave, about to deliver some very bad news. "No magic. I don't care what the other kids say; you know how much trouble it'll make for everyone if you show off, so don't let them goad you into it. Can I trust you to stay out of trouble?"

"Yes, Ivan." I mumbled, red cheeked at the merest hint that I might do something embarrassing.

"You know what? You were right about humans needing social time. I haven't been to one of those dances in years! I think I'll come with you."

"Ivan!" I protested. "I said I'd stay out of trouble. I don't need a nanny."

"I won't be anywhere near you." Ivan said, raising his nose. "Just … in eyeshot. In case. "

The dance was in Bowbringer's inn, the only place big enough for it. They were as regular as the seasons and I'd been to quite a few. In fact, my absence from the village center was unusual. I made it there most Market Days, as well as whenever I could convince my father to let me. I'd hoped to walk in as casually as ever and as if nothing had changed, but of course Ivan was right. He generally was when it came to how people would act.

"Hey, Zunvect!" My best friend, Misha. "My ma told me you were apprenticed to Master Solinsky now. Do some magic!"

"Misha, what do you think Ivan told me less than an hour ago?"

"No magic."

"No magic." I agreed.

"Aw, what a pain. Ivan never lets anyone have fun." Misha complained. I had to agree; Ivan had been adamant that I not learn any spells, despite him seeming ready to teach me them before the incident.

"He might be right," I had to admit, after an appropriately long session of groaning about how adults were boring. "The first time he tested me," I didn't have to tell him it was the only time, "I did almost knock down a tree."

"Really? Wow!" Misha was impressed, and I felt a lot better. "I thought your brother was the clumsy one." I stuck out my tongue. "That's a good look for you, especially with Dominka right behind you."

I worked very hard not to rise to the bait, and to turn only when my tongue was firmly in my mouth again. Dominka wasn't the only girl our age, but there certainly weren't many, and she was the one all the boys were most interested in. She was slim at that time, and just starting to fill out. Long black hair always wore frocks that were simple but obviously made with a lot of love and time by her mom. About two years older than I was, but that had never stopped me from hoping. She was sort of a one point two times magnification of a pretty young lady. It messed with your perception of perspective to realize that no, she wasn't as near as she looked. That is, it had that effect on people from outside the village. It was a common thing for us.

All the women were near or above two meters, and the men could usually replace a wagon wheel without help. It was a good trait for a self-sufficient farming village, and I didn't even know it was unusual until I left – I'd just thought that merchants were small since the caravan guards were usually as strong as we were. It must have been a decaying fragment of a massive physical enhancement spell from an old war. Our community was one of the very lucky ones. Most of the lost weapon spells did a lot worse than increase your size a little. From what I hear, you *still* haven't cleaned up all the contamination sites.

"Hi." I said. It was the best I could do on short notice.

"Hi, Zunvect." Dominka said. As always, she was surrounded by friends who made me feel like I was being judged for every move I made and found to be hilarious. "I heard you're studying magic with Ivan. That must be exciting."

"Uh, yeah. It is." I said. I tried to find some more words. "It's mostly sitting around and reading right now. I think I'm going to start doing real magic soon, though."

"That's nice." She smiled in a way that excited my twelve-year-old body, but in hindsight was more polite interest or perhaps the flirtation of a girl with a boy she knows she'll end up friends with. "I've never danced with a magician."

"From what I hear, Ivan's just having you stick your hands into pigbeds so he doesn't have to." Alexei said, walking over to us with his friend Ilia. They were closer to Dominka's age, and me and Misha had been in brawls with them before. Never anything serious; me and Alexei didn't dislike each other. It was just that whatever quirk of magic or nature that had made us big had also decreased the female birthrate, so there were never enough girls. A lot of men were single and got used to it. Those who preferred other men were pleased, though they tried not to act like it. Progressive, Idalia? Maybe if it were somewhere else, but for us it was pragmatism. With four men to three women, we boys weren't going to complain if two men took themselves out of the competition or found happiness in a different way.

For most of us youngsters, it seemed like a horrible fate to be left without a wife, so Alexei and I did our best to make each other look weak or stupid. I'm sure the girls saw right through it. "Or is that just something sorcerers like?" He glanced between me and Dominka. "I thought you magicians were supposed to stay away from women. It makes you lose your powers or something."

"That's a lot of horse manure and you know it." I said. "Anyone with any brains knows that's not how it works."

"Yeah, well I still say you may as well stop now." Alexei told me. "You'll go away to some fancy big school far away like Ivan did, and even if you do come back – which you probably won't because you'll be so besotted by painted harlots that you'll catch a fever and die – you'll take up like he has and never touch a woman again."

"That accusation isn't internally consistent." I said, trying to sound academic.

"You're not a proper sorcerer anyway. I heard you say you haven't even learned any spells. So there. If you dance with Dominka now, she won't have danced with a magician, so why don't you wait until harvest and let me dance instead."

"Do I get a say in this?" Dominka asked, both amused and annoyed.

"Yeah, does she get a say?" I said to Alexei.

"What he said." Misha added.

"You keep out of this," Ilia told him.

It was then that I realized I was angry, and I had to laugh. The floor was rock steady, after all. I was angry and the magic wasn't reacting at all.

"What's that about?" Alexei asked, heated and apparently believing that I was laughing at him.

"Ivan was right." I said, not wanting to let him in on the secret. I hoped I sounded mysterious and magical.

"Ivan doesn't know anything. He picked you as an apprentice, didn't he?"

"Careful, Alexei." Dominka said. She and her friends were looking nervously across the inn where Ivan was talking to Bowbringer and hoisting away what looked like lager. I knew it couldn't be. Ivan never drank!

"He can't hear me, and anyway it's all talk. All he ever does is cure animals. How is that proper magic?" Alexei argued. I wondered if *he'd* had something to drink. No one in the village talked about Ivan that way.

"You haven't seen what I have." I said.

"Bollocks. You're a faker and so is he."

"Come over here and say that." Ivan called, grinning widely. Maybe it really was lager.

The girls put their hands to their mouths and Alexei gulped. I saw Ilia edging away. So much for being comrades in trying to find a girlfriend. "I – I," he stammered.

"The thing about animal husbandry," Ivan said conversationally as he approached, "is that you learn so many interesting things about how all those bits operate, and the spells that make it all flow smoothly. The *most* interesting thing, I must say, is that the spell that makes a bull potent is not only reversible, but works exactly the same on all mammals, humans included. And if you put your back into casting the spell, it makes the relevant parts just drop off."

He looked grave. "It's a very unfortunate thing to happen, since only a qualified medical magician or a priest could possibly stick it back on." Alexei looked like he was going to be ill. "I was just thinking of teaching the spell to Zunvect since it's a routine operation and he'll have plenty of time to practice before most of the cows are ready again. Of course, I'm having a bit of trouble thinking of what he'd practice it on." He took a big swig of his drink. "So, what were we talking about?"

Alexei just stood there, gaping. "Come on, let's go." I said to Misha. "I heard you found a new place in the woods."

"I'll come with." Dominka called as we turned away. I had trouble catching my breath as she ran after us, hair streaming behind. "I think I could use some air."

"Don't give the town anything to talk about!" Ivan called after us, still smiling broadly. "Buck up." He said to Alexei. "I'll buy you a drink and tell you all about lambing season."

Misha led us deep into the forest to the south of the village. We were never worried about getting lost since the mountains always loomed to our left, and even if we lost sight of *those*, there was almost no chance of us ever failing to find the tower if we looked for it. I tried to keep up a chatter with Dominka, but after telling us that she thought most boys were a bit dopey and that Ivan was a hilarious drunk, she seemed content to enjoy nature and we fell into a silent march. The trees grew higher as we journeyed deeper in, and I couldn't help but worry about what we'd do if we met something.

"Like what?" Misha asked. "An Elf?" He laughed. "Nothing like that comes anywhere near us."

"I was actually thinking about a bear," I said. I wasn't. Misha could laugh, but occasionally we saw trolls, and we were swiftly walking away from the human lands. *Any* land that wasn't already settled with a town or a road belonged to someone else. The casual traveler was lucky to remain ignorant of who or what.

"Elves aren't what we'll find here." Dominka shuddered. "Trolls, werewolves. *Dragons*."

"We're not that far away from town." Misha assured us. "Dragons? Really? Dragons live on the mountain, not down here."

"Trolls and werewolves?" Dominka asked sharply.

"It's right over here." We'd followed an almost invisible track. Misha had better eyes than I thought if he could find what must have been a truly ancient path. His mother was a trapper, though, so perhaps it was no surprise that he'd learned to detect things in the forest that were hidden to most people. Every so often gray stone slabs emerged from the ground, meaning that wherever we were going, it had once been worked by the hands of a tool using race. As you know, that narrows it down to five or ten possibilities.

The path ended at a rock dome. It looked natural, as if something beneath the earth had blown a bubble in the stone, and the bubble had floated up until it reached the air and then stayed there. Misha led us around it to a low opening – even a normal sized human would have had to stoop to enter. Inside the ground fell so that we could stand up straight again in the small cave that had been formed by the rock bubble. This place must have been exceedingly old indeed, as what had seemed like a low door was in fact an opening at least eight feet tall, but with three feet of it blocked by the accumulation of earth around whatever it was. The dome was being slowly buried.

"What is it?" Dominka asked.

I swept the floor with my shoe. The earth had piled up high at the door, but inside it hadn't accumulated as much. The floor was smooth, black, shiny stone. "It looks natural, but it feels…"

I couldn't put it into words, and the others didn't seem quite as affected. The room was dark until Misha lit a candle, giving me the chance to see that whatever this place was, it was in some way linked to magic. The earth magic was bending around the room and the only place it came in was through the door. If the bubble sealed, there would be no magic at all inside of it. It was also much too big. I could walk around the outside in about twenty seconds, so the light of the candle should have reached the opposite wall. In fact, *daylight* should have at least given us some sight of it. Instead, the inside of the dome stretched into utter darkness, a darkness that felt much deeper than a few meters.

"I found it this spring." Misha said, proud of his find. "I don't think anyone in the village knows about this place. We could meet here and no one would find us."

"Have fun." Dominka said. "I think I'd rather have my fun anywhere else."

"Yeah, I …" Something about the bubble called to me. It was pulling at me. As if it wanted something. I felt myself moving forward, about to reach out to touch whatever it was. Then Misha touched my shoulder and I jolted back to myself. "Yeah, this is a neat place but a bit cold."

"I guess." Misha was disappointed, but obviously agreed with us. What had seemed exciting and mysterious was feeling ominous now. We left and returned to the village in silence. I don't know why, but I felt no desire to tell Ivan about Misha's find.

This may sound reckless, even idiotic. After all, these days if you found a strange geological formation that instilled a feeling of dread and seemed to be trying to get you to make magical contact, you'd naturally tell a mage about it. That's because you live in more civilized times. When I was growing up there were so many magical contamination sites that we just thought of them as places to find and then be sure never to go back to. My village was built on one. As I said before, finding cursed land was mysterious and exciting for youngsters. Occasionally someone got hurt, but that was because they were careless. Besides, who were we going to tell? Ivan would only tell us to stop being young fools and stay away from such places – and we knew that! If it was a really dangerous spot like a zombie patch or a werewolf generator, then he'd have to tell Lord Vectreon. We only brought *him* into the picture when things got very serious. I considered myself lucky to have never seen him.

Zunvect 4:

Veterinarian's Charge

It was winter of the following year when Ivan finally decided to let me try to cast a spell on an animal. I had turned fourteen that spring. I was over two meters tall and broad shouldered like most boys my age. One benefit I'd never really considered when I started learning from Ivan was that there was no one in town who ate better than he did, including Mayor Bowbringer. The post of veterinary sorcerer meant he was usually paid in food. Being the occasional protector of the village from things coming out of the forest added to those payments. Magic was hungry work and he ate more than many people who worked all day in the fields. I was a *teenage* sorcerer. You can imagine how much *I* ate.

I'd kept up on the farm work alongside learning from Ivan, who had arrested my swift rise in apparent magical talent by piling on the non-magical education. I was still meditating, exercising, and in fact doing everything to do with magic except for actual spells. The reason I didn't *use* magical spells was that I wasn't very good at controlling them. I remember the first real practical spell he taught me. It was a simple ignition spell. Useful for lighting candles or kindling the fire. A sorcerous trick that he deemed more useful for me than him since *I* didn't need to reserve my strength nearly as much as he did.

"Words and gestures, Zunvect, with the intent of terminating the final flick *towards* the candle wick. Your intention will guide the magic from there." Ivan said. As before, the book was propped up next to me and the candle sat on the stump outside his house and several meters away from me.

"Why are we practicing this outdoors?"

"Why do you think?" He asked, forcing me to do so.

"Fire magic indoors is a bad idea when you've never done it before?"

"There you go."

I sighed, rolling my eyes. Why would he think I would mess this up? How *could* I? I focused on the spell and it felt like second nature to make the motions in the correct order, the words coming to me easily now that I had practiced reading the phonetic script for hours on end. I ended with my finger precisely in line with the candle wick at the exact moment the words ended and the conduit formed.

They said that the column of flame reached the clouds, which is preposterous. It was supposedly visible from my own farm on the other side of town, which is just about possible. Ivan complained that he liked that stump, which was a bit unfair considering the state *I* was in after the pressure wave lifted me off my feet and threw me into a hedge.

"Next time we're attacked by trolls." Ivan said, picking the leaves off his trousers. "I'll be sure to hand them a candle."

"What happened?"

"What do you think?" He snapped. "You poured in enough magic to light a cathedral full of candles. There goes my table stump." He groused.

"It didn't feel like a lot of magic to me."

Ivan seemed about to say something sarcastic, but calmed himself. "In that case, I think we need to go back to some of the mindfulness exercises. See if we can get you to be able to hold back more." His beard was a mess and my shirt was torn but because of his caution, we had suffered no worse damage. "You may also benefit from reading this."

He went into his house and returned with a little red book, about thirteen by eighteen. The cover was plain leather with a sigil burned into it, which seemed familiar. I looked up. It was the same icon as the one on the keystone above Ivan's door.

The River and the Wheel

Author Unknown (believed ~1000 BXR)

Contemplate the River. The River flows from here to there, and that is all that many see when they look upon it. Contemplate the Wheel. It is both within the River and outside of it. It takes from the River and turns, and that is all that many see.

The River is the realm of the Thaumic. The River is many things. It is the spring, the ice melt, and the rain which feed it. It is the loam and stone of the bed, which make it rough here and smooth there; falling, foaming, flowing. It is the bank, which may be wider to make the river seem to dawdle, and narrow to send it racing. Whence it comes and where it goes is where you will find a Thaumologist. How it flows and why it races here and foams there is the place to seek a Thaumist.

The Wheel is where the Thaumaturgic meets the Thaumic. The Wheel is turned by the River, and sits with some of it in the River, hidden beneath its surface, and outside of it, where we might see it move as the River moves. It turns and in turning each part returns to the River again, unseen, and then to the air, where we once again observe the effects.

The Wheel does not turn for itself.

The Machine is the realm of the Thaumaturgic. The Wheel turns the axle, and the gears of the Machine are turned with it. The gears, some large, some small, meet tooth to gap and so the magician's work is done. Some Thaumaturgists care about just one gear, while others seek to fit them together into a greater mechanism. The Thaumaturgist may have many names for what they do, but lose not the sight of the River and the Wheel as you tend the Machine, for the Machine is naught but many Wheels all turning upon the same axle.

Without the Machine, the Wheel would have no reason to turn. Without the River, the Wheel would have no strength to turn. Without the Wheel, the River would be naught but a spectacular insignificance, beautiful as the flower, but pointless as seed with no soil.

The course in restraint was long and one of the most difficult magical projects I have ever embarked on. Every day after meditating on my magic, I would try to move a pebble. To be more precise, I would try *not* to move it. To hit it with so little magic that I failed to overcome the force of static friction. At first the pebble flew so far that we had to get a new one. After a few months, it was only going a few meters. I kept working at it, but progress was painfully slow, and until I could prove I was able to hold back, I wasn't to learn any spells.

Let's skip forward a year. A year of of me working almost every day to control my magical output. It was an especially cold predawn in Missus Herskorn's chicken field. She was standing, bundled up to her ears like we were, her foot tapping, obviously impatient as we made our examination.

"It's obviously an infection." I hissed. "A simple one at that."

"Of course it is. Enteritis, I'd say." Ivan replied.

"So the cure is simple. A broad parasitic reduction."

"What I'm tarrying on," Ivan growled, "is whether to let *you* try it."

"Me?" I said, loudly and forgetting that we were trying to keep it down so that the farmer wouldn't hear our conference. She threw us a narrow-eyed glance, obviously weighing whether that meant anything that could affect Ivan's fee. "I'm not a veterinary sorcerer."

"Yes, you." Ivan said. "I'm aware that you are not accredited to perform the task, but as you're my assistant, I do have some latitude. If I think you're up to it, simple spells are allowed."

"But – what if I…" I didn't want to say it aloud.

"If you do, then we'll owe her a chicken. You've been practicing on dead ones enough. I think you can do it."

I nodded, squaring myself for the task. My legs felt like they were going to fold under me as I moved my hands and said the words, willing the chicken to get well, for the parasites to all be burned away. You can guess what happened next.

For most sorcerers, that act of supreme will is needed to make a spell work. To put *meaning* and *intention* behind the work of pulling the raw power out of the earth and making it do what you want it to. For them it's like putting your shoulder behind a tree and pushing until it falls over. For a wizard, it's more like running at full speed into a field of springy new saplings and hoping to only knock down one. That's why our spells are structurally different. Theirs limits loss, ours limits gain.

The chicken let out a single, panicky squawk, and then burst. I am not too proud to say that, when I felt the feathers and blood plastering my face, I threw up. I'd seen animals slaughtered for food, of course, and even when they were horribly diseased. I had never seen one explode.

Ivan finished the job and paid the farmer for her lost chicken. The farmer was still complaining about lost egg production as we gathered up what bits we could find and trudged off to make a chicken breakfast out of the smithereens. Ivan didn't have to say anything as we ate in his cottage; he knew and I knew that unless something changed, I would never be a worker of small magic.

"On the plus side," he said, trying to cheer me up, "if someone needs battle magic, or to have their sails filled with wind, I figure you'll have no problem. Maybe you can get work mining. They're always causing all manner of mayhem as they burrow into the ground." He saw my expression and patted my shoulder. "Were I a war-mage, a miner, or a seaman I wonder if your reaction would be the same on finding that you were better cut out to be a veterinary sorcerer. Imagine that! Me, a big strong fire throwing siege sorcerer and your expression when you realized you were better at seeing to the horses than casting down fortresses."

I smiled weakly. I knew he was right. It would take awhile for the disappointment to pass, but it was the disappointment of having a path closed. Soon would come the excitement of the paths that were now open.

Deftness and gentleness are linked in magic, as I am sure a demonologist who conjures a god would know. My great strength meant that there were spells that Ivan had in his books that only I could cast. Turning winter to summer in a secluded dell – that is, I raised the temperature of about ten thousand cubic meters around me by twenty degrees – and moving the boulders that occasionally rolled down the mountain were favorites in town. Imagine having an outdoor fete in midwinter with no need for warm clothes, the snow falling turning to mist as it entered your bubble of festive cheer, and then putting on your winter togs and waiting a few hours while all that water froze again and you could slip around and use barrel covers to slide at dangerous speeds from one end of the meadow to the other....

Idalia 2:

Alumna Meeting

The narrative slowed to a halt, and Idalia looked up from her notes to stare at Zunvect. The staff had gone dim, and Zunvect's eyes were emitting a strange light, warmer and more distant than usual. She got up and prodded at the wards around him, taking readings from their reaction. Something was wrong; they were reporting that there was nothing in the sphere of magic. "Zunvect!" She called. "Don't you fade away on me!" She bustled around the wards, hastily tweaking their properties to try to lock on to Zunvect's magical signature again. The staff burned white and so did Zunvect's eyes.

"Where am I?" He said, cotton-tongued and vaguely staring into the distance. "What's going on?"

"Come back!" Idalia shouted. "You're losing yourself."

Zunvect shook his head and his face tightened in concentration. "Oh … right … here I am!" The runes on his staff changed back to their previous crawling up and down, and he let out a breath. "Sorry, got lost in the mists of time there. I went all lyrical and started to see it like it was really there."

"I wondered about the poetry."

"A poor translation, hence the lack of meter and rhyme. Yes, I think someone must have written it back home and I was just remembering it. I don't recall ever being artistic, though maybe I did write it during my studies as an exercise." He shook his head and rolled his shoulders. "I need a break. Why don't you tell me how you retrieved my staff? It helped you save me from whatever was about to happen just now, and I want to know how it was being treated in my absence."

"I thought you could see the minds of the magi. Can't you just take what you want?"

"Very diplomatic, *ambassador*. We both know that you're my mistress in this relationship, so your mind is closed to me. I saw it from your President's perspective, but only in patches. Her mind has … unfamiliar features."

Idalia shrugged. There was no reason to hide anything from Zunvect. He was her prisoner, and nothing she told him would leave the room unless she allowed it. "She's both President of the Unity Senate and Archmage of the university I went to for my education as a mage. Going to her office always felt like being called to see the headmaster."

Visiting the President had been as terrifying an experience for Idalia as her brief encounter with Lord Xetic-Nal. Returning to her old university – the seats of power in each region – had been jarring. She'd remembered the paths and roads within Huywer Regional University as bright and energetic places. They were often filled with magi of all ages and strength classes engaging in recreation between classes, or else strolling between the imposing buildings, the younger magi still restricted to using their feet to get from lecture to lab. As she'd approached Nicodemus Hall where the administrative and legislative offices had been located, the campus was subdued. The return of the God of Wizards was not the celebration the god himself would have wanted.

Even the ancient and not-so-ancient halls of magical education seemed afflicted with the uncertainty of the time. Overcast skies turned crystal spires dull, and the very enchantments which caused many a window and chimney to glow were damped down. The lurid shades of thaumic backwash were turned to sullen hazes. The President herself must have felt some of the pressure. The motion enchantments on the avenues were set to a crawl, and Idalia shivered at how plain and boring the grass fields were without their kaleidoscope of fractured continuity. No one was going to have fun playing volleyball when the trajectories of ball and player were so easy to predict.

For the first time in years, Idalia was painfully aware of her own appearance. She was dressed with her black and blue outer robe signifying that she communed with intelligences across gulfs of space and void. Her five gold First Contact medals shone from recent cleaning. She'd even gone as far as to wear the robe with all twelve of her patches for successful planetary exploration. Still, her brown hair might be well coiffed, but it was still dull and uninteresting compared to the riot of colors available. None of the students around her had chosen anything so drab. She'd done her best with her skin, but it was still pockmarked in places from an unfortunately acne-prone youth. She was also shorter, rounder, and wider than most women of her era. Magi of the First remained youthful most of their lives, and she'd had the misfortune to have her body stop aging before she'd gotten rid of all of her baby fat.

She'd worked with creatures with no concept of human fashion or beauty, and never had the time or inclination for the routine body modifications most magi engaged in. It was a mark of pride for her not to give in to the current craze of emulating a sort of humanly sexualized elven appearance. She'd had nothing but sardonic derision for being turned tall and slender, with those ridiculously bony faces and big eyes. Nor was she enamored of the trend in her youth towards narrow waists and big everything elses. Still, she reflected, it might have been nice to be a *little* altered for this meeting. It might have made her feel more prepared for the woman she was about to meet.

Idalia took a long Tunneling Step, bypassing the walks between her and Nicodemus Hall, and then another, skipping the entrance hall and foyer. Emerging from an almost imperceptible shimmer in the air, she arrived precisely one step in front of President Chronomarien's receptionist's desk. Her appointment having been confirmed, she was shocked again to be ushered directly into the President's office.

Every tenant had their own style, and Chronomarien was a renowned thaumaturge and enchanter, so it was no surprise that she favored an almost museum atmosphere. Idalia passed between glass fronted cabinets and display cases to the imposing Cherrywood desk of the most politically powerful human being since Nicodemus himself had united the Staff of a regional Senator, the bronze Key of the President of the Senate of Magi, and the pectoral Sunburst of the Lord of the Sun. Silveria Chronomarien was leader of a region, leader of all mankind, *and* the heir to the Sunlord in the Solar Conclave. Had she been born with the unique ability to sing, she might have perhaps become Conductor of the Sorcerous Symphony – ruler of the Symphonic Collective – and thus rivaled Xetic-Nal or Zunvect himself in power.

This was the person Zunvect had sent her to *haggle* with.

"Mage First Idalia Periscalitin," Silveria intoned, standing to shake Idalia's hand, "top ranked non-local entity communications concentration, specializing in binding and discovery. An impressive academic record." She touched a buff colored folder with the tip of a bloodless finger, her reflective silver eyes boring into Idalia. "Impressive achievements as well. Discovering twelve potentially habitable and *inhabited* worlds. First Contact with five different civilizations. Your career has been a credit to this institution. Now you're the bona fide owner of your own deity, who is decidedly *not* non-local. My, my, you may be up for my job one of these days."

Silveria gestured for Idalia to sit in the leather wing-backed chair across the desk, and then seated herself in an imposing high-backed swivel chair. Despite her demeanor and the loosely curled silver hair that she carefully arranged before sitting back, Silveria was as youthful in her face and body as any other Mage First – those who had once been called wizards. She was also not that much older than Idalia herself. Idalia was accounted on the young side of middle age for a Mage First, and Silveria was knocking on elderly for a Node, the mostly human and immensely powerful members of the Solar Conclave. She was also – very strangely – not physically modified by conscious intent, but bore instead the marks of someone affected deeply by unpredictable magic. She no doubt could have returned herself to what she'd been before, or something else entirely, but there was strength in bearing the scars of ancient and unpredictable magic.

"I remember when I was a boy," Silveria said, referring in her disconcertingly breezy way to the period when she was a male Node with a female Anecho, before that revived spirit of one of his ancestors merged with his body and the two had become a single person. "I dreamed of being a heroic Wizard-Lord, perhaps even the Sunlord himself. Zunvect, Grandfather of my race. How strange it is to speak to someone who has met him. If Xetic-Nal had not come to me this very morning, I would consider it a unique honor. If Xetic-Nal had not made his opinion clear as the Sunlord's own day, I would ask you to invite him to speak before the Solar Conclave. Ah well. Perhaps when the delicate matter of the resurgence of divinity has passed, we'll be able to mend those fences. I understand that you come with an offer from our esteemed Grandfather."

"Lord Zunvect," Idalia said, staying away from his legendary title of Sunlord and the familiar and private appellation 'Grandfather' that the Solar Conclave used, "desires his staff."

Silveria rose and, with a gesture that was both spell and pass-key, opened a tall display case that was in place of prominence just inside the door to her office. The two-meter midnight black metal staff zoomed down the aisle, flipped over Idalia's head, and came to rest in Silveria's hand. As if in recognition of the Node's kinship with its maker and true master, the Staff of Zunvect's twin Thau-mine spheres detached from the Obdurin and Ductin head of the staff and began to orbit it. The three metals of magic were rare even in the present day and had been priceless in Zunvect's time. Maker, Blocker, and Sender.

Silveria's regard of the ancient artifact was more reverent even than Zunvect's. "I'm sure you know, but I rediscovered the Staff during my student days. A colleague from the University of Miyaria showed me what she thought was a very old and powerful Staff of Expectation. It had been passed down in her family for countless generations. Since Miyaria was Zunvect's first viable grandchild and the first ever Node, I suspect that it had been in my friend's family for the better part of two thirds of recorded history. It's priceless, so of course I couldn't *buy* it. It's borrowed as a sym-bol of both the Solar Conclave and the Senate with Desora's bless-ing. She comes to see it from time to time."

Silveria gently placed the Staff on her desk, and again the silver eyes shining in the lights of her office seemed to look into Idalia's soul. "What you are proposing is that I give you an artifact as old as our civilization, more important than anything else the magi own, a priceless heirloom of Miyaria, the symbol of the Solar Con-clave's link to the founder of the magi, and something that isn't even *mine*. I deeply respect Grandfather Zunvect. I would like nothing more than to restore to him his property. I am left with a doubt, a question that cannot be dismissed. What is he offering that outweighs the very real political issues inherent in letting the most valuable thing on the planet walk out of this office in the hands of a woman whose actions have resulted in the end of Gotterdammerung and the extreme displeasure of Lord Xetic-Nal?"

Idalia was breathless, unable to speak. She had answers prepared, but now she wasn't sure she could force herself to say a word in answer to the rebukes in President Chronomarien's response to her. "I – he offers what the Solar Conclave has never had, what it has desired for eight thousand years." She took a long breath and gulped hard to fight down nervousness. Reaching into a Pocket Bag, she pulled out a staff that was as black as the Staff of Zunvect, but with more complex Ductin inlay which took the light and returned it in a dizzying array of ever changing channels. *Four* Thaumine spheres orbited its crown, which was a sharp sunburst rather than a simple rounded top. "This is the true Staff of the Sunlord, as designed by Zunvect. He had to decrease the scope of his original plans because he couldn't afford the materials. He offers this in recognition of the Solar Conclave as his representatives and emissaries. Zunvect the Sunlord offers *legitimacy*. When you open the Solar Conclave with the Staff of the Sunlord, it will be official that the Nodes are the true heirs of Zunvect's authority." Idalia placed the offered arcana next to the item Zunvect had told her to obtain at all costs.

For the first time, Idalia thought she had the advantage. Silveria looked with longing at the Staff of the Sunlord. "Millennia of strife and doubt. He's offering to end the rumors that we took our roles as opportunists and not as his true children." President Chronomarien gripped the new staff in pale fingers. "The University board will be livid, the Senate will vote to expel me, but the Conclave … the Conclave will have what it has fought to keep for eight thousand years." She looked up at Idalia and whispered. "Deal. Take it. It's yours. My friends will hate me for this, but I am a Node first, a Node before anything else. My people are what matters, not the history of a pseudo nobility, or the silly one-upmanship between universities. Zunvect knows his children well." She stroked the Staff of Zunvect once and the black metal seemed to recede along the neck where the shaft met the head. A gold band that seemed to flicker and writhe appeared, then expanded to slide off of the original Staff, moving to take the same place on the newly made symbol of the power and truth of the Sunlord's children.

"Interesting." Zunvect said, in a thoughtful purr that made Idalia's hackles rise. "I know that the ring that she showed you was the more valuable of the two, and that's a remarkable achievement. It recognized the staff like the staff recognizes me. The ring was acting as a sort of symbiote. I imagine the President used it to control the staff so that he – she, I really must stop using her persistent mental image to determine her gender – could access portions I reserved for myself. Camouflaged as part of the staff, so she's trying to hide it from the others. I wonder what it could be…"

"I have no idea what you are talking about."

"Sorry. Old habits. Whenever I find out someone's being sneaky, I find it safest to assume I'm involved. Egotistical, but life saving when correct. Right, I was just telling you about how I was better at amusements and amenities than saving lives or keeping the stock healthy."

Zunvect 5:

Rough Enchantment

In this, as in many other things, I found myself more popular though less respected than Ivan, especially by the youth of my village. I tried to act like I was just doing a job, and that magic wasn't such a big deal, but I couldn't help but revel in their adulation. It was especially exciting when young women smiled at me and asked for spells. I had to refuse more often than not; I just didn't have the time. Though I never felt very tired after casting spells, I knew it meant a lot to Ivan that I pace myself. Besides, though Ivan tried to be supportive, I knew he was pained by how the villagers complimented me and were so much friendlier than they were to him. He saved their lives, but I brought the carnival.

It was enough to keep me from complaining about how there were only piddling small jobs to do in our village – most of the time – and to stop veterinary sorcery once and for all when I attempted an impromptu flea cure as a favor to Misha's father. The shepherd was getting creaky in his old age and didn't want to walk all the way to Ivan's cottage, but his prize sheepdog was getting the itches and doing poorly at his job because of it. No, Idalia, I didn't kill the dog. It *smoked* for an hour or so after I was done, and the poor animal's fluffy coat never grew back in some patches, but it lived and certainly didn't have any fleas anymore.

Occasionally I snuck into the forest and tried this or that spell on the local wildlife, but eventually my father and brother said they had enough squirrel meat packed away and I was getting sick to my stomach every time one flopped off its tree still steaming. I was a farm lad and familiar with slaughtering pigs and even hunting small game, but it felt wrong to inflict death like that on the local rodents.

There was one other major reason not to be profligate with my magic – apart from the secret reason Ivan never told me – which was that eventually I would leave. I had to, since in our region the regulation on sorcerers was that all natural magicians may be trained up to the age of seventeen by a competent and licensed sorcerer. At any time before, and firmly at, the age of seventeen, a magician, whether trained or untrained, had to present themselves to Lord Vectreon in person and request a license to practice. Most regions had a power limit, above which one was classed a sorcerer and required to have a primary and secondary license. The primary allowed you to practice for as long as you were enrolled in a magical college, and the secondary was awarded on graduation. Our region's bar was quite low, but no matter where I lived there was no doubt I would have to be educated officially in a structured curriculum by an accredited institution. Everyone knew that and the wise ones refrained from asking me for more help than they could afford. They knew that anything I could do that Ivan could not was a temporary arrangement, and that they'd have to live without me very soon.

In power, I had outstripped Ivan from the first day. As far as complexity went, I eventually had Ivan flummoxed there as well. It took me *months* but with daily practice I finally managed it. I produced a heatless light source. This is of course a misnomer. What I'd done was produce a very *low* heat light source, which is simply a matter of efficiency rather than violating natural law.

However, for generating light in a productive manner – that is, without blinding myself and everyone nearby – I still relied on candles and the like. The more efficient the source, the less energy it needed and so I found myself unable to produce a heatless source that wasn't exceedingly bright. This meant mastering fire, which was still hard for me. As I said, I *could* manage to light a candle without blowing myself up, but as seen on the chicken farm, I needed to concentrate very hard and be extremely calm. Casual or stressful casting still led to far more power being used than I wanted.

"Look here," I said, pointing to a page in one of Ivan's books about magic, "it says that many strong sorcerers employ a focusing device. Maybe I need to make one of those. There are mentions of it in multiple locations, but I can't find anything beyond a superficial description. It's strange. They're all made of wood. Magic flows very poorly through wood."

"I can think of a few reasons, but I only ever met a handful of sorcerers who used wands and staves as they seem to usually be. That instructor I told you about who was a yellow-zone was one. He had a great big staff made of oak. I never saw him use it for anything other than clouting people over the head and knocking on doors, so there's every chance that the very fine and polished wooden staff was only a prop. I know he carved runes into it, and every source I've seen has dismissed rune magic as nonsense. I don't think you're going to find a solution in enchantasy. Not in this village, and not from me."

Still, the idea had stuck in my head and I started looking around for big sticks and woodfalls. I had a strange notion that a branch might call out to me and transfigure itself in front of my eyes into a tool of destiny. It was a storybook notion of how magic worked, and I ought to have known better. Thank goodness I didn't!

Before I tell you that story, I should tell you this one. Not that either have any bearing on each other – not in the least directly – but because this happened first, and it tells you a lot about the state of knowledge in those days. I was fifteen, and it was summer. These two things conspired to mean that Ivan had to make the lessons more interesting in order to get my attention, so he turned to geography. A dangerous topic indeed, as maps in those days were inextricably linked to *stories,* and though he loved to tell them he knew he had to hold back lest he tell me all the apocryphal tales he knew and ran out of things to use to get me to remain interested in mathematics, science, and other things which were interesting enough but not nearly as much as the amazing things which happened to other people in places further than I would ever travel. Tall tales that were just plausible enough to be true.

"We are here." He said, pointing to a place neither north nor south, but west of west. The western shore of the western continent – labeled 'Ismun' on the map - to the west of the great mountains on which our Wizard-Lords built their towers. I knew that there were beaches not far to the west of our village, but I had never been there.

"Instead of moving intellectually," I said, "why don't we move physically?"

"What, you mean point to a place on the map and suddenly appear there?" Ivan laughed. "That's a touch beyond us."

"No, I mean go to the shore and look at the encircling mountains where the west and east meet."

"You wouldn't see much. It's just a wall of earth and rock, and only visible on the clearest day as a darker haze in the distance. It may be taller than any mountain hereabouts, but it's still just another mountain from our side. If we were foolish enough to cross the channel, we'd get a better look, but we wouldn't be able to go further. The Bowl is unclimbable, and its face reaches the water line."

I pointed to the place on the map where it was blank, the only such gap in human knowledge of our world. It was a ring of mountains on the eastern continent – Bomarie - where it drew close to our western one. East and west are of course rather vague things in a spherical planet, but it made sense that we were west. The only way to reach us was from the east, after all. The rich cities were on the eastern side of the mountains that divided our continent, and there was a lot of superstition around the channel between us and the Bowl.

The Bowl was the name of both the mountain range and the land that sat within the ring-shaped mountain range. Within the Bowl, there was nothing, and no one returned from it. Even being near them was considered bad luck. No ship would sail into the shadow of their western wall, and there was nowhere to port since no one would live within sight of them. On the other hand, all the stories spoke of how nothing left the lands ringed by the highest peaks in the world, so in truth it seemed a very safe neighbor as long as you didn't want to visit.

"Fine, then let's go back to our own land." I said. "The rest of the eastern half is boring."

"Yes," Ivan drawled, "I can see how trackless deserts full of powerful spirits, forests so deep that the hearts almost certainly contain something ancient and strong, and jungles where even Wizard-Lords find their powers tested against the beasts within would be *boring*. Just because the borders of the Wizard-Lords' territories meet and cover the land, don't think that they *control* all of it. Not to mention that we are not the only two major landmasses. But yes, let us ignore the near limitless east, mysterious islands, and remote south, and focus on the long and narrow isthmus that we live on. I take it that you are similarly bored with the center, despite the fact that the mountains are home to Dwarves, the seas to masters we haven't even a name for, and the forests are filled with the live remnants of the last true magical war fought. So, north or south?"

"North." I said eagerly.

"Of course." His finger traveled up until it reached a peninsula where the channels on either side met at the Sea of Songs. A peninsula where the mountains dividing us ended, and a wide plain was said to stretch as far as the eye could see. "An empty place, but for the Singing City. What better place for a rebellious teenager than the only human government in the world that does not recognize the authority of the Wizard-Lords?"

Excerpt from the Introduction to *A Dream of Endless Music* (3446 [XR³])

No polity has ever been so vexing to the society of well governed magic than that of the Singing City. It was said that when the Wizard-Lord Sol Viexta first laid eyes on it, he believed the translucent, shimmering walls which straddled the only river on the plains to be a mirage. On closer inspection, he concluded that it was a settlement of Elves that had maintained hope for almost three thousand years and were still building crystal cities as if the Uidrana has never left. This is what he reported – erroneously – to his fellows to the south, and under the assumption that elves had made a hard and open claim to the peninsula, the Wizard-Lords' conquest ended at the cliff face where the final mountain fell to the plain. It is said that Xetic-Nal knew of this, and made no attempt to enlighten the 'reclamation crew', instead letting the dangerously large group of sorcerers in the far north continue to self-govern, and more importantly to maintain an independent state where any sorcerer could go and find freedom from the regulation of wizards. Though many are annoyed at the freedom given to those who live in the flat-lands on the *southern* end of the continent, the Sky Vision is agreed to serve a valuable purpose while the Singing City's utility remains a topic of debate.

---

³ XR added for clarity – Ed.

In modern times, the Singing City is seen by its wizard proponents as an efficient way to deal with turbulent sorcerers. Let them gather, the Wizard-Lords say, in one place where they won't be a nuisance. We will trade with them, and leave them be, and they will be alone. Any sorcerer who cannot be governed may find a place there and let them spend the rest of their lives singing for their supper.

The opinions of the sorcerers of the Singing City is not known, as they do not speak of politics to outsiders, though it can be guessed from merchant caravaners' talk that the sorcerers find this a pleasant arrangement, and the ability to not only work without a Wizard-Lords' writ, but also to build magic upon magic in the harmony of the collective is something far more valuable than living in 'society.' What few Wizard-Lords will admit is that this very harmonic collective is what makes attempting reclamation distasteful. Who wants to be the first to try their single magic – powerful as it is – against the combined mental and thaumaturgical presence of a hundred thousand sorcerers all casting the same spell?

My lust for stories – especially for the fruitless speculation about what happened to the north and south – was never sated. Though I scorned the east for its soft civility, the islands for their lack of history, and the far south for its irrelevance and remoteness, still I was more than willing to hear about what happened there. The far south was still an almost total unknown in that time which was mainly due to the climate rather than the defenses around other hard to reach places, and the islands were already becoming a very strange place, each one strange in a totally different way.

It was with a head full of stories that I sometimes wandered the forest, trying out magic I knew Ivan would disapprove of or wish not to be seen by the town. There I could call forth light which washed away the false color which overlayed the mundane world. I could heal small animals without farmers to jangle my nerves and spoil my control. It was in the forest that I was able to feel as if the mysterious world outside the village was close, and that magic which lived only in Ivan's stories might come to me even without a spell to hand. I searched through the months for a tree branch or a stick or even a twig that would call out. In the deepest winter I trudged down the old tracks which few in the village dared tread – their excuse was dread, but their real reason was that they enjoyed the beer at the tavern more than a trek through woods to some ruin which didn't do anyone any good these days.

It was in that winter that I went off the tracks I knew and found a new one. It led to a clearing, small but bright with winter sun. There was a sapling in the middle and from it grew a perfect branch, crooked and yet straight in my mind. I plucked it from the tree, and I could feel magic in it. With a flourish of the branch I called forth the summer and it came, and the tree seemed to thank me. I also loosened an icicle from a much taller tree with an over-hanging branch above me and I almost impaled myself. So much for the perfection of destiny.

I noticed, as I left, that the branch was starting to char near the end, and the few withered leaves from the previous season were turned to embers, the ash drifting in my wake. I saw that the tip was alight as if it had been thrust into a fire and just removed, and when I let the summer spell go, it dimmed and went out. A wisp of smoke rose, and the branch was just a branch again. I hurried back to Ivan's, fearful that my perfect wand wood was going to go up in flames before I could do anything with it.

Ivan was no help. He didn't have any books that even hinted at how wands and staves and other foci were made; only that they were wielded to great effect by many legendary sorcerers. I went home, dejected, and put the branch up on a shelf above my bed with the books I was reading and a stuffed cow my mom had made for Mikel and had been handed down to me. I shoveled the walk in front of our house clear of snow and thought about any way I might make a wand with no practical experience. I should mention that I used a shovel because dad didn't like me using magic on our farm. It wasn't that he disapproved of magic, but he'd been brought up and lived his life as a solid, no-frills man. Now that I look back, I don't blame him for his attitude. If I made his life too easy while I was there, would he still be in shape to do the hard work once I was away seeking my fortune? He was glad I had a profession, that I would be a learned and influential sorcerer one day, and that he wouldn't have to divide the farm. On the other hand, Mikel was going to inherit one day, and he needed to keep in shape as much as dad did so he could do the job right. Mikel was even likely to be married and have children – so that put grandkids into the plan!

No, best that magic be kept for emergencies like when the pigs got salt poisoning – and we didn't even need magic for that one – or dragons came down from the mountain. Not that a dragon was likely to ever bother us. They were mostly in the north or high up in the mountains. They rarely came down into human lands, and never without a Wizard-Lord catching wind and chasing them off before they could do any harm. In that, a Wizard-Lord's job was a bit like Ivan's. Ivan kept away the little things like trolls and the Wizard-Lords chased of dragons, elves, and all other manner of terrifying monster.

I went back in the house and couldn't help but fetch down the branch again. Once upon a time, wands had to have been made without the sorcerer knowing anything about the craft. At one time, someone – most probably a wizard – must have made the first and so learned it was possible. What was the small matter of making an enchanted object without knowing anything other than it could be done next to the achievement of doing it *first*?

I stared at the branch, falling into my meditation routine with ease. Ivan let me do magic unsupervised all the time now. I was sixteen and careful enough not to cause harm. The branch grew in my vision until it was all that I could see. Like all things, it had some small amount of magic. I tried to work with that. Nothing. It would move, bend, and twist but nothing would change fundamentally. The branch remained a branch. I picked it up and swung it towards a candle, arresting my motion in time to keep myself from casting the spell and probably burning the house down. My frustration grew with the shame of almost doing something really dumb and I stomped off with the candle and the branch.

My father was still in the field trying to do a little bit of ground preparation despite the hard-frozen earth. Anything to keep his hand in. Mikel was seeing to a pig that seemed determined to bite his neighbors in the pen. I was alone on my doorstep. I placed the candle well away from the house and this time completed the spell, branch in hand. The candle lit easily and with none of the usual bursts of flame that often melted them before I could stop the flow of magic. On the other hand, all the leaves on the branch fell off, and the twigs sticking out along its length flared and fell to ash. However, the proto-wand itself only turned darker, as if the flame had licked it but done no more, and the end glowed like an ember and then went out. It gave me an idea.

I put the candle back and tried casting a spell of light instead of heat. The wand grew hot and I pulled back the power of the spell a little. A brilliant speck much dimmer than my usual dazzling sphere appeared near the end. The wand's tip glowed, but I noticed that it never seemed to actually *burn*. No material was consumed. It was a type of feedback, but I didn't know what. I kept casting spells – mostly harmless ones – and the wand seemed to work best when I wasn't using much power. Still, even my usually leaky performances when distracted were much improved. I had an arcane focus. I don't know how I knew this was the right wood, and perhaps some unknown sorcerous instinct had drawn me to it in the first place. I didn't know what I had really done, apart from use it to cast spells, and how *using* it had really worked, apart from the fact that I'd gestured with it in my hand. I only knew that it did work, and I had made it. *I had an arcane focus.*

Ivan was amazed as I cast spell after spell using it. "You're just adapting the standard motions to having it in your hand?" He asked.

"Aye."

"And you say you just made it without any knowledge of how? That you used it to cast spells without prior awareness of how this was done?"

"Yes, Ivan. It's a splendid mystery."

"It's borderline, Zunvect." Ivan muttered. "You did this by instinct and desire; the magic served your intention and your emotion rather than your intellect."

"It worked!" I said, growing hot at his implication I had done something wrong. "If no knowledge exists, then I make some."

I realized then that Ivan was scared. "Zunvect, that is illegal."

"What?" I laughed. "How can it be illegal to learn things I don't know?"

"Creating spells is a proscribed activity." Ivan explained. "The Wizard-Lords have very strict rules about what spells a sorcerer can use."

"That's silly. Anyway, Vectreon won't know. I've been practicing here for years and he hasn't said a word. Do you believe he can know what spell is cast?"

"Maybe, probably not." Ivan relaxed. "You're not quite old enough yet that I have to have you licensed, but the time comes swiftly. I'd recommend you not put it about that you've broken the law before you're even recognized and given your own marque to operate."

"Actually," I said, feeling a bit ashamed to bring it up now, but knowing I had to or else the opportunity might not come again, "that's something I wanted to talk to you about. Maybe I ought to go to Vectreon now. I have enjoyed these years with you, and I cannot think of a better man to have taught me to use magic with wisdom and understanding, but it seems close to time for me to go somewhere to find my path. The colleges of sorcery are where I belong now. You have taught me all you can teach me, all that someone like me can learn from you. Even if I were cut out to be a V.S. like you, I'd need to attend the College."

Ivan's eyes had been turning misty as I talked, and he nodded in assent. "Aye," he said huskily, "it does seem to be nearly time. Give it another year, Zunvect, and you'll be old enough to attend without any bars. I know it seems a long time, but it's for the best." I squeezed his shoulder and left, not knowing that his emotion was not just because I had complimented him and because I was leaving. He was resigning himself to never seeing me again, perhaps even to my death. Not many wizards survive their first meeting with a Wizard-Lord.

Zunvect 6:

Light Threats

Ivan had seemed so distressed that, at first, I stopped using my wand entirely. After a few days, though, I felt like I was wearing heavy greased gloves whenever I did magic. Every time I used magic, I had to fight to keep it from escaping my grip, and there were small adjustments that I was unable to make at all. I couldn't take it, so I started using the wand again. No thunderbolts fell on me to punish me for my presumption, but I remained wary. It was seeing Misha at a dance – he'd ended up with Dominka if the romantic engagements of a village trapper eight thousand years ago mean anything to you – got me to thinking. A couple years before, he had guided us to that strange cavern and we'd never spoken of it afterwards. I remembered … it had seemed like magic was shut out of it. Maybe the eye of a Wizard-Lord would be blind to whatever happened there. I had no idea what I'd do, except that it would be mildly rebellious and show those Wizard-Lords what I thought of them.

The cave-dome-cellar was not so hard to find a second time. In my wandering around the forest, I'd occasionally stumbled on it, always feeling a sense that I should get away as quickly as possible. This time I sought it out intentionally. Not that it was going anywhere, but if the dome was driving people away with magic, then my intention to go might alter its behavior. My projecting didn't seem to have an appreciable effect, but the feeling was manageable as I entered, and fell away within a few minutes of ducking through the half-buried door.

This time I had a much better means of pushing away the darkness and I placed my light spell at the end of my wand *before* going very far in to make sure that it remained. I need not have worried; the power I needed was minimal and I was able to draw plenty through the door. No Wizard-Lord was liable to see me in this shielded place. The dome itself seemed totally insulated, and the Wizard-Lord would have had to peep through the door to see me. I judged this unlikely since by all accounts no Wizard-Lord knew of my hideaway and the door's orientation meant that Vectreon would have to be on ground level to see through it. I was safe.

The light didn't travel as far as it ought to have; my circle of illumination ended abruptly in a straight line on the floor. The far wall was solidly refusing to become visible. On the other hand, nothing had jumped out to eat me. I decided that if it was going to leave me alone, I would do the same, so I resisted the urge to jam my wand right into the darkness. I was afraid of what might happen and equally afraid that nothing would, that the dark wall would devour my wand, or me, or be illuminated and show me something I didn't want to see. I had no magical experiments in mind that day, so I decided that my brief observation was experiment enough. It was a place I returned to often while testing out ideas.

In the spring, I got up enough nerve to put my wand aside and call up the most enormous ball of intense white light I could muster. I threw it at that far wall, and it vanished completely, less than a meter from where I estimated the physical wall should be. I could feel the spell continuing to draw magic from me and from the earth beyond the dome, but no sign of it remained. I called the light back and it emerged as if passing through a solid wall.

There was no way I was going to stick my hand in there to feel around, so I set about thinking of ways to pierce the shadow with magic. It was a project which took until summer, which was fortunate because it was near to Harvest when we needed just that kind of spell.

I don't remember exactly how I came to decide to try it, but I do recall reasoning that any spell over an area had to have a strength measured in terms of that area. That is, the more pressure applied in one place, the more likely I was to break through. A lot of mechanical talk for the idea that a rock won't pierce leather, but an arrow will. Same force, smaller area, more concentrated piercing power. I needed to *see*, however, so fire was no good. The one thing Ivan flatly refused to tell me about was lightning – I think because he worried about how much I'd call down at once, which was sensible. It had to be the light spell. Ivan didn't have a magnifying glass, but they were mentioned in a few places, so I knew that light could be concentrated in one place. There was my grand experiment, the one that would be harmless enough but also dangerously illicit. I would concentrate light until I could see through the dark curtain in a spot and then run it along the wall until I knew what had been hidden. Yes, Idalia, I was dangerously and willfully moronic. Thank you for stating the obvious. What was that about calling a god into a summoning circle again?

The wand helped immensely in my visualization of the concentrated light. All I wanted was for the sphere or speck which radiated in all directions to radiate the same amount but only in the direction pointed by the wand and, if possible, with no more than the wand's diameter. This visualization was by itself nonsense, but it helped me feel out how the wand interacted with the light spell and how to change it by mixing in parts of other spells. Sometimes I'd do something very wrong and feel like a hammer had struck me in the head. Occasionally I'd get closer and the ray would tighten for a moment and then lose cohesion. Every failure was a lost day and every success a silent celebration. I dared not tell Ivan about it, so it was my secret. All that he and my father knew was that I was working harder than ever for them so that I could leave early and disappear off to some secluded location. I'm sure it puzzled them mightily since there were so few youngsters in town that they knew for certain that it wasn't a girl or boy I was meeting, but since I always came back unharmed they decided to let the teenager have his secrets. I'd work it out of my system eventually.

Shortly before Harvest, I pierced the curtain and saw the wall. I was deeply disappointed and thought all my efforts had been wasted. The wall was carved with a script which looked ancient and menacing, but was totally incomprehensible to me. Catastrophe! Whoever had hollowed out this cave and placed the chilling enchantments on it was either educated in foreign languages or had come here before the Wizard-Lords turned Trade into the only language I'd ever heard spoken. Both ideas made the place more exciting, but I'd also reached a dead end of understanding. Dejected, I didn't bother to try to read more than a few of the letters, an alphabet unknown to me. It was impossible for me to even sound out the words. The secrets of this cave I had made my own were doomed to remain secret forever. Angry, I ignited the air – an act both thoughtless and ignorant. As I learned later, you can't just burn air.

The impossible fire's edges were tinged black with my frustration, and I threw the fireball at the dark curtain. The ground shook beneath my feet, tremors brought on not *by* my magic but in reaction to it. I stumbled out of the low door, cursing myself for my slip of control. The mysterious dome did not like being attacked by angry sorcerers. Fearing reprisal, I sprinted away but no revenge struck me; the dome was either dormant or simply warning me off. Either way I was done trying to force it to reveal itself to me.

A few days later we were just beginning to bring the wheat in when Mikel came running from the east side of the field. He was wheezing and only managed to shout, "Dragon!" as he passed. I smelled something burning and then a huge shape passed just above us, nearly knocking us over with the wind of its passage. My father ran up from the house and helped us stagger back towards it.

I looked around and saw the dragon clearly for the first time. It was about two meters long with another meter and a half of tail, big but not as big as I'd been told dragons were. The reptilian snout and wings with their skin flaps and bone ridges were definitely draconic, however. It swiveled a cat-like eye at us, and turned its long, sinuous neck. The dragon's scales were grayish-green like ancient verdigris and yet glistened in the sun. A dragon is a beautiful creature, but we were focused not on the majestic wings and shining scales, but on the sharp white teeth and pink tongue. I dove away from the direction it was pointing its mouth and my father and brother followed a split second later. Ivan had taught me that the most important thing, if I ever saw a dragon, was never to let it draw a straight line between its mouth and me. Nothing passed in my normal sight, but it was pouring out a torrent of something in my magical vision. The wheat above us boiled and burst into flame.

"It's young." I gasped. "Probably not very smart. Keep low."

Dad and Mikel nodded their understanding and we crept through the tall wheat. The dragon passed several times and then veered towards the village, wings flapping to get it more altitude.

"I can't let it go!" I hissed. "It'll burn down the whole village before they can do anything." I left unsaid that there was nothing they could do apart from run.

"What can you—" My father's question was cut off as I stood.

"Run!" I told them, and did the same, pushing myself to the limit to reach the house. They did the same, although I should have been more specific in telling them to run *away* from the flammable wooden building. I needed to go there. My wand was in the house.

The dragon was distracted enough to turn back and we scattered, which bought me more time. The dragon was momentarily confused by its prey going in three different directions and overshot us while it tried to make up its mind about which of us to chase. I was in the house and back out with my wand in time to see my father dive aside of another boiling stream. This gave me enough time to realize that I had no idea what to do next. Fire was useless; a dragon is above all things flame proof. I didn't know how to call lightning, and throwing kinetic energy at it might batter it, but the dragon needed to only get lucky once and I wasn't confident I could pull it down quickly enough. Rocks were similarly out; I was just as shaky about my aim in the situation as I was about my control of force. I needed something accurate and energetic, and my new light trick came to hand with the ease of daily practice. I played it along the dragon's side, and managed to give it a good shine in the eye, which naturally drew the beast's attention directly towards the annoying piece of uncooked meat with the glowing stick.

After another narrow escape, which ruined another half-acre of our crops and set the roof on fire, I was up on my feet with the dragon banking for another run. With my cover burnt away and nowhere to run, I let my power flow with no regard for my safety or the tolerances of my wand. It felt *blissful*, as if I'd relaxed or stretched a muscle for the first time in years. The wand was overloading badly and burning my skin, but it was better than what would happen if the dragon was able to close on me. From a point just beyond the tip erupted a focused light ray so bright that I had to close my eyes and rely on my overwhelmed magical sight to guide me. The power of my spell washed everything out, but the dragon cast a shadow where the light struck it. The air was burning around me, but the dragon seemed to absorb the magical attack without harm, though it overshot me again, confirming that I had at least blinded it along with myself. Whatever senses it had were not up to locating me, and when it was all over, I found out that it had almost struck me several times. Luckily for me, it couldn't send a blast straight down the vector made by my light ray since that would have required it to open its mouth and instinct was enough to tell it that this was a bad idea.

I tried to keep the dragon squarely in line with my wand, which I could feel was turning to ash in my grip. As my aim wavered, my power dissipated, but not before I happened to cross a spot I should have been aiming for the entire time. A dragon may be well protected in many places, but that much focused energy could still pierce certain vital areas like the roof of its mouth … or the taut skin of its wing as it flapped and banked. The shadow twisted and then fell to the ground as I tore a hole in one wing and it lost control, its bulk throwing sod up into the air with the impact. I opened my eyes and staggered in the direction of the crash, frantically blinking the spots out of my eyes. My father and brother had hidden their faces almost as soon as my light ray had started and were in better shape, so they reached the dragon before I did.

The animal was in pain. I looked behind me, smelling burning, and saw that in addition to much of our fields, the house was now fully engulfed. The dragon thrashed and I knew I could do nothing to help the house while it lived. I imagined the stuffed cow my mother had made, consumed in flame. As I vividly saw the little button eyes fall off, rage, grief, and pity for the brainless beast that had done so much damage all welled up in me. The wand was still in my hand. It was stuck there by baked blood. The dragon opened its mouth and at that moment all my emotion flooded down my poor, abused wand. I abandoned myself to the pain, letting it flow through me and then with a scream, I forced it to flow through my wand. I'd already cast aside Ivan's warnings about using too much magic, and the dragon deserved my hate. It was justice that it would share my pain. I hadn't touched that cow in years, but it had been *there*; it had been a reminder of her love and now it was gone.

Something dim and shadowy engulfed me and then spread to the dragon, which suddenly choked on the blast it was aiming at me. The creature's neck stretched as it screamed with me, and it beat the ground in helpless agony as I spent my loathing on it, making it suffer for what it did to me. I felt a hand on my shoulder and looked away from the dragon to see my father's understanding but disapproving gaze.

"Best if you finish the job if you can." Embarrassed and ashamed, I returned the familiar emotional barriers and, with so little magic that it didn't even make my poor disintegrating wand smoke, I burned a neat hole through the roof of the dragon's mouth. With its brain vaporized, the dragon collapsed with a sigh which felt like insects scrabbling around inside my body.

Ivan arrived in time to heal my burns without scarring but not in time to save the house. Mikel and dad were cut up and a little red from the dragon's sigh, but Ivan declared them well enough to help him carry me to Bowbringer's Inn. I protested, but was overruled, and so they found a wheelbarrow and took turns pushing it until we got to town. Some had seen or smelled the burning field from afar, and there were loud cries and a lot of talk when Ivan informed them that there had been a dragon and I had dealt with it. Some tried to stand me a drink, and Ivan told them that what I needed was plenty of water and a bed. What *he* needed was ten strong helpers and a hay cart. The dragon needed to be moved to his cottage so he could study it. The murmuring swelled back to a roar with this news. I had *killed* a dragon? Unthinkable!

Even as Ivan and his helpers went off to get the dragon's carcass, the word was spreading and as they put me to bed. I heard something that would be repeated at first quietly in private and eventually shouted openly in town meetings. Where was Lord Vectreon? If the village was attacked by a dragon and defended by a *sorcerer* then what good was a *Wizard-Lord*?

Excerpt from *Testimonies of Zunvect*, a manuscript of collected interviews and personal writings released in 8126 MR by Xetic-Nal

An approximate account of the Wizard-Lords during Zunvect's battle:

Around the world in every tower of every Wizard-Lord, the arcane map was showing the same thing. An enormous source of energy had just been detected in Lord Vectreon's territory. It was far more than the elderly lord himself could have produced, and more than he would have even if he could. The hedonistic Vectreon was well known for having abandoned research years ago when he'd noticed the first signs of the Fade taking him. As many Wizard-Lords were wont to do, he prepared for his death by sampling all the things in life that his scholarly pursuits had denied him these past two hundred years. Wizard-Lords were often vigorous to the very day the Fade took them and Vectreon used his supernaturally youthful body to its fullest in feasts, fights, and ... other things beginning with that letter. The question on the minds of the Wizard-Lords was not just 'Where is Vectreon?' but 'What has happened, and why haven't we been informed?'

In the tower of one Wizard-Lord, the answer seemed plain. "Good grief. The idiot's *died* with no heir or plan for continuity of rule, and I'm going to have to clean up the mess. As always." One good thing was that if this source was *untrained* then it meant that it belonged to a very strong wizard indeed. Much could be done if he was right. Revise that statement: much could be done. He was always right. The Chronoculum had once again shown him more than mere thaumaturgical sensors had shown his peers. This was what he'd been waiting for.

Zunvect 7:

Learn or Die

I woke up a hero, with all the beer and food I could ask for ready at any time. Our farm was lost, but as the new 'protector' a new house was being built for me, and I would not want for anything for as long as I kept the dragons away. Ivan said he gave it a week before the villagers started to change their minds, and I agreed. Of course, this meant reveling in their adulation as much as possible since I knew it would be gone soon and I would have to help my father and brother rebuild. Dad worked as he always did and disapproved of me taking advantage of my newfound glory. "You only did what you had to." He said to me. "It's any man's responsibility to do what he can for his neighbors, and you did just that. Mind, I don't disagree that we saved them a heap of trouble and they owe us as much as it takes to get us on our feet, but I don't hold with all this hero business. You did your job and you'll be rewarded for it, and that ought to be the end." My teenage self thought that he was jealous, or uncomfortable because he had never done anything worth high praise. Now ... actually, I agree. Not in anger but in understanding. Dad was a plain farmer and parades in the square were more than he thought anyone deserved. There was a job, there was doing it, and there was being paid for services and that was all there was to it. If he saw someone drowning in a river, he'd jump in with no hesitation and do all he could to save them. He did right and expected everyone else to do the same. He didn't expect praise for doing what was right, and only grudgingly gave it. That man held the world to a high standard and was often disappointed but never discouraged. The older I get, the more I admire that.

My wand had survived, though it had gone from light brown to jet black and was constantly flaking. For the first few days it was also covered in a layer of my skin. The deterioration was severe. It worked, but would not survive another abuse like the one I'd put it through two days earlier. If I wanted a wand that could survive battle magic levels of usage, I would need to make another and find a way to strengthen it.

There was also the matter of the spell I'd used to kill the dragon. My secret was revealed; I had been training with an illicit spell for months. I had to tell them that much because it was obvious, but I didn't tell them why. Ivan asked, but didn't seem too put out when I told him I was interested in focused light and had found a spot where I could practice without worrying about failures. Since I hadn't been caught yet, there was no point in lecturing me about the law. Besides, it was becoming plain that Vectreon didn't care. The rest of the village thought that it was grand to have their own battle-mage. Since Vectreon seemed to have left us entirely, then all the better to have someone able to protect them who had grown up with them and would stay to help. Not only that, but given my age I was liable to remain protector for decades to come.

"They're fooling themselves," Ivan told me when I'd grown bored of being praised and went to see how the dragon autopsy was going. "Wizard-Lords do not relinquish territory except to one another as a result of war. We are still ruled by that tower," he pointed up at the tower clearly visible at the top of the mountain. "It is a mystery, though. Bowbringer and I have been worried for awhile. Do you remember the last time the taxes came due?"

"I think so." I said. "I was a little boy."

"Yes, about ten years ago." Ivan mused. "The tax collector is very late. Most have celebrated this, but it's a bad sign. Have we been *forgotten*? It's more important than ever that you present yourself to Vectreon soon. Light spell or not, it is intolerable that we are left on our own out here like a singing sorcerer or a prophet. No matter what folk say now, we need a Wizard-Lord. Baby dragons are nowhere near the worst thing that will come if it becomes known that there is no Wizard-Lord protecting us. That's my finding, by the way. This is not just a juvenile, but probably less than five years old. It must have gotten lost and hungry, and came down from the mountains in just the wrong spot to go hunting. It was a freak accident and even more of an accident that it came down right on top of you. Thank goodness you're a disobedient young thing. With more experience you might have been able to drive it off with wind or force, but nothing I have in my library could have outright killed it without a lot of luck. Here, hold the knife. We've reached what I think is an organ that produces or controls the dragon's breath mechanism and I'll need both hands and my magic to make sure it doesn't rupture."

There was less time for getting away from things with the farm to rebuild and winter coming soon, but I stole away occasionally to visit the dome. I was a hero now, and in my seventeen-year-old mind that meant I had to keep doing heroic things to keep my title. Defeating a millennia old protective wall and forcing the long-buried artifice to tell me its secrets sounded like just the sort of thing to maintain a reputation. I was committing the second line to memory so I could write it down later when someone said, "That is the most beautifully overcomplicated piece of spellcraft I have ever seen."

I whirled and behind me stood a man. I only just remembered to stop the flow of magic before I burned him to a crisp. I stood speechless. He was a stranger, he was in *my* private place, and he had snuck up on me while I was at my most vulnerable, concentrating not only on magic but on memorization of the foreign letters as well.

"You used Nagoma's illusion focusing method." The man continued, walking slowly towards me. He was no more than a meter and a half tall, with a cap of white hair and a very short white beard. He was dressed in black robes trimmed in blood red along the collar, placket, and cuffs. The light caught his buttons, and with a chill I realized that they were silver skulls with tiny red stones in the eye sockets. The way his robe moved and caught the light announced that his clothing was made of material finer than anything other than our wedding dresses, which were expected to last five or ten generations. The robes fell to the floor, obscuring shoes which clicked as he walked, and covering all but the tips of his fingers. The eyes looking out at me from small spectacles were alight with curiosity and intense interest. "Easy to set up, but it must take a lot of concentration to keep it going. Nagoma wasn't meant to keep up a coherent stream like that. You'd have to focus each segment by hand and keep it focused with a constant stream of manual adjustments. Effective if you don't know any better, but ultimately only useful if you have nothing better to do with your time or mental faculties."

"I've gotten used to it." I stammered. "I can hold the spell even while memorizing these inscriptions."

"Two bad ideas in one." The man replied.

He was getting close and I pointed the wand at him. "Stay back!" I was scared. A stranger who seemed to know how my spells worked by a brief inspection felt dangerous. He was also dressed far too well to be a wandering sage or a vagabond. What was a sorcerer of such extraordinary skill and wealth doing wandering the woods and how had he found me when I was so well shielded?

The invader reached out and in fear I shot him through with a ray of light. The ray split when it reached him and bent around his body, rejoining at his back to spray harmlessly out the door. I had seen these sorts of light shows when I was young. Ivan had entertained the youngsters by throwing flour to show where the light was going and then making it wiggle all over the place, but I couldn't believe this man had defended himself so quickly or against so much power. He took the wand from my hand and examined it even as I tried to fry him with all the fire I could call up. The flames streaming from my palms vanished before they could reach him. "Pipe down, kid, or you'll wake up the enchantments." He said, gesturing towards me. My hands fell to my sides against my will and I stood motionless as he turned the wand carefully, examining it from every angle. "Interesting but unnecessary. Like your light spell it is magic which is impressive but only useful because you don't know better. You would have made a wonderful addition to my group back when I started out. We loved overcomplicated spells that used intricate and flashy spellcraft rather than straightforward solutions" I was freed from his grip in time for him to pass me my wand back. "I'd tell you to leave it here, but then the enchantments might start sniffing at it and decide you're a threat."

Panicked, I bolted for the door and I made it about two meters before I turned my head to look forward and there he was in front of me. There was no sign that he had moved from his previous position, no sound or motion. He was just there. I stared at him and he returned the gaze impassively. "Aren't you going to ask me the most important question?"

This was the kind of prompting I had grown used to as a student of a magician. "Who are you?"

"Who do you think I am?"

"You defeated my spells with so much ease…" I was going to ask if he was a professor at the regional college, but by that point I finally was calming down from my panic and something in my magical sight looked wrong. His skin, in fact all of his visible flesh, was not visible outside the standard range of human sight. My vision pierced what I now realized was an illusion more sophisticated than those I had learned from Ivan as the beginnings of my focus spell. Who else could be a walking, talking, spell critiquing skeleton? I fell to my knees. "I beg your pardon, Lord Xetic-Nal."

"Oh, don't go all old style on me." The ancient Wizard-Lord said. "Then again, it's good to be able to look you in the eye. You're as tall as a tree! That was a very direct guess, young man. I suspected that you might get as close as figuring out I was a Wizard-Lord, but how did you know it was me?"

"Your … semblance – that is you created an illusion that doesn't go beyond the chromatic range." I said.

Xetic-Nal grabbed my chin and looked into my eyes. "You're sensitive to a larger range of frequencies. Interesting. Is this a permanent condition?" Somewhere in this sentence, the illusion fell and I was left with the skeleton whose eyes were like embers in the otherwise empty sockets.

"I've been able to see magic for as long as I can remember." It seemed best to answer his questions directly. Wizard-Lords were always to be obeyed, and now that I was in his presence, I could feel why their chief was treated like as a god. He'd brushed my spells aside like they were nothing!

Xetic tilted his head and his eyes glowed brighter. "The powers of a Wizard-Lord *and* a magical mutation." He put his hands on my shoulders, emphasizing my big frame. "Perhaps more than one. I'm glad I got here first." He clapped his hands, which made a sharp *clack* rather than a clapping sound. "You will be leaving this … edifice very soon. You will either walk across that threshold and fall down dead at that instant or you will be my apprentice."

"Is this a test?"

"No, young man, it's a question. Do you want to be shut in a tower for years learning the most exciting and terrible things so that you may never be the same person again and will shoulder the responsibility of hundreds of thousands of people, or do you want to die? It's a legitimate question ... what was your name?"

"Zunvect, Lord Xetic."

"Zunvect, right. Some people really do prefer to die. I mean, I've never *met* them, but I have met a lot of people who said they'd have preferred the death option afterwards. It's actually a bit unfair. They also get really annoyed when I offer to kill them. I think it might be rhetorical, but I thought I'd ask anyway."

"I'd rather live."

"Excellent. Pack your bags and say goodbye to your loved ones. I'll be back in a week."

"Wait!" I blurted, trying to forestall him vanishing again.

"What? We've established you're my apprentice now. I think that pretty much takes care of everything."

"Wha – what?!" I asked, surprise, confusion and a large helping of excitement rendering me incoherent.

"If I hadn't seen you adapting Nagoma, I'd think you were a thick as two planks. You ... are ... a ... Wizard-Lord. *My* Wizard-Lord. I'm taking you on; be back in a week." He looked ready to disappear without further remark, so I risked rudeness in my haste to get answers before he was gone.

"What about Vectreon? I'm in his territory!" I knew how it worked. Wizards were either eliminated or trained by the local Wizard-Lord to be their successor. The eternal Wizard-Lord didn't need an heir!

"You'd rather learn from him?" Xetic asked. "That knuckle head? The moron who *died* before he could train his replacement? Even if I were minded to resurrect him, I'd only do it to tell him he's got as much sense as an albatross and then promptly kill him once I'd made it clear how much of a disappointment he's been to me. I grant broad autonomy to my oligarchs because I expect them to be responsible. Leaving a territory unguarded without a word to me or anyone else is perhaps the worst thing he could do short of letting a portal blitz reach the eighth advancement or betraying us to the elves."

"Lord Vectreon's dead?"

"Well, yes. Generally, only dead Wizard-Lords are so derelict as to leave a dependent community open to a dragon attack, and let a wizard of your power wander around free. Wizard-Lords do not *delegate* their responsibility to protect the territory, so he had to be dead if you were filling in as dragoncatcher. I had a few words for Vectreon's seneschal and regional governor, you can count on that! Imagine not telling anyone. Their excuse was infuriatingly logical, of course. They didn't tell anyone because Vectreon was dead and so he couldn't instruct them to. That's the problem with the oligarchy; no one talks to anyone but me! Listen, I haven't got all day to hang around in shadow temples telling my apprentice everything he doesn't know. That could take centuries. You'll get a better idea of the situation once you've started your studies.

"Now, if you haven't got any more pressing concerns that can't wait, I'll be back next week to pick you up. I don't want a big hullabaloo, but if your headman insists on a festival or something, tell him I enjoy tea and not to worry himself otherwise about my comforts. If I want something else, I'll arrange for it personally. Oh, and make sure your current instructor is present. I'll want to discuss the handover with him. If he could find the time to prepare a precis of your curriculum and progress in each subject, I'll be obliged." Before I could reply, he was gone. No rush of air, no loud bangs or flashes or puffs of smoke. Just gone. Along with my believe that my life was in any way under my control. I was walking home when I realized that he had done every bit of his magic by mental concentration alone. His hands had not moved and he had made no sound other than continuing to talk to me as he deflected and absorbed my spells. He'd even teleported without betraying anything visibly. I'd seen the magic flow around him, but the patterns were so complex that I couldn't make anything of them.

I told Ivan about what had happened, and he was as speechless as I had been. I let it sink in as I tried to find out anything I could about Xetic-Nal from his library. The information on him was sketchy at best. "Nobody knows much about him." Ivan said as I tore through his book, wincing every time I literally tore a page in my haste. "I don't even think the Wizard-Lords do. There's a lot you can get away with when you're immortal and invincible."

"How can he be more powerful than eighty-four other Wizard-Lords combined?"

Ivan favored me with a crooked smile. "I don't know. Perhaps that's the answer to the question of why there are only eighty-four in addition to him. He can't beat *eighty-five*. Joking aside, this is ... I don't know how to react. Vectreon is dead and you are being apprenticed to Lord Xetic-Nal. We don't know much about him, but his apprentices are legendary."

"Legendary for only being three in number." I said. "Three in four thousand years. He's picky."

"He picked you." Ivan said. "I don't think I'm going to get over the shock soon."

"You'll have to get over it in less than five days." I grinned. "He wants to talk to you. I think you're supposed to formally hand over my apprenticeship. I imagine there's a protocol and ceremony about that."

"The way you describe his behavior, I think we'll skip the ceremony." Ivan replied. "Go and tell your father, Zunvect. There's no point in you hanging around here watching me gulp like a fish on land."

As I expected, my father was stoic. "It's a big job." He said. "You say he only takes on one apprentice every thousand years or so. Big shoes, son." What could I do but agree? My brother took it as yet another air for me to put on. "Oh, fantastic. You're even better than a sorcerer now. Does this mean you're going to be ruling this territory?" It was a good question and one I hadn't considered. Xetic wouldn't need an heir, but *someone* had to take over Vectreon's vacant seat. "Maybe." I said, not able to help teasing. "Imagine having to pay taxes to your little brother. Don't worry, though. If I have to raise the militia, I'll be sure to make you a corporal."

Mikel took advantage of my position a lowly sorcerer, for another week anyway, by tackling me to the ground and pushing my face to the floor. "Gotta get in all the whaling I can before it's treason." He said cheerfully, ignoring my threats to have him horsewhipped and jailed. Of course, I could have thrown him across the room without effort, but that wasn't the point of brotherly wrestling. If I don't talk much about my home life when I was a child, it's mainly because it felt so normal, and because I know that you and the wolves and the magi all like to hear about magic more than wrestling and planting potatoes. My whole life up until then, dad made sure we had a lot to do and Mikel deflated my ego by being bigger and stronger, growing up to be twenty centimeters taller than me and ten broader. I miss them both.

Bowbringer shared the feelings of just about everyone else in the village: terror, pride, and panic at having to arrange a state luncheon for the highest ranking human being to ever live. For a man who had never met anyone more important than the tax collector, it was so overwhelming that he probably would have gone mad if everyone hadn't pitched in with suggestions. He'd wanted to make it dinner, but I'd interpreted Lord Xetic's behavior as suggesting that he wasn't going to stay long enough to reach dinner. That seemed fine to the town since it meant that we could have a day-long fete and since he'd said he only wanted tea anyway, he could show up whenever it pleased him, and they'd welcome him then. No sense in wasting the whole day by setting up elaborate pageants and speeches and then having to wait until he arrived to start the festivities. In retrospect, I have to think that old boney grew up in much the same circumstances as I had, because neither of us appreciated elaborate ceremony.

The day arrived, and my entire body felt loose and tense at the same time. The festivities started early, and I danced with every female above the age of ten and most of the men too. It was sort of like having your wake before you die. Everyone wanted to say goodbye and to tell me how proud they were that someone from our little village could produce a Wizard-Lord that Lord Xetic-Nal himself wanted to train. I was sort of like a sports team. Everyone felt that my success was their success. Ivan was drinking and this time he wasn't restricted to beer. I think I saw him put away more vodka that morning than he'd had in his entire life. A little after noon there was a loud bang and a billow of white smoke on the mayor's stage, from which Lord Xetic-Nal emerged. The festivities paused. Everyone looked at him. He looked at them. Bowbringer was with his wife. He tripped coming onto the stage and then had to clear his throat loudly before commencing. "Welcome, your mighty lordship. Um, it's an honor to have you here and that you'd take one of ours to learn from you."

There was a long pause and total silence from the crowd. "Wait, is that it?" Xetic asked.

"Oh, and we have your tea for you, sir." Bowbringer said. "It's, uh, right on the table there. We found you a silver cup."

"Capital. So no speeches then? No parade or flowers or native dance or anything like that?"

"We didn't know when you'd arrive, your most high lordliness." Bowbringer said, trying to throw as many titles in as he could and sweating profusely. The instinct to run from the undead horror, and the terror of possibly offending the most powerful wizard in the world were taking a toll. "I'm sure if you wanted to –" He was cut off as Xetic pumped his hand furiously. Xetic turned to the crowd and spread his arms dramatically, his sleeves billowing in the breeze. "For this I shall grant your village a boon!"

"What'd he say?" Mrs. Androski asked, seemingly unperturbed at being addressed by a centuries old corpse in a robe that cost more than her cattle ranch.

"He said he's granting us a boon for not having to hear Bowbringer give a speech, Anna!" Nyetrusha bellowed, forgetting his own fear in the familiar ritual of repeating everything to his aged aunt.

"Good on him!" Androski cackled. "What'll he give us if I don't give a speech?"

"Silence!" Xetic boomed, with a rolling thunderclap for good measure. "Head man. What's the name of this village?"

"We don't have a name, your lordship." Bowbringer said apologetically. "We've all lived here our whole lives, sir. We don't need a name for it."

"Then I shall call you the village of Hamlet since that is slightly more original than what you've got right now."

This was too much. "Isn't that like calling a city 'Bergopolis'?" I called up to him. Death threats notwithstanding, I was a smart mouthed teenager and had a week to get used to the idea of Xetic-Nal's presence.

"You're the backwards hicks who haven't bothered to call their one-horse town anything." He shot back.

"I'll have you know that we have four horses, twelve mules, and sixty-eight head of cattle here." Nyetrusha said, and then tried to melt into the crowd when he realized who he'd said it to.

"Listen, I'm giving you salt of the earth types a boon, so get on with telling me what. Village of Hamlet, name your boon before I give in to temptation and provide you with what you really need: a great big blasted library."

"Well, your highness, Zunvect used to warm up the air for us so we could have outdoor festivals in winter. Now that he's going, we won't have that. If you could give us a charm to let us have a warm winter festival, we'd be very grateful."

"Cripes you people are easy to please. So it is asked, so I shall grant." He held out his palm and a metal sphere with a post sticking out of it appeared in it. He pressed it into Bowbringer's arms. "Shove it in the ground, air gets warm. Pull it out, air stops being warm. There, boon delivered. By the way, are you always this meek around Wizard-Lords? I know I've got a reputation, but we *are* supposed to be your protectors and governors. Was Vectreon mistreating you?"

"Sir, your lordship ..." Bowbringer trailed off, looking terrified.

Xetic looked around and then down into his teacup. "Oh for – I thought I fixed that before I left!" With an annoyed grunt, he was again clad in illusion that only I could see past. Everyone seemed to relax a little now that he was a little old man instead of a fire-eyed skeleton. He even managed to get another handshake from Bowbringer before the mayor decided to make for the vodka jug.

Xetic walked off the front of the rough wooden platform, slowly descending as he came towards me. "That was thoroughly embarrassing. I usually don't give my students menial work, but one job you'll have is to tell me when that happens. I'm always forgetting the illusion. Sort of like how I never seemed to have my hat on back when I needed one. Which one's the sorcerer who gave you the basics?"

"Him." I pointed at Ivan, letting the somewhat disjointed observations and instructions wash over me. "Ivan Solinsky, MRCVS. He doesn't usually drink this much, but I think he's scared you'll disapprove of his teaching."

"Nonsense!" Xetic said, loud enough for Ivan to hear as we approached him. "He's done as good a job as any sorcerer training a wizard could. You've got decent separation from your emotions, a healthy amount of curiosity, and you don't cause earthquakes when you sneeze. The spells he's taught you are wholly inappropriate, but there was no way he could know that." The lich stuck out his hand and pumped Ivan's with even more enthusiasm than he had Bowbringer's. "Good work. Most sorcerers who are saddled with a wizard to teach manage to botch the job early on and get themselves incinerated, crushed by rocks, or otherwise horribly killed. Tell me, when did you first work out the boy was a wizard?" Ivan blinked to clear the fog and Xetic noticed his inebriation. "Allow me."

Ivan reeled and when he regained his balance, it looked like all the alcohol had been purged from his system. "Wow. I mean, first week of working with him, Lord Xetic. I tried him out on a testing device I got from the college and he scored outside its range."

"Did he really? In the first week? I must see what you used. I'm sure the assembled … land workers won't mind if we pop off for a few minutes while we talk about Zunvect's magical history. Oh, let me just – " he poured himself a cup of tea, "off we go."

The transition was instantaneous and jarring, and I felt horrendously dizzy at the change from a bustling fair in the middle of town to the cleared dirt plot outside Ivan's cottage. "I felt the stones on my way in," Xetic explained by way of how he knew where to go. "Yes, teleportation can be a bit rough the first hundred times or so. Something to do with the senses being presented with a discontinuous event where all the stimuli change at once. It will pass swiftly and then you can show me your testing device." My dizziness passed first, so I ran in and grabbed the cylinder, only realizing that this meant I'd left Ivan alone with Xetic outside, so I worked hard to be quick enough to keep the Wizard-Lord from asking Ivan any more questions. "Oh, fabulous." Xetic enthused when I gave him the device. "A Hoch-Sköberg Thaumodynamic version six point eight. This came out what, about four hundred years ago? They didn't make many of them. You're lucky to have gotten your hands on this one. There are some people who have said that the H-S 6.8 was the most elegant design, though of course Yukanso's Thaumbox is considered the standard these days. What were you programming it with?"

Ivan dashed in and got the spell book. "This one, sir. One of my professors let me have it when I took the device."

Xetic made a disapproving sound where the back of his throat would have been. "Oh, I can't let you keep doing that. The poor thing's meant to be set up with a four-ten or higher. This spell is a good thousand years too old for it! Here." A page of text and figures appeared inside the book. "Use that from now on. I know that sorcerer spells can be slow to promulgate, but really using a two-six on a five-three substrate! No wonder it overheated when Zunvect tried it out. Here, I'll use the wizard version and we can see if Zunvect's got as much punch as he thinks he does." Xetic set the device on a table which appeared underneath it and cast a spell so fast and complex that I could only get the barest glimpse of its structure. "I'll try you out on the Thaumbox four point six later, but this ought to be a pretty close approximation. Here's the wizard version of the compatible direct link." He gave me a page of notes. "In your own time."

The wizard spell felt odd after so many years of casting sorcerer spells. Instead of trying to pull magic by force and then use my body to control it, I was instead taking the flow which I could naturally divert from the river of magic around me and crafting it into a spell without ever having the magic pass through my body. It felt right, and the flow was smoother and less turbulent to the touch. The spell itself was more words and fewer gestures than sorcerer spells, and I could already feel it in an intimate way. Sorcerer spells always felt remote, and I had trouble using them without going through all the motions. I already knew wizard spells would become part of my instinct more easily. It was a pleasure to tell the magic what to do, and it jumped to my call with ease born of both practice and the more appropriate spell structure. The device went almost immediately to yellow.

"Good, but we both know you can do better." Xetic observed. It turned green. "Come on, Zunvect. You killed a dragon, kid. Have some pride." Blueish green. "Slowing down already? You *know* you can do so much more than that." I was feeling the strain but goaded, I forced it to pure blue. "If you really worked at it, you might just be able to make the H-K warm." I pushed hard and the energy I was channeling was enough to have sent an inferno to the heavens. Xetic's version of the containment spell was so much more demanding! It was all psychosomatic, but despite myself the muscles on my arms were starting to stand out. "Cut the drama and you might achieve another stage right here." Xetic deadpanned. "This is about your mind. If I wanted you to churn butter, I'd have asked." I was determined now, but apart from a brief flutter of periwinkle, I couldn't go any further. My head spinning, I dropped my hands and the device slowly cycled back through the colors.

"Not bad for someone trained the way you were." Xetic said. "Mr. Solinsky has done well to bring you this far. For your reference, most Wizard-Lords at the height of their power can strike purple on that scale and go on to around green on the next one up. I expect you to exceed midrange on the *third* scale by the time we are finished together. Now that we've had our fun, it's time for me to examine your education in other fields. Mr. Solinsky, if you would be so kind as to either bring me or draw up the topics you have gone over with Zunvect. This may be the most pleasurable apprenticeship I have taken on. It's so gratifying when they've already covered the basics. I must have an idea, however, as to how *much* of the basics you've covered."

The sorcerer and Wizard-Lord spent about an hour in close conference, and I was relieved that Ivan seemed to be relaxing as he reported in exhaustive detail on my education so far. I chimed in once or twice, but I spent most of my time on the other side of Ivan's yard. I was still coming to terms with the fact that it wouldn't be much longer before I left my childhood home behind, possibly forever. I hadn't strayed more than ten miles from home in my entire life and that was only on the trip Ivan took me on to go see the ocean. Now I was going to be whisked thousands of miles in a step and sequestered in the oldest and most mysterious human habitation. It seemed ridiculous. Until a week ago, I'd thought that the cities the caravan traders talked about were exotic and remote! Now I was going to be inducted into an order that probably thought of them as backwaters, and didn't even consider my own village as more than a wide spot in the road. In fact, with the exception of Lord Vectreon, they probably had no idea any of us existed.

"You've done a splendid job." I heard Xetic-Nal saying as I returned. "Absolutely top shelf considering how far out into the sticks you are. With your dedication, you ought to be *teaching* magic, not slaving away for a bunch of … people like them."

"I enjoy being a big fish in a small pond." Ivan said.

"You won't if you end up doing it for a thousand years!" Xetic chortled. "All right, since I've been throwing boons around like copper bits I may as well give you something as a token of my appreciation that you're turning over an apprentice who is reasonably civilized and unlikely to set the tapestries on fire." One of these days, I thought, I really would blow something to pieces just to prove these old codgers right about something. "What can I get for you? Oh, how about a cure for something you haven't got yet.

Swine fever? Demodectic mange? How about a spell that extermi-
nates listeria? I'm sorry I can't do anything about foot and mouth
but we haven't nailed that one down yet."

"A curative spell for swine fever would be …" Ivan seemed at a
loss for words. I knew what the problem was. There really was
nothing that encapsulated just how much it would impact the
community. Swine fever was a highly infectious ailment in pigs
that was almost always deadly and usually required the slaughter
and burning of all pigs in a wide area around the infection site. We
hadn't had an outbreak in a generation, but there were stories told
of the village going decades without pork because we had to kill
every pig we owned and then save up to have more brought in by
the caravans.

"Outstanding," Xetic said when the silence had grown awkward. "I'll tell Lord Mycontree to handle the translation. He's a
lazy old sod and hasn't produced a single paper worth reading in
six years. He's been too busy attempting to eat his way through the
entire *Field Guide to Flora and Fauna*. It'll serve him right to be put
on legacy spellcraft. No offense meant, but nobody likes doing the
grunt work of translating a spell from our books to yours so you can
cast them properly. We'd make the apprentices do it for practice,
but *some people* –" he didn't elaborate, "are careless enough to leave
out key terminators and we end up with dead sorcerers, so now only Wizard-Lords can do it. If one of my full members does something like that, they know what I'd do about it." His eyes were
starting to burn so bright that they were spilling out of their sockets.
He opened his mouth to continue and saw our expressions. "Right,
old annoyances. It's amazing how bad people are at details. Anyway, I'll have the new spell and the latest edition of Soong's Manual
of Thaumaturgical Cures sent over. Zunvect, I think I've done everything I planned on." He looked up. "I'm very happy with how
prepared everyone here was. Given how most mayors and governors and the like try to take up my valuable time. Maybe I'll drop a

sack of gold or something in the town square as a bonus." He looked at me. "Any last minute matters you need to attend to?"

There were a million things I wanted to do. Kiss Dominka, have a beer in Bowbringer's tavern with my friends one last time... Xetic seemed to be constantly rushing around and I knew he'd either refuse or make a big deal out of it if I spent half the day doing all the things I'd thought I had my teenage years to do. There was one thing that I needed, though. "I'd like to say goodbye one last time to my father and brother." I said. I couldn't leave without that. We'd been whisked away so quickly and I wanted my last sight of home to be them.

"Fair enough. We left the party abruptly, so I can't blame you for not doing that beforehand."

In a sickening instant we were back in the town square. I didn't have much time. I ran up to my dad and hugged him. "I love you dad." I whispered. "Goodbye. I'll – I'll come back when I can."

"Do that." Boris said. He held me at arm's length and then gravely shook my hand. "You'll grow up a good man, Zunvect, if you remember your teaching and mind your new master. I can't say it won't be strange to think of you sitting up there one day looking down on all of us and doing what Wizard-Lords do, but it's a relief to know that the boy I raised is watching out for us."

"Try not to raise our taxes!" Someone called from the crowd. We ignored them. Mikel clapped me on the shoulder. "My brother's a Wizard-Lord." He said. "I guess that means I get the whole farm." He punched me and I punched him back.

"Wow. A whole farm. What will you do?" I teased. "And here's me with only a small territory. Why, my four cities and a merchant fleet look pretty paltry next to all that wheat."

I don't remember if we went on for much longer. I only recall going back to Xetic-Nal – on his fourth cup of tea – and waving goodbye as he took hold of my arm and teleported us somewhere I thought I'd only visit in my daydreams.

Excerpt from *Faith in our Founder*, the definitive collection of the myths and legends of Zunvect the Sunlord, 60th ed, revised 7943 MR

Zunvect is Discovered, the story of Zunvect's first meeting with Lord Xetic-Nal. Predominantly sourced from the *Sunlord's Canon* by Lorn Malthaum. Acknowledged to be entirely apocryphal[4].

In his youth, the mighty Zunvect was the son of humble farmer, and had few cares. As he walked upon the only road in his village, he found twilight coming faster than he expected. He called the light, which was ever his friend, to show him the road and guide him home. A hundred times he had called upon the light, and seen what few mortals could, in the realm of magic so deep that even wizards dare not look upon it for long. This time, the light grew and revealed a man upon the road, cloaked and hooded though it were summer.

"Good evening to you," Zunvect said, always polite to his elders even though this man was unknown to him.

"It is indeed." The man said, and threw back his hood. Beneath was a skull, which grinned at Zunvect, and the fire within the skull's eye sockets burned to look upon. "For this

---

[4] I think I can take a guess that the full analysis provided by Xetic was "You may acknowledge this to be entirely apocryphal, or else." This story is typical of Lorn's way of seeing the world, by the way. All I said was, "I would have beaten the old bastard if it had been a fair fight," meaning, "if he hadn't known everything and I nothing." Somehow Lorn spun it into some big fat mystical duel. - Z

is the evening which you shall either perish or become my servant."

"I should prefer neither," Zunvect replied. "I go to help my father at his farm, and could not do so were I dead or in your service."

"Yet one or the other shall be so. Your magic is too great to be allowed to remain here, and so you must either serve me as my apprentice, or leave this world."

So, there was a grand battle of magic, for even in the first flower of his youth, the power of the Sunlord eclipsed all others. Yes, his might would have overcome even Lord Xetic-Nal, had the lich lord not stooped to low and cunning means to attack and bind Zunvect to his service with fell words and sinister spinnings. When the battle was over, Zunvect bended his knee to the lich lord, the first and only man who would ever be called 'master' by the Sunlord. Both knew that the bindings would be broken in time, but for now the lich lord ruled Zunvect as he ruled all in those days.

Thus, Zunvect was taken from his home and brought to the lonely tower where no living man may dwell. Bound to service, knowing that he would learn the lich lord's secrets and turn them against his master one day. Zunvect was content to wait and study, for his first lesson was that men like Xetic-Nal were plentiful and took what they liked without regard for who was hurt. The world needed Zunvect, and he could never walk without a care while the Wizard-Lords' evil ruled.

Idalia 3:

Doubts

"This is ridiculous." Idalia told Zunvect. "Mother died in childbirth, killed a dragon before the age of eighteen, a taciturn but extremely upright father who dispensed solid advice. I'm surprised you weren't tutored by a hermit in a cave."

Zunvect cracked one eye open and relaxed his grip on the staff. The tantalizingly familiar looking runes faded, turning to a complicated chasework of hair thin lines that zigzagged up and around the length and circumference of the shaft. "You don't believe me, Idalia?"

"No." She said, crossing her arms. "I think you're not content with the things you did later in life, and now you want to start myths about your youth as well."

"Make up your mind. If I did them, they're not myths." His tone was more controlled than before, less manic. The light that came from him had become a warm summer day instead of the furnace flash he'd emitted before he started. "Why would I lie? Self-aggrandizement?" He scoffed. "I'm a *god*. My story is apparently compelling enough to bring veneration and worship from a group of people who were atheists when I was alive. Anti-theists, even."

"Maybe you want to have a new story so that the Brotherhood will keep us safe. It could be fear, Zunvect. You haven't fared well in this time period."

"Idalia, that was a mistake I'm still trying to understand. Maybe at some point in the story I'll remember why I had the urge to strike at Xetic like I did. Think about it from my perspective. All these clichés I talk about and you accuse me of conforming to? I know they're major story elements from the minds of the magi. We had different stories in my time. Think about that, oh puissant one who captures gods in bottles. I'm from eight thousand years ago. My life isn't conforming to narrative structure. *It's* conforming to *me.* I'm the ur-example, girl. I was there first. We're getting close to where your contemporary sources will be more able to corroborate my story. Try to reserve judgment until then."

Zunvect 8:

The Basics

Xetic-Nal was ten steps ahead of me when he noticed I'd stopped. "What's the hold up?" He asked. "Did you forget your luggage? I thought it was strange that you weren't bringing anything, but I thought maybe you were just dirt poor and it would be impolite to mention it."

I shook my head, keeping my eyes tightly shut to keep the enormous chamber from spinning around me. I sat down on the smooth stone floor and rubbed by face. "Dizzy." I ground out, ashamed at my weakness.

Xetic was next to me in an instant, kneeling and prying one eye open. The illusion around him was gone, leaving me staring at his naked glowing eye socket without any cloaking haze in the chromatic spectrum. "You're stillsick. It's a bit like being motion sick – which on balance I guess you probably wouldn't know about – but the other way around. Take a minute and your senses should recover."

"I was fine the first couple times."

"You thought you were. Adrenaline rush finally wearing off; it's a good thing because it means you're relaxed. That's ... actually really special. Not many people can feel relaxed talking to a fire-eyed magical skeleton after only a couple hours, as well as dealing with the certain knowledge that you'd left your home for good in order to rush headlong into something totally unknown to your – oh, or maybe you're just now coming to grips with all of it." He added as I started to show signs of throwing up. "Normally I'd recommend rest and mindful meditation on all of this, but I haven't got all day to nurse your multifarious adjustment issues so..." I felt a jolt, like ice water flowing through my veins and the dizziness disappeared. "That should get you back on your feet long enough to recover somewhat while we deal with the particulars of your re-location." He gestured, and I was lifted to my feet. "Let me know if you start to feel woozy again and I'll give you something to sit on. It does remind me, though, that I ought to do a physical examina-tion on you. You've got some odd magical bric-a-brac floating around in you, and anyway I'd hate to spend all this time getting you ready only to find out you've got a heart disease. If you keeled over on graduation day I'd never forgive myself for wasting all that effort." The marvelous feeling of clarity reawakened my curiosity – and I didn't want to even consider what it would be like to have Lord Xetic-Nal treating me like Ivan treated a horse - so I looked around for the first time to take in my new surroundings.

The space we were standing in was much larger than the town square and it took some time for me to accept that it was a *room*. The stones beneath my bare feet were warm and smooth, and the wall we were standing next to was made of the same smooth gray stone. Behind me rose a door at least twenty meters tall, made of oak and bound in steel. The keyhole was bigger than my hand and I stifled a laugh at the idea of the great Xetic-Nal having to lug around a key that would undoubtedly pull his trousers down. The room was windowless, and I looked around to try to figure out how it was so brightly lit, finally seeing the massive crystal chandelier high above my head. The wall curved away from us, sharply meet-ing a squared off section in front of us and to either side. I'd seen wizard towers from the outside and even at the great distance I'd known they were circular. My mind shied away from the concept that not only was this room big enough to contain most of the hous-es in town, it wasn't the only one on this level.

I also began to realize what one of the causes of my earlier diz-ziness was because it hadn't gone away when Xetic cleared my head out. The entire tower was awash in magic. Every stone of the walls, floor, and ceiling were charged and enchanted so densely that they seemed to swim in my vision. Spells surged in complicated patterns between and within the heavy stones, and it seemed like half the fittings and furniture were enchanted as well. Having so much magic flying around me was disorienting and I had to work to force the permanent enchantments on the stonework to the background of my awareness in order to pay attention to everything else. Ivan's cottage had been similarly fortified, but only with one or two spells for each brick. The tower's stonework looked like layers had been added upon layers until it was impossible to tell where one spell ended and another began. It was a continuum, a river where Ivan's cottage was a creek. I did my best to focus on the chromatic spectrum and hurried to keep up with Xetic.

The stone entry gave way to tiles and it only took a moment to recognize that they'd been laid out in the pattern of a skull with fire in the eye sockets. I looked up at the door we were approaching and above it hung a banner depicting that same flame-eyed skull on a black background with a red border. Xetic-Nal's emblem and colors. "Gauche, isn't it?" He said as he opened the door. "I was an insecure young lich once upon a time. I'd change it to something elegant, but the others would complain. I get enough grief from them about important things without going looking for trouble about pointless nonsense." We passed down a long corridor ending in a staircase. "I'd almost forgotten where the stairs were." He said. "I almost never bother with them. Some people like to have theirs run all the way around the circumference," he said conversationally, "and then square off the rest. It means they can have a very shallow ramp, but it also wastes so much time to go one floor up by having to walk almost four hundred meters. I'll show you where your living space is, and then we can go through some of the facilities," he continued as we passed the third floor landing. I was already breathing hard. "It's all the rage now to have apprentices do menial tasks like washing the floors or dusting. I'm not sure how that applies to doing magic. Of course I still want you to be tidy. Until you learn the spells for it, you'll be maintaining your own quarters – such as they'll need it. I think that it's important to keep fit too. A Wizard-Lord's mind is always sharper if they're healthy. So I put your room ten stories above the library and five below the labs. I also recommend trying to climb the tower every day. You may never reach the top on foot, but you'll get plenty of exercise trying. See, you're already slowing down and you spend half your life doing manual labor. Let's see, are there any burning questions right now? I know you must have a lot, but what's uppermost right this second?"

My mind was spinning with things I wanted to know. Most of them would probably be easy to look up later on if Xetic-Nal's library was as extensive as I imagined it was. There were several that I worried might offend him – I'd sassed him once and he hadn't seemed to mind, but now we were alone in his tower I was feeling isolated and worried about having to live with him for the years it would take for him to teach me wizardry. There were also quite a few questions I shied away from because I was afraid of the answer. *'Why me?'* was uppermost on that list, followed by *'Would you really have killed me?'* I decided on something relatively innocuous. "Why tea? I mean, I saw the wet spot under you; it was passing straight through your body."

"Doesn't mean I didn't taste it." Xetic replied. Proudly, he continued. "It was a priority project post-mortem. I mean, imagine the complexity of having to create a means of tasting simply by using an analogous means of analysis of the food and drink and then turning it into the same kind of signals to my newly created immortal mind construct. Not only that, but having to do it all swiftly enough that I could accurately judge the tastes produced before I forgot what they all were. Even finding baseline foodstuffs was a challenge. Anyway, all villages do food in about the same way. Turnips, onions, beef, whatever. Tea is different everywhere. Not to be too critical except yes, I will be, because – let's face it – what you people drink isn't really tea, is it? It tasted distinctly medicinal."

"You mean tea from the tea plant?" I wheezed. We were passing the seventh landing now.

"Yes, that is why it's called *tea*. What you drink would be called herbal mélange. Mint works, don't get me wrong, but *oregano? Bay?* The lavender was an interesting flavor. Tell me, do you just dump every edible plant you find growing in the woods into a cauldron and hope for the best? I think there might have even been pine needles in one of those mugs."

"Sir, we only ever drink tea when we're ill." I said.

"Keep drinking that stuff and you'll never get better." He replied. "And good thinking; 'milord' is a bit much and 'master' is just dumb. Sir will do nicely as long as you're with me."

I felt like my lungs were going to shrivel up and fall off by the time we reached the twelfth floor where Xetic-Nal had put my living space. I expected a stone cell like I'd seen in illustrations of where ascetic scholars stayed. Comfort didn't seem like something a long dead wizard considered. What I saw when he opened the door was a sitting room as big as Ivan's cottage with couches, armchairs, and a plush rug in front of a fire with no wood. Cherry shelves lined the walls and the doors on either side of the fire were made of walnut while the ones to my left and right were oak. I wasn't even sure what the writing desk was made of. I was getting the impression that Lord Xetic's taste was 'whatever looks about right and I've got a piece of.' Not to say that the rich red carpet and green leather sofa wasn't an elegant match, just that paired with a blue damask armchair and another armchair upholstered in something yellow and slick looking made it seem as if he'd gone to a bazaar and picked the six most expensive things he saw and then threw them together. I could hardly complain; at the time I had no sense of color coordination either and was used to burlap and homespun. My family was lucky to have linen sheets.

"Another reason I picked the twelfth floor," Xetic said as I goggled at the furnishings, "was that there wasn't much on this level anyway. May as well not have to move too much around, eh? Let's make sure I haven't forgotten anything. Heaven knows I don't want you feeling too embarrassed to ask how the toilet works." So saying, he went to the door on the left and opened it. I'd heard of indoor privies, so I was expecting something like a fancier version of what we had. A seat with a hole in it, a method of flushing, a bathtub, and a water basin. No doubt you grew up with modern bath fittings, Idalia, but I thought Xetic had given me an entire bathhouse. I'd read about them in a history book. There was a time when even the city people didn't have running water in their houses, you know, so they all piled into municipal pools to wash. That's what it felt like when I entered the tiled bathroom. The tiles were bright orange incidentally. I wonder if old boney messed up something in his chromatic sense when he became undead. If he'd scrambled his perception of color, it would have explained his taste in interior decoration.

Anyway, the tiles were orange, the bathtub was four feet deep in the center and as wide as my room back in my old house – incidentally tiled in alternating black and white. The pullchain on the porcelain toilet looked like it had been gilt, and the basin had six knobs on the faucet. I worked out H and C easily enough, but I had to try – hesitantly – B, I, S, and T to find out what they were. Xetic-Nal really liked tea, and apparently iced tea as well, because B was for boiling, and I was for ice. S was steam - I remain unsure why that was considered necessary - and T was for a substance I have only recently learned is toothpaste. For the entire duration of my study in the tower, I thought it was an extremely strange tasting dessert. It's probably for the best that I didn't eat much of it. Stranger still, I will add, because he didn't provide a toothbrush.

Not that I would have known what to do with it; the minds of the magi are somewhat vague on when toothpaste became prevalent, but I can tell no one would have believed it was around over eight thousand years ago. In retrospect it makes sense. When all that's left of your mouth is your jawbone and your teeth, you want to take good care of them.

The door on the right of the sitting room led into a bedroom with – what else – a bed, and naturally one bigger than any I'd ever seen. Yes, Idalia, I'm feeling like this is getting repetitive too. Let's just take it as read that everything is bigger than whatever I had before and move on.

The bed was big, with lots of pillows and covers and thankfully mostly done in scarlet and gold so it wasn't distractingly colorful. There was an empty closet on the righthand wall, and a few chairs and low benches strewn around, as well as a night table with a large pitcher of water and a fireplace much like the one in the sitting room on the near wall. The very first window I'd seen in the tower was on the lefthand wall, letting in rays of bright sunshine.

I was thirsty from my climb and everything had been so wonderful so far that I was barely surprised to find that, when I poured the ice-cold water into a cup next to the pitcher, there was just as much in the pitcher when I put it down as when I'd picked it up.

Xetic was looking in the closet. "I thought you'd bring your own clothes, but this works out." I was about to look out the window to see just how big Xetic's own capital city was when I saw magic flowing out of the corner of my eye in a pattern unlike that of the tower. I was beginning to get the knack already for telling the difference between the immediate sight and feel of a spell being cast and the slow churn of the ever-present enchantments. I moved towards Xetic, who was walking slowly into the closet, stopping every step to gesture at the metal rails on each side. Each step left behind a pair of garments. The first few hangers held simple black robes with scarlet around the sleeves and hem, and lines of scarlet up the front that curved around the neckline. I felt the sleeve, seeing a tiny red skull on each shoulder, and guessed it was silk.

"Some casual wear to start with." Xetic said over his shoulder. "Let's see. Something to work in." The robe he conjured was thicker, padded and the outer portion felt slick and tough. It had similarly reinforced breeches on the same hanger. "Undergarments … maybe trousers in case you feel the need … socks … slippers. Don't worry about cleaning them. A quick rinse in the sink should do the job for most of these. You'll need an outfit for when we have visitors." He was near the back and the last thing he produced was a robe which looked like it was going to be very difficult to wear well. The shoulders flared out in layers of starched red linen, the material falling down the sides of the robe in flowing bunches. The lower half was silk, with a diamond shaped leather panel in the front and back. Both were black with red tracing around the edges and a large red skull in the center. The sleeves would go well past my hands, opening wide at the end and were made of something black with a red sheen. The ends of the sleeves had little black skulls embroidered in a circle. I imagined I would need some practice walking and sitting in it before I would be allowed near guests. I hadn't thought of it, but it made sense that the other wizards would come to him rather than him visiting them.

"All it needs is a magically supported cape." I murmured, thinking of illustrations in old books about Wizard-Lords.

"You get that when you graduate." Xetic said. "There; that should take care of everything. Come on."

I followed him back into the sitting room and into the lefthand door. I felt a little more relaxed in the kitchen. It wasn't all that different from what Bowbringer had at the inn with a brick fireplace, cast iron pots, and various other pieces of cutlery. Like everything else it seemed much too large for just me, and I'd never seen an icebox before but the use of it wasn't too different from a very cool cellar.

"A bit old fashioned, but I thought you'd better have one place that's like home. When you're settled, I'm sure you'll get the hang of something modern. If you need more provisions, just bang the table and say what you want." He slammed his fist on the heavy wooden table. "Corn porridge and beans! I thought I'd give you something like what you're used to."

A pair of bowls appeared in the middle of the table and filled with the familiar staple of our diet. "There's some variety to what you can get, but mostly it only does raw ingredients right now. There's a list in one of the cabinets. If you want more you'll have to learn how to do it yourself and make changes to the enchantment. Consider it an incentive."

"Sir, I'm from a small farming community near the very end of the caravan route. I'm used to eating the same thing most days."

"Wait a minute, I'm seeing a pattern." Xetic's flaming eyes shrank to pinpoints. "You only call me 'sir' when you're being impertinent!"

"How is it working, sir?"

"Disturbingly well. Don't get too full of yourself, youngling. I'm – how old are you again?"

"Seventeen."

"About four hundred times older than you are. That's like an old man talking to a newborn in your frame of reference."

"I was wondering about that. If you're really that old, then how come you're in such a hurry? Surely a few minutes or even days doesn't mean a lot to you?"

"Let's sit down." We went into the sitting room and – big surprise – sat. He took an imposing wingbacked chair and I lounged on the sofa. Very appropriate image. "Thought experiment, young Zunvect. How long is it until winter festival? I assume you have one."

"About six months." I said.

"How long does that *feel* like?" Xetic pressed, his eyes growing in my vision. I felt at that moment like I could be consumed by the avid curiosity and intellect in them. Despite being balls of red light set in a dark abyss within his skull, they could be very expressive.

"A little long?" I hazarded

"Fine. Ten years ago you were seven years old. How long was it then?"

"Still six months. But it felt like a lot more." I blurted, not wanting to seem pedantic.

"Good. So, here's the question. Why? It's six months either way, but when you were younger it felt like longer. Everything did, correct?"

"Yes. I guess it's because I have more to do."

"That's part of the answer. Also experience. You're more than twice as old now as you were then. You've seen many more winter festivals." Xetic sat back and looked past me and into the distance. "The older you get, the more things you realize you need to do. That progression is roughly linear. Unfortunately, it also has no bounding function. To me, a year passes in an instant, but the days still have the same number of minutes as they always did. Since I died, I've been able to devote more than twice the time I used to into working. At first it was wonderful, but age and experience quickly take that away. In answer to your question, I'm always in a hurry because I'm constantly aware of what needs to be done and how little time there really is in which to do it. When your project schedules can be measured in centuries, you start to get a very deep appreciation for getting on with it. After all, imagine all the time I could procrastinate!"

He let me rest for a couple hours with strict instructions to bathe, dress properly, and eat in the meantime. I admit that I asked the table for corn porridge and beans to start with, and that I spent a very long time in the bathtub, having never enjoyed more than a cauldron of hot water's worth of bathtime. All that *and* I got my first view of what was outside the tower through my bedroom window. It was an enormous letdown from all the wonderful things Xetic-Nal had deluged me with in the short time since I'd arrived. My spirits sank as I realized I wasn't in Xetic's city-state of Ydrasia, capital of humanity and legendary in song and story. I was in one of the other two territories.

The tower stood on a low hill, which sloped gently down to a broad grassy meadow. By leaning out the window I could see that there were five hills spaced evenly around the tower. Given that they were spaced in a very clear pattern, I guessed that there were three more on the other side of the tower, finishing the eight points around a circle. They were all exactly the same distance apart and the same distance from the tower, placing us at the center and the other hills marking a constant radius of about a kilometer. The hills not only marked a circle, they marked a boundary, and one that I didn't learn the purpose of for a very long time. Beyond the circle was forest stretching out to the horizon. Xetic-Nal was not ruling his city. In this tower, he didn't rule anyone besides the other Wizard-Lords. There would be no slipping out to spend an evening at a tavern or discovering my sexuality with a girl at the inn. No joking with guards or finding a best friend during an entertaining tavern brawl in which I only used a hint of magic when no one was looking, and revealing dramatically over a beer that I was the apprentice of the Wizard-Lord who ruled *them*. I was the only living person here, sitting in my aerie within a pinnacle which pierced the heavens. A single man in a monolith.

At first my disappointment was sharpened by how much it reminded me of home. A clearing with forests keeping us penned in. Then I thought that this forest surrounded the tower on every side. Where I came from there was the mountain reared up to the east, a stone wall which blocked all sight and all travel except on wizard business – like the tax collector. My home also had the north-south highway, bringing merchants and news slowly through all the villages on the west side of events in the metropolitan east. Unless there was a road on the opposite side of the tower – and I firmly doubted that – the forest was totally unbroken. No one approached Lord Xetic-Nal on foot or horseback. The mighty oaken doors were entirely for show. The only people who came to his tower did so by magical transport, bypassing all physical barriers to arrive in his front hall. Staring out at the sea of green and inhaling wind that was warmer than any I had ever tasted before, I realized that I was alone and was going to *be* alone for a very, very long time.

Xetic collected me and on our way down, I counted each landing with the sinking feeling that comes with knowing that I'd have to walk back up at some point. I refrained from asking which floor the library was on since I got the impression that smalltalk wasn't something my new master enjoyed and that he'd no doubt ask me why I cared if I knew now or in five minutes when we arrived. I was feeling relaxed from my brief rest and didn't want to get into a long discussion of why I asked a question I was imminently about to get the answer to. It turned out that the library was on the second floor. Sort of.

The door itself did not prepare me for what I saw when I went in. It was like all the other landing doors. Wooden with a unique pattern of banding, paint, and inlay which was either how Xetic-Nal read numerals or – much more likely – a completely random result of making or buying a door of the correct size at some point and putting it wherever a new door was needed. At first, I stood in one place, not quite seeing what I was looking at. The tower was big. I think I've adequately communicated that. Exactly *how* big around it was had not been apparent since even the main hall wasn't actually the entirety of the first floor. The floors – more than one – of the library had no dividers other than the shelves, which had aisles which reached from one outer wall to the other. It also did have windows, though curiously they appeared to have metal shutters which were now open, and were glassed with no means of opening them. "When I don't have visitors I replace all the air with argon." Xetic commented when he saw me looking at the deep-set window frame. Deep set because the tower's bricks were at least a third of a meter thick. "Tell me why."

"Argon." I frowned. "It's a gas?"

"No," Xetic said caustically, "it's a non-wet liquid. Yes, it's a gas."

"Inert." I guessed. "So the books won't age."

"Basically correct. Chemistry wasn't something the sorcerer had stressed much, I notice. It didn't look like he had the materials for it, to be fair. Yes. When almost every manuscript is an original and you want to be able to read them again in a thousand years you need to keep things stable." He looked at me sharply. "So make sure to wash – and dry! – your hands frequently. I'll have to install a sink for the duration so you aren't tempted by laziness not to go upstairs to do so. And make sure you use good page turning methods. You're going to have times where you'll be going through the pages quickly to find something and you're going to need to practice to make sure you can do it without tearing. You'll be starting on common reprints and you won't be allowed to work with the good stuff until we're confident you're treating the books correctly."

"We?" I asked.

"Yes. Your day to day education will be handled by my librarian." I must have looked hopeful at the idea of there being another person in the tower. "She doesn't breathe either, so the argon isn't a problem for her. In fact, I'll leave you to meet her now. Let's see. Is there anything about me or the tower that you're particularly curious about? I need a hook for your first report and it may as well be something that interests you. I'm confining you to questions about your current surroundings since this is to be an example of critical thinking rather than research and so I need a question with an answer I am absolutely sure of." Now that he mentioned breathing, I was coming to realize that Lord Xetic spoke very quickly, not having to ever pause for breath between thoughts. The longer I knew him, the faster he talked.

I decided to think it through carefully. I had a hunch that Xetic wanted something interesting *from* me as well as something that interested me personally. A question that showed I wasn't just saying the first thing that I was curious about. "There's a very odd discrepancy in your biography." I said at length.

"Good grief. I'm not surprised; I usually tell people sniffing around my life story to bugger off. I wonder which of those half-rate hacks you were reading."

"It's a very basic fact." I continued. "The book said you're seven thousand years old, but that you were born shortly before the Uidrana exodus four thousand years ago."

"You want to know which is true since those are mutually exclusive claims. How about this: Come to me next week with at least six possible reasons for this claim, not counting the author being horrible at math or unable to keep his own facts straight. Let's assume I told the idiot both of those things and he took my word as truth despite the manifest impossibility. Why would I say that? Try to think of creative reasons." He disappeared.

Did I mention how the library was colossal? Because it was. Over four hundred meters in diameter and now that I was walking down one aisle, saw that the shelves went through the ceiling and could just make out that they seemed to keep going through to a third story above that. At the center was a completely smooth column about five meters wide made of what at first seemed to be stone, but didn't look or feel quite like any kind of rock I'd seen before. It was also totally opaque across my entire range of vision. Around the column were chairs and tables for studying, the chairs ranging from simple wood without arms to very squishy armchairs. The tables were either broad flat surfaces or smaller angled ones with stops on the bottom so books could be propped up. Curious about the column and with nothing else to do – it felt impolite to start browsing when I'd yet to find the librarian and Xetic had told me to keep my hands off most of them – I walked around to try to find a door. It was totally featureless all the way around, slick to the touch and cooler than its surroundings.

"That's where he keeps the books whose titles are dangerous." A female voice said. I turned around. "Good afternoon," the librarian said. "I hope Lord Nal remembered to feed you. The last boy could barely think for hunger the first time I saw him."

"Uh, good afternoon," I said, flustered. "Yeah, he showed me the kitchen before I came down." Having resigned myself to a monastic life for the next few years, and before that to never finding a girl until I left town to seek my fortune, it was a shock for Xetic-Nal's librarian to be a beautiful woman who looked to be in her mid-twenties. I knew Wizard-Lords remained youthful most of their lives, so I guessed she was much older.

The librarian emerged from the stacks on the far side of the reading area. Her light blue robe fluttered around her ankles, the black webwork of an unfamiliar design seeming to highlight parts of her I tried not to stare at. Her raven hair didn't move at all as she crossed the floor, seeming to be suspended in its own world. She glanced down when she reached me and quirked her lip, fixing me with pale and slightly slanted eyes over sharp cheekbones. "It wouldn't be a very satisfying lay for either of us." She sidestepped through a table and for the first time I realized that her robe hadn't been disturbed as she moved. She hadn't been walking and now that I looked at her, I realized that her entire body was magic. There was no material substance at all. "I've got some leeway physically, but you'd feel no more than a breeze and I haven't felt anything real since I came here." She was the first person I could remember who had an accent, and spoke in that same continuous way Xetic did, though her syllables were clipped while his words tended to flow together.

"So, uh, you're … oh, you're dead too." Her frankness had reduced my already badly damaged conversational skill.

"Lord Nal prefers his assistants permanent. I think he'd go crazy if he had to train a new researcher every two hundred years." She bowed shallowly. "I am Aika Chimamire no Kata. You've probably read about me."

"You were Lord Xetic's second apprentice." I said. "I'm Zunvect," I added.

"The fourth." Aika observed. "Welcome to the collection of all human knowledge."

I'm sure you have your own books about Lady Aika, but to help you understand my initial attitude towards her, I'll tell you of what *I* had learned from Ivan's history books about the second – and arguably most magically successful – apprentice. Yes, Idalia, I was thinking 'until me' but I was trying to be polite. As you'll learn later on in this story, I have a lot of reasons to be very kind towards Aika.

She was … incredible. After her, no one took the colors seafoam and black out of respect for her achievements. This was unlike the *third* apprentice, whose colors had been struck as a remembrance of his villainy. Aika had been the first Wizard-Lord to claim one of the large islands in the south sea. At the time, the archipelago which stretched across half the world in the southern oceans had been independent nations, sometimes in loose confederacy, sometimes in empire, but rarely in harmony for long. At the time, most of the Wizard-Lords ruled Crescent Bay, and were just beginning to expand north towards the Crooklands, the massive isthmus to the north of the Crescent. It was that protected cove where Xetic established the first Wizard-Lord territories and they had been expanding outward ever since. It was an easy ship crossing even then to get to Ismun – though it was another thousand years before they expanded in that direction – and the arc almost six thousand kilometers wide sent arms out into the sea creating a not-quite-enclosed warm water port which aided sea commerce.

Overland routes were difficult then, and remained so during my lifetime. Several Wizard-Lords had founded regions on the horn which formed the southern end of the Crescent, and separated it from the southern coast of Bomarie, an area we called Anchorage Horn. As the march of civilization spread to the south coast of Bomarie, they also looked across the sea to the islands.

I didn't know then where Aika had been born. All I knew was that she'd been trained by Xetic-Nal and decided that rather than settle in the south to help tame the summoners or go north and put pressure on the Elves, she decided that it was high time that the Wizard-Lords expand their remit to the seas beyond their coastline. The largest island was about a thousand kilometers south of the Horn and was the port of choice for pirates who had been raiding Wizard-Lord commerce fleets for the past four hundred years. Repeated strikes from the wizards had done little to dissuade the pirates and after an enormous blast of fire which killed thousands of people who lived there and barely singed the pirate base on the opposite side of their island, Xetic had put a moratorium on punitive expeditions. Instead he waited for another century while the wizards grumbled and then sent Aika to conquer the big island, which she renamed Zile. Aika took a native name to rule under and there was massive immigration as she turned her islands into wealthy shipping hubs. By the time her successor took over Zile, all trade routes had ceased hugging the dangerous coastline, and instead zigzagged, using the islands as waypoints between the far-flung territories of southern Bomarie.

You probably know better now than I did when I first met her *how* she came to rule a peaceful and prosperous island territory which grew to encompass six of its nearby neighbors before the Wizard-Lords established another four towers along the length of the archipelago and formalized who owned what. Her political skills were important, but her prolific magical research also contributed heavily. One of Ivan's books said that she had invented and perfected some of the sea-based spells still in use. Navigation, propulsion, durability, size, and defenses were all revolutionized in the Wizard-Lords' deep water fleets.

In addition to her maritime magical innovation, she had integrated much of the local culture into her court manners, and the etiquette she adopted spread and was still used on formal occasions by most Wizard-Lords. Aika was learned, cultured, and possibly the most influential mortal human in history. To find her as Xetic-Nal's ghostly research assistant and librarian was very strange. The books hadn't mentioned anything about a mysterious disappearance, or in fact anything to do with her death at all. I had assumed she'd died a relatively natural death two thousand years ago. Now here she was, telling me that I wasn't going to be having sex for the first time after all and making sure I wasn't hungry.

"You're probably getting pretty tired, Zunvect." Aika said. "It's your first day and you've been running around probably since dawn. You're from out in the far west, right?"

"Yeah." I swallowed. "About as far away from the big cities as you can get without losing the protection of a Wizard-Lord."

"You've been up since dawn, then. It's almost eighteen now and even if you've had dinner, you're probably not up for the strain of a new beginning to your studies. We'll have a quick walk through and then you can come back in the morning. I don't sleep, so let's make it six since you're probably going to stay on your old schedule for a few days at least."

"Where's the clock?" I asked. The only one in the village had been inside Bowbringer's common room, high up on a shelf so no one would disturb it.

Aika looked at me with an expression of such outright disbelieving rebuke that I flushed. Then she burst out into a raucous, immoderate laugh. "Of course! Lord Nal the Rushed, Lord Nal the Punctual, Lord Nal the Microsecond Retentive didn't give his apprentice a clock for his room. I am going to *enjoy* pointing that out. Don't worry; you'll have one by tomorrow." She was still giggling as she showed me how the angled desks lit up when a book was placed on them so that I could study after sunset. This was followed by a rapid overview of which section was which, what books were in them, the order, and where I should start. I caught very little of it, being exhausted, amazed, overawed, and still slightly attracted to the ghostly librarian. I tried to pay attention when she told me where to find the books I would be starting with, not wanting to fail such a simple task. "Not that it matters right now," she added as she finished ticking off the sections of the library. "I'm your day-to-day tutor, so I'll pull whatever I think you should be reading." I at least managed to fix the locations of the six internal helical staircases, as well as the basic concept of how the shelves were laid out. "You're falling over. Time for bed." Aika said when we were back down in the first-floor study space. All three of the library's floors had them, but I grew fond of the one on the first floor and did most of my work there. "Take this and make a start on it tonight if you can. If you're as far along as you seem to be, it ought to be light reading. We can discuss it when you've gotten a couple chapters in." She raised her hand and a moment later a book zipped down one of the aisles and slapped into her palm. She handed it to me. "This is the first thing any wizard reads. Once you understand the ethos that underlies this book, you'll truly have begun your apprenticeship." I looked at the title. *Us by Lord Xetic-Nal, W-L1 ThD MFCSR FURI etc etc etc*

Excerpt from the Introduction to *Us* by Lord Xetic Nal, 74th ed. (3893 [XR])

You are a Wizard-Lord. Congratulations and condolences. Congratulations because you are beginning your journey of becoming one of the most powerful eighty-seven human beings on the planet, with access to knowledge and resources far beyond anything you've dreamt of. Congratulations on being alive; few confirmed wizards survive to be apprenticed. Congratulations on being chosen and on being judged able to learn what we teach. There are few who are responsible enough to use what you'll learn wisely, to protect and advance the interests of humanity.

Condolences because that's what you're going to do. You will learn some things that other humans only fear and suspect, and others that they are happily unaware of. You will oppose gods and repel monsters. The reason there are Wizard-Lords is because the world is dangerous. Condolences because as of now you are responsible, and when you take up rule in your territory you and you alone will bear the weight of governing, guiding, and protecting thousands or millions of your fellow human beings. They will submit to your authority, look to you for aid in crisis, and expect you to be wise, strong, and caring at all times.

No tower has fallen in the history of our organization, and precious few wizards have been found wanting. That is the burden and the legacy. I'm sorry it has to be this way but as you will soon learn, we exist because we have to. I've spent a very long time trying to think of an alternative. Trust me; I don't want to be in charge of you any more than you want to be in charge of them. Some of you are thinking that being in control will be fun or in some way fulfilling. The luckiest and best among us enjoy being servant-leaders, but don't expect to find yourself one of them once the realities of rule assert themselves. It is extremely rare to enjoy both politics and thaumaturgy. Most will find the responsibility burdensome and so I will stress this advice several times in my introductory volume: do not solve problems of state with magic. It is the easy solution the first day, but eventually your territory will come to rely on magic and that is a dangerous situation. You must remain somewhat apart from the day-to-day running of your polity in order to maintain vigilance – and if you're lucky, to do some magical research. Spells don't write themselves yet, and every advance in magic improves quality of life even if there isn't an application in your lifetime.

Magical research is your secondary priority in my view. Primary is of course to keep our various neighbors' predations at bay. To learn more about magic, the world, how everything works. That is the best task for us. There is so much still to learn, to understand, to figure out. I hope that you will revel in expanding your magical skills, and in expanding the sum total of our knowledge, despite my warnings and your other burdens. Retain your curiosity. Find something that you really want to do but can't. Don't let your government monopolize you. Enough warnings, hopes, and vague instructions. The rest of the book is a mixture of philosophical considerations, ethics, and the bylaws of the Wizard-Lord hierarchy. There are a lot of rules, and whenever possible I'll direct you to a historical reference as to why we have them. Some are amusing, some terrifying, but most are frankly infuriating. One boundary Wizard-Lords are very good at pushing is that of legal semantics. That's why chapter 6 comprises over half the book with over 1,600 headings and a total of 23,000 subheadings. This introduction only deals with the key regulations. Assume that if you think you ought not to, you probably shouldn't, and feel free to page through *Compendium of Thaumaturgic Regulation* if you ever feel the need for a laugh or to check on whether your harebrained scheme is original. Odds are someone a few hundred years ago has already tried it. If they haven't, *please don't.*

Idalia 4:

Another Tower

"Speaking of which," Zunvect said, "I wouldn't mind a little tour of my new home. I perceive by your pained expression, and the constant rubbing of your fingers, that perhaps we ought to take a rest. Since you had me in that box when we arrived, I'm a bit behind the times on our hosts and their world." He looked around. "They obviously like bare stone as much as Xetic-Nal did."

Idalia put the pencil down, stood up, and stretched. "I'm starting to get hungry, too. Not that I'm looking forward to our host's cuisine."

"It's funny. Lord Xetic was a food addict, but he never tried to get meals from offworlders even when he had the opportunity."

"He wouldn't like what they serve here. The word 'Lupine' is very literal. They're the creepiest example of parallel evolution I've ever witnessed, and I'm a demonologist. Giant bipedal wolves are something that takes a long time to get used to; I keep expecting them to try to eat me. The predator instinct thing may be why they're so cut-throat about getting the story first. It's something like the freshest intellectual meat to them."

Zunvect looked around the windowless stone cell, making it clear that he was doing so to call its deficits to Idalia's attention. "I hope I can buy us some furniture while I'm at it."

Idalia snorted. "I have some in my room. It didn't seem necessary to give you any. Even if I brought you a chair, I'd risk breaking containment to give it to you. No, Zunvect," she said, anticipating his next argument, "the wards must remain. They're as much for your safety and stability as my peace of mind. The Lupines are adamant that you not be allowed to wander free, and your manifestation is still unstable. My suite is very nice, thank you, though the bed is a bit deep, the chairs are too low, and the desks too high. You wouldn't like the view, either. Their towers aren't like yours were. Have a look." Being an ambassador and demonologist meant knowing Tunnel magic well. Idalia opened a shielded portal in the wall, showing what was on the other side without letting in the elements beyond.

They were in a high turret, surrounded by a vast complex of stone and wood. Thick, brooding black clouds hung over the Emerald Citadel, a perpetual storm where the rain and wind never let up. Towers like their own speared upwards at intervals, each one surrounded by even thicker clouds which sent green lightning bolts searing down into metal rods attached to reservoirs where a glowing green fog swirled biliously around. There were no external walkways.

"There's something about the magic they do here in the Emerald Citadel that causes this weather." Idalia said. "They spend a fortune on keeping the place from eroding away in the gales and downpours."

"Dreary," Zunvect said drily. "You couldn't have found us refuge on a planet with more … salubrious environs?"

"This planet is fine; it's the Citadel that's the problem. Unfortunately, the Orders of the Ruby and Diamond declined my request – their magic doesn't churn up the local weather. You can trust my judgment that the Lupine Orders were our best hope of asylum. It was a nail biter when two of their three centers of magic turned us down. If the Emerald hadn't stepped up, I'd have had to take your containment bottle even further afield. I was *not* looking forward to trying to strike any deals with non-humanoids, or of risking our necks in a civilization that the magi could easily extract us from. As it is, it's very uncomfortable. The Order of the Emerald is strictly males only, and if there's anything more disconcerting than getting my lunch from a commissary full of nine-foot-tall wolf-shaped magicians, it's getting looks which suggest that some of them are regretting the monastic lifestyle. The archmage assured me that they don't find humans attractive, but that's not the impression I was getting."

"And I thought my own culture shock was bad. How's your hand?"

"Well enough."

"In that case..."

Zunvect 9:

Litany of Law

I should have slept very badly on my first night as a Wizard-Lord-apprentice. I was somewhere completely different, doing things I'd never thought possible, and being given warnings that made it sound as if I had the worst job in the world. The only two people in a tower that seemed to go on forever were dead and they had continued working regardless. I could have worried about a thousand things, about a hundred people I'd not see again for years, or gone over every experience that was now denied to me. Then again, twenty-four hours ago I'd gone to bed on lumpy, poorly stuffed bed with no pillow and a draft strong enough to blow away my blanket. Now, I was lying in the softest bed in the world, so wide that I could roll over again and again without reaching the other side. It was warm, I'd eaten an enormous dinner, and it seemed as if the only work I had to do was walk up and down a lot of stairs and read a lot of books. I also wasn't given to anxiety when I was that age. At seventeen I hadn't had that much to be anxious about. Nothing that wasn't familiar to everyone else. Still, the farm doesn't leave a man that easily and I woke well before dawn.

I immediately noticed the ticking sound when I entered my sitting room. The mantel now had a very large clock on it, and underneath was a note. I could already hear Xetic-Nal's bone dry sarcastic humor in the words. 'Of course you wouldn't think to ask for your own clock, you dirt-grubbing bumpkin. It makes me wonder what else you were too damn salty to ask for. Get it through your skull that you're as good as the richest person in your wildest dreams and start having a bit of ambition – or at least avarice. With the deepest and warmest regards, X."

I decided never to mention that I'd been too gobsmacked by everything the day before to ask where the door across from the bathroom went. No doubt he'd berate me for being an uncurious lump of meat and so on and so forth as a screen for having forgotten to show me what it was himself. I peeked in and found something totally unexpected – a flight of stairs going up and to my left. I decided to have a wash before I climbed them, and so was very clean when I emerged on the floor above. I was very unsure of what I'd found. There were no inner walls, no dividers on this floor. Just row upon row of granite topped tables, interspersed with steel shelves, sinks, what I later learned were slateboards, and racks full of tools and bottles. With apprehension, I noticed another note on the nearest worktop. 'Finally, a bit of curiosity. This is your lab; I didn't show it to you yesterday because you used up all the time I'd blocked out for introductions on eating and bathing and whatnot. You probably won't get much use out of it now, but have a read through the various guides when you have a chance, and remember the first rule: Always use the isolation circle. Deepest regards etc, X.' I wondered how many more of these notes I'd find lying around.

I walked around the big laboratory, marveling at how Xetic expected me to use all this space for magical work. Surely there couldn't be that much experimentation to do! I caught my foot on something and finally noticed that every table had a circle of inlaid metal around it, and that at the far end there was a clear space with circles of varying widths spaced out. I assumed 'isolation circle' meant some kind of protection against unexpected magic. That seemed sensible. Between two of the shelves were hung a set of papers which turned out to be guidelines for safe experimentation, which I decided to come back and read when I was more likely to need them. It had been half past four when I came up, so I grabbed *Us* and hurried down to meet Aika.

The week passed swiftly and in discussion which began hesitant and swiftly became spirited and enthralling. Eternity had driven my master to become a manic worker always aware of just how much time can pass unless you use every moment of it. In Aika, it had instilled a calm and patient serenity. Where Xetic was a caustic and dry wit, she enjoyed how ridiculous the world was and the people in it. I was already falling in love, but I didn't know it. She did and she knew it wouldn't go anywhere. I cherish those moments when I leave a conceited immortal speechless, and none more than when I disproved her about *that*.

"There are so many rules!" I complained one day.

"Of course there are; there are so many wizards trying to find a way to get around the rules to achieve something momentary, pointless, and notorious."

"I've tried looking it up and I can't find a proper reference. *Why* does Lord Xetic track every single stone? Three hundred twenty-three million, three hunded and sixy thousand bricks, and precisely three point seven-six per tower. Why? Why track them so carefully?"

"Zunvect, critical thinking. What would happen if there was one more brick than the current count?"

"Someone's added one." I said. "Their tower is bigger."

"Exactly, and that can't be allowed. You can have whatever you want *inside*, but the outside is fixed. No one is bigger, no one is better, no one has more space to fill."

"There has to be more to it than that."

"There is, but that's a very … advanced question. Let's say that it resides in the central library and leave it at that. The most I can say now is that that's the amount we started with. You can tell that easily enough."

"From the protocol on starting a new tower." I said. "When you do that, everyone has to contribute until they're all equal again. You can't make more."

"Right. And what would it mean if there was one too few?"

"Someone destroyed a brick."

"Good. Wars can be as destructive as you want, but the tower is inviolate. It *must* be passed to the next Wizard-Lord. We leave, the towers remain."

"All right, so let me critically think a bit. What is so special about these bricks? If they've always been here, then that means Lord Xetic either made them or found them and his original towers were … well, too big to stand up."

"Assumption!" Aika chided.

"They used to be wider."

"Better. It's dangerous to know, but not dangerous to speculate. Consider the approximate size of a tower back when it was only Lord Nal's original three. Figure out the volume and you can play around with the dimensions to see what might have fit."

Then there was the report. The day I was to present my six possibilities to Xetic, I found a note under my clock. '10 AM – X.' I was, of course, early, even after going all the way down to the library to ask Aika where Xetic's study was. It was on the twenty-fifth floor. I was in for a long climb. The door off the stairs was unremarkable save that it had a small skull at eye level and no handle. It swung open at what I assumed was 10 AM precisely. "Good morning. I trust you have been reading my book." Xetic said as I looked around. "I hope it wasn't too heavy handed for you. I despise the tone of the introduction, but I find that many apprentices require a hammer to the brain to take anything seriously. I hope that you will not require such vulgar prodding."

"I will be sure to take any advice you give me seriously." I assured him. The study was surprising in how ordinary it seemed. His office was carpeted in plush plum, and the fireplace never seemed to be without a crackling log. Xetic's desk was a heavy wooden affair with a high backed seat for him and a less impressive one on the near side for me. The righthand wall was mostly window looking out on the seemingly endless forest. On the left was a set of odd looking wooden cabinets with labeled drawers instead of doors. There was a pen, inkwell, and paper on Xetic's desk. I couldn't quite imagine him writing. He seemed to prefer conjuring paper with the words already written on them.

As I entered, he took a steaming pot of tea from an alcove behind him. Every time I went to his office, he had a mug or a teapot somewhere nearby. I always drank when he offered, but never appreciated it like he did. He had thousands of varieties, but I could rarely taste the subtle differences. To me black was black, green was green, and I liked mint in mine. After tasting what my village called tea, I think he was afraid I might say I preferred mine with pine cones or mushrooms, so he never asked my opinion.

"So, let's hear your six ideas." Xetic said as I sat across from him. He steepled his fingers and placed his skull on top of them. I'd thought I'd gotten more comfortable with his manner, but those pinpricks in his sockets were unnerving in that pose.

"Right. Idea one: You were lying. You told him contradictory information because you wanted him to leave or had some other purpose in deliberate misinformation about your true age. It's the most plausible because it's the simplest. No need for any elaborate invention."

"A good reason for placing it first, but perhaps a more concrete one would be better. As you progress, I hope that you will be able to discard simplicity in favor of evidence."

"Idea two: You had no interest in deception, but instead wanted to see who was paying attention. I place this below idea one because I cannot see any benefit, nor would there be many opportunities to make use of planted data since it would require someone to notice, interact with you, and choose to bring it up.

"Idea three is related: It was an inside joke. I also find this less likely than an outright fabrication because the author lived in the mid two thousands, a period when you were very unlikely to have any friends who would read it and so far as I have seen, you are not prone to nostalgia so using an old joke is unlikely."

"You correctly predict my sense of humor." Xetic allowed. "Nostalgia, however, is conjecture based on too little observation. Once you get to know me, you may find otherwise or you may not."

"Ideas four and five:" I continued. "You were referring to both objective and subjective temporal experience. Four is internal, five is external. In concept four, you refer to how long you have had continuous consciousness, taking into account long periods spent in an accelerated mental frame. This is consistent with you being in a hurry all the time. Placed lower because the last three ideas require some magical explanation. Concept five requires manipulation of time. You are both mentally *and* physically three thousand years older than you would be had time flowed normally in your tower. We are getting into very unlikely scenarios since I have never even heard of magic which could affect the flow of time."

"In that case, your sixth idea must be quite farfetched." Xetic replied.

"It is. The sixth possibility is that you were predicting your own end and that in three thousand years you will cease to exist. Seers and prophets are well known in the Skyland and it is plausible that you have learned their craft. I place this last because I do not believe you would ever reveal such critical information in that way. All accounts, and my little time talking to you, suggest to me that if you were absolutely sure that you were going to die permanently at a fixed point that you would either tell no one until the correct moment. Alternately, you would tell everyone immediately. Hiding an announcement like that for people with a paranoid bent to try to work out isn't a worthwhile strategy."

"Ah, but what if I had foreseen that the right person would figure it out?" Xetic countered. "Once you factor in situations of flexible causality, anything could happen."

"In which case there is no point in thought experiments." I retorted. "You cannot outguess someone who knows the future."

"Certainly not someone who can see as far ahead as – what would have been at the time – five thousand years with utter clarity." Xetic agreed. "Prophesy is a bit of a dead end, Zunvect. It suffers from a damaging inverse principle which I'll cover when you get to learning that branch. Very creative overall. I like your organization scheme. Work on the reasoning; you're falling into the trap of valuing simplicity above all other factors. For next week, I want you to explain a fundamental paradox – or refute it. The assertion is thus: No universe can maintain a situation in which immortality and time travel coexist in the same civilization.' Since you posited that I am altering the flow of time, I want you to think about why that particular concept may be impossible beyond the simple dismissal that time magic is unknown and thus not plausible."

"There are a lot of rules about wizards fighting each other." I commented as I sat in the library, making my slow way through the innumerable statutes and ordinances which governed wizard behavior. I was starting to think that I'd been better off as a sorcerer. If I lived somewhere with a well-disposed Wizard-Lord I'd probably have fewer rules to follow. None, however, would cause me to laugh out loud when I read them.[5]

"Lord Nal lived in a violent time." Aika replied, bringing me back to the question of the intricate Wizard-Lord battle rituals. She had little to do except watch me read, and occasionally answer when I got bored. In my boredom, you see, I would often begin questioning or criticizing the laws.

"He had a romantic notion back then that Wizard-Lords would be constantly getting into duels over protocol and etiquette. What they really did was give each other hells about border disputes, and write scathing academic criticisms in the thaumaturgical journals. We've had more duels break out over accusations of poor experimental practices than all the protocol questions combined." She snorted. "Anyway, they're not much used these days. Things are much more settled now, and most Wizard-Lords prefer to fight at a distance using those same scathing articles about each other. It's much more civilized. The majority of combat issues are now about trade wars, border skirmishes, and the odd ignition of a city wall.

---

[5] An example I remember to this day: 'Pyromancy – the manipulation of heat so as to produce a fueled flame – is henceforth prohibited within 10 meters of a haystack.' A law followed by 'Electromagnetomancy – any manipulation of electricity of magnetism – is prohibited within 20 meters of a haystack.' And finally 'All magic is prohibited within 50 meters of a haystack.' [5]

[6] Xetic's note – I try not to break into this because it's his story and I want him to tell all of it before I publish a rebuttal, but I just want to clarify something. I don't know why so much magic was being done in proximity to a haystack, but after the five farmsteads, two stately homes, twelve cottages, and sixteen city blocks burned down, I was sick of it. I was one conflagration away from banning *hay*.

Wizard-Lords aren't supposed to directly cause collateral damage, and using the regional militia to fight each other is only for the direst of disagreements. Lucky us; we have a lot of non-human enemies to keep us away from each other. Of course, we had all of that when I was alive and there were still many more wars than there are now. The creation of the Peacemaker Lineage fifteen hundred years ago has helped to keep tensions down. We're still who and what we are, but with a tower dedicated to interterritorial diplomacy, there's a resource to go to before matters escalate."

"Why would Wizard-Lords be so ... confrontational?" I asked. "If we're surrounded by foes and united by our common research goals as well as spending so much time governing, why add to that with fighting each other?"

Aika smiled. "For you, politics was something that happened in rumors and stories. For us, it's personal. A Wizard-Lord *is* their territory and they live vicariously through their people and land. If one sees that their neighbor is more prosperous, they take it as a personal failure. Someone else is doing better for their territory. There's also the personal issues around research goals. Usually the territories are all doing different things, but on the occasion where two or three are looking at the same problem, there are accusations of plagiarism, and attempts to beat others to publishing through slipshod magical methodology. The rules say that those grievances must be settled formally and personally, but often one can manufacture a territorial issue and bring it to open war. Wizards are like anyone else; there are a lot of petty and easily angered people. We're not immune to those demographics."

"I suppose." After all of the warnings in the introduction, I couldn't imagine going to war over something trivial. "Most of the dueling infractions go to 'permanent arbitration.' Is that execution?"

"Got it in one. If Lord Nal finds out a Wizard-Lord has broken a law, he usually just kills them. It seems harsh but it saves a lot of time in the long run. He's found that the recidivism rate for Wizard-Lords who aren't severely dealt with is very high and there aren't many other options. He can't confiscate or fine them much because a Wizard-Lord's belongings are part of their tower legacy. Imprisonment is pointless since then he has to appoint a regent, who will likely decide they want to keep the job, and will poison the offender as soon as they get out of jail. That's perfectly legal, by the way, so pay your cooks well."

"I had noticed that assassination seems almost completely unregulated."

"It can get messy if you bump off a Wizard-Lord with an apprentice, but otherwise it really only affects Wizard-Lords who aren't careful. We don't want careless wizards." Aika replied. "And of course if they're *caught* and the evidence is airtight, then you can issue a swift challenge to the wizard responsible for trying to kill you. That means you teleport behind them and blow their head off with a spell before they can react, by the way. It has to be airtight because if you do that without conclusive evidence, then Lord Nal will do the same to you."

"Being a Wizard-Lord sounds dangerous."

"Only if you live in a very active incursion zone or you make enemies out of other Wizard-Lords." Aika said airily. "We have a lot of rules to make sure that these situations don't happen often and are dealt with in an orderly manner when they do. You'll read about the Peacemakers soon; they are often consulted and usually succeed in calming everyone down. I think you've made enough progress for one day. Take the afternoon off and explore. I'm sure you haven't been past the thirtieth floor yet."

As a matter of fact, I hadn't really looked around beyond my own quarters, the library, and Xetic-Nal's office. That left most of the tower below the twenty-fifth to see, and the seemingly endless levels above it. I'd dutifully exercised daily by climbing the stairs, but by the time I fought my way up – always trying to get at least one more step than the day before – I wasn't in the mood to try the door. With Aika's assurance that I would be unable to open any door I wasn't supposed to, I set off to see what I was allowed to see.

At first it was a great disappointment. The doors leading out from the sixth all the way up to my own rooms on the twelfth and thirteenth floors were locked. I recalled him saying that there were labs five levels above my quarters – I guessed they must be more advanced versions of what he'd equipped my suite with – so after making sure that the doors in between would not open – and they didn't – I finally reached someplace I was allowed to go. The isolation room on the seventeenth floor.

I could tell it was a protected area as soon as I walked in. The door was very thick, and the inside was covered with something dull and gray which was opaque in every way I could discern. The squared off walls of that full-floor room were the same. I felt the same chill emanating from it as I had in the cave back home and knew that if I closed the door that I would be shut off from everything. I did so. It was the first time I could remember being truly at peace. Not that there was any enchantment pumping good feelings into me through psychomancy, just that I'd never been without my magical sight, never been anything but aware of the mighty roar of Ry-Kel's magic surging around me and through everything and of the sharper, brighter pinpricks of spells.

It took me a few minutes of hard looking to notice the circular patterns on the floor. For the first time I had to rely solely on chromatic vision which wasn't as sharp as most people's. Using magical sight all the time was an eyestrain, and if I relied on my physical eyes more, I'd have needed spectacles. Probing one with my finger, I found a depression in the center which gave way to my push, slowly opening a hole in the blocking material. A geyser of magic erupted out of the gap in the protective layer, slowly filling the room. I guessed that this was a way to control the inflow of magic so that it would feed only the spell being cast and no more than that. I closed the hole and peace returned.

After a long time sitting and seeing how much more effective mediating was when there wasn't a maelstrom around me, I departed the isolation lab. Above it were six more floors of lab spaces with equipment that looked specialized, complicated, and sometimes a bit dangerous. I should clarify that in this case the doors opened but I was unable to enter the room. My magical sight registered a tight mesh of lines which filled the doorframe on the inner side. I was allowed to look, but not come near the blackboards covered in writing, active isolation fields, and bubbling retorts. The twenty-fourth floor was, as I'd expected, locked. Faced with the prospect of yet more climbing and an almost certain series of locked doors above Xetic's office, I returned to my quarters to struggle through more laws.

Excerpt from *Us* by Lord Xetic-Nal, 74th ed. (3893 [XR]), Chapter 2: The Fundamentals of Rule

By what mandate do the Wizard-Lords rule? Those of you disposed towards reflection have no doubt already asked yourself this – or will consider it at length in the future. The basic answer to this question may not seem satisfying. Wizard-Lords rule because they can, and because no one can physically stop us from doing so. 'Might makes right' may seem immoral at first, but consider our world beyond the comfortable confines of a city wall or Wizard-Lord's magical reach. The elves seek to restore the Uidrana or to take their place, and the dragons consider all property communal and will eat your livestock. There are stories of sea serpents eating ships, sirens pulling sailors into the depths, trolls dragging children into the deep forest (that one was our fault), and innumerable other dangers beyond the ken of most human beings to defend themselves from. Most of these things aren't even imaginary. There are real dangers in the world and our culture wouldn't survive more than a few years were we limited to force of arms in combating them.

The question I hope you are asking: Why do we need to rule in order to repel monsters, invaders, and other magical incursions? Authority seems unnecessary when we could just sit in our towers alone and be a service rather than a government. Strictly speaking there is nothing to prevent us from doing just that. We would need a very keen incentive to be *paid* for it, however. A well-prepared Wizard-Lord requires economic investment in the range of 10% of the productive output of a territory, and human nature suggests that secular rulers would be tempted towards stinginess, which would degrade readiness and threaten later generations. Wizard-Lords must be constantly researching new forms and methods of magic, and that takes time and money. Rule also has the benefit of giving a Wizard-Lord the weight of law. An evacuation goes smoothly when the Wizard-Lord has the authority to order it on his own. Yes, there have been evacuations; sometimes a territory faces an incursion so great that they have to withdraw the entire population either out of the territory or into the tower until the threat can be eliminated.

My experience as a wizard in the days when the rulers were hereditary aristocracy – or in rare cases, democratic republics - was that they preferred to spend their money on immediate concerns and call up a draft when matters got rough. This attitude was doomed to failure, and without a frankly heroic effort on the part of me and my contemporaries at the time, there might not *be* a human race right now. To them it was the way things were and we alternately basked in the praise of those saved and the vituperation of rulers who thought wizards were dangerous pests, fit only to kill the even less desirable monsters before fading away. Wizards were meant to fight, win, and disappear without a fuss. If they didn't, then they were labeled as 'dark lords' and 'evil that must be fought.' To me it was an intolerable state of affairs, and I took very firm measures to alter the balance of power. The benefit of immortality is that one need not argue, but merely wait until those who would form an opposition die of old age. Their successors grew up not knowing the world was any different from the one I made.

Of course, all this leaves the Wizard-Lord with the responsibility of being the autocratic ruler of their territory. We are academics by and large, so administration is often not a natural strength. We must cultivate this, however, or risk becoming the pawn of an able minister. The remainder of this chapter will be general advice on how to rule, defend, and research without becoming a figurehead, a warmonger, or a hermit.

Zunvect 10:

A Version of History

Xetic was in exactly the same place as before when I entered his office, and I realized that there was going to be a fixed routine to this. I sat. "I tried to refute your assertion," I began, "but then I realized it makes perfect logical sense. If a person is immortal, they'll live until the end of time, and if they can time travel, they'll return to the beginning rather than continue into an uncertain rebirth or permanent death. Being immortal, they'll live again through everything and go back yet again. From their perspective, it will be linear, but from an outsider's view, it will be as if at the instant of one ability meeting the other that the entire universe is instantaneously filled to bursting with time shifted copies of that individual. Thus the two cannot coexist within the same person because if they did, we'd have observed it occurring."

"Unless anyone who does so eventually realizes that paradox themselves and so does not take that path." Xetic countered.

"In which case only responsible immortal time travelers can exist?" I retorted.

"That, or there's someone who is much more powerful keeping them in line."

"Like you do with the wizards. No, that's untenable. There's always someone more powerful eventually. Or a situation which forces the issue."

"Perhaps." Xetic allowed. "Though 'there's always someone stronger' and 'always a situation that changes things' are unprovable axioms. Well thought out overall, and I agree provisionally that no absolute law can be upheld permanently. Consider that for next week. Consider what is to come after I can no longer adequately enforce my conception of good conduct on the wizards. I trust that you have completed your study of what that good conduct is."

"I have, sir."

"Good. I think the next topic to pursue is history and geography. That way you can better understand where we are and how we got there. In fact, it would be better if you had rather more background for this question since it's a practical one rather than a pure thought experiment. Make this one a written report and be ready to submit it in two months and defend it on the same day."

"Two months?" I asked, astonished at the sudden gap in my assignments.

"This is a question I want a very good answer to." Xetic said. "That and every time I sit down and get to grips with something, you walk in and present a report. It's giving me a headache."

"Would it be diplomatic to mention that's impossible, sir?"

"There's that impertinent 'sir' again. Two months, written report, be ready for a discussion. Good morning, Zunvect."

"Good morning, sir." I said, privately thankful that I wouldn't have to dodge his attempts to examine me medically *or* magically for two months. These tests of reasoning and critical thinking were fine, but I wasn't enthusiastic about him poking around inside of me.

Even when I was alive eight thousand years ago, we had a lot of history: Four thousand years under Lord Xetic and a murkier period beforehand. Since Xetic had taken over, records had been kept and maintained so that just about every event of more than local importance was recorded and remembered. Most of the primary sources – the letters, newspapers, and journals – resided in the library. It was through these lessons that I learned that there were five levels of the library above the third floor I had access to, which was the repository which contained the most important of these records. The rest were much further up, and took up a lot more space. "It's very rare that you will need any of them," Aika told me. "Most of the time the chroniclers and historians summed everything up adequately. Most of the archival material kept in the proximal archives aren't worth it, in any case. Magical research has many dead ends, and experimental records are nine tenths failure, one tenth incremental success. You're better off skipping to the conclusion until you start doing your own thaumaturgical development."

We started early, as far back as possible. The oldest surviving manuscripts dated to a staggering quarter million years ago, and weren't written by humans. These documents were the imperishable ceramic tablets which had appeared all across the world just prior to the arrival of the Uidrana. The Uidrana had been as faithful about maintaining documentation as Xetic, and had charged their Intendant Races – the elves, dwarves, dragons, and aqueous – with doing the same. If it happened in the sky, on the ground, below the earth, or in the ocean, the Intendant Races knew and, through their reports, so did the Uidrana.

Few of the tablets fell into human hands, and only four were known to be still extant. Xetic had two, one belonged to Lady Xenos, and the last was held by Lord Marinvect in the Unusual Arcana Trust. Their message was well known for being the shortest declaration of conquest in history. 'The Uidrana come. This world is a protectorate. Adapt.'

A handful of Intendant Race reports had been taken by Lord Xetic during the upheaval surrounding his rise to power, but few were of note. What they showed, however, was a strange schism in the Uidrana themselves. It seemed as if half the time they were attempting to keep the world exactly as they found it, even suppressing natural events which would have altered the ecology and geology of the planet. The other half was spent remaking life and the world to fit an image they never shared with any of the natives. Their motives and powers were inscrutable because every Uidrana looked, sounded, and acted identical. There was no way of knowing how many there were, nor even if there was one present unless it wished to be seen. They were featureless cloudy-white spheres atop a shadowy column which looked like a humanoid body in a shapeless smock. My first week was spent studying them with the aid of books stuffed with speculation and almost devoid of fact.

The facts were these: The tablets arrived, followed by the Uidrana two hundred and fifty thousand years ago. They remade or recruited the Intendant Races to be their stewards of earth, sky, and water. They were either preserving or remaking Ry-Kel to fit an unknown objective. In the process they introduced what we consider to be modern magic to the elves and possibly the aqueous. Their true nature and the extent of their ability to manipulate magic was unclear, but certainly greater than ours at the time, and probably significantly more advanced than what we are capable of now. They left four thousand years ago, throwing the Intendant Races into chaos and opening the way for Xetic to rise to power. The elves insisted that they would return, the dwarves and dragons didn't seem to care, and the aqueous were – as always – impossible to gauge. Everything else was open to speculation, and the subject of many theories and innumerable myths. We got through all of it in the first week with time to spare to begin on geography – which turned out to be more about the politics of who owned the land than what that land looked like.

"These are the original three territories." Aika told me, pointing to three marked towers on the map. One was Crescent Bay, about a thousand kilometers long and over a hundred wide. The other two seemed to be no bigger than the field outside my window, pinpoints on the map smaller than the tower icons themselves, positioned deep within the continent and out on the northern Crooklands. It didn't surprise me that we were in the tower that was deep within Bomarie – the only tower for hundreds of miles in all directions. "The territory in the Crescent was a draw for thousands of people seeking safety from the suddenly independent Intendant Races. It was also where Lord Nal promulgated his philosophies of modern magic to the first Wizard-Lords, and where he sent them to expand the safe zones. They provided sanctuary to tens of thousands more humans who were unable to reach the first territory." She reached out and a slim book flew into her hand. "Each of these period maps has a companion." She explained.

"There's a gap there." I said. "The last book said that modern magic was brought by the Uidrana and given to the elves and possibly the aqueous. How did Lord Xetic get that knowledge?"

"Like a few questions you've been asked or asked yourself, that's one that can really only be answered by you as you learn more. All the clues are there, but you need to be … sophisticated enough to figure it out in order to properly appreciate why the answer is hidden."

"That sounds surprisingly mystical." I replied. Xetic rejected any kind of fuzzy thinking as being inimical to his concept of how magic ought to be.

"We could judge when you're ready," Aika begrudged, "but this way is simpler. Once you know, it means you were ready to know. It's like the books in the central column; the knowledge is so dangerous that even its name is best not disclosed. *How* humanity came to possess the Uidrana Magical Logic – UML – language is something that shouldn't be widely known. The topic could cause a lot of trouble for many people should it be openly discussed. Everything you need in order to figure it out will be provided as your education progresses. By the time you realize it, the answer will be very obvious. Aren't you late for your meeting with Lord Nal?"

"No, he told me to come back in two months."

"Two months?" Aika seemed surprised. "Either that's a very hard question he wanted you to mull over or Lord Nal is getting lazy."

"He wants a written report." I explained. "Backed by examples from throughout history. He wants to know ... what should come after him – us, I guess."

Aika looked annoyed. "He's getting impatient." She blew her hair up out of her face and her lambent eyes turned steely. "He didn't even broach the subject with me until I was six years into my conquest, and he only asked Matt because he needed to talk him down from doing something foolhardy." Aika snorted. "That situation didn't last."

"Is this some kind of test?" I asked. "A trial to see if I'm worthy or something?"

"Sort of. My advice is to fail. Lord Nal's constantly carping on about how he hates being the adult in the room and corralling a lot of fractious Wizard-Lords into being productive. It's more ego than anything else; he assumes he's the only one who can do it and that it needs doing. He's wanted to retire almost since the day he realized he was sitting at the top of the pyramid, and that everyone expected him to tell them what to do. He's afraid, though. Afraid that we poor ephemerals – well, you poor ephemerals now – are going to screw up and ruin all his good work. Two women and two men have been asked that question. So far he's never been satisfied with the answer."

"What did you say?" I asked, stomach in my mouth. It seemed like a very private thing to ask, but I was getting scared now. *Being*

Xetic's replacement was a responsibility so big that I could barely wrap my head around it. I was feeling dizzy just thinking about it.

"I told him that I was far too busy to take it on, but ask me again if he planned to make me immortal." Aika said. Is it ruining the suspense to tell you that this was a lie? It did? Well, too bad, because it was. She quickly went on. "Matt said that the hierarchy should transition to a global republic structure with a bicameral legislature made up of elected representatives in the lower house and wizards in the upper house. Lord Nal was not impressed with the notion. Matt tried to force the issue. You know how that went."

"Sort of. I know he raised an army of undead and marched on Lord Xetic's tower. He demanded that the newly formed revolutionary movement's demands be heard and Xetic let him in. He was never seen again and his army disintegrated shortly after he vanished."

"Yes, well... We'll cover a more thorough view of that when we reach that part of your history lessons. There was, of course, one more."

"The first apprentice." I said, barely breathing. None of Ivan's books had done more than mention her and I was intensely curious.

"I don't know what she said or did, but it was apparently so disappointing that she barely merits a mention anywhere in any study of her time – which was shortly after Lord Nal became a lich, by the way. Consider that while you draft your response. She was asked about a hundred years after the towers first rose. Then came me two thousand years later, then Matt fifteen hundred after me, and you a mere five hundred after him."

"The calls for an apprentice are coming with a decreasing interval."

"Yes." Aika said, sounding bleak. "Lord Nal may be getting a bit desperate. Or he's seeing something coming soon that will necessitate a dramatic shift. Either way, I again recommend that you answer honestly, but also do your best not to make it look at all as if you want the job. I can't say that it will save you from it in the end, but it can't hurt." As you might imagine, Idalia, I learned later that the last part of her statement was also a lie.

The remainder of my history lessons were very wizard-centric. Many other events were glossed over ("We'll cover the Symphonics and the Seers in a different unit"), simplified ("All you need to know is that magic of the time was crude and harmful and so Lord Nal's message was well received. We'll get to the specifics when we cover the concepts of emotional thaumocontrols"), or completely ignored ("The divine kings will never come again. If you're very curious, then study them later on your own time. For now, we're going through the core concepts of history").

Despite this, two months didn't seem like nearly enough time to learn about the Wizard-Lords, their territories, and how they came to be where they are. There were also the handful of custodians of some specific magical topic, and each was a special case. As you might imagine, my keenest interest was in Aika and my immediate predecessor, Matthew D'Angkou, who came to be called 'Black Matthew'. She had spent only a little more time on her own life ("Let's get through the overview before we dive too deeply on specifics") and I was badgering her to tell me more about Matthew.

"Doesn't it help to know how you and he answered the question? I can learn from your examples."

"Zunvect, no matter how cautious you are, you still have to be honest." Aika chided. "Crafting your response based on ours is disingenuous because it has to be about what *you* think should happen given the historical context. What we *wanted* was immaterial, but what we *did* is important. You know very well what my method was; I was an expansionist and a believer in sea power."

"And killed a hundred thousand pirates, according to stories." I said.

"You know that's not true." Aika said, smiling back at my grin. "There was really only one group that was making most of the trouble, and maybe ten thousand pirates in total, most of whom gave up voluntarily when I put my foot down about their activities. So, my response to Lord Nal was to expand and diversify, trying to bring all humans under our remit and to take the water as well as the land." She pointed to a modern map we were using as a reference. "As you can see, even if I did not replace Lord Nal, my proposal has been adopted."

"Wasn't it just natural growth?" I countered.

"Someone has to do the growing." She replied. "Back to the period we're studying now. The circumstances that led up to Matt's time, plus the changes he made, are more important to history than he was. If you want to understand his motivation it was a mixture of frustration and pride. He and Lord Nal are very similar people, even down to a talent for necromancy. Things were going very well for the transition when Lord Nal unilaterally withdrew with no explanation – not even to me. Matt took it hard. He said that the rule of Wizard-Lords had become outdated and corrupt." She went over the events of Matthew's revolution, who had supported his aim to overthrow Xetic-Nal, and how he wanted to institute a republic with the vote open to everyone, regardless of magical ability. Entire territories had fallen to him as he raised an army of tradesmen, merchants, and artisans augmented with the animated remains of friends and enemies alike.

"Even some Wizard-Lords decided to join him. Most were on the path between him and Lord Nal, but some had other motivations – few as high minded as Matt's. He'd promised them that they could research banned topics after the revolution had succeeded, and that brought him many allies. Most, though, were frightened at how Lord Nal was doing nothing to stop the march. Matt hadn't broken a law yet, you see. He had a license to practice necromancy, and everything else had been very carefully done within the rules of war. When the time came to enter Lord Nal's tower, though, no living human would stand with him. He came only with his undead, and they burned in place less than an hour after he entered Lord Nal's tower. Afterwards there was an amnesty and -"

"What happened to Black Matthew?" I interrupted. "He enters the tower, and then his army is destroyed. What happened to *him*?"

Aika shook her head. "Zunvect, that has no bearing on the history of the world. His fate was to disappear and as far as the development of society goes, that's all that mattered. All else is ... prurient interest."

"Come on, Aika!" I was almost laughing at the evasion. "Of course it matters! It matters to *us*. How can you hover there and tell me that what my master did to my most recent predecessor doesn't make any difference?"

"It doesn't. Not to history, which is what we're studying." She said, turning severe.

"This is another one of those things I need to be more 'sophisticated' to understand, isn't it?" I said bitingly. "Isn't it interesting how many of those are directly related to His Mightiness upstairs - and you! He's ashamed, isn't he? And has forbidden you from talking about it."

"What he did to Matt was ... not ideal, but it isn't about what he did, it's what Matthew did." Aika replied.

"Other than the revolution." I guessed.

"Yes. Although, sans revolution, he might have been forgiven. Now let us move on to the amnesty. Non-wizards were pardoned unconditionally. The understanding was that it would be impossible to try so many, and impossible to be sure who was coerced and who joined voluntarily, The Wizard-Lords, however..."

Wizard-Lord history was as much sketched out in the published articles as in events themselves. Development of a new spell often drove some new twist in politics or society with its use, and the permanent research towers – the lineages tasked with a single area of magic like Neryk and Vinura. The Trusts, as they were collectively known, were licensed to practice magic which was considered too dangerous to be unregulated. For example, Neryk, as I've mentioned earlier, studied enchanted objects that did not originate on Ry-Kel. I took all of this into account as I began writing ideas. At first, I thought that Xetic had forgotten paper and ink when he made my suite, but of course I had simply not been curious enough to open every drawer. My writing desk, in fact, had an endless supply. Despite this, I spent most of my time in the library, so I could ask Aika questions and check the facts as I put together my outline. One question turned out to have a very upsetting answer.

"Aika," I said pensively, looking at a particularly bold suggestion for reorganizing the Wizard-Lords' resources. "Every tower is occupied, right?"

"Of course; they have to be. With the exception of yours, of course, which is currently claimed as a temporary protectorate. That happens on rare occasions when a Wizard-Lord dies suddenly, or an apprentice isn't trained in time."

"But there are always enough wizards."

"Oh, that conversation." Aika sighed and gestured, a chair pulling itself next to me for her to settle in. "The approximate estimate is two and a half percent."

"Estimate of what?" I asked, afraid to speculate.

"The number of wizards in the population, of course." She said. "Again before you ask, there are roughly a quarter of a billion humans. So that's nineteen million wizards."

"Nineteen million wizards and only eighty-three towers for them to occupy?" I felt like I was going to choke. Ivan had told me that all sorcerers and wizards had to present themselves to their Wizard-Lord, which meant … "What-"

"What happens to all the others?" Aika looked down. "That depends on the territory. I know it's an evasive answer. I think about a third of territories neutralize their wizards by thaumacide. The others are a mixture of power limiting spells and a registry which tracks the location and identifying information about the wizard. Breaking the limit spell, willfully using magic while on the registry, or attempting to escape notice is severely punished. So, what word are you going to use for this? Monstrous, terrifying, sickening? I've heard them all. We all have. It's perhaps the most contentious subject we debate on a regular basis. The only good part is that most wizards never realize what they are because unlike sorcerers they rarely if ever accidentally use magic. With greater natural control comes a very big drop in unintended expressions of the power. That helps; we only ever identify one in forty. That's still half a million, but spread out among the territories, we're looking at less than six thousand each at that point. That's still a one in sixteen thousand chance – give or take – of your child being positively identifiable as a wizard. Families who discover a wizard among them usually move somewhere more liberal if they find themselves in a kill on sight territory. Nobody stops them."

My mind was blank. It was too much, too sudden. I said the first thing that came to me. "Good gods. If that's something you're willing to tell me, how bad is the stuff you're keeping secret?"

Aika laughed hollowly. "Bad. Believe me about that. There are many that find the practice *comforting*. The secret knowledge is much, much worse."

"Why?" It was the only question I could think of.

"Nineteen million wizards. Think about how much would change if suddenly one in forty people were able to do what we can. A trained wizard can cross distances instantaneously, open cracks in the earth to swallow cities, call down hurricanes of fire, and speak to creatures on other worlds which make dragons look like housecats. Eighty-four wizards can be controlled by organizational pressure; nineteen million would be a plague."

"There are protections, aren't there? Spells to stop that kind of thing? And if they need training, they'll still be part of an organization."

"It's a numbers thing." Aika replied. "Everyday life would change drastically when every house requires enchantments to keep it safe, secure, and private. When stories of rogue wizards are the norm and even *insane* wizards. We have enough external pressure without subjecting ourselves to that kind of societal instability."

"Eighty wizards keep most of our external threats at bay. Nineteen million would make us invincible." I argued.

"Feel free to include it in your proposal. You're going to need to think of every argument, for and against, that you can. Lord Nal may want change, but I've known him long enough to be sure that he'd be strongly opposed to training all the wizards. Or maybe I'm just a dusty old relic who can't see the way of progress." She smiled and floated back towards the stacks. "Matt certainly had some strong opinions, and I did before him. It's the nature of this particular fellowship to have big ideas."

There was nothing else of any groundshaking import. I imagine that in these enlightened times, we are thought of as barbarians.

Sitting in that chair, my mind roiling with the realization, I certainly thought so. Other influences came earlier, but if you want to put your finger on a single moment in time, a formative instant, it was in that library as I looked uncomprehendingly at the book in my hand, my mind a long way away. Imagining a poor little boy being dragged off in chains because he was considered inherently dangerous for being what he was. I could see my own face on that boy, and many other faces besides. One in forty. There were more than forty people in my village. I might have been more comforted had I known basic statistics back then, or perhaps not. All I could think of at the time were two questions. 'Why?' and – much more concerning – 'Who?' Why was 'who?' more concerning, Idalia? Think about it. I was going to be Wizard-Lord. I was going to be the one who sat in judgment. I might have to execute someone I'd known my whole life not because they'd done anything wrong but because they *were*.

Excerpt from a letter from Lord Xetic-Nal to Lord Matthew D'Angkou 3267 [XR] (restricted reading):

Yes, Matthew, I am aware that – long term – what I'm doing to humanity is no different from what the Uidrana did. In the long term. You may say that I am trying to change humanity to fit my ideal. I submit, however, that I am the closest thing you'll ever meet to a human unmodified by social, magical, or genetic meddling, which means that ultimately, you're arguing in favor of humanity being *more* like me. Remember that next time you call me a petty, selfish, vain, egotistical dried up old husk of a man, whose time passed centuries ago. And that I can hear you, even when you're talking to your latest sexual conquest in bed. Good night, Matt. Pleasant dreams.

Zunvect 11:

The Question's First Asking

"Ambitious." Xetic said as I settled in. "Oh, and do remember this time to remind me at the end to do that workup. I really have to see how your brain works without the tedious intermediary of questions."

"Humane." I countered, staying on topic and not even acknowledging his request. "Yes, sir, I will." I added, deciding that conveniently forgetting at the end of the conversation was better than annoying him and possibly goading Xetic into performing the procedure immediately.

"Oh, I don't mean your insistence that any future society refrain from the wholesale slaughter of our fellow wizards. One generally tries not to commit genocide on one's own kind. It rather makes it harder to find more of them in the following generation." Xetic replied, spreading the pages out in front of him. "By the way, work on handwriting. It's going to be awhile yet before you learn how to write with magic." He pulled a sheet out and read it again. "You propose that we freeze our borders and look inward to improve ourselves. It's been suggested before. Never in the context of attempting to find and train all of our wizards, though. Usually I get the non-expansionist argument framed as either pacifism or as a prelude to economic reforms. Let's start at the beginning. You wish to entirely abolish the Wizard-Lords as an organization."

"Our structure at present emphasizes division over unity, and squanders our greatest resource." I said, leaning forward eagerly to make my case. "It seems like everything I read is framed by how we're under siege. Everyone hates us, and we have to stay vigilant and paranoid. I lived in an unprotected community for ten years as it turns out. We were attacked once by trolls, so that's no attacks *at all* from outside agents. I think we're safer than we like to think we are."

"Lady Xenos would tend to agree." Xetic replied evenly. "So, we entrust ourselves to what appears to be a safer world – temporarily, I understand – and reorganize into larger polities with some kind of wizard council. An executive council made from representatives of each larger regional polity is elected from the ranks of the local Wizard-Councilors. Zunvect, you're very close to describing the kind of devolutionary government that Matthew did."

"I'm not throwing out a good idea because of the person who had it."

"What you're too polite – or too afraid – to say is: You won't throw out an idea because I'm having a bit of a row with the last person who floated it. You're right inasmuch as the messenger should not pollute the message."

"The improvement here is that my concept goes further than his. Matthew D'Angkou made the mistake of trying to curry favor with other Wizard-Lords by retaining their overarching oligarchy as an upper house – which could only mean retaining their *numbers* as well. Who could handle a senate of nineteen million?"

"I remember senates that could barely manage nineteen." Xetic chortled. "Yes, it does appear as if there is a certain … lack of egalitarianism in your plan."

"With respect to wizards, of course there is. If we expand our numbers so much, then we become a special interest rather than a ruling class. That means that while we would likely retain political power because of our utility, we're better off being more like a guild or a merchant house in our structure. Not all wizards are equally suited to rule. You've said so yourself." I was getting into the argument now, my practice with Aika paying off. "Perhaps some sort of executive council or agency will continue to exist with wizards as the predominant members. We are, after all, likely to remain key to the wellbeing of society."

"I'll want an answer to this later, but for now let's skip over the *how* of this proposal. It *will* result in all-our war unless you're careful, but you're perhaps not quite ready for that part of the plan. We'll focus instead on one more thing: What is your place in it? Let's assume I've decided to retire in favor of your plan to turn us into a guild, having come to the conclusion that humanity no longer needs me to maintain a direct interest. Maybe we should go over how, in that case. Since your position would be influenced by the method of making your framework a reality."

"I don't know." I admitted, thinking as I spoke to try to come up with something. "I couldn't possibly say what my place is or how it ought to be done. I don't have the experience. Were I forced to take a position right here in this room, I'd start by increasing the apprentice count to two, and having each apprentice begin training more when they have enough experience to teach the basics, but not enough to be a licensed wizard. The current Wizard-Lords retain their territories for now, but each fully trained apprentice is immediately placed in charge of a city or a town – or even a bureaucracy with more than one wizard if the cities are large. When the current Wizard-Lord dies, then those presently active as governors elect a new Wizard-Lord, but one without absolute authority in all matters. Instead, they'll preside as executive. The other wizards act as an advisory council with majority veto power and the ability to replace the Wizard-Lord at pre-determined election times. The Wizard-Lords in turn elect a president over their own council. Eventually each territory is likely to form its own hierarchy, but as long as the highest level remains a coalition of territories, I can hope that eventually they will begin to amalgamate into bigger blobs of land."

Xetic cut me off as I tried to think of more. "You're getting into *how*, and that's not something you're ready for yet, as evidenced by your response. Hope is not a strategy, and you haven't said what *you'll* do. How do you intend to convince the current lords to do it, whatever *it* is? They may retain their power in their lifetimes, but many will oppose your guild concept on principle or in hopes of getting something in return for endorsing later."

"The tempting thing to say is that I will use my own apparently immense magical strength combined with superior spellcraft derived from my studies here to force them. Of course, that won't work; we've seen it tried in the past. It would be even worse than your own rise to power, because now there is an entrenched thaumocractic system in place. I couldn't hope to win that war unless I was willing to sacrifice millions. With all due respect, sir –" I saw his eyes narrow as he expected an impertinence – "I find the question extremely premature. I know enough history to guess at what might be a good idea to come next, but how can I give you anything close to a good answer when I don't know my own capabilities? I don't even know what magic can do. I know that the wizards collectively have enough power to tear the world apart, and that you can somehow counter all of them at once, but I don't know what *I* can do about it." I was getting upset and scared of what my outburst might provoke in Lord Xetic. He was regarding me silently as I grew louder, and I felt myself turning red with passion.

"Good." He said. "It *is* premature, and your answer is the most interesting of the four I've gotten so far. Not necessarily original in the design, but astonishingly honest in the implementation. You understand things that few who have not already spent years as a Wizard-Lord do. Let's see how that answer changes when you've learned some magic."

I felt like someone was squeezing my heart. I didn't dare hope. "Does that mean I'm going to learn wizard magic now?"

Xetic's eyes flashed. "You've been learning wizard magic since the day I first met you." He said, and with deep amusement he continued, "right now you're about to start learning the truest magic, the most baffling. A power so arcane that most humans can barely conceive of it, and their minds break at even the basest explanation. You're going to learn *real math*."

"Like Numerology, Arithmancy, that kind of thing?" I asked, hesitant. To be dropped in the deep end of magic like that sounded terrifying.

"No, those don't exist the way you understand them. Much, much worse. You're going to learn something far more arcane than simple combinatorial chicanery or the pitiful permutations mad monks do when they look at all the numbers in the world and try to make them fit together. None of those actually *do* anything. They don't even reveal any knowledge. No, what you're going to learn are things like covariance, epipolar geometry and – if you've got the brains for it – inverse kinematics. Once you've solved a problem in state-space by hand, the eldritch terrors found on the other side of ancient portals will seem like one of those fluffy mountain ponies you probably couldn't afford to have in that tiny spit on the road you called home for fifteen years."

"Is every conversation with you going to involve insulting my hometown, sir?" I asked, giving in to a flash of anger. I'd never been *proud* of the village, but it still felt like home even after a few months in the tower. Besides, he'd forgotten to examine me again, and keeping the subject firmly away from me and on my village seemed the best course of action.

"Yes. If you can't have a laugh in seven thousand years of reading academic drivel, then you're in really big trouble."

Aika seemed strangely disappointed, or maybe depressed, when I told her about my conversation with Lord Xetic. I was afraid to ask why. The teenage me was like most boys that age in that I feared rejection more than ignorance and more than whatever might have come to pass if I'd known that Aika had been very disappointed, but not for any reason I'd have understood at the time. She'd just sealed my doom, you see, and was quite conflicted about it since she'd sealed it in entirely the opposite direction from the one she'd intended.

Excerpt from *Excruciatingly Difficult Sums and Why We Need Them* by Lord Jariavect, 58th ed. Introduction, ~3500 XR

It may amaze you to learn that to do magic you need to learn a seemingly unfair amount of math and natural law. The reason is that magic follows the same laws of nature as anything else. There are shortcuts, but even we cannot produce something from nothing (excepting a few instances which came to a very bad end), and our spells are not nearly as clever as we are, so they need to have things explained to them. Take the color red. You know what it is. How does the spell know? How does one *describe red* to an unthinking thaumaturgical construct? Intelligent spellcraft requires such things. Humans are born with the ability to track objects in space. How to tell a spell, then, 'look at this and not that and keep looking at it even when it moves?' True, a wizard can use their own brain to control spells, but if you want your spell to handle anything but the most primitive of stimuli, you need the formulae, methods, and algorithms listed in this book. If you ever have the question 'why am I learning this?' or 'how can I symbolically explain this concept to a spell?' then this is the textbook for you.

Zunvect 12:

Time Flies

A year later, I looked up from *Fundamentals of Linear Algebra*, a constant companion as I delved deeper into multidimensional mathematics. It wasn't the fun kind that ends with creatures covered in eyes and tentacles, or in a room with ten sides and six vertices, but instead the kind that begins and ends with a bracket. Rubbing my eyes, I looked out at the snowswept hill beyond the window. When the leaves fell, I'd begun to see more movement in the forest beyond, creatures far too large to be anything other than magical denizens. Aika had convinced me to start reading for fun, hence why I was still somewhat sane. It was no mean feat after over a year cooped up with only her, and occasionally Xetic, to talk to, and little to do but run up and down the stairs. This was when I wasn't doing ever more difficult math problems.

Early on I'd mingled my math studies with the far more interesting bestiaries compiled by wizards down the ages. If Aika hadn't told me that the early works were mostly wrong, I'd have wondered if it wasn't a Forest Dragon or a Foliage Fiend prowling the borders of our island of human dominion. The only thing in modern books that was big enough and might live in a deciduous forest was a giant, and the silhouette didn't look human. It also moved so ponderously slow that I thought it might be a giant turtle, except that those would never have wandered so far inland.

The smooth white expanse reminded me of something I'd been meaning to do. "Aika," I said, knowing she was always listening. When I'd realized her awareness was such that she knew everything that happened in the tower, I'd been so embarrassed that I hadn't bathed for a week. Then Xetic had told me not to be a bumpkin and Aika had pointed out that she was twenty times older than the oldest granny in my village, and observing teenage boys in the bath wasn't something that interested ghosts much. The twinkle in her eye and the fact that she'd had her fingers crossed had not helped, but I'd given up and started washing again. The woman seemed to be getting younger and more familiar with me every day.

"Trouble with the Derivative Inverse again?" She asked, appearing next to me.

"No, I'd just like to ask if I could get a calendar." I said. I'd read about them in a journal Xetic had let me borrow from the Upper Archives. It had been very entertaining reading the accounts of a Wizard-Lord named Terina twelve hundred hundred years ago. She had a hilariously acerbic way of writing about her peers. It turns out she was the current Lady Xenos – ambassador to the Intendant Races. I wasn't sure if I wanted to meet her or not – she'd either be extremely amusing or even more of a pain in the butt than Lord Xetic.

Aika's smile widened into a grin. "You're finally starting to work it out."

I looked at her with studious indifference. "Work what out, Aika?" I asked in my best 'bored academic talking to the librarian' voice, which I'd cobbled together from reading several books by wizards who'd had living human librarians.

Aika's punch to my arm almost hurt. I'd begun to take secretive notes of these instances, and was developing a hypothesis about that too. "You know exactly what I'm talking about, Zunvect." She rushed off, giggling, and came back with a thick folio. "Xetic circled today's date." She winked. "Have fun with the Jacobian," she said, in a voice that told me she knew I wasn't going to be working on it until I'd satisfied my curiosity.

Of course it wasn't that easy. I was suspicious, but I also had no idea what months in the modern calendar corresponded to time as I knew it. Ivan had referenced the true calendar, of course, but never pressed me to learn it. I knew that there were twelve months – of course – with three for each season, and a shorter thirteenth month to mark the depths of winter. The folio followed this convention as well, along with the five-day week and five-week month, excepting Midwinter. I could guess from the depth of the snow outside that it was Midwinter, and the circle was around the fourth day (the calendar called the month Dwin and the day Jalday) of the fourth and final week. Almost my father's birthday.

I say I'd been studying math for a year. It definitely *felt* like it. The leaves seemed to take ages to fall from the trees and the snow had been on the ground for so long that I thought maybe the sun had started to cool down. Ivan had said that might happen one day, but he'd also said that I'd be dead, buried, dust, and the dust itself turned into much finer dust by the time it did. If I'd learned anything from the drawn out - and sometimes painfully dull - study of stochastic processes, it was that weird things happened. I knew I shouldn't be too surprised when they did, because weird things were always happening. That and the still baffling realization that if someone offered to play me in a shell game and then took away one shell, I'd for some reason have a better shot at winning if I then changed my mind. I'm not sure I ever really believed that while I was alive.

The calendar, I hoped, would in some way anchor me to reality a little better. That, or prove a hypothesis that was frankly insane and proof that I was starting to be affected by the long isolation and mental fatigue. I felt like I'd been studying for a year. According to calendar and season it, had been more like four to five months.

Xetic, in an uncharacteristic display of empathy, called me up to his office shortly afterward. "You haven't had any human contact in quite some time." He looked at me and forestalled my protest.

"Aika and I don't really count. You could do with some air, and a talk with people who were born in the same millennium as you. Come on, it's a bit early, but I may as well help you and get this over with." He ambled out of his office with no further explanation, but instead of going onto the landing, the door led to a dark room with straw on the floor.

I knew he was trying to goad me into asking a question, so of course I didn't. Xetic treated my youthful pride the same way he treated any foible of the living, by ignoring it until he found it funny to make a clever and droll remark about it. In this case, he didn't need the remark. He just looked at me, smugly sure I was going to *have* to ask. He *knew* that I wouldn't be able to keep up the pretense of disinterest. "Where are we?" I asked, immediately regretting it. He was about to get his own back.

"What does it look like?" There it was. The extremely dry wit. We were self-evidently in a stable with more horses than I'd ever seen, and a set of carriages resting in the far end. I didn't know what a livery stable was at the time, so after he grilled me in hopes of seeing how much I'd be able to work out for myself, he filled in the gaps.

"Of course, I'd normally just teleport directly to our destination, but in this case I'm banned." He said, knocking sharply on the stable door.

"Illusion," I said just before the top half of the door opened. Xetic was fast enough to cover himself in his usual 'kindly old scholar' appearance before the man at the door saw anything, but shot me a dirty look. I regarded him with feigned innocence, as if I'd only just thought of it.

"Have my usual ready in an hour." He said to the bearded stablemaster, giving him a silver coin.

"Yes, milord." The man replied.

"They're very fast here," Xetic explained, "but I thought that you might appreciate a change of diet for the afternoon. Personally, I've never had any complaints in the sixteen hundred years I've had my coach parked in the stable."

"That's a record." I said, unsure of what else to say. My experience of taverns was only one and nobody complained to Bowbringer because he and his wife could only make four things. That was two more than most of *us*!

"What's on the menu this century?" Xetic asked with a disconcerting red twinkle in his eye when he settled in a booth.

I goggled at the woman serving us at first – give me a break, Idalia, I was seventeen! – but they were all dressed the same way and every single one of them seemed to be equally well endowed. As an aside, I have no idea how this happens. I traveled quite a bit later on, and every tavern I went to had a complement of large-breasted wenches serving the food and I can't for the life of me remember any difference between them. It's like there's an enchantment loose on the world that changes them the moment they decide to work in a tavern. What? Shut up, Idalia, I'm not a sexist lich. That was Xetic. What? Lech? Oh. Well, give me a break, Idalia, I'm technically only thirty or so. Well excuse me if that's long enough to learn better in *your* time. Fine, I won't talk about the waitresses at taverns anymore, but I still think there was something weird about the whole thing and it wasn't my memory. Huh? Tavern keepers only ever *hired* women who made men spend more money than they planned on? So now *everyone* in my era is – you know what, maybe you're right. What I learned later from Aika about why only six of the Wizard-Lords were women was the dumbest thing I've heard in both my lifetimes. Anyway, by the time I pried my eyes off the staff, Xetic had ordered and I had the best meal of my young life. Moving on to after the extremely good meal which by the way was chicken in garlic sauce followed by a raspberry tart in case you were wondering. Xetic abstained, saying that the menu hadn't changed in a hundred and fifty years and he'd already had everything.

Without lunch to distract me, I gave in to the pressure within a few minutes of climbing into the dim interior of the carriage. "Banned, sir?"

"Yes, banned," Xetic said. He had a habit of picking up conversations where they left off even after weeks had passed, and I was starting to do the same, much to the later frustration of my peers and servants. "Extrapolate, Zunvect. Who could possibly ban *me* from doing anything?"

"Yourself." I said.

"A neat trick. Not in this case. Wouldn't help, anyway, since I'm notoriously bad at following my own rules."

"The gods?" I asked tentatively. His relationship with the collective deities of Ry-Kel was legendarily turbulent.

"Yes." His response was diffident, and he'd started that slight drawl that meant he was talking about an old and distasteful topic. "We've come to an understanding after a long argument that's burned itself into the better part of written history. This understanding unfortunately has applications to all wizards. I thought I'd show you some of them firsthand. One very important part is that magic is forbidden within fifty kilometers of the Bascilicas, the capital churches of each god. I'm obliged to make a visit to one in particular every sixty years. Drotaka."

"The death god?" I asked, dimly remembering what little education I'd had in holy matters.

"I should hope so!" Xetic laughed. "There aren't many other people named that. Good grief, imagine the presumption of naming your child after a *god*. A death god at that! They'd have to grow up to be all grim and sepulchral and get jobs in mortuaries. It'd be a whale of a jarring experience to meet someone named

Drotaka who was a grocer or who sold middens. Goddess, incidentally. Last I looked she was female, but then again the gods tend to have very fluid sexual identities. It comes of not having reproductive systems. Well, not anymore. I dealt with *those* shenanigans."

I knew better than to follow that line of thought. "Why do you have to visit?"

"Part of the treaty. I'm considered a touchy subject for them. I mean, I'm an eldritch abomination in their books. Undeath is a bit of a problem for a church built on the idea of a peaceful transfer of spirit from the material world to whatever afterlife Drotaka has cobbled together to keep the masses happy. Huruum is also peeved because I'm not alive but I'm also not dead by the strict scriptural interpretation, so as a life god he has to constantly deal with people using me as an exception to the rule in theological arguments. Finally, I specifically and wizards generally are a constant thorn in the side of Valya since she's supposed to keep the natural order and we are decidedly unnatural in her estimation. The upshot is that I'm considered a sanctioned exception to all the rules as long as I show up occasionally and pay lip service to their supposed dominions. It saves me the time it would take to deal with a holy war, and they can rest easy knowing I'm not going to try to nobble them. There's an element of gratitude as well. The old pantheon was a mess and I helped them clean it up and make religion into something decently respectable. Look up the Shadow Gods sometime. Around the fourth century of my unlife." The conversation lulled and then Xetic sat up. "Did I ever tell you what my name means?"

"No." I said, curious despite myself. It was rare to learn *anything* about Xetic that wasn't in the official biographies.

"It means 'Not Xetic.'" He said. "Imaginative, huh? My brother was named Xetic and I was Not Xetic. I came from an extremely … disadvantaged part of the world. My village had only just worked out that round things rolled. They were expecting a girl and all the boy names had already been taken in my old village, so since my brother was Xetic they decided it was easier to tell us apart and not cause confusion with the other families to just call me Not Xetic. It looks like we're almost there." He was looking out the window. Naturally he was facing forward, forcing me to stick my head out and crane my neck, letting draughts of frigid air into the carriage and exposing myself to a biting wind. It was worth it. For once my reaction to seeing something unfamiliar was a shared experience with much of the growing traffic on the road, mostly pilgrims on their first and only journey. We were approaching a city that even a hardened urban dweller would have stared at.

The first thing that struck me were the walls. No, Idalia, I did not accidentally make one fall on me. You've been getting very testy lately and I think it may be close to your bedtime. We can pick this up tomorrow.

Idalia 5:

Lupines and Leadership

Idalia yawned, and set aside the lap desk she'd made when she got tired of sitting on the floor next to the growing pile of pages. She'd been keeping her own notes alongside the pages of dictation, trying to connect events he'd witnessed to ones already known to the magi. "How do you know what time it is?" She asked. "There aren't any windows, and even if there were, the Emerald Citadel is locked in an eternal twilight of impenetrable cloud cover lit from below by the Citadel's towers. It's beautiful at first, but it wears on me. The Lupines might be nocturnal, but perpetual darkness really throws off my sleep cycle."

"Isn't it grand to have a god looking after you?" Zunvect said smugly. "I can see into the collected thoughts of the magi, remember? It's evening in Huywer, so you may as well get some rest. I'd pass you a clock set to your local time, but ..." he gestured downwards.

"No need," she said, her instincts aroused. She was always suspicious when something *inside* started suggesting things that would make it easier for them to get *outside*. "There's a standing Tunnel to The World. I may be an exile, but that doesn't stop stores from taking my money for delivery. I can get my own clock, thank you."

"Cripes, you people are jingoistic. 'The World?' It was the only planet my people knew, and we still had a *name* for it."

Idalia shrugged. "It's the world to us. Ours."

"Yes, and it means that people who aren't from your planet either have to call it by that ridiculously self-important name or come up with their own. It smacks of cultural conquest."

"Speaking of world domination, was Xetic-Nal really planning to pass the title of First Wizard to you that early?"

"Idalia, it's the only reason he taught apprentices." Zunvect replied, a smile curling at his lips. Idalia was puzzled by how the question seemed to have amused him. "Well, not to pass the title *to* so much as *away*. He'd been trying to retire since the first day. That's what apprentices are for. In my case, the strict answer to your question is 'no.' He'd given up on finding someone to take over the oligarchy. His plans were more ambitious than that. He explained it to me at one point, and I'll fill in the gaps when we get there. I'm still fading in and out, and trying to reach forward in the process will only jumble things up worse."

"Is that why you want a rest?" Idalia asked, suddenly concerned. "You need to consolidate your essence again?"

"I'm not going to lose focus again, if that's what you mean. I got foggy because it was a time I idolize in a sort of golden haze. I was important and powerful within my tiny sphere of influence, but not worried about the future. As much fun as I had in my early student days with Xetic, I'm content to leave that part of my past where it is. Go on, go to bed. It's not like I'm going anywhere."

"Do you sleep?" Idalia asked.

"No," Zunvect said wearily. "I can subsume myself in the minds of the magi, though. There's so much to catch up on."

Idalia left the containment room and hurried down the corridor to her own suite. It was no more than a sitting room, washroom, and bedroom, but it was more than she'd expected. On her way, she met a Lupine in a pale yellow vest and tan trousers. "Good day, Mistress Periscalitin."

Idalia bowed slightly. "The same, Master Imastadun." She couldn't help feeling intimidated by him, despite his status being lower in the Emeralds than hers was among the Magi. Most Lupines were taller and broader than she, built along the same lines as Zunvect himself. That alone would have made her feel like a child in a house full of adults. In addition, they were covered in fur which ranged from shaggy to fluffy, and colors mostly in the browns and grays, though the younger Lupines - like human youths - often tried out brighter hues along the entire chromatic range. Imastadun himself had longer fur of a medium gray. He – like all Lupines – also had a long muzzle filled with sharp teeth, digitigrade legs which made Lupines seem even taller, and vestigial claws at the ends of his otherwise humanoid fingers. Idalia forced herself to see the differences rather than the similarities. They weren't *entirely* like giant bipedal wolves. They didn't have tails, and their eyes were remarkably similar to her own, though tending towards being more yellow and red than green and blue in the iris. Their speech was always surprising at first, their voices smooth and deep rather than the growls and snarls a human might first expect on seeing their appearance.

How Lupines were able to form human phenomes at all remained a mystery, since their long muzzles didn't seem capable of it. Most magi assumed that they had a low energy field effect of some kind that automatically translated their language, since no human had ever heard them speak anything but human Trade. As Imastadun patiently watched Idalia, she became aware that she'd sunken into a reverie. "My apologies. I have spent a long day with my charge, and fear that I'm not as swift as I should be."

"It is understandable." The Emerald Lupine said evenly. "His story progresses well?"

"Very. I have heard much that was previously unknown, and he hints that he knows things that will significantly alter our view of the founding of our order."

"That is well. You have no doubt surmised that our meeting was not by chance. The archmage is restless," Idalia wished inwardly that the Lupines could have picked a name for their leadership class that wasn't identical to those of her own people. "Your magi pressure us, but neither to keep nor return you. It is most perplexing."

"They're likely as confused as you are. I don't think they know what they want right now. To let you keep me is to leave their own god – and a valuable political tool – in your hands. To insist that I return is to bring even greater chaos. It is bad enough that the gods of the ruled stir and speak again. It would be madness for the ruling class to invite the man that they've revered – and sworn by – to return. What if he disagrees with their policy? It could tear us apart."

"I am glad," the Emerald said, "that I do not need to concern myself with that. I will never comprehend why your magical caste has taken on the additional burden of leading your species. I will take your good news to the archmage. I'm sure she will be pleased to know that a story about your people will be known to us before it is even known to them."

"Good evening, Master Imastadun."

Idalia rose early, as was her habit. She only knew this, however, from the pocket watch which had been left in a parcel in front of her door. Quartz oscillator timepieces were rare on the World, since most people could consult devices which were updated magically from a central source. It was within Idalia's power to open her own permanent Tunnel to the World, but not her authority. It was bad enough being a political exile without being wanted on charges of creating and maintaining an illegal inter-planetary Tunnel.

She spent an hour before breakfast in one of the too-low chairs at a too-high desk sorting through and annotating Zunvect's account. Again, it was within her power to alter or replace the furniture, but, in this case, it would have been impolite to her very generous hosts. Idalia mused momentarily on how wrong Xetic-Nal had been all those centuries ago. He'd thought that so many wizard (or wizard-equivalents as the Magi Firsts were) would be ungovernable. How wrong he was! Most people were basically polite, and most followed the law. As for the rest, there were enough Firsts to crew an investigatory body which took a very hard line with people who abused magic. Their professional skills were augmented with a suite of nearly unavoidable surveillance spells. Perhaps a member of the Senate could get away with murder, but no one else had the power or skill to evade the mage-constables for long.

Idalia was adding clarifying notation and references to the relevant passages when she saw the footnote. She shoved the stack of volumes which comprised the current state of research on Zunvect's life to one side. The footnote wasn't in her handwriting, and it was signed 'X-N.' Despite being a prosaic clarification on why there were multiple consecutive rulings on appropriate use of thaumaturgy in proximity to haystacks, her blood ran cold at the sight of it. *He was watching.* Xetic-Nal, a man who remained the single most accomplished human thaumaturgist, was reading along with her. It had been a faint hope, she realized, that he might lose interest or balk at acting within the jurisdiction of another sapient species, however distant.

Then again, this was perhaps good news. If he was going to the trouble of adding his own notes to hers, it meant that he felt that the exercise had some merit. He wouldn't waste his time jotting down footnotes only to kill them both and destroy the manuscript. Of course, he might kill them both and *take* the manuscript, but if so, why bother with footnotes now? Idalia sighed. This wasn't her area of expertise. At least she was safe until the story ended – or so she assumed. She entertained herself with the ridiculous notion of asking him to review it for the dust jacket.

The realization that Lord Xetic-Nal was so close at hand – along with the morning news summary from the World – put her off her breakfast. Not that this was very hard. Lupine food was edible, but mainly meat-based and often undercooked. Her hosts did their best to find alternatives, but as she contemplated a barely warm sausage and a bowl of something analogous to but not quite porridge, she thought that perhaps she should add groceries to her list of things to have imported from the World.

Zunvect was where she'd left him, suspended within the wards, unable to touch any solid surface. His eyes were closed and his face slack, and he didn't move as she edged around the outermost circle. The light from the wall crystals shone on the reflective surface of the conductive ink, a shimmer seeming to follow her around as she moved. She picked up her lap desk and conjured a chair. There wasn't enough room for a table to put her notes on, but she was sick of being uncomfortable, and was growing more used to the presence of her supposed god. As she settled in, his eyes opened, tripling the brightness of the room.

"Good morning, Idalia," he said. She hated that he addressed her like his servant. "Did you have a pleasant breakfast?"

"Enough," she said shortly.

"Jolly good. Any news from my chosen people?"

"They're not yours," she said firmly, "but yes." She was relieved not to need a pretext to avoid mentioning Xetic's surveillance. "I'll show you." She held out her palm and a shifting ball of light expanded outward.

"Oh, that's clever. Immersive photomantic journalism. Very flashy." Zunvect enthused. "Oh, and it has sound, too. I'm sure this is much better than reading about events."

The room was transformed, turned into a much larger space. It was now paneled in hardwood, brass fittings, and gold leaf. Three tiers lined in raised tables and high-backed chairs faced a multi-tiered enclosed podium. Thirteen men and women, all marked as Magi by their youthful faces, hard expressions, and authoritative bearing, sat in the seats of the Senate. Facing them, hands resting on the chest-high wooden podium, was Silveria Chronomarien, President of the Senate. There was a gold disc on the ebony box she stood in, bearing the words 'Senate of Magi' on top and 'First in Unity' below. The emblem of the government of the Magi was in the center of the disc, Zunvect's staff imposed over a globe. The globe was outlined, and four spokes radiated out into eight points around the circle, forming the Wheel, with the River underneath. At the either end of each spoke was the symbol of one of Unity's major members. The Wheel turned to indicate who was represent-ed when they took the rostrum to speak. Silveria represented a ter-ritorial university as well as being President, so the Wheel had turned to place the broken tower of the Magi First – the successors to the wizards – uppermost. On the other spokes were a musical note, a spiral inside a stylized sun, a tree, two clawed feet holding a coin between them, a circle of hands, and a contract on the end of a pick. Wizards, Symphonics, Nodes, Elves, Dragons, the Republic, and Dwarves.

"I call this meeting of the Senate of Magi to order," Silveria in-toned. "Our only order of business today, regretfully, my own vote of no confidence. As is my right, I choose to defend myself after the other remarks are made. I recognize the Senator from Sularat." It was no surprise to her that her greatest detractor, and strongest op-ponent in the Senate, would speak for the faction that wished to see her gone. She knew he was the one who had instigated the vote. The Wheel didn't turn as he took the rostrum, though a section of the globe to the southeast of Silveria's glowed instead.

"Madame President, honored colleagues in the Senate," Mage First Golaran began, "You know my views on the honorable Madame President. I do not need to rehash old arguments, arguments that have never been quite enough to sway this esteemed body to the regrettable action we take today."

"Good grief, are they all this windy?" Zunvect asked.

Golaran continued. "I have often stated my view that President Chronomarien has a split loyalty. In her role as leader of the Solar Conclave, she holds a position of authority over the only agency with a direct check on this very deliberative body. She is a Node. This is not bigotry or racism, but fact. She is not human, and her loyalty is not to us, but to her own. This is right and proper, and demonstrated perfectly by her decision to *trade* the symbol of human unity and power for something that is only for her own people. It makes sense for the Conclave to give away the oldest relic of our people, the creation of the man who paved the way for our society to become what it is. Even this would not be a crime worthy of expulsion from the Senate. After all, it isn't a crime to disrespect our heritage and to cast away that which symbolizes the passing of authority from the Wizard-Lords to the Magi. The crime, my colleagues, is theft. Pure and simple. The staff may belong to humanity, it may belong to the family who has passed it down since Zunvect died and Lorn took it up in his place. It may even belong to that one woman, Desora, daughter of the lineage of Miyaria, heir of Lorn, heir of Zunvect. One thing is certain, honorable Senators. It did not belong to *the President*. Mere theft may be a scandal, but this was more than theft, more than the grandest of theft. For that reason, I urge you to vote yes, and take this extreme but necessary action to show the degree to which we censure this heinous act."

"Most of the speeches against are the same thing," Idalia said, flicking her finger and making the people jerk to new positions, the Senators sitting and Silveria standing again. "Even her supporters don't have much to add. But President Chronomarien had this to say for herself, and it was … interesting."

The illusion moved again. Silveria stood with her hands shrouded in the depths of her gray robe, bent over the rail of the rostrum as if with the age she was no doubt beginning to feel. Her hands emerged and she gripped the rail as if it were the only thing holding her up. Her mirrored eyes swept the room, that piercing stare pinning each one in turn. "Honored Senators. You have heard the arguments. There are but two when simplified. First, I offended against the very concept of Unity. I could refute that, but it is not the crime that this vote is predicated upon, and my arguments against it would be premature. Should I remain your President, I will present my findings in due course, and after considered research on the new symbol of Unity." Her lip curled in a self-deprecating smirk. "Even if I am voted out, my findings will be published. You have entrusted me with the ultimate authority over the defenses of humanity. Please trust me with another month to make sure that my findings are solid and correct." She took a deep breath and swept the room again, reaching up to brush a long strand of silver hair from her face. "The crime, then. The honorable representative of Sularat calls if theft. No one else has been so bold, but theft is a good enough word. It encompasses the malfeasance without trying to sugarcoat it in euphemistic legalisms. Theft. I am accused – effectively – of selling the Staff of Zunvect, which is owned in this marvelous chain that Senator Golaran has outlined.

"Theft, he says, from Desora – a friend of mine, though a friendship strained of late." A low chuckle from some of her supporters. "Desora, heir of Miyaria, heir of Lorn, heir of Zunvect. Zunvect. The progenitor of the Magi, and my own race. Honorary founder of the Solar Conclave. Mage-Guardian of the Symphonic Collective. The only person who could have been described as both a Mage First and Second. He was a wizard *and* a sorcerer. Most importantly, *he's not dead*." These last three words were delivered with such emphasis that some of the sleepier Senators jerked upright in their seats. She continued in the same harangue. "I am accused of *stealing from a thief.* Oh, Lorn didn't know he'd stolen the Staff. He thought it was his by right. He took it from the rubble of Zunvect's tower, he was Zunvect's chosen. It was obvious to him given his condition as the Ur-Node. He was heir to Zunvect's power, so he must also be heir to Zunvect's arcana.

"Unfortunately, you cannot inherit from someone who is still conscious. We have well established case law stating that the differently vivified have the same rights as the living, and that their estate is not inherited until their consciousness ends. Zunvect has returned, and claims that he never ceased. Thus is the chain broken. I didn't *trade* the Staff. I didn't *steal* the Staff. I *returned* the Staff to its rightful owner!" She slammed her fist on the rail. "It was my duty to give it to Zunvect, and he generously rewarded me with a newly forged and updated version of his most renowned creation. It is here," she gestured, and the four-sphered staff appeared in her hand. "The Staff of the Sunlord, the symbol of true Unity, as you will soon see. I give this Staff to the Unified Human Cause. Not to the Firsts, not to the Nodes, not to the Collective, but to all of us." Silveria sent the Staff back into the pocket it had emerged from. "But not until I have understood it, and understood the message it brings. In one month, honored colleagues, you will hear the message from my own lips. Whether I continue to represent the Unified Human Cause or not."

The illusion faded. "She won the vote." Idalia said. "Ten to three."

"I'm so glad," Zunvect said. "Not just that one of my successors in magic has succeeded so well, but that some things don't change. Dangle a nugget of knowledge in front of a wizard, and they'll do whatever you tell them. I think that this isn't quite the end of proceedings, however. If you would care to give me your newsball." He held out his hand.

"You're not tricking me that easily." Idalia replied.

Zunvect grimaced. "I'm not trying to trick you at all, Idalia. Are you always this uncooperative with your captives?"

"When they're asking me to allow them to interact with objects outside of their containment zones." Idalia replied, settling down on her chair.

"What possible harm could I do with a photomantic record? You know what, I don't even need it. Just give me a trickle of magic. Enough to use photomancy myself. You *know* I can't do anything dangerous with a few rays of light."

"Tell me again what your name means." Idalia said with false sweetness.

"Are you honestly telling me that in eight thousand years, you're still not sure how much damage I can do with light? I'm not a g – all right, I am a god. You captured me once, Idalia. Trust me this far."

Idalia looked up at him. "If I trust you with this, I might go further. It's the slippery slope strategy. They teach it as a fundamental mistake of demonologists." Sighing, she reached down and tapped a ward, which rose off the floor and spread out in front of her. Her fingers danced along the geometric shapes. "Enough for photomancy, and it expires in ten minutes."

"Long enough." Zunvect stretched his shoulders and spread his fingers. "Here's a trick I picked up in the firmament. I was never any good at this when I was alive. It's so much easier now."

Idalia rolled her eyes at the crass showmanship, but was grudgingly amazed when the room expanded. The floor became dark marble, reflecting the ice-bright stars in their field of purest black. The stars were visible through a window which wrapped around the semicircular chamber. Idalia recognized it from photojournals as the atrium of the Unified Human Cause capitol building.   A woman stood looking out at the stars and the planet below.

Silveria stood alone, contemplating the World. She'd stood in this place so many times, and yet her thoughts rarely changed when she looked down at her homeworld. Her first thought was always that down was relative to the frame of reference, and it was fitting that society's homeworld-centrism extended even as far as down always being toward the World. Her second thought was that it was ridiculous that the Magi couldn't agree on a location for the UHC Capitol building, so they'd had to wrap it up in a bubble of recycling atmosphere and throw it into orbit.

People appeared and disappeared all around the atrium, many emerging from or entering doors placed on the flat wall behind her. The Commons continued its work even as the Senate – and the World itself – was in turmoil. The interminable committee hearings would continue, she was sure, even if there was only one human left to call them to order. Day-to-day governance of the World was all about inertia and momentum. As long as the slow grind of the hearings and legislative calendar remained intact, the bureaucracy that enforced it would never flounder. The doors themselves were just guides, of course. The only part of the Capitol that was in orbit – the only part that wasn't located in the pocket of vacuum that most large structures occupied these days – was the atrium. The rest hung in deep space or nothingness or whatever lurked on the opposite end of a Tunnel with one too many spatial dimensions. For security reasons the only way in or out of those chambers were the standing Tunnels. Of course, she thought with a twist to her lip that was almost a smile, with the Staff of the Sunlord she could probably breach any of them. Once.

"Contemplating our next conquest?" A deep, quiet voice intruded on her musing. Golaran joined her at the window.

"I'm not expansionist, as you well know. We have enough difficulty keeping our own homeworld secure without looking to dominate others. Our motto ought to be 'Every Session is an Emergency Session.' There's no point in taking over other worlds while our government has so much difficulty with this one."

"Leave it to the slow march of economic imperialism, huh?" Golaran smiled. "For a Node, you have a remarkable preference for soft power."

"Zunvect himself used soft more than hard. He understood that if someone follows you willingly, they stay longer." They were opponents in the Senate, but Silveria couldn't help but respect Golaran. They'd never be friends, but both understood that the other acted out of genuine belief that their way was the best for the security, stability, and prosperity of the UHC.

Golaran looked out at the World, and Silveria wondered what he saw when he looked at it. Did he see the deceptively peaceful swirl of cloud and water? The texture of mountains that she could almost reach out and touch? All the people: human, elf, Node, dwarf, dragon … Or did he just see the humans? Or even just the Magi? They both looked for a long time in the silence of two people who both admire something, even if for very different reasons. "Damn good speech you gave in there." He said.

"Thanks. It got the result."

"I'm surprised you didn't say anything about how stupid it would have been to change leadership during a crisis."

"I didn't need to. I made the pure legalistic argument because the crisis is on everyone's mind. I'd have looked weak if I said that the reason I ought to stay is because we need to keep ourselves in one piece during an emergency. Like I was using it. I'm surprised you put it up for a vote right now."

"No better time." Golaran said. "I wasn't blowing smoke when I said this proved the point."

"Yes, and your words will be spilling from the mouths of a thousand streetcorner bigots within a day." Silveria said with asperity. "Attack me if you want, but please don't fan the flames of anti-Node sentiment."

"It needs to be said, Silveria. You *are* a Node, and your loyalties are split."

"More than you think." Silveria said. "At this very moment, I am the only member of the Solar Conclave absent from the Parliament Building on Katzunvect. There's an ongoing general meeting of the Conclave. Every Node in the World is there. All but me."

"I'm surprised the Nodes feel so affected. I thought you were supposed to be apart from it all. I thought you'd be celebrating the return of the man you credit as your ... progenitor."

"We love the Grandfather deeply, but it's *because* of his return that our position has become so unstable. Do you know what the Conclave *is*, Golaran? Or are you blinded by your obsession with our differences?"

"You are the check on our power. The Senate is responsible for the security of the World and acts as a veto when the Commons makes a law which may – usually for thaumaturgical reasons – be detrimental to the common good. The Senate also deals with matters of highest magical import. The Nodes are our check, the ones who make sure the Senate does not overstep their own authority and try to become like the old Wizard-Lords. That's the conflict of interest that worries me most. You lead the Senate, and so speak for humanity and for the Magi. You also lead the Solar Conclave. In a plausible emergency – such as the gods waking up and the World being forced to deal with a newly emergent divine presence – you could take emergency powers in the Senate *and* Solar Conclave.

You'd hold authority almost as great as that of the First Wizard, and effectively be the most powerful person in the World by having direct command of the military forces of the Magi and the Nodes."

"All this is true." Silveria replied. "I could, but I won't. Besides, the Conclave would never stand for it, and neither would the Senate." She took a long breath, feeling her age in her joints as she had in the Senate chamber. Golaran was fifty years her senior and likely to live fifty years after she died. Zunvect had gifted his children with four times his life expectancy, but it still seemed paltry compared to what the Magi enjoyed. "We have that check because historically we've been neutral. We stood between the armies of the successors to the wizards – including the early Magi – and the Penitent Crusade of the recently somnolent gods. We helped keep order. We saved the lives of those without magical defenses of their own when the wars raged during the Rebuilding. We've spoken for the elves who refuse to vote, the dwarves who cannot, and the dragons who are no longer a culture but a remnant. We stand for all and none. Mage First and Second, Node and non-human. We have tried to *be* Unity, whether you agree or not. There is historical and thaumaturgical legitimacy behind that position."

She closed her eyes. "Zunvect has destroyed that tenuous claim. We are adrift, fighting to remain balanced, and yet inexorably pulled away by public opinion." At Golaran's confused look, she blew air hard out of her nostrils. "*Think* about it. You think the *Magi* are put in a bad position by having someone claiming deific mandate over them? A parishioner may refuse to attend their church, and even repudiate it." She looked at him, her eyes reflecting stars and planet. Tired, open. "A parishioner may leave. A *prophet* cannot. If you are his subjects, we are his priests, his evangelists, his chosen representatives. He made us, Golaran. The scales have now tipped hard, and the ecclesiastical conferences are pushing hard to claim us as members. If we refuse, we seem to be anti-theist. If we assent, then we stop being outsiders, and we become just another special interest."

Silveria pushed against the window, stretching her back. "Now, Golaran, you can tell me I have a conflict of interest until you're blue in the face. Ask yourself one question, though. If I am loyal to the Solar Conclave - which I lead and which is now facing its greatest trial since the Rebuilding- why am I *here*?"

The illusion faded. "She'll find that I've made provision." Zunvect said smugly. "I'm a lot better at playing the game than I was when I was young. Speaking of which, I believe I left off just as we were entering the Capitol City of the Goddess of Death."

Zunvect 13:

Mors Media

I was describing the city. Mors Media. It had a wall which looked twenty meters high and at least two thick. Great blocks of limestone which had been smoothed and joined so well that it looked like one great line as far as I could see, with a projection at the top so no one could climb over. It was yellow in the afternoon light, almost glowing gold. The gate straddling the road we were on was open, though I could see the doors, great black and gray things with rivets and bands over them. If they'd been closed, I could only imagine the force needed to open them again from the outside. I wondered if I would ever be able to wield such forces.

There were towers visible above the wall, poking out above the helmeted heads moving back and forth along its length. Not like the solid, matter-of-fact impossibility of a wizard tower, but something seemingly as impressive despite being so much smaller. Spires that looked to be made of several towers twined together or which rose in narrow spikes to pierce the heavens. There was one that was vertical and yet looked like it ought to be sideways, and another which appeared to be a corn stalk growing out of the skyline. Above all of them was a tower swathed in shadow, ominously crooked as if the builder had decided several times to change direction, and peaked at the top with a skeletal torso and skull which seemed to loom over the city and all of us on the road.

"Dreadful, isn't it?" Xetic commented, seeing where I was looking. "I keep trying to make us into a respectable species and then people build something mind numbingly gauche. The others aren't any better, of course, but they save their most flashy and depressingly representative architecture for their own capitals. Can't overshadow the church in charge!" I looked back at him and he was regarding the view with stiff-backed disdain as far as I could see. The illusion had gone and I still hadn't gotten the knack of reading his subtler moods from his skull alone. I drew breath to remind him and he waved me away, seeing my concern. "The illusion is pointless now. The law is that no deception may pass the gate nor be perpetrated within the walls. Splendidly hypocritical given how much self-delusion they engage in. I'm minded to give my theological lecture here and now but we haven't got time and, despite my contempt, it would be in poor taste to proselytize for atheism inside a holy city."

We'd nearly reached the gate and a bored looking guard – a rather overweight one, I thought – with a skull over a setting sun on his tabard was going down the line. He knocked on the door of our carriage. "Name and business, please."

Xetic's eyes blazed so brightly that I thought the carriage might catch fire, and then shrank to nearly invisible pinpricks. He gestured, and the window exploded outward, throwing the guard into the verge. Xetic waited for the poor man to sit up and then he stuck his head out the window. "Look at the livery and then take three guesses, pinhead!" He shouted, and then gestured rudely. He settled back in his seat and the glass of the window sprang back into place, appearing after a moment as if it had never been broken. "Townie guards." He grumbled. "I've hated those jumped up imbecilic wastes of space since I was alive."

"Won't that cause trouble?" I asked as the guard scrambled to his feet and ran back to his guardhouse. I thought I saw a wet spot on his trousers and not where he'd landed on snow pack. After the terror he'd inflicted on the man – who was just trying to do his job - Xetic's comment about the guard's peaked helmet seemed very unkind.

Xetic's eyes flashed. "I surely hope it does. *They* asked to see *me*. I wouldn't mind one bit if this meant they gave up on this asinine ritual of theirs. I'd like it even more if the fool came back with a squad to try to turn me away or arrest me. Never let them see you're afraid, Zunvect. Always be confident, aloof, or even arrogant. Most of the power of a wizard lies in projecting the air that no one is above you and *everyone* is below you. Make it clear if they want to make something of it, that it would be your pleasure to hurl them bodily through the nearest grove of trees, and be there to box their ears and kick 'em in the goolies when they land. In all but a handful of cases, you need never fear the question 'you and what army?' That said, actually carrying out the implicit threat is a last resort because it's usually messy and people carry a grudge if they think it was personal. It looks as if we're being let through. If you had any money to gamble, I'd bet you that they'll take their helmets off when we pass."

They did, which made Xetic an even more insufferable traveling companion. We traversed the straight lanes and radial boulevards towards the center of the city where all the towers were. I assumed they belonged to churches.

I'd only ever met the itinerant healers of Huruum. They were calm, gentle, and often cheerful individuals who went from village to village, hoping to catch people who were terribly injured or ill, and then restore them to health. Not that they were ever disappointed to find us all in perfect condition under the rough ministrations of Ivan. We were always public spirited about it. We gave them a free room and dinner, and a coin if we had one to spare so that they could go on to less fortunate communities. They learned that the less they preached and tried to convert us, the more alms they got. It wasn't that we were atheists or anything, but that we were happy to leave the gods to places where they could get a better reception.

We prayed occasionally to Nenya the goddess of agricultural matters. Most of the prayers were something like, "Listen, tought bitch. It han't rained in a fortnight and what are you playing at?

We'd very much like a bit of weather so that the potatoes don't all shrivel up and if a priestess ever passes by we'll throw a few bits in the hat, so get on with it." Our attitude had been that we got on with our jobs, so she should do the same. We'd never starved, so we assumed she either paid us no mind or didn't care if our prayers were phrased in the same way we talked to sows or merchants.

The roads outside the walls had been packed earth, turning to cobblestones as we got nearer. Inside, they were smooth and unmarked by traffic. The houses, too, looked well kept, almost uniform in their appearance. "I'll hand this to the priests," Xetic said by way of explanation via backhanded compliment, "they do drive an economy. Over two hundred thousand people live here and most of them aren't in holy orders. The local churches send tribute from the donations given by believers, and they take in a lot themselves right here. Souvenir shops, public houses, inns, larger donations from those who can afford to make the trip for some special request. You saw the hundreds of people streaming in along with us. Many of them are making their way to the same destination as we are, but with very different business.

"The Capital Church of Drotaka is *the* place to go if you're nearing the end, or if you have a relative who is and you're a bit concerned about their next life. Once in a very long while you can even prevail on them to grant an extension. Usually the argument is made by dragging in a cart filled with treasure. They're always preaching that you can't take it with you. Opportunistic jerks. They're just mad at me because I offer a glimmer of hope that there's another way. Indefinite extension without having to pay a cartload of gold per year of extra life. As if I'd grant *that* request." He snorted, which was an achievement for a man with no nose and no sinuses.

"The roads are very good." I observed, and winced as I set off another tirade.

"For them, but no one else!" Xetic grumbled. "Not that they *can* extend it much further." He said with self-satisfaction. "It takes a priest for every mile to keep the road repaired. They have to come out here and chant at it once a week. Not like if *we* built it."

Knowing I was going to regret it, I asked, "Why don't we?"

"Expense." Xetic grunted. "You haven't done any really serious enchanting, or even much more than a very rough instinctive focus rod. Something must hold the energy that powers the spell of self-repair, or else it's like with the priests and you have to constantly come out and fix it yourself. Power distribution systems are very costly, and even with the threat of the most unpleasant form of magical execution you can think of, there are thieves willing to try to pry the energy gathering devices out to try and sell. There are some territories that build extensive highways, but they never build magical ones past their own borders. Great, now you've made me compare myself to the priests." He opened the window the proper way and called to the driver. "Leave us here. My apprentice needs to see the sights on foot. Meet us at the Sanctified Cheesery around the corner." He threw the driver a large coin. "Get yourself something to drink in the pub across the street but be ready to pick us up in no more than two hours. That should give us time to look at all the wretched architecture." He said to me. "And you can talk to a few bishops or whatever important people are loitering with nothing better to do than pass the time of day with us."

He stumped off, me following in his wake and wishing he'd let me get a coat before we left. We wound our way the quarter of a mile or so to the open plaza at the center of the city. This was paved in brick of the same glowing golden-beige of the walls and many of the houses and shops we passed. With some effort, I finally realized that the stone itself was a very dark gray rather than cream and that the glow hadn't been the sun at all. The stone was heavily and uniformly enchanted, so much that the enchantments blocked out the stone itself unless I looked carefully. I felt a bit silly having not guessed, but my annoyance with myself ended with a literal crash. We'd entered from one of eight avenues feeding into the cathedral plaza and the edifice next to us on the right was starting to sound a series of sonorous bells. There were far too many being rung all at once to make out a melody and Xetic heard it only as noise so there was no point in questioning him. "Time for the show." Xetic opined.

I looked around and saw that the bells had drawn a crowd and that the plaza, already packed, was filling up even more. It was a tight fit for most, and I looked around for a reason why I wasn't being jostled and squeezed by the pilgrims and supplicants. I noticed the air was discolored and that the people around us seemed to be pressed up against something about a meter away in every direction. Xetic didn't like crowds and had put some kind of barrier around us, which thankfully helped hold in some warmth so I wasn't freezing. There must have been something similar around the entrances to each towering temple because the throng ended abruptly at the front step of each one.

The church with the bells was also the one with the twisted green spire. Its façade was a lighter green, carved into scenes of people being cared for in beds, on battlefields, and by the side of the road. It opened on to a breathtaking peaked veranda, held up with alternating bright red and green columns and lined with lifelike statues that held their hands out in welcome and offering. Out of the twenty-foot-tall verdigris doors marched a line of green robed figures, chanting high and long in a language that made my skin crawl. They banged small gongs which were inaudible in the continuing tolling of the bells above. Some of the supplicants stumbled through the barrier, and each one was met by a smiling priest, who touched them lightly on the forehead and gently ushered them back through to the other side. Those met seemed transfixed by the touch and then ecstatic. I could see them straighten and walk with renewed vigor even when they'd looked ready to collapse when they arrived.

"Huruum." Xetic said as the echoes of the bells faded away. "Nice chap all in all. All those statues are saints; he prefers to take care of his entire responsibility personally so no demigods for him. Of course, those lucky people in the front row are no doubt going to dedicate half their earnings for a year to the church, and they don't do serious healing on the stoop like that. Coughs, limps, those they'll fix up if you're fortunate enough to be picked out of the audience like that, but if you need something more, you need to talk to the vicar in charge of the donation box." It was hard to pay attention to my teacher's constant cynicism when so many of those chosen seemed so genuinely relieved. Even if there was a monetary factor, at least people were *helped* by it.

"I regret," said an elderly, bald man in a green monk's habit, "that he has a point." I started, surprised that anyone could get so close without us noticing. Xetic's bubble of warm calm should have given us warning of the monk's passing through the otherwise empty space even if it didn't keep him out entirely. "The church's overhead is unfortunately higher than I would like. I'm reliably informed that the finery and art are necessary to drive further worship and donations. We do *try* to divert as much as we can towards charitable works, though. You, lad, have met some of our traveling healers." He smiled warmly at me. "Your village may have its own doctor, but few are so fortunate. Paying for our brothers and sisters to travel the highways to heal the sick and injured across Ry-Kel is expensive."

"Is it fair that your most devoted followers subsidize that?" Xetic asked without looking away from the healing spectacle.

"Come now, Xetic. You're not being skeptical *enough*. How many people in this square have visited from a distant land? Almost all of them. Forgive me for playing the odds with lives at stake, but even if they're only coming as far as Mors Media and not Panaceplis – the healing church's capitol," he said for my benefit, "they have enough to donate to the less fortunate."

There wasn't time to argue further because the temple on our left was now tolling out in two very distinct melodies. I guessed that they would trade back and forth along the circumference of the plaza until they reached Drotaka's capital church, which was opposite us as we entered. Saving the best for last as Xetic might have said.

This church had the corn sheaf tower and was a mixture of colors, mainly wheat gold and leaf green. It had only a wide, open courtyard in front, where representatives of each arable crop were visible, along with some small animals in neat pens. The front of the church was split down the middle, however, and I realized that the gold and green with its carvings of pastoral scenes, fine weather, and depictions of plants and animals was on the near side to us. I craned my neck and saw that the other half ended much lower and with a conically peaked dome next to a rounded tower. It was in richer reds and purples, with carvings of people and animals in more active poses. The courtyard was filled with, "Beds?" I mouthed.

"You've heard of the twin goddesses, haven't you?" Xetic asked, amused. "You dirt grubbers pray to *Nenya* all the time. She tends to work mostly on her own with a few representative nature spirits, but *Valya* has a whole armful of demigods keeping her company."

Nenya was indeed the only deity our village really paid much attention to. Her sister Valya was the ultimate example of a goddess for foreign parts. Of course, all the activities she was best known for were participated in by just about everyone in town, and often quite enthusiastically. That said, hers was a type of fertility we didn't discuss when we could help it. Her sister kept us fed, our crops growing, and our animals healthy. Valya was responsible for everything multiplying.

Double doors opened and, on our side of the church, walked priests in long yellow robes, half with green sashes and the other half with purple. They sang cheerfully in that skin tightening language as they watered their plants and fed the animals. On the far side strutted their counterparts in sky blue and purple robes – if you could call them that - which often failed to cover nearly enough to be called decent by the folks back home, and at whose beckon the barrier became momentarily permeable. They were joined by as many of the eager travelers as could scramble across the threshold before the barrier snapped back into place. The priests in blue didn't seem to mind who or how many joined them. This time around it wasn't some vast bizarre conspiracy of barmaids, but real and solid magic that led to me stare at the women who called and laughed as they were borne down onto the soft mattresses to copulate in front of an audience of hundreds. I had to look away, feeling my face coloring but the image of those ladies made into my perfect sexual fantasy by divine intervention stayed with me for years. Don't blame me for this one, Idalia. A goddess herself was enticing me. I know because every one of the women was identical and I didn't spare a single look for the men.

"It's enough to make you lose track of what the other side is doing." Xetic said.

I risked a look, trying to ignore the orgy occurring just on the other side of a shallow drain between the two groups. A calmer set of pilgrims had brought ailing pets or bags of seeds to the priests in yellow-green, who cured the animals and blessed the seeds with a kind word and then went back to their duties. "Take a good look at that." Xetic said. "Scattering corn for those chickens and what don't they have?"

"A bag full of corn?"

"Right. Pure bloody materialization without any fanfare. That isn't how we do it and remember that as hard as you can. Priests can get away with making something out of nothing, but you'd get the Fires down on you if you tried that." I opened my mouth to protest. "Your food and clothes and everything else I make is done by rearranging, not *creating*. Aika will teach you the difference. They're also cleaning the pens by simply making the muck cease to exist. It's disgusting."

"Zealotry, Xetic?" The monk asked, amused. "Intolerance of something because it fails to fit your view of the world?"

"It's wasteful," Lord Xetic shot back.

"How can there be waste when she can make or destroy at will?"

"I'm more concerned by the other side." I said, failing to keep the scandalized tone out of my voice. The discussion between the secular and the divine was a buzzing in my ears. What the priests of Nenya were doing would have distracted me even if Xetic declared there and then to teach me a spell.

"I know. Huruum hates it because they cure people of venereal disease while they're having their fun." If Xetic could differentiate between grinning and his normal expression, I felt sure he would be. "Many Wizard-Lords keep harems, you know, so you'll have to get used to this kind of thing eventually or else you'll be frustrated for your whole life. Nobody likes a frustrated Wizard-Lord; that's why we have Peacemakers now. Do you know what they're doing?"

"I have a pretty good idea." I said sarcastically.

"Idiot child." Xetic said affectionately. "When there's more than one with a priest, it means they're being helped to conceive a child because one or the other cannot. Alone, they're after a cure, solace, or are asking for a blessing to carry back to their farm so that their stock will grow. All for a price, but it isn't about fun for most of them. Not that you can't make an offering and have a good time with a holy harlot, who will never give you the itch and knows exactly what you want. Wealthy families whose children are either bashful or scornful of the opposite sex often get sent to Valya. There's nothing like being bedded by someone who knows everything there is to know to give you confidence, and nothing like a supposed sexual conquest who is supernaturally tireless to give you a bit of respect. It's all a bit grotty, but no worse than the other services. That said, I've always taken strong exception to how most of their iconography is of very attractive women, their deity is a goddess, and they mostly market to men with all that giggling and mincing around. You'll note – or not since you can't seem to get up the strength of will to look at them with an objective eye – that three quarters of those who've taken the blue are female. There's something deeply sexist in that and if I ever work out which sex they're denigrating with it, I intend to have a word. You can look again; most of them have their clothes back on."

"I resent the implication that I would disapprove of *any* healing," the monk said stiffly. "What I dislike is that it takes away the consequences of poor hygiene. Valya ought to be promoting awareness; when we find a plague, we *teach* those we heal how to avoid being infected next time. As for the gender imbalance, try looking at your own organization, Xetic. Whether we like it or not, you wizards drive many norms and values in society. You are unwittingly promoting patriarchy, decreasing opportunity for women, and putting the onus of sexual desirability on females. So, if you want to have a 'word' with someone, try talking to yourself."

"I'm ignoring him right now because he's right and I've been trying to do something about it for a thousand years," Xetic murmured to me. "Although," he said loudly, "the imbalance in the *church* has existed since well before the issues amongst Wizard-

Lords began. Valya can use our troubles as an excuse and a rein-forcement, but it didn't *start* with me."

"Speaking of imbalance," the monk said, "this is all your fault. You pruned away too many gods, and now we're all doing multiple duty, and often doing so well outside of our mandate. Take Valya. Her priests may be all about human reproduction here in the city, but the local churches often have to do everything a veterinary sor-cerer does. It's not Nenya's problem if there's a rough lambing, or a pig won't conceive. Sometimes Valya's stuck doing *all* the animal work if it's a bad year for plants and Nenya's staff are busy helping to make sure there's enough grain for winter. Heck, if a community can't afford to support three priesthoods, either me, Nenya, or Val-ya have to do it all!"

Xetic sighed and waved dismissively. "Yes, yes. Agreed. I couldn't kill sex, death, or whatever Hylentor is, and so I left six gods who are horribly imbalanced conceptually, and overworked too. I'd hoped, you see," he said to me, "to get rid of Nenya and Valya, and just leave gods of life, death, knowledge, and chaos – and I wasn't too keen on the last part. Unfortunately, it turns out that it would have been a lot worse to have a balanced pantheon. Some urges were too great to be eliminated and would have resur-faced anyway. If sex had somehow beaten out life, then there would have been a terrible gap in the middle of everything."

"You should have left us with at least twenty gods," the monk grumbled.

"I'd have preferred none at all."

Since the next church to put on a show was going to be on our right anyway, I declined to watch the retreating backsides of the sex priests. My imagination was bothering me far too much already and I was afraid I might pass out if I ogled any more. There were no bells on the church I looked at. None that I could hear. It was the one with the tower that was standing up straight but looked sideways. The entire church looked twisted around, as if a whirl-pool of brick had formed around a central point and then frozen in place. There was a door, but it was at a steep angle. There were no carvings or iconography at first, but the longer I looked the more I felt like there was something there but for some reason I couldn't see it properly. I tilted my head, squinted, and craned my neck but couldn't make any sense out of it.

The door opened and a portly man in a stained gray cassock hurled a brass instrument with a very large bell down the stairs. It crashed several times, falling end over end until it fell at just the right angle to trap one of the lay people watching the ceremony in-side the bell with his arms pinned to his sides. A woman, in equally shabby vestments, sprinted down the stairs and delivered a sharp kick to the trapped pilgrim's shin. "That'll teach you to stand in the way of our holy tuba!" She shouted. Then she blew into the in-strument, producing a deep *blat*, and kicked the man again. He fell, and she turned on her heel to march back up the stairs and into the church.

The pilgrim was helped to his feet and the instrument – a tuba I assumed – was pulled off. Long hair spilled down the pilgrim's back, and he looked very confused. It was a long way off, but I was pretty sure that it was now a woman standing there. She looked around and wandered away, still with the expression of total be-wilderment, holding the tuba to herself as if it might contain an-swers.

"Hylentor." Xetic explained. "Some people use the male pro-noun, but that deity is most definitely an *it*, and most certainly *not* from this planet. I don't know where it originated from, but I know that humanity did not, in its collective psyche, decide to form a god that combines cosmic entropy, tricksterism, and slapstick comedy amongst other similarly ridiculous concepts. Having your sex changed is one of the tamest things that will happen to people who decide to pray to that thing. Only the terminally bored stand in the front section when they do their daily ceremony. I once saw a woman end up with eleven eyes, a puppet for a left hand, and a halo made of infinitely replenishing beet soup. Hylentor's gifts can't be cured, either. None of the other gods are strong enough to make a dent in its enchantments." As I turned away, I saw a priest in red and yellow body paint jump out of an upper story window on an elastic rope, grab the tuba from the dazed pilgrim, and spring back through the window.

"Don't ask me." The monk said when I looked at him expecting a comment on Xetic's explanation. "Hylentor simply *is*. Its nature defies further questions."

A single gong rang from a church with carvings so fine that I didn't know what they were. They ran along every visible inch of the squat, rectangular building. It was the least impressive looking of any of the cathedrals yet, though the procession that exited - swinging censors and carrying thick tomes - were richly dressed in deep blue and silver vestments. The lead priestess rang a bell in a wooden frame, which echoed the single deep note across the circle. "We certify that the following statements are, in their entirety, factual." She sang. The priests all opened their books in unison and the one behind her in the line stepped forward. "The practice of cow tipping is an urban legend. Cows do not sleep standing up."

The next one took his place. "The word cashew refers both to a nut and a fruit which grow from the same tree." She called in a melodious chant.

"Magnesium floride occurs naturally in sellaite."

"A giraffe has as many vertebrae in its neck as a human."

"The three bones in the human ear are the malleus, incus, and stapes."

"The escape velocity of the planet Ry-Kel is 11.42 kilometers per second."

"There is a man in this city who will die in a ham sandwich."

"It's mostly rubbish." Xetic said as the priests returned to the church. "The human imagination is sometimes drearily literal. Garliem is the god of knowledge and has hundreds of attending spirits and demigods who are almost all more useful than he is. The problem is that he isn't the god of *useful* knowledge, so his priests mostly just babble about everything. Each full priest is attended by four scribes who take down everything they say. The entire capital church is dedicated to the filing system needed to keep track of it all in an organized way. That and the frescoes. His knowledge isn't necessarily causal, so they're constantly painting the future. Absolutely pointless because the moment anyone tries to puzzle out what the pictures mean in advance of the events occurring, they become meaningless. Inverse law of prophetic stability. You'll cover it in your studies if you're very good. Anyway, the demigod in charge of stationary is more useful than he is, and all *she* ever does is miraculously keep your ink from running out and ensure that your paperweights never slip. Here comes the grand finale. Hold on to your grannies and anyone with so much as a limp."

The capital church of Drotaka, opposite us as we looked across the plaza, was tolling a single deep bell. The sound rolled across us, absolute silence following in its wake. The bell tolled again, and the dull, gray doors swung back into the absolute darkness within. At fifty meters tall and over a hundred wide, there was a lot of swinging to do before they were open. The clothes of the onlookers were blown towards those doors as if pulled into the hungry void. The gray textured walls of the basilica shivered. The giant skeletal torso that surmounted the supernaturally shadowed spire opened its arms in macabre welcome. The cloud around the spire grew until the entire city was shrouded in darkness. The mood of sepulchral dread was broken only by my teacher grunting in annoyance. "Playing on the fears of uncertain mortals."

There were no shields around the doors of the dominant temple of this city. Nothing to prevent people from crowding as close as they liked to the steps, or even to try to climb them to the gray paved pavilion in front of the doors, lined in grim statues whose eyes glowed red. The crowd was drawing back, however. The statues were turning to look at the doors, the grinding audible even to us at the far end. Tens and then hundreds of priests filed out, absolutely silent. Some wore gray, others blood red, and the last ones to emerge were wearing light-swallowing black. All were long and trailing, hiding the feet and hands from sight, and those in black wore deep hoods which showed only pinpricks of red where their eyes ought to be. Those with heads visible looked pale and gaunt as if they were near to the grave already, and all had shaved heads. They lined up in rows and raised their arms above their heads, looking up at the skeleton above, which crooked its finger. A scattering of pilgrims stepped forward, most supporting someone who was aged or infirm, bent and doddering under the weight of their age and illness. As the first party reached the top of the stairs, a voice boomed from beyond the doors.

"We face death alone. There is strength at the last. Say your goodbyes at the threshold or else join them in their journey."

Each group hugged and spoke a few words before those who had come to meet the priests went on and crossed into the pavilion, where each was met by a priest who took them into the basilica. None of those who were guiding a pilgrim wore black, and most wore red. As I watched, a red-robed priest dashed down the stairs and into the crowd, which began to churn to try to get out of the way. Amidst the screams and panicked shoving, a piercing yelp echoed across the plaza.

"Excellent, a show." Xetic said. "You don't usually get to watch this."

The crowd was drawing back from the red-robed priest, who was now trying to wrestle someone to the ground. The man was dressed in a fine coat, and had the soft face and well-kept, longer hair that bespoke wealth. He was calling out to someone on the edge of the circle of people – I guessed a servant. The woman was shaking her head, wide-eyed and terrified as the priest pulled a staff out of nowhere and started beating the man. He drew a knife from his boot, and made it to his feet to fight back. The priest expertly caught a wild swing with the staff and knocked the knife out of his grip, following up by hitting him on the head with a crack that was audible where I was standing. The priest then dragged the man up the stairs and threw him bodily to a black-robed priest, who carried him inside.

"Assassin," Xetic explained. "That unfortunate fellow must have angered someone with a lot of money. Damn silly of him to come to Mors Media, but he must not have known. That's the death church for you. They preach that everyone needs to go when their time has come, but they're not above taking a fat sack of cash in one hand and then moving the hands of the clock with the other. Some of their upper echelon live ridiculously long lives. I've always suspected that they're balancing it out by using the lifespans of the people they're hired to kill."

"Don't worry, son," the monk said. "They don't take contracts on wizards. Your boss-man here keeps that from happening, though I doubt they'd do it even if he weren't. I'm not thrilled to pieces about the practice, and I try not to pay much attention to it, but even I know that few people have enough money to make it worthwhile to try to assassinate a Wizard-Lord."

With words of encouragement, the priests with willing pilgrims started ushering them forward again. As the last one entered the cathedral, the remaining priests chanted a deep, bone-chilling litany in a language that sounded painful to speak, then retreated. The ground shook as the doors slammed shut behind them, the shadows returned to the spire, and the skeleton at the top returned to looking out into the distance.

"I swear I think they emulate *me* to try to scare people." Xetic said at the end. "All those skulls with eyes just like mine. I should charge royalties for the use of my image!" He looked around. "Bah! No decent time left to give you a better look inside each one. It's getting towards dinnertime already and Aika will be wondering where we are. Come on." We started crossing the open space between the churches, occasionally jostled by someone who glanced at Xetic and drew back hurriedly with a muttered apology or a look of terror. "They make these laws just to annoy us." Xetic continued to grumble. "No magic indeed! I ought to have them all properly expunged and be done with the entire farce."

I looked back and the monk in green waved to us. "Tell that liar that I'll make an exception to the rule and let either of you use that bubble spell he had going *in the middle of Mors Media* in Panaceplis as long as you're with him." With that parting shot, he disappeared into the crowd.

"Insufferable old wiseacre," Xetic groused, kicking someone who wasn't fast enough to get out of the way. "As if *I* ever have a reason to go to his stupid capitol cathedral anyway."

"He didn't look like a high-ranking priest." I said. "Was he someone you know?"

"He doesn't look much like a *god* either, and yes, we go back a little." Xetic replied. "That was Huruum." I stopped, and he grabbed my hand, pulling me along. "Don't get awestruck; you're moving in exalted circles now. Huruum thinks of himself as a wise and worldly philosopher, so he never misses a chance to start an argument. Since you were here, and I was explaining the facts of life to you, he had the best opportunity in centuries to get in a few poorly conceived 'thoughts' on the relationship between divine idealism and secular realism. Try not to be too moved by his 'humble philosopher' schtick. He's as venal, self-important, and obsessed with pomp and show as the rest of them. Give him an inch and he'll be looming over you like some third-rate Uidrana impersonator and giving you strictures and commands."

"But ... he's a god." I said faintly. You may have the gall to conjure one, Idalia, but to me a god was something to be feared and avoided whenever possible. "He's ... well, he's a god."

"Gods are just like us, only dumber." Xetic said. "Oh, all right, not exactly like us. I don't want to get into the whole divinity lecture here, but I suppose you have a right to be a bit awed. I wasn't expecting him to pop up in any guise. Feel proud. I don't like gods, but it's a good sign when one takes a shine and invites you over for tea and cake. The ones that are left are very powerful and it's good to get along with them. In fact, if it came to blows, I'm not too proud to admit that I doubt I could take any one of them directly. Thank goodness that they keep each other busy and for the most part out of our way. Right, well, at least I don't have to worry about you lagging behind because we have to deal with a few steps." We'd reached the stairs leading up to the pavilion, which were far taller than they'd looked from afar. They were made of something I couldn't quite place at first, and carved with names.

"I didn't know there were only five churches." I said to try to distract Lord Xetic from his recitation of grievances and insults. "I thought there would be a lot more."

"There used to be. It was thoroughly untidy." Xetic replied. "In my day there was a god for just about everything, including individual lucky boulders which happened to fall down off the mountain and crush someone you didn't like. Most of the important aspects are still demigods working for one of the big ones. Even the gods engage in unfair trade practices and building of monopolies. Some of the really big things are shared, like how sunlight is either Huruum, Nenya, or Hylentor depending on what it's doing. Sort of like conjugating verbs, you get a different god depending on how you use it."

I remembered a few offhand comments made in history books about deific consolidation. This seemed to be what they'd been talking about. "And murder? Thieving, hatred? The worst I've seen so far is death. There must be gods for bad things as well as good ones."

"Not any blasted more there aren't." Xetic said with satisfaction. "When you're old enough and wise enough that I'm sure you won't run your mouth to the wrong person, I'll tell you what happened to them."

This seemed like a very unkind comment given that I didn't have much opportunity to talk to anyone. "Like who? I live with you and Aika in an unreachable tower in the middle of an empty forest!"

"Empty he says. Bless your ignorance, boy. Replies like that convince me you haven't matured yet. You'll learn far more than you want soon enough. You'll probably hear more than you ought to just in this meeting."

Fuming, I fell silent, not giving in to my nervousness as Xetic rapped on the enormous doors of the basilica. Now that we were closer, it was plain that the textured walls were made of bone. Frescoes depicting scenes of death in battle, of illness, even a person dying with the horn of a bull impaling them. All picked out in every type of human bone. I tried to pretend to ignore Xetic when he spoke again, but it was hard not to be interested. "Their tithe is not just in gold but in bits." Xetic said. "Thousands of people come to Drotaka every year for a 'peaceful transition' as they call it, and the price is that they get tacked up to the wall or turned into furniture. Only the finest bones are sent here, of course. No osteoporosis, no poorly knitted broken arm from when you were five and fell off a donkey. First rate from the healthiest specimens only, please. Preferably those who died of something fast when they were in their prime so that the bones are in peak condition." He addressed the door. "Open up, you morbid scum or I'll forget my manners and break down the door!"

"Lord Xetic-Nal. Always a pleasure to hear your cheerful greetings." A smaller, serviceable looking entrance was placed discreetly to one side of the colossal frame of the main doors and a priest was sticking her head out. "Has eternal life finally started to claim your memory or are you cursing at our ceremonial gateway for fun?"

"It's my right as a visiting dignitary to enter through the main gate." Xetic insisted.

"Visiting dignitaries usually arrive with an entourage, their best clothes, and don't hurl abuse because they've forgotten where the door went." The priest replied acidly. "You, on the other hand, have shown up with one teenage boy, a robe that looks like you dribbled on it, and are kicking a door that can only be opened by the power of our Lady. I've often wondered if the phrase 'keep a civil tongue in your mouth' was inspired by *you*, seeing as how you have neither civility nor a tongue. Neither of us enjoys these meetings, but our Lady does insist." She stepped back, gesturing for us to join her inside.

The interior of the basilica was surprisingly bright. While the side facing the street was unbroken bone, the other three had high, wide stained-glass windows illuminating a nave and an altar, which unsurprisingly had a skull on it. The windows naturally showed more scenes of death, though a few seemed to be showing people dressed in Drotaka's robes *fighting* the dead. There were more grim statues and no sign of the supplicants who had passed through the main doors to our right. Sarcophagi lined the alcoves that ran the length of the basilica beside the nave, each one with a statue a person – I assumed the occupant. I noticed then that the floor tiles each bore a name and set of dates. After some thought, I guessed that there were urns under each one, containing the ashes of some noted person. Worshipers sat silently in pews as low music played, for the time being ignoring the empty pulpit. I shuddered at the thought of what might be said during services. Everything from the chandeliers to the font were made of interlocked bones. "Gierna, this is my apprentice Zunvect. Zunvect, this is Ianor Gierna, chief hypocrite of Drotaka and my case worker."

"You look young, so I hope that my advice to not believe anything this blasphemous blowhard says about us falls on fertile ground." The woman replied. "Nothing he just said was accurate except for my name and title. I am an Ianor of Drotaka's church, which means I am not at all the 'chief' anything. That would be the Capitalis, the senior mortal servant of our Lady Drotaka, who is Merendi Kinarl. I believe he is calling me a hypocrite for the flawed reason that, because I am over four hundred years old, I am failing to display adequate mortality for a servant of death. We all know what our final moment will be. I, for example, will be struck by a tibia that one of our novices has failed to adequately re-adhere to a mural of Saint Munstable near the ceiling, two hundred years from now. We get very few novices, so even that display of ineptitude will not see him expelled, and it is also the reason our Lady chooses not to call us until we have served her for a very long time. Finally, I am not his case worker, I am his liaison. Whatever he has told you about this meeting is probably slanted very heavily. We meet once every twenty-five years to make sure that the Pact is being upheld, and I report as much to him as he does to me. Shall we retire to my study? I'm sure you know the way, but just in case you get lost and start berating a bench, I'll lead."

"It's hard to tell since they all look like skeletons," Xetic whispered as we walked, "but a few of those murals include me. On their side more often than not. I knew old Munstable back when he was helping me clear out a necromantic temple. Reckless bloke; became a martyr during that raid."

We were led up a long stairway, taking us above the vaulted ceiling of the nave. The stairs turned from bone to wood, as did the wall paneling. When we emerged from the staircase, we were in a passageway that could have been in Xetic's own tower. It was somewhat gloomy and showed a great deal of bare gray limestone, but it had none of the overwhelmingly macabre feel of the public spaces below. Apparently even the servants of death grew tired of being surrounded by skulls and coffins all the time. We stopped at a wooden door with the Ianor's name on it and were let into a study with a bookshelf behind a wide desk. Gierna sat behind it and we sat in hard leather chairs opposite her. It was my first time getting a good look at her.

Like all the priests of Drotaka, she had shaved all of her hair, including her eyebrows, leaving her face to be defined by the jutting bones and sunken cheeks common to her priesthood. She didn't have the youthful look of a wizard, nor was she stooped and misshapen as a person of four hundred would be if they showed all their years. Her fingers were long, with carefully trimmed nails, and her gray robe unadorned with a deep hood. Her stick-thin arms swam in the wide, deep sleeves. Gray, I learned later, denoted go-betweens. Reds worked with the living, blacks with the dead, and grays straddled the boundary of death. Normally, grays were only consulted by the terminally ill and the bereaved hoping to get a message across. Theologically, Xetic was alive, but the priesthood had decided that a red priest was a ridiculous conceit, and that lichdom meant he was perpetually on the brink of death, which gave them a good excuse to assign grays to talk to him. Reds, after all, were trained to console and advise, and blacks were supposed to either inter or destroy. I heard that the gray priests disliked the duty, but acknowledged that as communicators, they were best suited to handle the difficulties, as well as being the only ones qualified to administer the test that I witnessed later.

There was a map on Gierna's desk, which she indicated with a sharp metal implement. "Do you want to start, or shall I?"

"Tell her what you saw, Zunvect." Xetic had been grumbling at me about how this was the kind of thing he had to deal with, but I'd been tuning it out in favor of looking around. Consequently, I'd missed something important hidden in the stream of annoyance.

"Sorry, what?" I asked.

"Crimeny. Never mind, Zunvect. Go on," he waved at Gierna.

"We've uncovered sites associated with Nalagash, Zoroktelitan, and Uberiub." She said, indicating spots on the map – all in the Crescent – with each name. "All sites dormant, possibly dead. We judged that they were more trouble to clear away than it was worth."

Xetic took the spike from her and rested it in the western half of the map. "Alok'derosh." He said. The Ianor gasped. "Don't be dramatic, girl. It's hardly surprising that some of his were still standing, even after I had a strong word about it. The site is active, which is the really worrying part, but apparently in some sort of defensive position. It's been subject to repeated thaumaturgical perturbation and not reacted at all. Judged to be waiting for something that will never come. I chose to leave it be since I had more pressing matters. More importantly, it might try to protect itself if I meddle."

"You can't just leave it there." Gierna insisted.

"Of course I can, and you will do the same!" Xetic admonished. "It's near a population center, and you know what the old boy was like. If we come huffing and puffing and trying to knock it down, the site will wake up. We'll be up to our eye sockets in zombies before the day is out. I say it's not surprising that Alok is still around because I know for a fact that he's still got cults, which means his sites are not only capable of being active, but aggressive. Squashing the heretics is your problem; I can send a list if you need it, but I expect better of you than that. Good old fashioned ecclesiastical espionage can't have gone completely out of fashion." He settled himself. "Anyway, on to the next bit of bad business." He detached his skull and laid it on the table. "There. You can check for yourself."

Gierna acted like this was a regular occurrence but it was very disconcerting to me. I turned away so I didn't see what she did, but it didn't take long before Xetic was whole again. "I certify that your soul has not left your body." Gierna said. "You are still, legally, alive."

"I certify that I have detected no unlicensed necromantic activity in my organization, nor have I detected it in yours." Xetic replied. "There. Everyone is still clean." He got up. "I'll see myself out. Unless your church has one of those tedious maze things that you were so keen on a few centuries ago, it shouldn't be hard to find the door."

"It's been a pleasure, you foul spawn of the worst heresy. I hope your stolen power backfires and sends you straight to the moon." I wondered where that was.

"Likewise, you hypocritical upstart. May you one day realize it's *you* who is being robbed." They bowed to each other and Xetic swept out, with me rushing to follow. "It's all so silly." He said, taking the stairs faster than I'd ever seen him go. "I mean, really. This hierarchical nonsense. It's all an attempt to impose a global oligarchy on the whole world. If they had their way, they'd rule everyone."

I couldn't help myself. "Yes, I can see how a global oligarchy of the magically empowered could be a real problem."

Xetic clapped, producing a horrible clacking. "You ought to be a barrister, or possibly a court jester if there are any of them left." He looked up at the ceiling of the nave, which had been vaulted to look like ribs. "I suppose they're no worse than most of my own. All this flash stuff keeps the casual observer entertained and impressed. I don't engage in that kind of thing, of course," he said sanctimoniously, "but since you won't have my reputation, you might learn a little from it. Only a little, mind! None of this walking about chanting and giving out tiny bits of magic like they're sweets to a good child."

We found the driver waiting for us. Xetic's instruction to wait in the public house had been assiduously followed. He looked like he might fall off the seat if we went too fast. He controlled the carriage well enough, though, and we made it back to the gates without running anyone over. I hoped he would be all right. I doubted we would be staying in the carriage all the way back, so he'd be on his own.

"She was more unpleasant than I remembered." Xetic commented. "Still, the church has its uses. They think we're all heretics, you know. Supposedly we steal their divine juices."

"They think the earth magic is stolen?"

"No, they don't believe in the earth magic!" Xetic chortled. "They believe that all magic comes from the gods and we're somehow siphoning it off, like some underhanded farmer who goes in the dead of night and digs a canal from someone else's waterway to his land. They blame me for it, of course. They blame me for everything that goes wrong. I'm the holy horror, the one who assails them with doubt and false promises of power. If they only knew how many of their priests were wizards."

"How many?" I asked.

"Almost all of them." Xetic replied. "Whenever we find a spare wizard, we tell them to take holy orders. The gods suck the power straight out of them, and then they give it back in drips and drabs based on - oh, something silly. Importance, devotion, something like that. It's a terrible waste, but it's better than the alternatives. The spells to stop a wizard from casting are usually far too finicky for most of our order to do on a regular basis, and jail would never work. We can convince some to just stop entirely, but most decide it's easier to pick a god to bend their knee to. It ensures they'll never be tempted again. It also handles the *very thorny* problem of those who figure out they're wizards later in life from the obvious clue that they stopped aging before they were thirty. Once their powers are yanked out, the age retardant fades away. Why? Did you think we *kill* wizards who don't become Wizard-Lords?"

Idalia 6:

Explanatory Notes

"So, who was right?" Idalia asked, standing and stretching, the latest stack of dictation jumping up from her lap desk as she rose. The pages streamed out the door to join the growing pile in her sitting room down the corridor.

"What about?"

"Thaumacide, of course! Did Wizard-Lords kill potential rivals or didn't they?"

Zunvect's brow lowered. "Who said anything about rivals? They were dangers to society if left untrained, and even bigger dangers if turned loose without the moderating influence of institutional pressure. In answer to your question 'did we kill wizards?' the answer is: I don't know. Or, more properly, I don't remember." He absently twirled the length of the staff in his hand. "I'd recommend that you tune the fourth consecutive ward's eighth harmonic just a tiny bit higher. Yes, thank you." He said as Idalia knelt and made the adjustment. "I'm reconstructing this as I go along, you know. I'll only harm my own stability if I try to leap too far forward."

"Wonderful," Idalia said drily. "So much for being able to include explanatory notes to indicate what was a lie and what was the truth."

"It will all be cleared up eventually."

"Why would either of them lie?"

Zunvect's expression cleared and he smiled fondly. "Now *that* I remember a little better. They both had an idea of the kind of wizard I ought to be, and Aika was in two minds about it, at that.

Don't bother asking what their motives were; I'll get to that eventually. The explanation is better done when I've fully rebuilt my recollections. Anything else bothering you?"

Idalia brushed off her robe. She'd worn one with a simpler pattern that day, and she'd left off the medals. Her hair, too, wasn't as carefully styled. There didn't seem to be much point in being more than clean and neat. The Lupines didn't care, and Zunvect was preoccupied. She turned her gray eyes up to try to look into Zunvect's, but it was like trying to make eye contact with the surface of the sun. "A few clarifications."

"Get on with it," Zunvect sighed. "I do want to get back to the narrative, and progress with putting my life back together."

"Yes, and you're skipping over things. For instance, I can't believe you just stood there while a man was beaten up and dragged to his death." Idalia said primly.

"Bystander syndrome," Zunvect replied. "I might have taken a step, and Xetic might have told me there wasn't any point. Mainly, I was surprised. I kept expecting someone else to do something about it. I had yet to grow that carapace of arrogance that lets a Wizard-Lord walk calmly into any situation assuming they're the best person to handle it. In retrospect, there wasn't anything I *could* do. It was their city, their law. I caught my share of the priests dedicated to the demigod of assassins, the Chapel of Expedited Fate as they called themselves. They got away with murder often enough by making it look like natural causes, but whenever I caught one of those criminals hiding behind an ecclesiastical mandate, I – well, I almost remembered something out of order there, but now it's gone. Well, maybe we'll see it later."

"Fine, fine," Idalia said, resigned to his fitful memory. She noted the terms and events that he'd described. "I'm afraid to ask, but was the church of Valya really that ... erotically oriented?"

"No, no, no!" Zunvect said. "Oh, gracious me, look at it from *my* perspective. I was a sex-crazed, socially starved teenage boy! Xetic knew that, but since my attention was firmly fixed on the sexual angle, he used that against me to score some cheap points against a priesthood that – as Huruum said – often cared for the physical wellbeing of the entire community, regardless of the activity they were engaged in. Valya *was* the goddess of sex, and had become preeminent based on a mistake that Xetic made while on that idiotic anti-theocratic crusade of his. That's something else that will have to wait until we reach it, but rest assured that she and her demigods were not as narrowly focused as it seemed to a horny teenager and his prejudiced teacher. Oh, I'd better give you an example just so you don't think I'm making this up. Let me see."

Zunvect thought for a long time, dredging his memory for events that were in the subjective future of where he was rebuilding his mind from. "I've got it. Take it as read that Nenya was almost entirely focused on the health and wellbeing of plants, specifically those eaten and raised for agricultural purposes, but with some broader aspects since we didn't have a god of the forest. Huruum mostly cared about humans. That left animal health to Valya."

"I thought you said Nenya's priests were the ones blessing animals." Idalia replied.

"Oh!" Zunvect said. "I see where you got mixed up. Right, the delineation was like *this*. You remember that the priests in yellow had one of two colored sashes, and the ones in sky blue all had purple sashes. Well, the ones with purple sashes were Valya priests, and *they* were the ones blessing animals. Their counterparts were Nenya priests who were the ones *feeding* them. See the difference? Those in sky blue could technically either have purple or green, but it was terribly rare. Most Nenya priests cared for plants no matter what stage of the life cycle they were, but there were occasions where specialists in seed production and fruiting were needed, and they were Valya priests working with the reproductive cycles of plants. All clear?"

"Yes," Idalia said. "It sounds a bit complicated, which priests of who did what."

"Yes, that's why I didn't get too deep into it," Zunvect replied. "To be honest, Huruum was always the most confusing to me. God of life, so he wasn't *just* about healing, but the concept of life covers a lot of ground. Anyway, does that cover all your questions?"

"You mentioned a few different gods in the conversation with Gierna –"

"Later, Idalia. That's *definitely* something I'd rather talk about in the context of Xetic explaining it to me."

Zunvect 14:

Wizard Magic

I told Aika about our trip, leaving out the final conversation. I still wasn't sure how to ask Aika about the difference between her account of wizards being summarily executed and Xetic's incredulity at the idea. Thinking back to my conversation with him about governmental reform, I wasn't sure he'd ever acknowledged that such things happened, only that they were a bad idea. The only thing Aika seemed to find remotely interesting was my reaction when I teleported back to the tower. "Teleportation sickness shouldn't get *worse* with repeated trips." She said with concern. I'd been in bed for almost twelve hours sleeping off the nausea and headache. Xetic had been forced to lift me with magic and take me to my quarters himself. "Then again, your body has some very odd quirks."

"Thanks." I said flatly.

"Being unique is an advantage." Aika chided. "It means nobody will know what you might do next."

"Including me." I retorted, going back to my reading and hoping she'd drop the subject before it reminded her to remind Xetic to do that long overdue magical and physical *he* occasionally brought up and *I* always deflected. Aika had let me take a holiday from math, and I was making my way through natural science. It was almost as boring in some parts, but most of it was a refreshing change from endless equations. The science books had some of their own, of course, but they seemed trivially simple compared to what I'd been doing. Aika said that some science was just as hard, but we wouldn't reach it for a long time and most of it was so theoretical that it had little application in magic.

Aika spoke to Xetic during the next couple days, and I found that the unused laboratory space above my apartment had been filled with the accoutrements of scientific inquiry. It almost felt like magic, cranking a handle and watching the sparks fly out of the little metal spheres attached to wires, or pouring the contents of glass jars into bigger glass jars and noting down the results. I spent weeks trying out all the combinations I could find in the books Aika gave me. One day Xetic came down to the library to tell me he was going to take me to the top of the tower to drop a metal bead and an iron sphere as big as my head off the side.

"Don't tell me you don't want to try the gravity experiment?" Xetic said when I asked why. "Aika can't do it as well as I can." He sounded almost eager, as if he enjoyed showing off.

"I believe it, though." I said. "It makes sense."

"Pfah!" Xetic shook his head. "You don't *believe* in natural law, Zunvect. You *test* it!" The two metal balls jumped into the air and in an instant we were up on a stone platform with only the sky around us. The top of Xetic-Nal's tower had no railing or wall, a smooth stone disc that was as easy to fall from as taking a single step. I sank to my knees, feeling so ill that I could barely see. What little of my intellect that was able to break through was amused at the idea of what might happen if I threw up over the side. Another part interrupted to tell me that my knees would freeze soon if I didn't get up.

"Good grief. I'm so glad I don't have a stomach anymore. Come on," he hauled me to my feet and flooded my senses with clarity. "I can't teach you if you keep on falling over every time we go somewhere. Still, I can't really *teach* you if I don't *understand* you. Must be a real ego boost for a teenager, having someone as old as me admit he doesn't understand you."

I'd never been to the top of a Wizard-Lord's tower before, so I was too distracted by the view to pay attention to Xetic's needling and nattering. There was a *cloud* going by right next to us. The ground seemed so far away from almost nine kilometers up, and the trees so small. I'd never climbed anything taller than a hill at home – the only mountain nearby had Vectreon's tower on top so I wasn't keen on going there - and the highest I'd managed to make it in the tower so far by climbing was the forty-sixth floor, though I was making more progress every day. I'd make it as far as the personal journal repository soon. Aika had promised that if I could walk there, I could read whatever I liked. I assumed that the idea was that it would take me long enough to become that strong that I'd gain an appreciation for proper treatment. The only other possibility was that only people with strong hearts and legs were allowed to read primary sources. The archives directly above the library, she'd told me, were not closed for the books' safety, but for mine.

The view was making me dizzy and the wind was picking up, chilling me to the bone, so I stepped back. Xetic was waiting impatiently. "Yes, it's a nice view. One day you'll be able to go much higher. Come on." The balls floated in front of him and he took a confident step over the edge – showoff – and then let them fall. "How long have we got before they hit the ground?" He asked, suddenly turning towards me.

"Ummm..." It was terribly unfair for him to ask me to do the square root of six hundred in the space of a few seconds!

"Come on, before they hit the ground." Xetic said, tapping his foot on the stone and making an eerie, hollow sound.

"About twenty-four seconds!" I said hurriedly.

Xetic raised his hand and chopped downward, and the air parted. I didn't have time to think about what he'd done before he pulled me through, leaving us standing a few meters away from the base of the tower. The snow had mostly gone, but despite my calendar telling me we were in the first month of spring, the cold wasn't letting up very fast.

"Tunnels don't affect you badly." He said. "Good. Our test subjects should be arriving shortly."

The big iron ball hit the ground with a thud that embedded it in the not quite thawed ground. Xetic looked up, looked around, and then looked at me with a piercing stare. "All right, what happened to it?"

"I didn't do anything!" I protested.

"I'm not accusing you of somehow pickpocketing the sky or spiriting it away with magic. I'm asking what you think happened to our smaller ball."

I thought about it. "Wind resistance?" I hazarded.

"More like an updraft or a gust partway down." Xetic said. "Right! That didn't go quite as planned." He gestured and a gout of earth heralded the violent retrieval of the larger iron sphere. "Let's try that again, only this time we're making sure that the air doesn't get in our way." I followed him through the hole in the air back to the top of the tower and watched as he reached out a hand and conjured an iron sphere about a meter across. "That should do it." He threw them both off the top and we returned to our vantage point at the bottom of the tower.

This time the impact was felt as well as seen and heard. The ground shook as both spheres struck the ground at the same time, the larger one sending up a spray of earth. I was thrown from my feet, but of course Xetic just stood there as if nothing had happened. When I got up, the earth clods were all around us, but none were closer than a meter. Some fell in a ring pattern that told me that he'd stopped them. "That's why I didn't want to start with the big one." He said conversationally. "Still, we can manage a few observations from it." He strolled over to the crater the larger ball had made. "How much kinetic energy do you think that was?"

That was too much even for me. I could do a decent job of remembering a formula here and there but what he wanted to know would require me to either guess the mass of the ball or know the density of iron. I knew neither, so I answered. "Quite a lot. Sorry, sir, but calculating the mass of the ball is a bit much in this weather."

Xetic looked around, and then back at me. "It's cold?"

"Very, sir." I said drily.

"I really do miss feeling temperature sometimes." He started, and stared at me. "You're not wearing a coat! No wonder you're freezing."

"You never gave me one." I told him.

"Good grief, man, why didn't you ever mention it? We were out in that square a few weeks ago for hours – oh, I was heating the air so you were only half frozen by the walking around – but still you should have said something." I was impressed. I'd never seen Lord Xetic-Nal flustered into nattering before.

"So can I have a coat then?" I asked.

"Right, right." He gestured and a heavy black woolen coat that almost swept the ground appeared around me. It had large black buttons on the front and a wide lapel. "Speaking of that trip." Xetic said, looking at me sidelong as he prodded the upper half of the sphere embedded in the earth. "Were you able to observe anything … familiar?"

I frowned. This was an odd question and odd questions from Xetic deserved careful thought. "I'm not sure I understand the question." I said at length. "I'd never been in a city, but the people looked like people anywhere. Maybe not always the same *hue* I'm used to but –"

"Not the ethnic makeup!" Xetic said shortly. "I mean did you notice any spells being cast? Enchantments?"

"The walls were glowing amber." I hazarded. "So were the roads near the center, and the stones of the plaza itself."

"I see." Xetic nodded, digesting the information. "What about the churches and the ceremonies they performed? You can hear music. Could you hear anything special about *that* music?"

I took my time recalling what I could. "It was all so odd. I was watching their performances and rituals more than paying attention to the outer spectra. I did feel very strange when they chanted, like magic but very remote and ... not weird." I ended lamely.

"Even in the church of Drotaka?" He pressed. "You saw nothing of magic in there?"

"I was paying attention to the architecture." I said.

"Bumpkin." He muttered. "Rubbernecking the blasted decorations and not paying a single bit of attention to the really important matter – " he cut himself off with a sigh. "I shouldn't blame you," he said to me. "The principal intention was for you to see a bit of the world and you did. Next time, please do me a favor and have a discreet look at everyone and what kind of magic they're trailing around." I opened my mouth and he held up a hand. "Your eyes are natural, an anomaly. Their alarms and wards don't notice you because you're one hundred percent you when you do it. If any other magician tried to peer around in those spectra, they'd need a spell to do it. That's detectable. Anyway, we'd better be getting inside." He slashed his hand downwards, opening a new rip which seemed to suck air through it at the same time as a wash of heat rippled the air around it. With a gesture, the other tear leading to the roof of the tower disappeared.

We were in Xetic's study. I instinctively took my accustomed place in the guest chair on the door side of his desk. He remained standing and after a moment walked over to his window, staring out of it. A moment later the fireplace with its simple wooden carvings over the mantelpiece burst into a crackling blaze. Likely for my comfort after the session out in the winter cold. An absolutely gut-wrenching, sickening, revolting noise emanated from him. The old lich was running his teeth against each other and then grinding them occasionally to add a further point to whatever thought he was having. The sound is annoying enough when there is flesh to dampen it, but bare bone *resonates*. I was almost ready to ask him to stop when he turned around. "It's time. Really time. No teasing or slipping out of it. You'll need to continue your other studies, but you're ready to begin on magic. I only need to ask you a question." I braced myself for a mystical test or intellectual exercise. Perhaps a question that bound the hearer to answer their deepest thoughts. "Why haven't you used magic in my tower?"

As with many of my master's questions, I was blindsided. "You told me not to." I blurted, too excited by the idea of finally learning to be a wizard to consider my reply carefully.

"No I didn't. I *never* forbade you to use sorcerer's magic in my tower. It's admirable that you haven't. Fine restraint. Very impressive for a male of your age. Teenage boys almost never do anything as wise. Why?"

"You said sorcerer's magic didn't work right for wizards." I said.

"Not quite but I suppose you could have misconstrued it that way."

"There were other reasons." I said defensively. "A big one was that I wasn't starting magical education, so it seemed like practicing magic would not be appropriate. Also, what's the point in practicing sorcerer spells when wizard ones are better?"

"So just because of that you didn't cast any spells? Not a single bit of practice of the thing you spent years learning, which was your life until you came here? I'd have known if you did and you did not. That is perhaps the most interesting thing yet. I am amazed by your restraint."

I was convinced by this point he didn't believe me. The problem was that he couldn't think of a reason I'd lie to him. There was a very good reason I hadn't used magic. For one thing I really had been scared that he would disapprove. Since I wasn't learning magic yet, I was worried what he might say if I asked if I could use magic here and there just to keep in practice. The long hours of study had helped distract me from the yearning to feel the power flowing through me rather than around me, though all those enchantments were something of a comfort as well. Surrounded by magic, I hadn't really felt much of a craving in truth. The most important thing, however, was that I didn't want to draw attention to myself too much. Our discussions were one thing, but if I used magic, I might have reminded him that my magic was a bit different and that he had yet to study me up close. His casual references to my musical and visual talents made me think I'd been foolish to think that.

"Putting that issue aside," Xetic continued, "it is indeed the right moment for you to begin your magical studies. Our field trip wasn't enough to keep you from being antsy – don't deny it. It's understandable that the mental strain and isolation is likely becoming a distraction to your studies. Aika's been telling me you've been losing focus more often lately. The field trip may have even been the wrong thing to do since it reminded you that there's a world outside." He tapped his finger bone on the window. "I assume there's someone literate in your one-cow gathering of hovels. The sorcerer at least can read. I will provide you with a box, and him with its partner. Put a letter in the box, and it will be transported to the other box. I should have given you this earlier, but the psychological needs – well, you know how it is for me."

"I wish you'd stop saying things like that about my town." I grumbled, angrier than I was letting on but holding it in so he wouldn't retract his decision to have me learn real magic at last.

"The phrase 'I wish' is a surprisingly dangerous one." Xetic replied in his lecturer's voice. "I'd recommend not making a habit of using it. There are … entities out there which respond to 'I wish' rather literally, or which provide your desire and then take their payment whether you like it or not. The box will be in your sitting room by tomorrow and Aika will begin your training immediately. I'd say tomorrow morning, but then you wouldn't sleep for anticipation and then you'd be in even a worse frame of mind for the first lesson than you are now. You have achieved a milestone. You may ask a question." He said magnanimously.

I thought hard. I'd started writing my questions down in a notebook, but I didn't have it to hand. I asked one that had been bothering me for a long time – almost since I'd arrived. "Was your tower originally wide enough to reach those mounds out there?" I asked, pointing to the hills which had been arranged with geometric perfection to mark out precise forty-five degree angles around a circle with the tower in the center. "It was a mental exercise Aika suggested a few months ago." I said by way of explanation. "I'd ask her, but since it was one of those issues that deals with your past and those usually are restricted…" I trailed off. His eyes had turned into rotating, four-pointed stars. I'd never seen that expression before, and I quickly learned that it was cold fury.

"Did she? Did my librarian point out to a novice, a boy who hadn't even been with me for a year, that there were enough stones to stretch out that far? How very interesting." He said softly, coldly. I shrank back in my chair, now terrified he might lash out and reduce me to a pile of ash in the process. He mastered himself.

"Yes, that's a restricted topic. A very restricted one. Aika is over-stepping herself. The answer is yes, and the why of that answer is something you will only need to know if you come to a position where you have authority over Lady Xenos. This is one of those situations where knowing something even *is* is a danger. Please do not mention it to anyone else." He sighed. "That was a fiasco. Please try another – preferably not relating to my past – question."

"Well." I hesitated. "This sort of does, I'm afraid."

"Oh dear." Xetic sat down. "Well, out with it. You need to start with that kibitzer Aika and I need to get back to work."

"I – the calendar." I stammered. "I've revised my estimations regarding the first question you asked me." Xetic leaned forward, the sparkle that of curiosity and pleasure rather than anger now. "I think – I think that the question of a time-based discrepancy is more likely." I finished. "Am I close?"

"You're very close." Xetic purred. "And I think that the answer to *that* question should wait a little longer. Until you're *sure* of what you're observing." He sat back and the door opened behind me. With great relief, I left Xetic-Nal's study and ran down the stairs to begin my first wizarding lesson.

Excerpt from *Testimonies of Zunvect*, a manuscript of collected interviews and personal writings released in 8126 MR by Xetic-Nal, Appendix A[7], Transcript of Disciplinary Meeting between Lord Xetic-Nal and Lord Aika Chimamire no Kata (Ret. Dec.)

---

[7] Appendix A was obtained by serving a notice under the Lore Retention Act of 7840 to Lord Xetic-Nal via his librarian. Sidenote: She was giggling when she gave us this

XETIC: Why?

AIKA: I'm not going to clear my conscience just because you asked me an open-ended question, Lord Nal. Why what?

XETIC: Why did you assign Zunvect a critical thinking exercise which pointed him straight at the protective measures which once secured the Vedn Marbles?

AIKA: Don't use that razor tone with me. He asked why the number of stones was important and had already deduced that the stones exist as part of an unbroken chain back to the first three towers. He asked why and I gave him the most innocuous non-answer I could. If I'd told him that something that glaringly obvious was the result of a restricted topic, he'd get curious. You've now fired up that curiosity.

XETIC: Zunvect is much more obedient than you were. Almost suspiciously so. He will not pry.

AIKA: Lady Xenos will tell him if he ever meets her outside of your supervision. He's curious enough to go looking for her.

XETIC: By which time I hope he'll be ready for the answer. Regardless, it was not your place –

AIKA: My place is as his primary educator and instructor. Unless you would care to take over from here?

XETIC: Do not make me force this. You are immortal for as long as I say you are.

AIKA: So, you're throwing that in my face now? You own me so I have to toe the line! Don't tell me you're going to replace me. The idea is laughable. I'm not even sure you could if you wanted to. That stasis chamber isn't exactly yours to command anymore, is it? If I still had the full strength of my magic…

XETIC: If you had that, then Drotaka would eat you. Return to your work, Aika, and do not try to place yourself above me in his estimation. His life and career belong to me. You are in no place to try to scheme your way into influence again.

A long pause is observed in the transcription

XETIC: Thankfully.

Transcript ends

Idalia 7:

Adjustments

"Honestly, I'm glad I didn't live in your time." Idalia said, standing up and knuckling her back. "It sounds very complicated, and your education was far more difficult than it had to be."

"Yes, it's so much better now." Zunvect drawled. "Instead of eighty scheming Wizard-Lords bickering about who traded with whom and trying to peek at each others' research, you've got two hundred million Magi Firsts, and almost a billion Magi Seconds. All of them argue about the minute points of arcane science while your Senate tries to backstab each other on a daily basis. Not to mention the extraordinary level of specialization you've forced yourselves to endure." He smiled. "Then again, perhaps I'd trade this maddeningly fast paced world of yours for the mental augmentation spells you've developed. Sorry, I should say the standard function library. A million spells every mage can cast, requiring that only one person in the whole world knows how to do it in their mind. Gradient descent, inverse kinematics, and even that nasty probabilistic stuff all done for you. I don't know whether to be disgusted or envious."

Idalia used the pretext of checking his summoning circle to examine her captive god. As he'd told his story, the odd shapes on his staff had glowed in turn, climbing the length of it slowly. They were paused less than thirty centimeters up. He had a long way to go in his life, but it was progressing faster than it ought to. At the rate he was going, another few tellings and he'd be all the way to the top, where the polished metal spheres spun lazily, following a complex path that occasionally forced them to pass through each other. At those moments, his hand tensed just a tiny bit, the knuckles going white briefly and his mouth tightening, the words coming just a little bit harder to his lips. He was becoming less agitated, though she'd been forced to do all her editing and research in another room. She'd tried to bring some of her work in to help keep him company, but he refused to shut up. He'd start mumbling even when she told him to be quiet, talking to himself. Saying something about a person waking up but taking longer about it than they should. She assumed he was referring to himself. Gods were like that, using the third person.

He hadn't tried to escape, though. Zunvect the Sunlord seemed perfectly content to hover in his little slice of existence. Whatever bluster he might put up, he was terribly afraid of Xetic-Nal finding him again. His outburst earlier had proved to him that his old master was as potent as ever. Idalia was sure that Xetic was, in fact, much more powerful than he'd been in Zunvect's time. He'd killed gods in his first thousand years of post-life. It was, objectively, almost eleven thousand years later, and nobody knew how much longer subjectively for Lord Xetic-Nal. The retired dictator of the world was someone whom the magi were grateful they rarely had to interact with.

In fact, not counting Zunvect's taunt, Xetic-Nal had been left to his solitary pursuits for about fifteen hundred years. A millennium and a half since anyone had dared ask the Senate to authorize a question to be submitted to him. The last answer was still a controversial one, an answer which Idalia had made very good use of in bottling up her own god. She considered this. The way Zunvect talked, Xetic-Nal was an inveterate politician as well as all his other feats. A schemer. Could he have set all of this up over a thousand years in advance? Provided an answer to a question that rang down the centuries to inspire a talented, and underappreciated, demonologist to use that answer to capture and detain his last, most powerful apprentice? Idalia shivered. She wanted to *hear* the story, not become part of it.

"I'm going to get something to eat, and then we can continue." Idalia said. "Do you want anything?"

"A serving wench." Zunvect replied absently. Idalia glared at him. "Hey, I haven't had sex in the entire history of your civilization. Sorry if I've got it on the brain right now. I just finished telling you about my first encounter with a busty barmaid and the first time I got within a hundred meters of an erotic priesthood. Or is the word 'wench' not appropriate anymore? Vulgarity and inappropriate language evolves so quickly. Anyway, I don't need to eat, and I'd rather not find out just yet what happens when a god incarnate who cannot *dis-incarnate* tries ingesting food."

"Don't go away." Idalia teased, closing the door before Zunvect could find a retort.

Zunvect 15:

The Fade

I burst into the library, Aika's name on my lips before the door had even completely opened. She appeared at once and seemed as excited as I was to hear the news that I was to begin learning magic. "So soon?" She exclaimed. At my look of deep consternation, she smiled. "Pardon me, but I was a student of science and mathematics for more than two years before I started with magic. You'll have to continue that," she said sternly. "This is *not* going to be full time instruction until both I and Lord Nal are satisfied with your understanding of the mechanics not only of nature but of society as well. Come on, then. We'll have to start you off in an isolation room. I believe you know how to set one up." I grinned at her back as she floated past me, maintaining the polite fiction of needing to join me on the stairs rather than flitting directly through the ceilings and floors. It also meant that we could speak on the fifteen-story journey up. I was now well past the fiftieth floor – the start of the personal journal storage section – in my exercise regimen, so holding a conversation while ascending left me only a little breathless.

"Why the full isolation room?" I asked. "I've used magic before without causing anyone any harm."

"Sorcerer's stuff." Aika sniffed. "Even with your potential, that magic was made for those much weaker than yourself. The limitations of attempting to use their spells decreased your likelihood of losing control. The difference between accurately controlling the course of a creek with that of a river. Ultimately you may manage to send the same quantity of water somewhere, but it takes a lot longer and there isn't as much at any given time."

"Why do you call him Lord Nal?"

"That's what you ask me?" Aika looked at me as if my eyes had turned into cabbages. "You're about to return to being a practicing magician and you want to know why I call our master by his last name?"

"So Xetic is –"

"I should say that no one currently living knows in what order his name is or even what the hyphen stands in for since it was originally written in a different alphabet than our own. Styles of address change over time and that's why I call him Lord Nal. It's as simple as that, Zunvect. I thought you might have noticed that since you seem to enjoy reading old journals."

"They're more amusing than current academic texts." I retorted.

"Quite. Do you have any relevant questions or can we begin?" We'd reached the door.

"No, Aika." I said, trying to be deferential since she might take my facetiousness as carelessness and postpone the lesson. After the first few 'incidents' during my lessons in science, I'd learned that Aika could be flippant when discussing theory, but when it came time for practical lessons she was diligent, often pedantically so. I usually just breezed through lists that she went over item by item every single time.

"Good. You may enter first."

I had at first retreated often to the isolation room when I wanted time to think without being disturbed. The dull gray walls and absolute silence of the place had been ideal when I wrestled with particularly trying algorithms or questions of historical motive. Over time, however, I started to feel strange if I stayed for too long. Weak, almost feverish. The feeling passed almost as soon as I left or opened one of the floor ports to let in some magic, but since that negated the usefulness of it as a meditation room, I returned to working in either my suite or the library.

Aika stayed outside until I opened a port – I almost asked before I realized it was because as a magical construct she could not sustain herself if the ports were closed. When I was settled on the floor with my robe arranged as I wanted it, she began. It was mostly familiar material. The first steps of using magic were the same no matter what kind of magician you were. Wizards, however, had done what wizards did best and labeled everything about it. Instead of Ivan's vague descriptions of feelings and flows, Aika lectured from a book which went through things step by step.

"We'll start with a spell that should be harmless no matter what goes wrong." Aika said. She looked at me critically. "Almost, at any rate. The first thing – the very first thing – you must understand is that all energy is ultimately the same. It's fungible, Zunvect. Power is power, energy is energy. Heat, light, motion, electricity, magic. It's all about turning one thing into another. Is that clear?"

"Sort of." I said. "It's like how fire makes light which can make the air move?"

"A little. One type is rarely without another." Aika said. "What you're seeing is a byproduct, but you're understanding the very outermost edges of the concept. Byproduct like your body moving a great deal making heat."

"I've never lit up or started spitting sparks when I run." I laughed.

"You might be surprised there." Aika chided, eyes dancing. Then she was serious again. "Just remember that it's all translatable. There are six well documented ways of gathering magic, and you'll need to gather it before using a spell. Sorcerers cast out of magic pooled within them, which is slow to replenish. That is why thaumaturgy is tiring for them, and explains their overall weakness. We pull magic towards us and pool it outside. The further you can reach, the more powerful your spells can be. Because of this, our spells call out specifically how powerful they will be before they are cast. We modify the spell itself while sorcerers use the same spell every time but put more force behind it when they need it to do more."

"Our spells are more self-contained?"

"In a way, yes. Not to say you cannot control them with your will, just that you start off with a lot more defined, and then work from there. What's the most obvious question here?"

I grinned. "Aika, what happens when you try to cast a spell that calls for more than you can provide?"

"I'm glad you asked that," she replied, grinning back. "You'll notice most of our spells start with the same blocks. Those define what happens if something goes wrong, like if the spell is under-powered. With those blocks, it will either diminish on its own or give you a good poke to tell you it didn't cast at all. If you don't have those blocks, it depends on your mental state. It might fail, or start trying to gather from ambient sources. You, for example. The difference in scale will mean that if this happens, you die. Sustaining an underpowered spell by metabolic action alone is almost impossible, so it just kills you and *then* fizzles. So, don't rush the spell and never forget to have good error catching blocks to start off with. We'll start today by gathering some magic. You've done this a little bit, but since sorcerers look inward and we look outward, you've probably never gotten more magic than is immediately around you. With the floor port open to twenty-five percent you will be able to feel everything but won't be in danger of pulling too much of it toward you right from the start."

I closed my eyes and she described what to do verbatim from the book. There wasn't any need; I could feel what she meant immediately. She was cautioning me to start with the room, then the adjoining floors, the tower, and so on. I was young, strong, and as full of beans as a colt let out of the barn after a week. We have had thousands of years to explain how grasping magic feels. Wizards, sorcerers, magi, seers, symphonics, and even the warlocks of old have left us tablets, scrolls, and books of poetry, clinical deconstruction, and metaphor. I could repeat any of them and then move on, but I am, after all, the progenitor of modern magic – all right, Idalia, *a* progenitor – and until Lorn spread it around, my way was, as far I as I know, unique. To start with the clinical, it's a bit like proprioception. One is suddenly aware of *expansion*; of being much larger, and encompassing the space around oneself. To be aware of it as if the space inhabited is one's own body.

The room was easy. I was instantaneously aware of it and of striking a hard boundary. The walls were impermeable to magic, so I followed the flow, a feeling that was as if I'd gained a new sense somewhere between self-awareness, hearing, and sight with hints of touch as my mind half flew and half swam through the floor port. The tower was there, its shape starkly 'visible' to my expanded senses. Each stone was heavily enchanted, shining and humming to me in a tower-shaped framework. There were jarring, uncomfortable discontinuities: walls that were warded against magic, like the isolation rooms, and worrisome gaps where an entire space was 'missing'. Still I moved outward, feeling the difference between earth and sky, the whispering fuzz of trees, and the twinkle and spark of living things that could themselves touch magic. I moved outward, and downward. At first, I thought there was something wrong – I could not penetrate the earth. Then I realized that I could feel the earth around me but that there was a colossal discontinuity directly beneath. With effort, I could perceive it to be as wide as the ring of hills around the tower.

Pushing aside questions about the mysteries below, I kept going, kept feeling my way out. I was unpracticed in exploring my surroundings this way, and the nearest geological landmark I knew of was the mountain range thousands of kilometers to the south. Until I grew better at finding map references using these senses, I could only measure the distance I encompassed against the width of the tower's ring of hills. The going became difficult at about four times the width, and I started to pull magic to me as Aika had ordered. It was a big area to 'pull' at and the magic reacted sluggishly. I found it easier to induce a sort of torque, a joyous maelstrom of magic flowing around me and then with a firm and confident grasp towards me, turning the disc into a sort of cylinder. It swirled and spun, an enormous spout with me at the center. The room was heavy with the miasma of unused magic. I felt like I could almost breathe it in, a tangy sort of sharp smell like the aftermath of the worst thunderstorm you've ever been through. I needed to keep my eyes shut, though. In my expanded vision, the magic was a fog which hid the other end of the room and I'd get vertigo if I could both see and not see that far.

"I said directly towards you, not around and around!" Aika snapped. "You're supposed to be using the basic Form One. A direct siphon, Zunbvect. You were *not* instructed to form Mauldin's Whirlpool and attempt Form Four!"

I opened my eyes. "What? I was just seeing how far I could reach and then pulling the magic towards me."

"I can feel that." Aika said drily. "Lord Nal will want to explore the extent of your reach later. Right now we're just getting you used to how everything feels. So let Form Four go and just draw in a little of what you've already gotten and make it into a pool so we can try a spell."

"What's under the tower?"

"Eldritch mysteries now and we can save the really dangerous questions for later, Zunvect."

I should explain, Idalia, in case you or later readers aren't aware, that Mauldin's Whirlpool is now known as the Node Spiral in honor of my children. Yes, mine. We'll get to that much later. I learned later that it's not a very fast way of getting magic, and most find it so tricky to master that they never bother. The geometry is not intuitive since you're trying to induce a torque orthogonal to at least two dimensions without one interfering with the other. I never quite understood it in theory, but I always seemed to grasp the practical side quite well when doing it. Of course, that's because I look at the equations and then use a bit of common sense. The flows – you think of them as discrete vectors these days – are all of a length whether you're under the earth or up in the air, so there's no real gain in forming a sphere rather than a disc, which is what I do. Despite the headaches and confusion, it does afford the greatest overall magical draw once you can get it going. If one is engaged in fighting another wizard, it often ends up depriving them of magic if they are unable to create their own Whirlpool. The Form expands and draws in even those flows created by wizards using other Forms. Hence the belief of the magi that the Nodes command magic itself.

Making a pool is akin to forming your palms into a cup. It's really not necessary most of the time, especially if you're in the habit of drawing as much magic as I do. Aika was annoyed, so I remained obedient but eager. Xetic can bluster and protest about some insane supernatural calm all he wants, but I was as impatient and headstrong as any teenage boy in that moment. Aika had scolded me, but I'd almost forgotten already. She sensed this, and I sensed that she had, so I tried my best to swallow my hunger and project only mild enthusiasm to head off any lectures about safety and the dangers of being bold when using magic. She showed me the spell, and it was simple enough. The forms and words were similar to sorcerer magic, but the differences were such that I had to remain focused to keep from tripping myself up. I resisted a flourish as I conjured a fist-sized ball of soft white light which hovered between us.

"That block there," Aika indicated a section of the page, "is what tells the spell you can adjust it at will." She took me through making the light brighter and dimmer, and then changing colors and location. "You'll cast it several more times and I'll show you the various means to end a spell early or command it to stop when there's a clause for it – that block there in this case."

Aika had me not only practice premature ending, but also told me to use words alone to cast, focusing as I did on the *feel* of each motion that accompanied. Then we continued to replacing both words and gestures with the feeling and concept of each so that within two hours I was calling the globe of light in an instant with neither word or motion, though I felt an itch each time to do *something* even if just wave my arm a little. Despite my swift mastery, Aika's frown deepened with each casting until she looked positively thunderous. "Send most of the magic away." She commanded. I did so, puzzled as to what point she was about to make. "Pool the rest – no, tightly!" She corrected. "All in one place behind you so that there's only the flow to me and the pool for you. All right," she seemed to be holding her non-existent breath. "I'm going to turn out the lights and you're going to cast that spell one more time. Keep your eyes open this time!" She added shortly. "You must grow accustomed to doing so, and this spell does not require that much concentration." The ever-present illumination was extinguished, leaving us in the pitch black which was the norm for this room when the door and ports were closed, but which lifted the moment magic flowed to the light spells which were so much subtler than those I weaved that day.

"Cast!" She whispered. I resolutely kept my eyes open as I did so, and for a split second before the globe appeared, the room was thrown into stark relief, the shadows retreating with a harsh and sudden illumination, swiftly replaced with the softer glow of the light spell. Aika gasped. I never do that, by the way, Idalia. I don't gasp, I don't put my hand to my mouth, and I don't usually cry out. Never could grasp why anyone does that. Especially in this case when that someone had no functioning lungs. Aika's gasp was followed by a scream so loud that at first I didn't hear the words within. "Lord Nal!" She called, and I had to clap my hands to my ears. She looked ready to dive down the port and find him when the lich appeared in the room, sounding aggrieved.

"Good grief, woman, have some thought for the masonry! If you screech much louder you might disintegrate the joining and the whole place will tumble down. What could possibly be the matter-"

"Zunvect has Thaumic Saturation Syndrome." Aika told him, crossing her arms. "Is that important enough to disturb you?"

"Has your construct sprung a cognitive leak or are you finally succumbing to dementia?" Xetic replied. "Zunvect can't have TSS because no one under the age of *two hundred* can develop it."

"That's very nice," Aika grumbled. "I catch something you should have seen months ago and you accuse me of mental instability. Have a look for yourself if you don't believe me. I know the medical literature as well as you do. Of course, I'm just a librarian. How could I *possibly* diagnose the most common ..." Her voice trailed off as she disappeared in a huff.

That's when Xetic-Nal's continued insistence on a medical examination finally caught up to me. If I were a more egotistical – *even* more egotistical, thank you Idalia – man, I'd say that it was my evasions earlier that led to my case of the Fade being so acute. It wasn't; it was aggravated by going so long without diagnosis, but though that made the symptoms of my teleportation sickness worse, it had no effect on my lifespan. Nothing could affect the progression of TSS back then. It would be another thousand years or more before anyone found a way of slowing the tissue degradation and replacement. For those few in your audience who somehow don't know what the Fade is – or if your name for it has changed so much that it seems unrecognizable – Thaumic Saturation Syndrome is almost exactly what it says. An old wizard, who has steeped themselves in magic for centuries, begins to find that they cannot teleport without crippling debilitation. Their eyes and tongue glow, they become luminescent. Those are the early phases, as the softest parts are replaced with thaumic energy turned solid by their expectation of a whole and unchanged body.

A wizard can remain healthy and strong their entire lives, but the Fade is what they trade for it. The magic seeps in deeper, replacing muscle and even bone if the wizard is particularly strong of will, because as more of their body is converted it takes more mental effort to remain solid and intact. A wizard who dies of TSS simply *fades away*. Those with foresight allow it to happen in the end so that they can do so peacefully. Some lack that wisdom and try to hold on for as long as possible. Of course, a bad nightmare – or in some cases a particularly violent sneeze – can disrupt the concentration enough to make them lose their grip. Rather than a controlled evaporation, they discorporate hard, the energy bursting out all at once often with deadly results for anyone who is nearby. Only two types of wizard get the Fade before they're a hundred and fifty, and at the time I lived I was, as seems too often the case, unique. These days it's the bane of Nodes, who have to work almost from their first manifestation to keep themselves in one piece. When I was alive, it was absolutely unheard of. You can imagine Lord Xetic-Nal's … consternation on finding out he'd taken an apprentice who might not even survive long enough to finish his education. Not to mention my own … let's call my reaction consternation as well. So much less embarrassing than blubbering terror.

Excerpt from *Testimonies of Zunvect*, a manuscript of collected interviews and personal writings released in 8126 MR by Xetic-Nal, Appendix A, Transcript of Meeting between Lord Xetic-Nal and Lord Aika Chimamire no Kata (Ret. Dec.) regarding Zunvect's medical condition

AIKA: You agree then?

XETIC: Of course I agree. Pardon me if I was surprised that something that has never happened before has now occurred. Children are not supposed to get TSS. There's no precedent.

AIKA: How long does he have?

XETIC: A hundred years if–

AIKA: Bull.

XETIC: He'll be lucky to reach thirty. Thirty-five at most. I wasn't going to tell him that, though. How could I? I convinced him that it has a longer progression since he's a special case. This at least explains why he can't teleport. Having an appreciable quantity of tissue suddenly disappear would make any mortal ill. *Transcript records a pause.* This upsets everything. I'm never going to get this civilization off my hands.

AIKA: Yes, it must be so terrible when a young man dies and ruins all your good planning.

XETIC: Your sarcasm is noted. The strange thing is that the moment I found out, I checked the Chronoculum. He's still viable, Aika. Something about a black staff and a ham sandwich. Naturally I couldn't look closely.

AIKA: Naturally. Well since you're too busy trying to figure out how you're going to use a dying boy to further your goals, I'll go deal with said boy, who is probably in shock.

XETIC: Yes, good. Do that. I think I'll just have a jaunt across the water, Aika. It's terribly dangerous meddling where he might see, but I need to know how young Zunvect came to be what he is. Too many unanswered questions, Aika. Too many mysteries. The Chronoculum is adamant that someone with at least five thaumically induced conditions is going to alter the course of history. I smell another player, Aika. This could get interesting. It's been so long since I had an opponent.

AIKA: And they call me the heartless bitch.

Zunvect 16:

Physics and the Lantern

I wasn't in any shape to continue my studies that day or the day after. For once Aika came to my room and we spent hours in front of the fire talking about one thing or another. We laughed about how I felt that moaning to her about death was insensitive, and she took pity on my monotonous meal choices and convinced Xetic to add five more options to the enchanted kitchen table. I really didn't mind eating the same thing most days; in truth the table's ten choices were a wider variety than I got at home. Amazingly, even Xetic came to see me, and when I mentioned it to him, he said my village wasn't even worth calling a wide spot in the road since he wasn't sure there even was a road. I was feeling better and told him I'd walk out if he said that again, Fade or no Fade. That got more of a chuckle than I'd expected. He said that after everything that had happened he owed me a word and that word was Chronomancy. I wasn't to say the word where anyone living could hear it, but yes there was such a thing as time magic. He was evasive as to exactly what he could do, but I guessed after he left that at the very least traveling backwards was impossible. If he could do *that* then the paradox of the immortal time traveler had a solution and I could see none.

I lazed about for a week before growing so bored and restless that I took up my studies again. Writing letters using the box Xetic gave me didn't help because no one answered – I assumed something had gone wrong and found out later that week that Xetic had forgotten to send its mate to Ivan – so I decided that applying myself to learning everything I could was the only way to take my mind away from self-pity. If I was going to die sooner than other wizards, I was going to make up for it by achieving more in a century than they would in two and a half! At least, that's what I re-member thinking about it later on. In truth, I was likely just bored and looking to do *something* and the only thing left to do was study. I was only eighteen after all, and I didn't have a firm grasp on things like distracting myself.

Xetic himself arrived while I was still catching up on some natu-ral science reading. I had left it half-finished what seemed like years ago, when he had taken me outside for his demonstration of gravity. "I was having a think about you," he said. My blood turned to ice; that was not a phrase that sounded like it could end well. "The Fade is usually the result of using an enormous amount of magic. I thought maybe it had been triggered by your brief time as a sorcerer, but that's absurd. It's been historically proven that sorcery is not deadly to wizards. Maybe it could cause a blood pressure spike from how *slow* it is, but a boy like you wouldn't be affected by that. I wondered if maybe there was a good side to you having TSS. Maybe you have it because of uncommon strength. You never showed it before, but that was before you started really honing your mind. I think it's time we checked you on the ThaumBox." With that, my coat appeared next to me and a smooth ceramic cube fell into Xetic's outstretched hand. The moment I had my coat on, he opened the window and leapt out.

"I can't fly yet!" I called down to him.

"Crimeny, boy, don't you trust me to slow your fall?" He shouted up.

"No, Lord Xetic, I'm afraid I do not."

"Have it your own way." I ran down the stairs and then had to use all my strength to pull the door open and then close it, leaving me breathless. He was tapping his foot on the frozen earth when I reached him, a noise like pebbles falling down a rocky hill. "I ought to set you to some imaginative task that teaches you to trust me as your teacher, but then I remembered the time I got distracted by a butterfly I'd never seen and accidentally dropped a rather large brick on – well anyway, let's just say that I once had a friend who spent most of her life mistaken for a dwarf." As with many of Xetic's stranger reminiscences, I elected to remain silent and wait for him to move on to his next thought. "Now I think about it, I could have done this while I was waiting." He conjured a table to put the ThaumBox on, and then called up to Aika to give him the capacity testing scroll. A second later, a slim volume fell out of the tower and into Xetic's hand. He gave it to me. "This is the latest edition." He told me. "Much more reliable than what you're used to, with two to the power of eight times more resolution and eight times the maximum power ceiling. Why anyone *needs* to be able to test up to a capacity at least a hundred times greater than any human has ever achieved is a mystery to me." You're thinking something amazing is about to happen, but it isn't. "You just finished learning Standard Lantern One, so I suppose I shouldn't ask you to enchant your own ThaumBox yet. Always a tricky business, that. A bit like seeing how much upper body strength you possess by trying to armwrestle yourself."

I tried to follow the spell that Xetic cast as swiftly as I could now make a sphere of light, but its complexity in comparison to the lantern was like that of a pencil sketch to a mural. It was finished before I could grasp the first block, and he was waiting for me to begin. "Aika tells me that you instinctively used Mauldin's Whirlpool," he mused. "That's a good one to call on when trying to get a better result."

I took the hint and reached outward. In my youth I still wasted precious range on a spherical reach, encompassing the same distance that day that I had when doing my first introductory exercises with Aika. I allowed myself a few seconds to enjoy the expansion of my personal self, to really drink in what it meant to be enormous. Xetic was waiting and even in my half-meditative state I could feel the eternal flame of his gaze on me. I pushed hard in one direction, swirling the magic around and towards me. In theory, I could channel any magic I could feel. In practice, it was far better to concentrate it nearby. I waited for Mauldin's Whirlpool to bring in a large amount and then cast the spell from the book Xetic had helpfully suspended in the air in front of me. Big surprise, Idalia, I showed off. I cast it without moving my arms at all, earning a smirking glint from Xetic. When the words were out of my mouth, I felt the connection open between me and the ThaumBox. I had read about wizard magic; I knew what to feel for now. I had achieved blue when straining at my utmost with my two masters watching. This time it slid past green with almost no effort.

There was no need to hold my hands out. This wasn't sorcerer magic anymore. I wasn't a weakling only able to use what power my body could handle. I was a wizard, and one who had spent the better part of a year of my own subjective time engaged in the most demanding curriculum my time could offer. My mind was strong, and with an effort of will the ThaumBox was glowing purple and then cycled back to red.

"Any reason why you're taking it slow?" Xetic asked.

I grinned, "I was worried I might break the ThaumBox if I produced a surge that was too big." My grin widened with pride that the color only slipped a shade as I momentarily split my attention between talking to Xetic and the spell.

"Watch the snark, my boy. Magic can make you dangerously overconfident. Prolonged exposure is why I'm known throughout the world for my caustic observations. Get a move on. I haven't got all day."

I obliged and threw my entire mental strength at the ThaumBox. It swiftly turned yellow … yellowish-green. The second stage was much tougher than the first. I narrowed my eyes and glared at the ThaumBox. It turned a delicate sea green shade. I focused everything I had on it, my vision filled with the color, my every thought on seeing it move just a little more. It turned a very nice deep green and then the spell collapsed. I almost did too, rubbing the bridge of my nose and then massaging my eyeballs. It was the worst headache I'd had in my life and that includes the time I blasted myself backwards and knocked myself out with my first magical surge.

"You know what your mistake was?" Xetic said. I could hear the smugness in his voice.

"What?" I moaned.

"You let go of the Whirlpool there at the end. It's mostly self-supporting but you have to give it *some* attention." He was nice enough to lift me up and propel me through a hole in space back to his office. "You got so worked up at the end that you lost control of the magic. As Aika's no doubt taught you, that's why we include those protective blocks at the beginning of spells. If it hadn't stopped the spell when there wasn't enough magic to push through the connection, the backlash probably would have toasted you quite thoroughly. Here," he set me down in an arm chair that hadn't been there a second before and handed me a glass that hadn't been in his hand. I drank, and the room came into sharp focus as I nearly coughed my lungs out. "Well, you are supposed to sip, you uncultured goat. That stuff is two hundred and fifty proof."

Not knowing anything about liquor, I did not ask him how my drink came to be over one hundred percent alcohol. The answer would likely have brought back my headache. "I thought it was water," I gasped.

Xetic looked at the pale, yellow drink. "I'd hate to think whose water it was you were drinking if it looked like this. Water doesn't help when you've overdone it magically. That's why so many wizards are so consistently drunk. Well, there is another option of course, but I'm not allowed to hire concubines most places anymore.[8]"

I cannot express, Idalia, how sorry I was to learn what that word meant. As long as I remained ignorant, I wasn't tempted to research, or try to imagine, how it could have happened. "Green on scale two, though." I said, fishing for a compliment.

"Yes, you're coming along about as well as I'd expected." So much for a compliment. "Not that most magic is about who can hit the other harder, but it's always gratifying to know you can if you need to. While I have you here, we should discuss your course of study. The secular parts seem to be going well, but I'm always keen on trying out something new in thaumaturgical pedagogy. Aika's started you out on some nice sandbox stuff – oh wait, there's been a loss of couple weeks, hasn't there? Never mind, too early. We'll pick this up when she's taken you through a bit more." He stood up and I did the same. Then I fell down. "Ah, good. Starting in on that fine wizarding tradition of getting completely legless after pushing yourself too hard. Sit back and ..." I thought I was passing out, but instead I landed hard on my bed. Xetic had opened a portal under my butt. While I was there, I thought a mid-morning nap sounded like a very good idea.

Excerpt from *Testimonies of Zunvect*, a manuscript of collected interviews and personal writings released in 8126 MR by Xetic-Nal, Chapter 2, Report 4: Notes on Investigation into Unique Physiology of Apprentice [Name Redacted, assumed from description to be Zunvect's birth name]

---

[8] Too many jokes about 'boning' - Xetic

Magic's been sorting out some of it, but the boy's still far too levelheaded. One more outlier trait among many. It may alert either him or the conjectured second party, but I need to sort this out. It's worth the risk. Even if the fine and upstanding hovel dwellers tell their noble and somehow intellectually advanced scion of my visit, it will only look like I was taking an interest. I never do, but he doesn't know that.

Setting out. Will have to reign in my celebrated trenchant wit and droll observations so as to get the rock ranchers to talk as if they had average intelligence.

Speaking to father and brother. Trying not to amusingly deconstruct house boy lived in. I say house, more like result of hollowing out pile of sod. Just amusingly deconstructed house. Was told not sod, thatch. Haven't lived in squalor for centuries, no longer know what difference is. Lucky I didn't amusingly deconstruct literally. Probably would have made sound like breaking wind as it deflated.

Ho boy, that was an eye opener. The brother is halfway to being normal, but the boy's father is almost frightening, and I'm undead! I thought the boy was unnaturally calm, but all the father did was tug his forelock, call me 'your lordship' and answer every question as if I were being *polite*! The man would make the best butler in history if it weren't for the constant stream of folksy aphorisms. I think I could have juggled his pigs and he wouldn't have done more than ask me calmly and politely to put them down. He's not an imbecile, just ... extremely calm. Bones should not get the heebie-jeebies, but I got it from him! He said the house they were in was new – could have fooled me! – and had been rebuilt after the dragon attack. Apparently seeing the boy's stuffed cow being burned caused him to go berserk and somehow force a pain spell through dragon hide. It was a young dragon, but *still*. Ban on emotive casting aside, he probably wielded more power in that moment than he ever has since. I could imagine the whirling, painful emotions manifesting in a Form Four gathering. There's hope yet. Shame it was powering a spell built with Gramayre.

Gone into town. Mayor very proud of clock. Insisted on showing me clock and then giving me beer. He was proud of method of brewing beer. I said why not save time and go straight to the horse? Got a rise, but not near as much as ought. Children play, but not roughhouse or raise voice. Not even run away from skeleton with burning eye sockets. Scaring the willies out of me.

Observation: No one talks about boy's mother. I asked. They act like they didn't hear. I insist. They still don't hear me. I think I'll have to come back another time if I want to figure out *that* little conundrum.

Talked to vet sorcerer. No answers there. Not a local, so unaffected by whatever this is. Got sick of not finding answers so risked a quick probe down under town (wanting better term / found better term - 'dorp') square (wanting better term). *All right, now* some *of this makes sense.*

Filth and excrement. I forgot I gave the boy a Letterbox linked to the VS. If he finds out – oh, it's on my desk. Good. I can give it to the VS now and pretend the whole visit was about that, and I merely was taking an interest while doing so.

I settled back into my study routine and after two days of readings and questions under Aika's tutelage, she judged I was ready to go back to spending two hours a day learning magic. I remained restricted, however, to the isolation room. When I asked what possible harm I could do, I spent my entire morning reading lurid accounts of spells going wrong. Even the simplest test spells seemed to be prone to running rampant, demolishing laboratories in fascinating ways, and killing the wizard developing them. One stands out in my memory to this day – yes, other than the one that killed *me*, Idalia.

The Wizard-Lord Apontarvect – a geometrologist – was attempting to refine the means of connecting one place to another in the way that I had seen Lord Xetic after we'd stopped teleporting. Some quirk had led to him connecting two locations which were well defined in space, but not in the same frame of reference. Whether this had led to the discovery of an entirely new universe or just to a different usable coordinate system remained a mystery. The practical result for Lord Apontarvect was to open a four-meter circular aperture into hard vacuum. In the time it took for other Wizard-Lords to notice, Apontarvect, everything in his laboratory, most of the adjoining levels, and – what concerned the Wizard-Lords the most – an irreplaceable quantity of air had been sucked through. The matter was made more difficult by the fact that it had occurred inside a tower. They needed to not only breach the tower wall, which had amazingly held firm against the forces within, but also close the gate by force at a long distance to keep from being pulled through themselves. The disaster had been mitigated, however, by notes which had been stored much further down and detailed the spell itself. These had been the foundation of the first attempts – made within the relative safety of a sealed room that could be closed to magic within a few seconds by hand, or almost instantaneously by an emergency spell – to produce stable gateways to places much further than had ever been achieved before.

That was an entertaining morning, and one which convinced me that Aika was right. She usually was, but even after I outgrew my 'question everything' phase, I still insisted on evidence for most things. That's just common sense.

Do they go over the basics using just one spell these days? I think they must. The lantern is such a wonderful tool for teaching everything you need to know about handling a spell. That afternoon I went over the exercises again until I could gather and cast in seconds without moving or speaking. When I had proved my concentration to her, she taxed it further by having me cast more than one, first in series and then all at the same time. By the end of the week, I was changing their hue and intensity, again one at a time and then all at once. The following month taught me to change the properties of each one to something different, gaining in speed until I couldn't help but laugh at the complex patterns I ran them through. First a color would run the circuit around the room, then two and so on until I had every single lantern doing something different. A hundred different sets of properties all juggled in one mind. By the gods did I have a headache some nights, and there were days when Aika saw that I had pushed concentration too far and canceled our exercises for the day.

It was a matter of thinking about what I wanted, setting it to happen, and then pushing that to the back of my mind like a whispered mnemonic while I thought of something else. Done a hundred times over. I could never have done that with more than one *spell*. The difference would have been too great. With one spell, though, I could handle it, though only just. There were plenty of days when the pattern would turn to discordant flashes or entire lanterns would wink out entirely. Those were usually the days when Aika ended early, though I protested. She had all the time in the world, and I only had a hundred years or so, and nearly a fifth of that was already gone. Had I known that the number was closer to two thirds, I might have won more of those arguments.

"Very nice," Aika said two weeks later as I juggled spheres of light down in the library. I had only had one accident a month earlier, a very small explosion. One of the lanterns became unstable, and I got it far enough away that neither of us were hurt. Not that she could be hurt by an explosion, but I don't wish to be unkind by leaving her out. This demonstrated my responsibility, so she had finally trusted me to cast the most basic spell there was outside the isolation room, though whenever we did something new I still had to use one of the circles in my own lab. "You can move them, change them, and call them up in large numbers at will. Do you want to hear something depressing?"

"I still have many years left?" I hazarded.

"That goes without saying," she smiled. "No, what's depressing is that you almost never have to maintain a spell the way you're doing now. For the most part, you can define how many you want, their patterns, and almost any behavior in advance."

"Oh." I couldn't really think of much else to say.

"It's good to keep in practice, though. The one time you need to start adding spells *ad hoc* or maintaining multiple spells that need your full attention to continue functioning properly is when you'll be glad of the time spent learning how. Upstairs now, and I'll show you block manipulation."

Xetic's estimation of how long I'd spend on this 'sandbox' spell was already off by a factor of eight. Now it was going to be much longer before I learned everything I needed to know to rate learning a *second* spell. I complained of this to Aika as we walked up the stairs. "This is one of the few times when mixing one subject with another is a bad idea." Aika told me. "Much like in mathematics, there is a foundational aspect that cannot be neglected in favor of learning more advanced topics at the same time. Besides, block manip makes everything you've done up until now much easier, and it doesn't take nearly as much time to learn. Actually, about-face. You should read about it first before we do any practical demonstrations." This was the usual price of complaint to Aika. She viewed it as exposing ignorance, which was remedied by assigning further reading. I chose not to risk compounding the delay.

Idalia 8:

Misoverestimation

"When did you find out?" Idalia asked. "Find out that he'd lied to you?"

"Xetic-Nal seemed to have lied to me about just about everything in some way." Zunvect replied. "What specific lie are you asking me to skip ahead for?"

"That your case of the Fade was going to kill you at about the same time you died anyway, with five years before it was one hundred percent terminal." Idalia replied, stumbling back as a nimbus of white light surrounded Zunvect's body. "I mean, that's why you were so reckless, right? It didn't matter –"

"Do you mean to tell me that he killed me when I had less than *five years* to live?" Zunvect roared. "What the hells point was that then? That vindictive, petty, revolting *zombie!*" The conductive ink forming his prison was smoking and the spheres above his staff whirled so quickly they'd become invisible. "I should have learned this from the minds of the magi already, but I always assumed I knew more about my life than you did."

"He wrote about it," Idalia said in a small voice. "He said it wasn't too big a tragedy because you were at death's door anyway. That maybe it was the early effects that caused the accident." Worried that Zunvect might tear the room apart in his tantrum, she said, "Calm down! I thought you were a trained Wizard-Lord. You have less control over your emotions than *I* do."

"I *was* a Wizard-Lord." Zunvect said. "I'm a construct of Gramayre now; the rules are different."

Idalia decided to ignore that and stick to the matter at hand. "I take it most of that was a lie?"

"The parts about *how* I died, yes. I'm rifling through your collected lore now and it's all baseless conjecture if not outright fabrication. The sourcing on my particular case of the Fade is contemporary, though, not after the fact." Zunvect subsided, his personal luminescence fading away. "It makes a little sense, but that man was *cold*, Idalia. The Chronoculum must have told him that there was a tiny chance I'd ruin his grand design if I, or anyone who had been actively part of the Demolition, had *any* contact with it during the Rebuilding."

"What's a chronoculum?"

"We'll get to that soon enough." Zunvect said. "Well, not really, but before I finish my education. Let's just say that Lord Xetic-Nal only ever took advice from three places and he was two of them."

Zunvect 17:

Birthday

Excerpt from *Testimonies of Zunvect*, a manuscript of collected interviews and personal writings released in 8126 MR by Xetic-Nal, Chapter 2, Transcript 6: Transcript of Meeting between Lord Xetic-Nal and Lord Aika Chimamire no Kata (Ret. Dec.) regarding Zunvect's medical condition – thaumically induced

AIKA: You must have found something truly horrifying to keep you from needling me and Zunvect to hurry up. It's been positively delightful teaching him without your constant interference.

XETIC: I found something that'll wipe that grin right off your insubstantial face. Zunvect is the product of long term exposure to *at least* two malevolent rituals and an illegal ground enchantment. It's no wonder the boy's so messed up – he's got more residual yuck in him than anyone I've ever met and that goes for his entire town. It was enough to make me turn the Chronoculum around to find out if I could view the precise moments each casting occurred. So far it was easy enough to find the land enchantment, but the undesirable deities were around long enough that I'll probably never find out exactly what happened. Though it puts the Alok'derosh defensive chapel into a different dark. My best guess is that Zunvect's dorp –

AIKA: What's a dorp?

XETIC: It refers to the flyspeck on a map that Zunvect's home represents. Anyway, looks like it's at least a thousand years older than the rest of the territory. Built by Alok'derosh's friendly throat slitters and filled with altar fodder. They put a curse on the land that makes everyone who is born there docile and biddable so they'll walk right up to the blood trough and disembowel themselves if a cleric tells them to. That chapel must have been one of the last fallback positions and one I missed when I finally drove them below critical mass.

AIKA: That remains to this day a tasteless pun.

XETIC: It remains to this day a clever quip. Anyway, god stuff's notoriously tricky to read, so I don't know what else they did, but one thing it isn't is friendly. Probably mixed very badly with Zunvect's magical potential. The Wizard-Lord enchantment is a standard self-supporting infantry enhancement. The dorp's faithful followers must have been an irresistible recruiting ground for some war or other. On top of being cattle, they then became huge. Both spells are much weaker than they used to be, so Zunvect is merely an unusually large and unusually calm human, and the calm part seems to be breaking now that he's well away from the dorp and learning magic.

AIKA: In other words, you don't know why he's got the Fade, he's potentially the tool of an extinct evil god, and he might wake up one day with the fervent desire to run headlong into melee swinging a mace.

XETIC: You always see the bad side of things, don't you?

When letters had begun appearing in the Letterbox, I'd been ec-static. Finally, there was a way to communicate with my family and friends back home, the people I had grown up with and with whom I'd shared so much of my previous life. They were so *boring*! I tried, Idalia, I really did. These were my friends, my playmates, my teachers and mentors. I'd gotten drunk for the first and only time in Bowbringer's tavern. Ivan had witnessed me almost kill myself with misused magic more times than I like to recall. My *father* and my *brother*, Idalia. The people who I'd run into a dragon's maw to save. I thought I'd be happy to hear from them, but I wasn't.

Looking back, I see that something Aika said later on was right. Wizard-Lords seek out other Wizard-Lords as mates and lovers not because we're elitist or because Wizards are somehow more attrac-tive. It's because we understand one another. It doesn't matter who we were before our training because our education sets us apart and makes us something different. It's a bond greater than friendship and – as I learned that month – more than family in many ways. I love my father and brother, and my sister-in-law and niece. Even now when their graves are so old that the stones themselves have been ground to dust and the graveyard lost to time. I love them. Just don't make me try to tell them about my day.

Even when I'd been training with Ivan, I learned not to talk magic with the other townsfolk. At first, I'd felt secretive and mys-terious. Then Ivan had told me that I could tell them whatever I liked but it wouldn't matter. He was right. They were either bored, jealous, or unable to understand what I meant. Still, I'd had the dances and days in the woods with friends, and my work on the farm with my father and brother. No matter how much magic I did, I still spent more than half my waking hours beside Mikel and my dad hoeing, planting, or digging. Forgive the play on words, but it was a grounding experience and one that I lacked once I left. My letters to my family were met with one sentence answers and banal news of whether it had rained that week and when.

Ivan at least expressed interest, but was so painfully slow to understand a point that I swiftly restricted my correspondence to history and geography. History was especially interesting him, and it gave me someone to talk to who hadn't experienced half of it. Unlike Xetic and Aika, Ivan didn't have strong opinions on everything; it wasn't personal to him. It probably helped that he was by far the most comfortable with writing letters, the others not usually having anyone to send long letters to. Everyone they knew – apart from me – could be reached by walking a few miles. There weren't enough of us to push people out to seek their fortunes.

The saving grace was that since I was going at about half the outside world's speed, I could take twice as long to respond, and only had to deal with letters half as often as I normally would. At first I was disappointed, but after a couple letters back and forth to my father in which I learned the names of all the piglets and the current height of the turnips, I was relieved. It also saved me some embarrassment when it took me two weeks of my time to remember to congratulate Mikel on getting married, since it only seemed one week to them. It was spring outside the tower, and marrying season for the handful of girls in the town and the few boys lucky enough to get their attention. It was the first time in over a year of my own time that I'd given more than a passing thought to Dominka. Not to be too graphic, Idalia, but my teenage hormones were firmly fixed on the supernaturally arousing priests of Valya. I asked in one letter and learned that Dominka was still unmarried despite being almost twenty, an unheard-of situation in a town where women had the pick of at least five potential husbands. I'd wanted to be that lucky man less than a year ago as they'd reckon it. Now I hoped she wasn't waiting because it would get very awkward when I turned her down.

It was writing letters to my family which reminded me that it was almost my birthday. In the Tower, it was a double birthday since subjectively I'd have spent the better part of two years in study by the time the outside calendar made its way to the spring festival – when spring children were traditionally all celebrated at once. I mentioned it to Aika, which proved to be an embarrassing mistake.

"What a quaint and charming custom!" She said. I inwardly wished she didn't sound so sincere about it. "Of course you need to celebrate your birthday as you would at home. You're so young that I should have asked you ages ago so you could celebrate the eighteenth before it passed. Oh well, we'll just have to have twice the party."

Aika was bad enough, but I hadn't expected *Lord Xetic* to behave like – like – like an actual human being for once! "For thine birthday, I shall grant you a boon!" He said in that grandiose manner that meant he was mocking me by being pompous. "Name it, and it shall be so!"

I wasn't going to let him get away with it. "I seek knowledge!" I boomed back. "Grant me the answer to my question: What happened to Black Matthew?" It had been bothering me for ages that Matthew D'Angkou had entered Xetic's tower and never been seen again. I knew Xetic-Nal would never answer that question except in his own time, but he'd offered a boon in the traditional manner, so he had to answer.

"Cripes, kid, I was only joking!" Xetic said, eyes darting to either side. "You know it's much too early to be telling you what I did with that scumbag. You can't even light a torch with wizardry, much less understand the subtleties of –"

"You promised a boon." I said. "I named it."

"Name another one." He said. "Something not in the restricted library."

"Fine, I want … I want…" I thought about my life so far. Everything I really wanted was in the Tower. Of course, one day I'd leave. I said the first thing that came to me. "I want Aika when I leave."

"Done! Wait a minute, no!" Xetic was really flustered now. I couldn't believe it. I'd gone for outrageous and it had worked! Xetic-Nal was on the back foot conversationally for the first time in the two years I'd been his – on paper – pupil. It was like winning an argument with Ivan; I'd never really thought I'd do it. "That's not on, Zunvect. She's a lady with free will."

"Who happens to be stuck in your tower forever because, and I quote, 'the price of eternity is by its nature infinite, and so only payable with that selfsame eternal existence.' Last I heard, Aika was your indentured servant. Besides, aren't you the one who is always saying that the lives of mortals pass in but a single stroke on the clock that is your everlasting relative timeframe? I'm sure you'll barely miss her before I'm dead and she's back." I wasn't intending to win, nor – at the time – did I believe most of what I was saying. Slavery might have existed once, and from what I understand came into vogue again some centuries after I died, but owning people wasn't something I was ever familiar with. Aika was the only person I ever met who was owned body and soul by another intelligence, though Lord Xetic rarely exercised that authority beyond his ban on her going beyond the confines of the tower.

"You know what, go ahead!" He spluttered. "You can have the blasted witch on the day you get up the nerve to tell her about this. I look forward to her taking you apart, and then kicking your rear end clear across the ocean. She might just be angry enough to turn completely solid and apply the boot with more than words." He stalked off in a huff. I decided not to mention the exchange to Aika. When she'd been teasing me about my birthday, I saw her actually leave an impression on the chair she'd been sitting on, so I could believe that her anger at hearing me ask for her indenture to be temporarily given to me would be enough that she might be able to once again earn the moniker 'bloody shoulders.' A reference to how deeply she'd plunged her hands in when – as she once put it – 'getting to grips with power.' What was disturbing was that in an offhand moment she'd complained that she ought to have been 'bloody neck.' She felt that the time she'd started wading in had been a much more memorable moment. She hadn't repented out of guilt so much as zeitgeist.

Oh, she could moan up a storm about how she deserved eternal servitude without sensation or magic to comfort her, how her sins were many and she the most terrible wizard who ever lived. The thing was that when it came to particulars, she never admitted that anyone she'd tortured, killed, disemboweled, widowed, orphaned, beat, cursed, or otherwise mistreated in creative and malevolent ways hadn't in some way *deserved* it. She'd – is there an inverse fraction for 'decimate'? Anyway, she'd come nine tenths of the way towards genocide, and they'd all had it coming and everything she'd done had served a noble and necessary purpose. I loved and respected Aika, and she was a lovely woman when I knew her, but there's no getting around it. She was violently insane, barely acknowledged that non-wizards deserved to live, and had once possessed powers that had left her ploughing a bloody path across the pages of history. If Xetic-Nal had passed his office to her, she'd have been a one-woman extinction event. This is all by way of ex- plaining that while Xetic-Nal calling her a 'witch' was the deepest insult to a female magician and usually the prelude to a duel, it wasn't … entirely misapplied.

Getting back to the interesting bits – what? Idalia, no! I am *not* telling you about my birthday party. Yes, of course it was fun, but - Fine, fine. You're worse than I was at your age. Let's see, Aika's birthday surprise. One of my favorite memories as a matter of fact. Hasn't got anything to do with anything – and yes, me winning an argument with Xetic does, so hold your horses on that one – but I'll try to recall how the day went.

My sitting room being hung with banners, colorful wall hangings, and a giant cake in the middle on my sitting room table, combined with Aika shouting "Happy Birthday!" the moment I opened by bedroom door wasn't enough to even raise a flinch. I'd been expecting it, after all. Aika was disappointed. "Remember the time Xetic got all upset when he teleported right behind me and told me he needed to borrow *Foundation Listing* while I was pouring corrosive chemicals?" I asked. "I do, and I remember how you both told me I needed to be able to take jarring events in stride if I'm going to be a good Wizard-Lord." I was grumpy, but when Aika looked crestfallen I relented. "Thanks, Aika. I'd hug you if my arms didn't go through your body."

"I love you too, Zunvect." She said.

There was one big surprise, though, and that was that the streamers and cake were there at all. Aika couldn't have possibly done any of it since the only physical objects she could reliably manipulate were books. That meant Xetic-Nal himself had put up my birthday party decorations. I have to say that despite my differences with him, I'm a bit proud that I'm probably one of three people in the entire history of the last two social epochs to have a birthday thrown by that scheming blackguard. We hate each other, but it's a cordial hate born of close association. If he asked me to attend *his* birthday party, I would. I'd also be dumbfounded since as he told me that morning, "Don't expect to be attending mine anytime soon. I made it a point to forget those details so no one could hold it over me." I still don't know what that meant.

Not that I cared. It was my birthday celebration, I was one or two years older depending on your frame of reference, and because of the cake, I had just eaten chocolate for the first time. It's a common thing in your time Idalia, but a rarity in most of the world when I was alive. I'm not even sure I'd heard the word before studying in the tower, but I'd commented often enough during readings of various Wizard-Lords' personal journals that I wondered what all the fuss was about. I learned that day, and gained my first measure of the fanatical devotion to food that Xetic-Nal seemed to possess. In deference to my birthday, he made the ultimate sacrifice for me and chose not to be smug when he was once again proven right about something totally without moment. "Since you can't come up with a rational boon," he remarked, "I'll add hot cocoa to your kitchen table's menu." He then took a slice of cake, his sixth, so that he'd eaten more than half of my birthday cake. Do you know, Idalia, that I still hold that grudge almost as high as him murdering me? He doesn't even have a digestive tract! He doesn't even have a *tongue*!

Aika wasn't a complete ass like Xetic, so she noticed my disappointment as Xetic-Nal demolished my birthday cake. "Don't worry; I told him he'd do this, and he bet me he wouldn't. He can hide a lot of things about his past, but not that he was a colossal glutton with no self-control once he got started. It's why he usually only drinks tea now, and why he eats only once a century." She winked. "He lost, so now he has to give you a much bigger birthday cake. Right, Lord Nal." This she aimed at Xetic, whose eyes darted back and forth between his plate and the now empty cake platter.

"Hellfire and damnation, woman!" With an annoyed wave, the platter which had once held a chocolate iced angel food cake – it's amazing the details one remembers, Idalia – was replaced by a five-tier monster covered in hot icing, whipped cream, and with a different base on each tier. "I did it on purpose," he said to me in a stage whisper. "She said you'd be spoiled with anything bigger than the first one, so I got her to –"

"Moving on," Aika said primly, and then the room fell into an awkward silence. She hadn't had anything to steer to conversation to. "You're doing well with the lantern spell." She finally said.

"Well, that was worth interrupting me for," Lord Xetic groused. "I remember when rulers had their servants put in the stocks for that kind of thing."

"I remember when I had someone's ears –" Aika began nostalgically.

"Moving on!" Xetic said, cutting off one of Aika's nightmare inducing reminiscences. She'd started relaxing her rules about telling stories about her life. I'd been regretting pushing her to tell me them ever since. "Aika and I discussed more ... arcane rewards given your mostly good behavior up until now." I was never going to live down the chemical spill which was all his fault, nor the time I'd gotten names mixed up and come to one of his sporadic discussion periods with the wrong paper ready. "I made you this." He handed me an oddly simple stylus with no apparent means to fill the inkwell, and a nib far too small to dip. It had a card attached. *Your penmanship sucks – Xetic.* "Stand it on a page and you can dictate notes."

"Then I pointed out that it was more a present for him than you," Aika said, "and made him produce this." She pointed to a box wrapped up in ribbons. I opened it and pulled out a ceramic basin. "It's an enchanted foot bath." She explained. "Your exercise seems to be slowed by getting footsore by the eightieth floor. Put your feet in and it'll heal them."

"I thought that was a dumb idea, so I made this too." Xetic gave me a pointed black hat with gold thread along the wide brim. "It's a hat." He told me helpfully. "So you don't get the sun in your eyes when it's warm enough to walk around outside a bit."

Steeling myself, knowing exactly what was coming, I asked, "What does it do?"

"It's a hat!" He crowed happily. "What do you want, a piano concerto? Actually," he said, "it keeps you temperate no matter what the weather is. Oh, and it's a very nice hat."

"Thank you for all of it." I said to both of them.

The conversation moved on and it was midafternoon before Xetic-Nal finally brought things back to business. It's a time record I don't believe he's since broken, being relaxed for a whole six hours.

"I understand that you've just about finished up with the lantern." He said. "It's well past time we considered getting you on to block manipulation using something a bit more interesting. Traditionally, the four elements are what's taught next. It's a bit old fashioned, though. Tell me why."

I sighed.

"The four elements aren't foundational to matter or energy, not even close. They're just the four things that seemed like *good* things to form the basis of magic back before we understood mathematics, chemistry, and physics." I was surprised Xetic-Nal was bothering to quiz me on this. Opinions on classical elementalism were discussed constantly in literature. "You're going to ask for the arguments in favor now, which are that fire is a simple and common expression of heat which is itself a very easy energy type to begin with. Water, earth, and air are functional placeholders for the three common phases of matter, and so kinetic manipulation of them can be extended to kinetic manipulation of almost everything else."

"Smartass." Xetic said. "I favor the pro more than the con, but I'm old. Your call. Do you want to do that, modern energy conversion, defensive spells, or material reorganization?"

"Don't pick defense," Aika warned me. "I can categorically state that you're not ready for it."

"She hates it because I teach it personally." Xetic said.

I wasn't sure I was ready for daily instruction from Lord Xetic either. "Elementalism seems to teach the basics of both the production and motion of matter and energy, so I'll start there, please."

"Ah, the old wick lighting exercises," Aika smiled, "I loved those. So calming."

"In other news, I'll be zeroing out the temporal dilation soon," Xetic said. "We should equalize the flow in a week or two. I'm bringing us back into contemporary reality because it's past time for a few reports. I had to skip a couple last year to handle you joining us, so I'll do ten this year. It's boring but necessary. I think Xenos is on the roster this time around; that should be infuriating if not interesting. We'll start with the Wizard-Lords who don't have apprentices this year. Explain why."

"I haven't learned much magic, so I might feel inferior to them?" I guessed.

"Which will lead you or them to do something stupid." Xetic corrected. "You're a levelheaded boy, but most young wizards need to be amused or else they wander off. If you don't know anything that impresses them, they'll dismiss you and then make a nuisance of themselves in some way or other. The first sign that Aika was going to be an especially violent person was when some boy or other –"

"The oaf who eventually became Wizard-Lord Anjunvect." Aika supplied.

"Said that since she hadn't reached defensive wards or enchantments, she was boring and useless."

"So, I proved a fundamental point of wizardry to him." Aika said smugly, smiling at the memory. "The specific concept is that since most spells need a period of mental preparation, unless you know them extremely well, they're useless when someone is very nearby since the assailant can act much more swiftly. I illustrated this point by clouting him on the head with a chair leg."

"An object lesson which, while elegantly made, was made in the inelegant manner of bashing a man's brains out."

"I'd feel worse if I believed he'd had some."

Xetic left it at that and brought out the list of Wizard-Lords coming to see him that year. It was long because he had not taken care of most of the previous year's required interviews. I ought to explain that, Idalia. You may have worked out by now that Lord Xetic-Nal was ... a very hands-off kind of ruler. He held the title of First Wizard, in other words the Wizard-Lord who made and enforced the laws that governed all other Wizard-Lords. It was one of the many Foundations – we'll get to those in a little while – he administered. While we're at it, I'll have to remember to tell you why 'Wizard-Lord' is an abominable translation of the true term in my language.

So, the reports. Every Wizard-Lord was required to come when summoned and to tell Lord Xetic-Nal what they were doing. It was his responsibility to do the summoning and listen while they talked about whatever they'd done. With eighty Wizard-Lords, and Xetic having very little patience for meetings, the reports were made roughly once every ten years. They'd submit all their monographs and copies of notes for archiving, and then give him a *very* brief summary of progress made in magical research. He usually didn't care to hear about their personal lives, political problems, or wars as long as the war didn't spill over into territories officially at peace. In the rare event they'd strayed into a forbidden topic, they would be forced to turn over the originals as well as copies of notes and find something new to research. Those that administered Foundations would also report on anything directly impacting the Foundation.

The first Wizard-Lord on the list was Darrin Jones, lord of a territory to the northeast of the Crescent, at the southernmost end of the Crooklands. There were only nine towers along the Crooklands, including his and one of Xetic's. Thus, his territory was one of the fourteen which commanded ports on two major water bodies. The Halfin Sea, which separated the Crescent from Ismun, and the Droa Ocean, which ran almost unbroken across the north of Ry-Kel. You don't seem to use that name for our planet anymore, but that's what we called it. Sorry, I probably should have mentioned that before now, rather than just dropping the name in every so often.

Jones had been given a long reprieve on his report, but it was still good manners for notice to be given no less than two weeks before the day a summoned Wizard-Lord was to appear. That, combined with Xetic letting the dilation dissipate slowly, meant I had about a month before he came. After him, the Wizard-Lords would be arriving weekly. The dilation had never been and never was a problem for me since I never noticed it. Xetic had long ago built into that spell a dome of magic which simulated a twenty-four-hour day no matter what was happening outside. Weather could come in, of course, but the passage of the sun appeared the same no matter how fast it tracked the sky outside our bubble of altered time.

That month was spent learning about fire. Heat transfer, really. Heat transfer and the basics of block manipulation, which was one of the most important differences between wizardry and all other magical methods. Block manipulation, or UML, is how we created our spells back then. To be precise about it, block was the method and UML was the language the blocks were made up of, the vocabulary of things we knew how to do along with the syntax of how to put them together. The principle is simple, Idalia, and still used in magecraft. Your methods may sound like elves singing and incorporate far more of Gramayre than Xetic likes, but at the core you use wizardry and wizardry means block manipulation.

In my time, however, the blocks were much larger. Your understanding has increased so that you can alter your spells down to single words. In our time, we had to move them around in blocks. Sentences, paragraphs, sometimes entire pages and long gestures. It was just as modular, though. Once you knew what a block did, you could insert it anywhere in a spell. That was as much a danger as a convenience, as I learned in my first week of moving heat.

"Did you remember to bring a candle with you?" Aika asked as I entered the isolation room.

"Yes, Aika." I said, rolling my eyes. As if I would set myself the task of having to run all the way back to my lab to rummage through drawers. Candles weren't light sources in this paper-filled tower, but test equipment. I had not known that until I went searching for one and finally found it in with the Thaumboxes and reactive paper.

"Set it down and cast this with the wick as your target." She called up a book and reading stand from the library, and opened it to an early page. The spell was an easy one, which I mastered in a few minutes of sheer boredom. Lighting the candle, blowing it out, and lighting it again. "Why not learn some air as well?" I asked. "That way I don't have to keep leaning over to put it out."

"You'll get plenty of practice with kinetic energy once you've mastered heat. We're focusing here, Zunvect, but since you're bored it's good that we're going to use this spell for some block manipulation." Naturally we'd spent time in the library with me doing it without casting spells, but this was my first time moving the blocks for a spell I would cast. I was excited, Idalia. I was going to cast the first spell I had written, even if it was really just a simple edit everyone could make. Aika took her time deciding what to ask me to do. "Melt the wax without lighting the wick." She said. "And since we don't want to leave a lot of wax lying around on the isolation room floor, you'll have to run up and get a saucer to put that candlestick in." I had apparently been overeager.

I ran as fast as I could down to my lab, grabbed a bowl, and pelted up to the isolation room. It was only a couple floors, so I wasn't even winded as I hurriedly placed the candlestick in the bowl and returned to the book. It was shut. "This is an easy one, Zunvect, and you've memorized the spell for a highly focused heat transfer. I don't think you'll need to see the spell to make this change."

I raised my hands, saw Aika opening her mouth, and lowered them. Of course, I would have to tell her exactly what I intended to do before I did it. As fast as I could, I did my best to remember the swap needed. There was only one block that had to be changed: I had enough heat but needed to have it diffuse through the wax rather than focus all in the top of the wick. I explained my reasoning and then outlined the block transfer.

"Mostly correct, though had you tried to cast what you just described, you would have done so with an ambiguity which would have either meant melting the wax. Or you would have found yourself blasted backwards and probably cooked as an expanding fireball consumed all the air in this room – assuming it could find the fuel. You forgot that there is a syntactical difference between moving to a point target – the wick top – and a volumetric – the wax. You would have probably been all right since even UML pays some little attention to your desire, but if you were distracted – this is a spell you ought to be able to cast while holding a conversation - it might have gone either way. By attempting to do a heat transfer using a point target but specifying a volumetric space, the spell might have tried to run itself as occupying a theoretically infinite number of points within the volume and consumed as much magic as it could to achieve it. Obviously, you can't draw an infinite amount of magic, but since you're in the habit of building a pool much larger than you need to –" I was and remain most comfortable with the swirling Form Four which does indeed leave me magic to spare most of the time. "– there would have been enough heat generated to ignite a wick in hundreds if not thousands of locations within the small volume of the candle." She spread her arms dramatically. "Kaboom!"

It was a warning I had read several times and my enthusiasm waned at the simple but deadly mistake. Suitably castigated, I took more care in the other exercises and successfully melted the candle, followed by warming and cooling the room, and maintaining a small sphere of fire between my palms. This final exercise required me to run back to the laboratory to fetch some Dragon's Breath, because of course I'm not claiming I could sustain a visible flame without fuel. On our way back down to the library, Aika quizzed me. "What block is the most dangerous to change?"

"The first, because it specifies the safety parameters and keeps me from casting an infinite spell, or one that tries to draw on my own internal magical reservoir. Which I don't have because I'm not a sorcerer."

"What's the most important thing to remember when using energy based spells?"

"Energy is energy. All is fungible."

"What does that mean about the spell I showed you?"

I thought about that. "If all energy is ultimately the same, and block manipulation can change where it goes, the volume it inhabits, and even whether it is removed or added … there is only one energy spell?"

"Just so." Aika said, pleased. "We write down many different spells for this fireball or that levitation, but the blocks are all the same. Target, source, volume, type, and so on. The construction can be tricky, but the concept is the same overall and once you know the blocks that do something, there is no need to consult a spell for a specific application."

My progress was apparently swift and consistent enough that Aika became confident in my abilities. Rather than having me practice in the isolation room or in my own laboratory, I was allowed the freedom of the grounds. Such as they were. A circle of grass two kilometers across was at least a good place to run around in. My exercise in the tower of climbing up and down the seemingly endless stairs had kept me in decent shape, but with thighs like tree trunks and arms like string. My hopes of finding something to throw were dashed, however. Within the delineation of the five hills, there didn't seem to be anything larger than a pebble, at least to first glance. I remembered my overdramatic lesson in gravity and found that the iron balls were still sunk in the ground about ninety degrees around the tower from the door. Looking at them, I decided that even if I could dig them out, the smaller was about a hundred kilograms, much too heavy to throw around.

Being out in the warm sun unsupervised for the first time in years was exhilarating and strangely disorientating. I felt exposed at first with no walls, no barriers to freely running in any direction I pleased. I ran. I don't know for how long, but I just kept going around and outward until I was on one of the hills, looking down the far slope at the shadowed earth under the thick canopy of a forest that stretched to the horizon. I contemplated going into that wood to see what I might discover in a place where Wizard-Lords didn't hold sway. I knew my way around a forest. I could find paths and my way back when exploring.

It was the unfamiliar shape of the trees that turned me back. The leaves and bark which were different from those where I'd lived as a boy brought home how far I was from town. I was in what I'd have once considered exotic parts and anything could happen in exotic parts. There were probably fairies, or dragons or something. Never mind that I knew from my study that fairies didn't exist, and dragons lived high up or else in their own land far away. The shade of the trees made an impenetrable gloom not far in, and Xetic-Nal's dominion ended at that boundary. One thing I had never done was left Wizard-Lord territory, and the pounding in my chest told me that I wouldn't be doing it today.

Of course, I wasn't out there for the exercise or exploration. I was outside because it was a reward for demonstrating that I was not going to immolate anything. Well, nothing I didn't *mean* to. Fire spells sound dangerous, but they're safer than most as long as you don't get carried away. I amused myself by heating the air around me, fighting the wind that kept trying to take away my oasis. I couldn't figure out what block would make a spell last and I wasn't going to try to experiment with live testing blocks until one worked when I didn't have any precautions ready, so I couldn't keep the air warm while doing anything else. When simply warming air stopped being interesting, I tried cooling down sections of ground to see if they would frost if I did it quickly.

I mentioned Dragon's Breath just a moment ago; it's a good moment to explain that. I'd brought a canister of it with me when I went out because the best fire spells required it. There are legends of spells which require rare ingredients and burning powders. Most of the legends are probably due to the expensive tools required for enchantasy, but Dragon's Breath was the closest thing to a chemical reagent that wizards regularly used. As you well know, Idalia, flame without fuel isn't chemically possible. A lot of people see us throw great big gouts of fire and think that we're burning the air. Oxygen is, of course, a required ingredient, but most magicians will either just heat the air up until it *feels* like fire, and throw an illusory flame to give the appearance, or use something like Dragon's

Breath. The name you magi use for it is boring and unevocative, so I'll continue to call it Dragon's Breath.

Our name was not only descriptive of what it did – burn – but also it's origin. It was first discovered occurring naturally in dragons. Their digestive tracts include a process which converts some of the sugars they consume into a flammable gas, which is then absorbed and eventually stored in pressurized sacs near their mouths, so that when they use their natural heat emission trait, it ignites the gas which, being at high pressure, can jet up to fifty meters when the sacs are opened. We traded for a sample of their digestive fluids and over time we were able to cultivate the stock for all wizards' use. We were still studying the process when I was in Xetic's tower with mixed results. We were getting more yields, but we couldn't understand what was happening to cause it. With Dragon's Breath, it was possible to make laboratory equipment that could regulate the heat within vessels without needing a constantly renewing heat transfer spell. As we learned how to control and improve production, limited supplies were being sold to sorcerers and even non-magicians, who used it for cooking and entertainment.

What was the most fun, of course, was making shapes with it. Calling up ribbons of fire and swirling them around my head and far above, looping them and trying to draw figures and scenes before the trailing end took my lines away. I continually lengthened the spell until the sky was filled with a single line which made an ever-growing image. I'd say what I drew, Idalia, but the problem is I have no artistic talent so after failing to make stick men, I just made lots of curves, loops, and sweeps. Feeling daring, I tried to do with the fire spell what I'd done with the lantern and with some effort I was directing a pair of fiery streams across the sky, using my arms as guides to help differentiate them in my mind.

Then the meadow caught fire.

I'd lowered one arm too far and an arcing ribbon of flame had hit the grass, dry after a month of summer with no rain. In my defense, if I'd known how to move air, it would have been a lot easier to put out. Of course, if I'd kept a level head, I would have also realized that I could as easily remove as much heat as I could from the area on fire, and put it out like that. Instead, I ended the fire ribbon spells and tried to put the meadow out the way I'd been raised to. With my feet. It worked, and the wizard robes Xetic made for me were impervious to fire or soot, so the only thing left covered in ash, smelling like burning weeds, and slightly smoking was me. A bath sorted that out.

Well how was I supposed to know I'd left an ember burning? It was still daylight when I stopped, and I missed it in all the confusion. Magical sight sounds very useful, but it doesn't spot a few sparks in a bed of recently burning grass.

It's amazing how much you miss something once you get used to it. For most of my life, I'd considered roasted pork a luxury, and fruit pies something I got as a reward for doing good work for the widow Zarkov. I'd once told Lord Xetic-Nal that I didn't mind eating corn porridge and beans for every meal. Funny thing. I really *did* mind not having crispy duck, lace potatoes, and – most importantly – chocolate for the month it took Aika to forgive me for having to explain to Xetic why he'd noticed a strange light at the window and looked out to find half his property ablaze with smoke rising four hundred meters up the side of the tower. It was Xetic who controlled the food making table, but Aika who reminded him, after I'd demonstrated my contrition, that it was time for me to have my normal menu back. Despite his earlier assertion, you see, he was so obsessed with food that he couldn't imagine leaving me with so few choices. Whenever I'd given him a well-reasoned argument, he'd quietly added another entry in the book of things I could get from my kitchen table. I'd forgotten he did that until just now when I recall him temporarily taking away those marks of his approval. He wasn't as dreadful a landlord as he liked to say he was. At least when it came to the table he kept. Designed, rather.

All this led to me not being allowed to use magic outside either the isolation room or my lab's isolation rings until I'd demonstrated I could keep calm and use *magic* to solve problems. Aika was very dry about my stomping out a fire when, as she put it, "You're a gods-blasted wizard, you potato-grubbing, square-dancing, sheep-fornicating bumpkin! Your father must have had you breaking rocks with your head!" Suffice to say that I never quite got over having *Aika* turning her vocabulary of insults on me; I was used to Xetic's insults, but hers hurt the more for being unfamiliar. I'm not accustomed to making mistakes, and this one stung. Even then, I always tried to be careful. I admit to being both ashamed and sullen about the entire matter, especially since there wasn't time to *practice* Aika's safety procedures before Lord Darrin arrived, meaning that my first time meeting a living wizard would also be the first time I was being punished for thaumaturgical malfeasance. As I was reminded when I protested that it was a much stronger charge than I deserved – it was a death sentence in many cases – setting fire to a Wizard-Lord's tower without being in an active state of conflict was an illegal aggression under the laws. Illegal aggression *was* a capital crime. Being an apprentice and doing it to my master's tower was naturally not a crime at all, and it wasn't illegal aggression since it was a mistake, but it *would* have been malfeasance had I been a fully ranked Wizard-Lord. If I had made the mistake in another Wizard-Lord's tower, they would have been allowed to name the punishment. Letting your magic get out of control when the guest of another Wizard-Lord was *just not done*.

Zunvect 18:

Reports

The fateful day came when Lord Darrin Jones arrived at the tower. It wasn't all that important that I was meeting Lord Darrin, but for being the first living Wizard-Lord I'd be presented to, and the first time I'd be held to the strict codes of conduct and appearance befitting a meeting between Wizard-Lords. This meant the ceremonial robe. I gave you a brief description before, but that was the observations of a boy who had seen a lot in one day and was being chivvied along by a master who was in a hurry to do everything. The monstrosity which I hauled out and laid on my bed that morning deserves to be fully explored so you know how awkward it was to look at – and to wear.

When I'd first glanced at the robe, it was like nothing I'd ever seen. After standing under the forbidding heights of the Cathedral of Drotaka, I had something to compare it to. As that structure rose in ever more soaring layers, so did this robe. Whereas the cathedral often had curves which pointed inward as flying buttresses, this had ones which ran outward into points and wicked looking spikes up the sleeves, ending in a pair so large that they arced around the back and formed a not-quite-closed circle haloing my head. The spikes were crimson with black backing, as were the shoulder pads. I say shoulder pads, but later on I learned a much more appropriate term – decorative pauldron. They stuck out over twenty centimeters and were going to make walking through doors an exercise in caution. Skulls of either crimson or black marched along the sleeves and shoulder pads. I was surprised at this point that it didn't come with an enormous hat.

I've explained already the long, flaring satin sleeves, red high-lighted black with the little black skulls around the ends, as well as the diamond-shaped leather panel that went from my chest down to my thighs on the front and its twin on the back, each black with red outlines and a red skull emblazoned on them, making it difficult to tell front from back. The panels were attached to the main part of the robe, which was silk. There was also the heavier linen which fell from the shoulder pads in almost a cloak. I've always been big, and this robe made me look like a normal sized man with his head sticking out of a tent belonging to some blood-soaked deity of old. I was thankful that I was still young and stronger than most since otherwise my knees would have buckled under the weight of the thing.

As if that wasn't awful enough, Idalia, imagine a nineteen-or-so young man trying to figure out how to put something like that on. I'd glanced at when I was in my closet, but I'd never dared lift it down and wear it. Aika might come to see me at any moment and I couldn't have stood her laughing as I floundered my way through miles of silk and satin trying to find a way in – or out – of it. Find-ing a way to put it on was, in its way, a more stressful mental puz-zle than inverse composition. There didn't seem to be any buttons to undo, and lifting the whole thing up and trying to wriggle into it from below seemed destined to leave me tangled and possibly even asphyxiated if I didn't find a neck hole quickly.

Naturally, Idalia, you know what the problem was. This confec-tion wasn't *meant* to be put on. Wizard-Lords didn't dress in their finest with the haphazard method used by mere nobles. Not for them was the valet or maid who helps their charge into elaborate garments. No, a Wizard-Lord *conjures* themselves into a formal robe. It materializes around them and then is dismissed into its component parts when done with. With his usual lack of aware-ness, Xetic-Nal had provided me with a garment that was never supposed to hang in a closet, but instead appear and vanish at need.

Of course, I did eventually figure out a way to slither in from underneath by laying it down and trusting to luck and a few tries. The saving grace of something as covered in pleats and plates and the like is that no one can tell the difference between a wrinkle and an intentional crease. I'd given myself time, so while Xetic looked slightly put out by my arriving twenty minutes later than planned – and almost falling down the stairs negotiating them without being able to see my feet or reach the railing - there was another thirty left before Wizard-Lord Darrin was supposed to arrive. That time was spent with Lord Xetic telling me everything I already knew about the meeting and my place in it.

There was no danger of Lord Darrin arriving before he was due. It was traditional to give a convenient place for others to focus on when teleporting. Every tower had a location with a tile mosaic, a mural, or some other marker in the shape of the Wizard-Lord's banner. This was usually its own room – the teleportoire. Coming in through the front door was for local business or special occasions. Since visiting Wizard-Lords customarily arrived *inside* a tower, that meant that they had to wait for their host to momentarily dismiss the protections which kept anyone *else* from doing so at will. You can imagine the opportunities for slights and insults. Xetic opened the way at precisely the appointed time, and Lord Darrin appeared in the main hall – that was what the tile mosaic right inside the front door was for. Xetic's tower predated modern conveniences such as a teleportoire where a visitor might freshen up before 'officially' entering a Wizard-Lord's Tower. Wizards visiting Xetic arrived in the thick of things.

As I've mentioned, Wizard-Lords tend to remain youthful for their entire lives and Lord Darrin, at only one hundred and six, was no exception. He was not quite as tall as me, but tall for a normal person, of medium build with only a hint of eating a little too well. His merry green eyes seemed to sparkle beneath a mop of red hair, and his smile was impish as his bony, clever fingers drummed on his starched and embroidered robes. Far more sensible than mine, they were dark green with navy blue edging and embroidery – and oddly enough he also wore skulls as ornaments on his shoulders and chest. Like mine, however, they had thick shoulders with an actual cloak pinned at the front with a jade skull which matched his eyes.

We were stationed below Xetic's banner, the flame-eyed skull on black and red, with the door open behind us. Lord Darrin, being the inferior, would in most circumstances speak first, but this was technically a request for a meeting – not that anyone refused Xetic, but custom is about form, not substance. Darrin was a guest, so Xetic took a single step forward. "Welcome, Wizard-Lord Jones." He said. He wasn't fooling anyone; if I hadn't been there, he'd have dispensed with even the formalities around an informal meeting and gotten straight to business. "I recognize you as my guest. I promise safe conduct within my territory for as long as you remain so. I thank you for accepting my invitation to this meeting."

Jones bowed. "I greet you as my host, First Lord Xetic-Nal. I promise that I shall act as your guest and do no harm to anything in your territory. To accept your meeting was a joy – a joy I had no choice in." The last part in an undertone.

"This is my apprentice, Zunvect." Xetic said, indicating me.

It was my turn. I remained a step behind Xetic as was proper. "It is an honor to meet you, Wizard-Lord Darrin." I said. "I know that in our brief acquaintance, I shall learn much of what it means to be a Wizard-Lord."

"It is a pleasure to meet you, Zunvect. Indeed, I hope to teach you what I can in our brief acquaintance." That was the end of the strict formalities, so he got to have the first unconstrained word. "It's a tall order being the first *modern* Wizard-Lord you've met, my boy. Lord Xetic is the greatest wizard there is, but you'll be a wreck socially if you take all your cues from him." His was the third accent I'd heard in my life – counting my own and Aika's. I don't think of Xetic as having an accent; he just talked fast. Lord Darrin' was thicker, more musical and at first difficult to understand. He came from where the curve of the great bay of the Crescent met the jutting peninsula of the far northern Crooklands, and the difference between his north-central and my far-west was apparent just in the manner of his speech. Thank goodness that my territory was so recent that we all spoke Trade as our first language!

"My apprentices are known for blazing their own trail, Darrin," Xetic said with asperity. "Your own formal ways were pioneered by Aika."

"Aye, and thank the powers that Lord D'Angkou didn't live long enough to start his own trend, or else we might all be trading blood or something when we meet." The Lord of Angkoura replied amiably. "By the by, were you expecting me to try to shoot a crossbow at your apprentice or what? He looks like you've built a small fort around him! Is that a sleeve or a ladder hook or what?"

"You know the way to my study." Xetic said. It must have been a strain keeping from breaking protocol. It was improper to insult a magical inferior even if they started it. The strain was too much. "Perhaps I was concerned that your tongue might run too fast and strike him a glancing blow."

"That I do, that I do!" I wasn't sure what part of Xetic's statement he was agreeing to. We began our ascent and he turned to speak to me. I was behind him as was proper. "Tell me, do you ever get the urge to leap out a window living with him?" He asked me. "I can quite understand if you do. You seem a vigorous specimen, and if I hadn't been so distracted I'd have made a run to get you as my apprentice first."

"Are you trying to entice my apprentice away from me?" Xetic asked. "You're my guest, you know."

"Ah, I wouldn't be doing anything so impolite, no sir." Jones replied. "I was only seeing if the boy was happy being cooped up with only the unquiet dead for company. Besides, I thought you'd be happy for me to take the young man off your hands, Lord Xetic. You've told me often enough that even these two-hour meetings are a waste of your time, so the training of an apprentice for a vacant territory must be an inconvenience of the highest order. I'd be obliged for the practice, you see. I'll need to train my own replacement in a century or so, and I'd be glad for a first run."

"And if you turn out to like Zunvect and decide to make *him* your replacement and incidentally your assistant for a solid hundred and fifty years, even better." Xetic said coldly. "I have my reasons, Jones, and you can see how *unquiet* I can become if you persist on attempting to lure Zunvect away from my tutelage. He isn't for you, Jones. You wouldn't know what to do with him."

I didn't know what to make of this, but I didn't have time to think much on it since we'd arrived at Xetic's office. Naturally, Jones had levitated most of the way, Xetic had no lungs, and I spent my afternoons on the stairs, so none of us were out of breath. As they entered, Jones looked worried for the first time. "Are you sure you want your apprentice attending? I know it's traditional, but since I run the G2UML-N, I thought perhaps I was one of the rare exceptions to the rule."

Xetic looked briefly at me, and back to Jones. "True. He's not quite experienced enough for category N discussions. Especially after last week."

"Ah, and what is that?" Jones was sounding a little more jovial.

"Look out the window. That … desolation was his first session using pyromancy alone."

"Ah, well, we all make mistakes. It's youthful high spirits and that, and no harm as long as it was only grass, yaknow." Jones laughed as the door closed.

"I see you've met Joyful Jones, the Merry Necromancer." Aika said, rising through the stairs next to me.

"Isn't necromancy a banned topic of research?"

"For everyone but him and Lord Nal. You ought to read the registry more closely. Lord Jones administers one of the Foundations. In his case, the Foundation for Translation of Gramayre to UML – Necromancy, formerly the Post-Mortem Thaumaturgy Trust. He has a license to practice necromancy *and* Gramayre to try to find a way to make undead using pure Wizardry. So far he's had no more success than Xetic. His colors may be different, but he lives in the very same tower Matt used to, and does the same job. Lord Nal thought about revoking the license after Matt, but there wasn't much point. It wasn't the necromancy that corrupted Matt."

"I always thought of that kind of magic as dour and gloomy."

"You need a sense of humor to do what he does. That's what Jones says."

The door behind us opened a crack. "If you two are going to yammer and make a racket, you can wait in lab five. Don't let him touch anything he doesn't know what is!" The door slammed shut.

"Excellent." Aika said. "I assumed that if you had to stand there for hours on end that your robe might give you a hernia. You heard Lord Nal – let's get going. There should be enough time for you to go through all the precautions necessary when doing magic which may result in fires."

Lab five meant Xetic-Nal's own dedicated space, one of the facilities which had specialized thaumaturgical equipment specifically tailored to his needs. I was apprehensive about going in for the first time, and I wished that I was not under the cloud of having been recently disciplined for my clumsy use of magic. This wish – thankfully – was not granted.

Unlike every other time I had passed the topmost of the laboratories spanning floors eighteen through twenty-three inclusive, the door was both unlocked and unshielded. I hadn't looked the first time I'd been allowed a glimpse of one of the specialized labs, so I checked the doorknob on my way in. There was no bolt or mechanism, which shouldn't have surprised me. In Xetic-Nal's tower, the doors opened when he wanted them to open.

In layout, it was identical to my own. Slateboards at the front – and in his case lining the aisles as well. Instead of my shaky scrawl noting this or that about my assignments, however, his were covered in tightly packed, even sometimes minutely labeled diagrams which sometimes stretched up the three meters to the ceiling and across twenty or thirty meters of slate. They were almost entirely incomprehensible with only the smallest sections of mathematical notation familiar to me. The tables were jumbled with metal and glass tubes, flexible hoses, pipes jutting out and into the wall, and hundreds of knobs and dials. Two thirds of the tables' occupants were shaking, lit, or whirring. Almost all the isolation rings in the back were active and the air around them opaque, their warding set to a higher level than I had ever required. I glanced at the labels on the nearest stand of drawers and was surprised to understand what most of them were – chemical reagents and sizes of enchantable crystal along with rolls of wire. Like Lord Xetic himself, his lab was mostly incomprehensible and thoroughly mysterious while seeming like the most important and deep thing you ever saw.

Despite being surrounded by arcane bric-a-brac, my eye was drawn to the back wall which was draped in a map. I always did enjoy maps, even as a child, and this one was woven not just with mundane thread but with metallic as well, heavily and actively enchanted. It sparkled in a seemingly random pattern and several areas had a steady glow. Aika saw me looking at it. "You can tell

Lord Nal doesn't spend much time in his own study because he doesn't have one of those in it. An essential tool of a Wizard-Lord which you may have read about; most of us have – had – five or six depending on how many places we regularly spent time."

It wasn't just a map, but a MAP. A Magical Activity Perceptor. It was how Xetic had found me. A MAP plotted, in real time, every unshielded thaumaturgical event in the world, with the intensity of light tied to how much energy was released. Wizard-Lord towers sometimes, but rarely, showed up on a MAP. Towers were passive and acted as dissipators for the occupants, attenuating the signal and pushing most daily use below the threshold. If a tower blazed brightly on a MAP, it meant either the wards were down – bad – or the Wizard-Lord was using magic of stupendous power – very bad. The third option of a tower being directly assaulted by magic was an event so rare and catastrophic that it wasn't even contemplated most of the time. Whatever dispute Wizard-Lords had with each other, it was death to harm a tower. Wizard-Lords were tenants, not owners.

The sparkles, then, were sorcerers and perhaps dragons, elves, and other non-regulated magic users. What I didn't know was why there was a steady and continuous illumination across the northernmost and southernmost tips of my own home continent and why the Bowl had no emanations at all. Sensing that her lesson on fire safety would be better received after a lesson on thaumo-geography – and that I was less likely to poke a mechanism or hit something with my enormous robe if I was sitting still and looking at the MAP, she relented. "You should know well enough what's going on here." She pointed to the plains in the furthest north of Ismun. "That's the Singing City. All those sorcerers constantly spreading their magic around. As for the other end," she wrinkled her nose. "The En-cave – the unofficial nickname the Sky Vision gave itself. A terrible pun from even more terrible people. It's a high plateau – the Skyland – riddled with caves, and every cave has a Seer in it. In his infinite maturity, our Lord Nal has lowered himself to their level and calls them koan heads." This is an insult that in my mortal life I never understood, but I always let pass because I could at least tell it was an insult. "They've raised the level of background magic by constantly looking at the future as people give them obscene amounts of gold. We'll cover why they're useless leeches on society later in your education. For now, consider why being able to see the future is a mostly useless ability."

That left the Bowl – the ring of mountains across the sea to the west of my home and on the far east of Bomarie. Aika's answer was close to what I expected.

"That's where the elves made their final stand and continue to hold. Their magic is visible but only when they're in a hurry. They have some knack that we've never discovered that make it so when they cast spells, the emanations are sort of folded or curved in on themselves. We think they've developed some kind of manifold geometry that lets them redefine how magic flows, but it's just as likely that they have a ward that is itself warded so that both are invisible and make everything inside the boundary invisible as well. We also have trouble seeing under the ocean, which is why we cannot be sure whether the Aqueous are still alive. You," she rested her insubstantial finger partway through the MAP near where I grew up, "lit up like the sun for a few seconds."

She tapped the space contemplatively. "It was the final proof that Vectreon was dead. If he'd seen that, he might have wet himself but then he'd have done something about it, if only by complaining to us to deal with it." She turned to me. "If there is one single thing a Wizard-Lord *must* positively do, it is train their successor. Lord Nal was furious when he found out that Vectreon had not." She said, not quite a lie, but far enough from the truth to be misleading. "It's forgivable if one dies early, but Vectreon was over two hundred and fifty, and had always shown signs of recklessness. Leaving a tower empty of a Wizard-Lord means someone else must take on two apprentices. Territorial governments are disrupted during the period of training. Extremely irresponsible. Almost as irresponsible as using pyromancy without due caution." So the safety lesson began.

We were obliged to end without completing any exercises when we heard the door two levels above us open. The voices of Lord Xetic and Lord Darrin drifted down as they entered the stairway. I was ready when they passed and took my place behind Lord Darrin as he followed Xetic down. "- cannot see how you expect progress, First." He was saying as I took my place. "Transliteration is not feasible without some clues about how the process occurs." His brightness was turned to cloudy uncertainty, and his voice was grave.

"Your Foundation has had centuries to investigate." Xetic-Nal countered. "Your remit is not to expand Gramayre but translate the effects to Wizardry. Your current line of questioning is unproductive."

"I disagree. Surely if we cannot find a way to fit necromancy into the current framework, we should explore the art rather than continuing to try to shoehorn it into an incomplete scientific framework."

"I reject your appeal and that's the end of it." Xetic said.

Lord Darrin looked mutinous but fell silent. I saw him off without him speaking another word and before I even had a chance to ask, Xetic answered my question. "He thinks that by exploring the boundaries of necromancy he can work himself out of the puzzle that's been holding back his Foundation's progress since the day I sent the first Marque of Waiver to the first member of his little lineage."

"That seems perfectly reasonable." I said.

"It would be if I hadn't already tried it myself over three thousand years ago." Xetic replied mildly. "He of all people ought to know better than to go beyond the well-defined rites I provided to Angkoura's library when I first sanctioned a research necromancer. If the answer can only be found in proscribed necromancy, then it's best that we go without."

I was always surprised when the otherwise obsessively epistemophilic philomath said he didn't want to expand the sum of human knowledge, even if it meant making sure that what had been learned was kept secret. There were good reasons, and I would have agreed with them if Xetic had told me about them. He was in a sour mood, so I didn't ask, and he left me at the library to Aika's continued tutelage without further comment.

There is little that is more likely to induce terminal boredom than the presentations of an academic on their preferred topic when you yourself have no particular interest. Many who delve deeply are endowed with the ability to make even the most avid devourer of arcana yawn and wonder how much longer they'll have to listen to the droning and dry description. It is even worse when the presenter is only given the opportunity to discuss their life's work once every ten years, for fear that a misplaced word to the wrong colleague could see years of research wasted as the other person copies and then improves the tidbit in a way they had not considered. I will spare you from an account of the next four Wizard-Lords, who all arrived, were greeted, spoke to Xetic-Nal in my increasingly fidgety presence, and left without saying a word directly to me or in fact a word that was in any way interesting to me. I can only imagine how painful it would be for you, Idalia, if I were to relate their discussion of topics that are not only dry and tedious but now *out of date* as well.

It also helps that I have no distinct memory apart from staring into Xetic's fire and wondering if chronomancy could be achieved simply by funneling my boredom into magic. I believe that, at the time, I didn't even understand what most of them were talking about, being very early in my magical education. One of them might have been presenting his findings in how certain insects were able to stick to the wall, but lacking a demonstration of doing it himself, I cannot be sure.

Call me dense – Aika did – but it wasn't until then that a fact that was buried in the register of Wizard-Lords finally dawned on me. Could it be a coincidence that all the living Wizard-Lords I'd seen were men? I checked the register. There were only six women out of eighty-three living Wizard-Lords: Xenos (partly immortal and barely counting more than Aika now), Peacemaker (lineage based, so again an exception), Arrin, Linovitch, Terrengivect, and Katzuvect. When I was quite sure, I asked Aika why.

"A shade less than two years here and you just now observed this trend?" She asked. "It's your fault, you know. Men in general, that is. I've tried to convince Lord Nal to do something about it, but he's balked at going further than ending that asinine rumor that sprang up when Fyudin published their supposed 'research.'"

"Was their conclusion that there was some reason *not* to train female Wizard-Lords?" I asked.

"Yes. Fyudin claimed that the menstrual cycle induced instability in magic which could in extremis trigger a Cascade Reality Breach, and that women in general were not suited to magic because of those instabilities. All of this happened shortly before I was trained, and I never found out about it until I came back to be librarian here. Lord Nal executed Fyudin for actions which threatened the foundation of human civilization but by then the damage was done. Men stopped taking girls as apprentices – there were plenty who already felt awkward doing so and Fyudin's paper made that much worse – and even women briefly found themselves pressured to recruit boys rather than girls. This disrupted the flow of female apprentices and within a generation we were in the situation you see now."

Aika looked at the register of Wizard-Lords like she could send her hatred backwards in time and kill Fyudin before he published his infamous paper, *On the Feminine Cylce and its Effects on Grammatic Contamination of UML-Based Thaumaturgy*. The putz had been so keen to publish something controversial that he hadn't even bothered to check if the paper's title had been spelled correctly.

"The result of his foolishness is why the Peacemaker lineage is so politically powerful. Bella Peacemaker's diplomacy is bolstered by the fact that she's willing to fulfil the romantic and sexual needs of an almost exclusively male oligarchy. Most of them consider non-wizards to be beneath them, but they'll only trust Peacemaker among the female Wizard-Lords because she is bound never to act against the interests of those who she represents. If she and her predecessors weren't oathbound to only use the Peacemaker powers to induce love and fellowship, they would have by now implanted suggestions in hundreds of Wizard-Lords. A thousand years of *that* would have fixed the gender imbalance. Or not, since it might have weakened their position. The Peacemaker psychology is an odd one."

"I'll make sure and try to find a woman when my time has come." I said. That seemed to depress Aika, who shook her head and floated away. I didn't know then, of course, that I was only going to leave Xetic's tower when it was absolutely assured I wouldn't have enough time to train a successor. I put one over on Xetic *there*, but that's for later. We'll visit Peacemaker soon since she's the Wizard-Lord I met *after* Xenos, who was next on Xetic-Nal's calendar.

Excerpt from *Them* by Lord Xetic-Nal, 28th ed. (3645 [XR]), Introduction

You know about the wizards and the people we rule. Let's now get down to the details of the most important thing we do; protecting humanity. There are a depressing number of things that will likely attack you, negotiate with you, or get in your way. The Intendant Races are just the tip of that unpleasant spear. During your tenure, you will likely have to do short term deals with dragons and elves, sign binding contracts with dwarves, and be afraid of what might one day burst out from the depths of the ocean and eat all your ships if you have any. Your towns will be accosted by trolls and your cities overrun by therianthropes. The dead will rise from their graves and you'll have to bury them again. If you're *very* unlucky, you'll meet a Thul. If you're *too* lucky, you'll meet a unicorn. The Seers will predict your death and the Singers will steal your sorcerers. We live in a dangerous world and in the following chapters you'll find out just *how* dangerous. As you read on, remember this: Yes, it's too late to give up becoming a Wizard-Lord, so stop sniveling and keep calm. It could be worse; you might be a priest!

Zunvect 19:

Xenos

Two major events came before it was time to get the report from Lady Xenos. Oh, maybe I should add a quick note on translation since I just related my conversation on sex balance. The term 'Wizard-Lord' is a very problematic one, as it is not as close to what I'd like to convey in terms of a translation. The 'wizard' part is fine, it's the 'lord' that is an issue. For whatever odd reason, your language is a bit low on gender neutral descriptors that are close enough to the word we used. The connotations are guardian, ambassador, ruler, judge, and scholar. 'Lord' communicates an air of aristocracy that is at least associated with the ruler and scholar segments while also conceivably having diplomatic and judicial aspects. However, our word was gender neutral, probably invented by Xetic and added to the lexicon for his purpose. I haven't figured out why it didn't survive. You can probably guess by now from all the names – Zunvect, Vectar, Vectreon, Katzuvect, et cetera – that the word is 'vect.' What? Yes, maybe I was a little insecure, Idalia. I wasn't raised to be an autocrat. So yes, my regial name translates to 'Sunlord.' Not subtle, but I think the differences in our magical languages show that I didn't live in a subtle time. And yes, you think Vektar is spelled with a 'k.' Vektar thought so too.

Getting back to the two things that happened, the first was that I finished my penance and remedial safety lectures, yay me. When Aika pronounced me once again fit to use magic without supervision, she insisted that I go outside and play with ribbons of fire again. I was afraid, which was exactly her point. "Magic brings the greatest responsibility with it, so you have to have fun when you can. You also cannot afford overcaution because you made a mistake. Go out, have fun, do something reckless but with the knowledge, skill, and experience to be confident about it. A Wizard-Lord who has fallen to meekness is useless and weak. Magic is yours to command, so do with it as you will!"

This also led to going on to the other elements, but I'd only just begun throwing rocks around and making dirt mounds when Xetic called me to his study. This is happening number two if you're keeping track. I was to meet Lady Xenos, and there were things I needed to know before entering her presence.

"You've read history and analysis, but it's time you got some solid advice and perspective from someone who was there and knows the principals personally." He said. The study grew dark. I looked to the windows; the curtains were drawn. The fire had also banked. Xetic-Nal's eyes were the brightest thing in the room. "There have been seven intelligent species confirmed to have lived on this world. That's if you count the Uidrana as having *lived* in the way we do. Six remain." He held up an ivory hand. "I know. You are aware of five. The sixth does not figure into our plans, our scholarly work, or our awareness except in very rare cases so you may have even read that they do not exist. To keep your attention, I will speak of them last. We can entirely dispense with humans since you will spend most of your life becoming familiar with the habits and quirks of our neighbors and friends. That leaves the Intendant Races."

A gangly humanoid with webbed hands and feet, a crest running from the crown of their head down their back to a stubby fin between their legs, and wide blank eyes appeared between us, semi-transparent and slowly revolving. I recognized the three-dimensional rendering of the classical illustration of an Aqueous. "Retreated to the depths of the ocean, I hope." Xetic commented. "Of no importance anymore, and I'm the last witness to them having ever lived. There are two possibilities for their continued absence. Either they chose to leave the surface waters to others when the Uidrana left, or they were all killed by some horrible unknown force that lives at the bottom of the ocean. I'm an optimist so I choose the first option."

"You're a pragmatist, sir." I said. "If they were all killed by some horrible deep sea menace, what would we do about it?"

"As you've surmised, nothing." Xetic said. "Let whatever it is live down there, and we'll stay up here without bothering it. Moving on."

The next image was heart-stoppingly familiar. A winged reptile in a pose of stooping for the kill. Wickedly sharp teeth filled a maw that opened and fire filled the air in front of it. A dragon. "Unique amongst the Intendant Races in that it is not a modified human." Xetic continued. "Don't look so surprised, kid. Look up the word 'fossil' some time and read all the fascinating theories as to why there are no fossilized elves. Last time I had extensive communication with dragons, they liked to keep to themselves. They signpost their borders clearly, and it's a traveler's own fault if they walk across and get eaten. They're easy enough as neighbors, except that their young are allowed to hunt as they please. Dragons have an interesting cultural belief that a dragon isn't a dragon until they can pass a series of tests of intellect and wit, and so a young dragon is not bound by their laws. On the other side of that, it also means that many youths do not make it to the age of awakening to intelligence because they get killed by lucky predators, mishaps, and pissed off young *wizards*." I could almost hear a smile in his tone. "Negotiations with them are almost always about borders and airspace. Their magic is incompatible with ours, but much more complicated. If a dragon says they can do something, they can. They also adapt very quickly to their surroundings, so if you suspect a dragon might be around, you'll need a sharp eye to catch it. You will likely never speak to the same dragon twice because they have a habit of gorging themselves and then settling down for a few years to 'think.' They never reveal what they're thinking about. *I think they're just lazy.*"

The image of the dragon was changed to a humanoid again. This one had thick, short limbs, a wide torso, and an enormous beard which took up the entire face except for a pair of pale circular eyes covered in thick goggles. A dwarf. One thing I did know was that the beard wasn't hair. Dwarves had a thick mesh of fibers covering their face, which filtered out particles and purified whatever the dwarf was breathing. In an environment full of poisonous pockets and rocks that dissolved into killer fogs, regular nose hairs weren't enough. Dwarves, thus, have no visible nose or mouth, and communicated with outsiders using hand signs and the written word. Wizards believed that their language had a sound component, but was either inaudible or incomprehensible to non-dwarves. Their mouths are sealed except when eating, which is always done privately.

"Everything below three meters belongs to dwarves." Xetic said. "Dig your cellar too deep and you have to pay them rent. This means that all metals and precious stones are bought from a dwarf market. Lucky for us and for them, what's common up here is rare underground and vice versa. You can usually get very good deals on iron, copper, and the like by trading food. I don't know what they eat when there aren't any humans around but apparently, it's not appetizing. Anything more exotic will be expensive, but again not as much as you might think. Relations with them are strictly contractual. You hold up your side and they'll do theirs. Try to swindle a dwarf, and they'll make your life miserable by undermining all your buildings. Remember that to them the letter and spirit of a bargain are equally important, so trying to be clever about wording is an invitation to have your tower turned sideways. There's nothing you can do about it, either, because they're not just immune to magic. They stop it from working in a very wide area around their bodies, and they have a metal that blocks it out as well. That's one of the less useful exotic metals they produce."

Xetic's eyes sparkled and the lights turned to spiky points when the image became a spindly humanoid with long limbs and wide, liquid eyes. The elf's fingers were half again as long as a human's, with an extra knuckle joint. The bare feet looked capable of grasping, and they were occasionally pictured hanging on to trees or cliff faces. "Elves." Xetic said with disgust. "The most annoying thing in the world is an elf who thinks they have a good argument to present, and almost every elf believes they do. When it comes to border disputes, you will spend most of your time referring these assholes to Lady Xenos, and having to defend yourself in arbitration. They are insufferably arrogant and have a religious conviction that human magic is irreparably harming the environment. The Uidrana drilled that into them, along with a similar belief about their own magic. That's the only redeeming trait about them – they're advanced but terrified to wield the power the Uidrana left them."

I could read the predatory glee in his eyes. "I am proud to be the personal nemesis of their entire useless 'protectorate of earth.' As if the ground and trees and grass need protection. Elves constantly have grievances and will tell you about them at length. My advice is to tell them to shut up before they start talking, and to ignore any advice an elf gives you. The only thing worse than an elf is a prophet. At least elves have some conviction, even if it is based on the lunatic instructions given to them by the Uidrana back when we humans were marginalized and treated like children who would hurt ourselves if left to our own devices. Oh well, I may as well tell you what little I know about them too."

The illusion lost most of its detail. It became a towering mass of vaguely human shaped fog, totally indistinct below the shoulders that were topped with a spherical, luminous orb. "That's what they looked like. Or what they showed to us. They spoke as if there was one, but I know there were more. To give you a sense of perspective, I worked very hard in many arenas and in many ways to slowly and laboriously unravel gods one by one when I found them to be detrimental to the welfare of humanity. A single Uidrana could have swept them all – except Hylentor – aside without effort. I don't know where they came from, where they went, or what they wanted. They seemed confused as well. Sometimes they were conservationists. Then they'd suddenly tear up hundreds of kilometers of prarie or forest, replacing it with entirely different ecologies and climates. They set up the Intendant races to deal with the minutiae. I was a young man when they took off to parts unknown, and it wasn't for another three thousand years or so that I even got an inkling of how they left. *What* they left was a power vacuum, and I did my best to fill every nook and cranny of it while I could. The elves have not taken my opportunism well. Oh no they haven't."

He was sounding self-satisfied again. The more worked up Xetic-Nal got about elves, the more he let slip accidental truths about his past, like his age when the Uidrana left. Xetic-Nal in full control of his emotions would never have told me something so pertinent. I'm often mystified by his secrecy, especially about his personal life. It's beyond my poor political skills to turn four-thousand-year-old biographical details into a weapon.

The image vanished. "I have no reliable visual for our last neighbor on this planet. There have been no sightings since before the Uidrana disappeared. In fact, I don't believe they've made contact with a human since centuries before I was born, though there are always rumors. I know they're alive, though. Nothing can kill a unicorn. The few accounts that I found, back when folk memory was still fresh, say that they could survive the end of days, though I don't know what they'd do then." He saw my confusion in the gloom. "They are mythical, Zunvect, but they are not myths. There are too many reliable sightings, too many mentions in places that did not carry unsubstantiated hearsay. There are firsthand accounts. The likelihood of you meeting a unicorn – the likelihood of you meeting someone who has met someone who knows a person who has met a unicorn – is a grain of sand in a dessert as wide and deep as the ocean." Yes, I distinctly heard him pronounce it *dessert*. The century feast was near at hand, though I didn't know it at the time, and he was starting to get obsessed with the imminent tuck-in. "Still, I'll try to describe a unicorn, so you know it if you see it. Have you ever seen a llama?"

"No."

"A rhinoceros? A lion?"

"No, sir."

"You are an uncultured barbarian. I instruct you to read a zoological picture book. Fine, it's not like they look like any of those things anyway. A unicorn ... take a horse, no a donkey. Actually, split the difference and make it a mule. Mix it with a sheep, now a goat, now a cat and some elephant – not that you know what that is, you ignorant clod. Mix it all up good and forget it because that's not what they look like. If you ever have a very confusing conversation with something four footed and shining silver you've probably met a unicorn. It might have a big horn on its head but that's not confirmed. The one thing all the sources agreed on was that unicorns were indestructible. One witness claimed to see a unicorn withstand a direct hit from a Uidrana. I don't know what they want except that they want nothing to do with us."

"None of that is very helpful, Lord Xetic."

"I did tell you that you weren't going to meet one, so I don't have to be helpful. Just ... in case." He knew something and yet I have concrete and incontrovertible proof right now that he didn't. His preparedness could be as hard to understand as his description of unicorns, which oddly enough was right, even though I couldn't make sense of it at the time.

Lady Xenos was unique in many ways. The first incredible thing I learned about her was that, when it was time for a report, *Xetic* came to *her*. He shrugged off my reminder about illusion – "that doesn't matter in the least to Xenos" – but in deference to my condition he used a Tunnel rather than teleportation to take us to a circular room about four meters wide with the floor painted to resemble Lady Xenos' emblem. I refer to her, and her alone, as Lady rather than Lord because her title was somewhat different from the classical 'vect.' She bore an honorific that encompassed the much more important diplomatic aspect of her duties.

The diplomat in question was practically glowing when we emerged from the teleportoire and not in a good way. "Were you trying to give me a conniption?" She snapped when she saw there were only the two of us. "I thought you were opening up a gate to bring in a frigging army to try and steal a march on the Bowl. Damn stupid thing to do, but you've always been a reckless bastard when it came to the elves."

"I greet you as well, Xenos." Xetic said.

"Don't get all formal with me just because you've got the boy with you. Silly thing you've put on him and all. He looks like a blooming fountain ornament. No," her nose was almost pressed to my chest, "a pineapple. A particularly poisonous pineapple."

Lady Xenos was unique in another way that stood out the moment I met her. I don't mean that she verbally abused Xetic. A lot of people did that when they knew they were indispensable or otherwise protected; it was a natural reaction to how he talked to everyone. No, it was that Lady Xenos was *old*. She had gray hair, and a gauntness that suggested old age in a non-wizard. Her dark green velvet robe trimmed in gold almost hung off her, a formal robe which she had likely not replaced in the centuries that had left her stick thin. There was nothing of the dotard in her sharp, penetrating gaze or upright bearing, but in all other ways she looked like a particularly fit octogenarian. This was absurd, and not just because she was over twelve hundred years old. Wizard-Lords weren't supposed to grow old; they stayed youthful until they were taken by the Fade or some quick acting magical illness. It was, I learned, a sort of gift. One which Lord Xetic-Nal was bitter about, as with anything to do with elves.

"Come on, then." She said, retrieving a cane from a stand at the foot of the stairs. More of a staff, really, almost as tall as she was and topped with a brass dragon. The dragon's spiked tail wrapped around the top of the staff and it's ruby eyes sparkled with alien enchantments. "I don't know why you come here, Lord Xetic. It's a waste of time me telling you things when we both know you're of no mind to listening." She stumped up, Xetic taking his place ahead of me and appearing unphased by her lack of protocol and respect.

Lady Xenos complained about her hip and joints on the way to her fifth floor study but her movements belied such ailments. She sat in a high backed chair across a table from Xetic, and I was relegated to an armchair in the corner. I took the opportunity granted by their lack of interest in me to glance out the window. Like Xetic, Xenos had no subjects and her tower was her territory. The mountains outside that window were mind-bogglingly lofty even to me, rearing to thrice the height of those I had grown up near. They were the tallest mountains in the world. They were the northwestern wall of the Bowl, the land that no human had ever seen. A single step out of Xenos' door would place me under the governance of elves. The idea of being so near a non-human polity sent shivers down my back.

A white mittened black cat emerged from under her desk and approached me. It was strange because in my experience cats rarely wanted to have anything to do with people, but this one rubbed up against my leg and pressed his head against my hand in a meaningful way. He jumped into my lap and I pet the cat while Xenos and Xetic began their discussion.

"I can sum up most of what's happened in the twenty-five years since you last had the stomach to come visit me in one word: nothing. Our esteemed peers, the other Wizard-Lords have behaved themselves and avoided both contract disputes with dwarves and border incursions with dragons. My contacts in the Singing City tell me that they had some difficulty with a rambler who ignored the warnings, but since he was eaten before they found out about it, their options were minimal. The seas are calm and – as if you need me to tell you – the collected maidens of the world have once again failed utterly in attracting a unicorn. I will now lodge my routine formal complaint that you even require me to report that last part. It is absolutely preposterous, and I'm sure if I could make contact with a unicorn, they'd tell you the same." She shuffled some papers. "Not that you're here to listen to dwarven contract law or reports of the occasional devouring. How's the Temple of Termanicles holding up?"

"I don't know what you mean." Xetic said, sounding bored. I guessed that he'd heard the question before.

Xenos too acted like this was routine. "Yes, and I'm sure you have no idea where the Vedn Marbles or Ydrasn Manuscript are. I have no doubt that this is all a mistake and the elves merely *mislaid* three relics of the Uidrana."

"Did you tell them I'd trade?" Xetic asked.

"Yes, and the elves were – wonder of wonders – not inclined to make a one to one trade for the Engine of Ry or Book of Kel, and they most *certainly* made it abundantly clear that they thought that trading all three for the Museum of Everything was an even greater insult than all the other indignities they say they've suffered. In fact, though I hesitate to tell you, they seem to think that even mentioning the Engine of Ry was somehow taboo. There is one major development – I hear that the elves are trying to find something to offer the dwarves to make them annul the contract they have with you. The one that lets you have a hundred cubic meters below your towers –"

"That's enough." Xetic said. "There's no need to get into that kind of trifle. We both know the dwarves do not abrogate without consent on both sides." It was too late, though. I'd heard something I wasn't supposed to, and his interruption had only highlighted that Xenos had said something that was restricted. A hundred meters *below* a tower? What did he need that kind of volume for? The towers were already too big to be fully used and even the ancient Xetic-Nal couldn't have filled all three of his.

Their discussion moved on to an upcoming summit of all the sapient species willing to talk, which meant elves, dragons, dwarves, and humans. "I think we're going to have to give in to the dragon delegation this time and put lights on the towers." Xenos said. "I've had four of them here in the last century complaining about navigation hazards. It's my turn to chair, which means the elves are going to moan and complain, and then bribe me with *another* five hundred years of extended life so I leave a space for the eternally absent Aqueous and Uidrana. I'll get my own back by also putting out space for the unicorns. They'll never tell me what, but I know there's bad blood between them. The dwarves will threaten to take their business to the dragons but back down because the dragons don't have guaranteed delivery." She consulted her notes. "That should be all the *real* business. Of course the elves will make a big stink about something because it's what they do, and the dragons will apologize for all the trespassers they've eaten, but I'll forgive them because there's nothing else to do."

"Tell the draconic ambassador I want my lamp back." He saw me perk up. "Not a magic lamp, Zunvect, just a really nice table lamp I got from an artist I was friendly with a long time ago. The ambassador swiped it at the twenty-eighth conference."

Xenos sighed. "I will tell him no such thing. Dragons can't *swipe* anything."

"This one did. And my gold fountain pen."

"Well if you have nothing sensible to contribute-"

"Tell them I'll put running lights on the towers if I get my lamp back."

"-we can conclude." Xenos kept going, ignoring Xetic's interjections.

"Isn't there a pre-summit meeting today?" Xetic asked abruptly.

Lady Xenos put her notes to one side with great deliberation and looked out the window. After a moment, she returned to looking at Lord Xetic. "That's it, huh? That's why you came here today of all days. I presume this is for the apprentice's benefit. Fine, you two can come." She held up a finger in warning. "As long as you don't say anything to them without my leave. You put me here, and they've made it clear that I'm their preferred go-between. I will *not* have you set interspecies relations back by a millennium because you are pathologically compelled to taunt every elf you see!" She got up and leaned across the table, hands splayed on the tabletop. "Agreed?"

"I've been dealing with elves for -"

"Immaterial! I'm the ambassador now." She smiled coldly. "I know you hate that they granted me living immortality. You think I'm on their side. I'm not; it's just that I'm the only wizard to take up the Local Sapient Species Outreach job who wasn't racist. You mistake impartiality for favorable bias. Your concept of 'dealing' with elves has been to keep us in a cold war for the last four thousand years. This isn't getting hot while I'm ambassador. Are we clear?"

There was an unfamiliar note of respect, even submissiveness, in Xetic's voice. His eyes grew dim. "Very well. The boy can talk, though. Ask him if you like; he has no preconceptions."

"I'll trust that in the scant time you've had him, you haven't yet made him irredeemably pigheaded about it." Xenos allowed. "I'll go ahead to warn them and you can follow in my carriage." With that she was gone. The cat jumped down and followed her out.

"Lady Xenos is an obdurate and relentless woman." Xetic said into the silence that filled the room. "Onward then, Zunvect. It's impolite to linger in a tower when the Wizard-Lord is not at home. The elves are adamantly against human magic within twenty kilometers of them – I think I signed a treaty at some point – so we will have to take Lady Xenos up on her generous offer of a carriage trip."

My impression that Lady Xenos' territory ended at her front door was exaggerated. There was a gravel path in front of the door and a low stone wall with an opening for it ringing the tower at a distance of about half a kilometer. A narrower path split off and into a stable, which was already open as Lady Xenos had evidently taken a horse and ridden hard to get ahead of us. "Damn good thing, too. Don't want to surprise the elves." Xetic said. "One of the worst things in the world, a surprised elf. They're a bit like rabbits that way. Timid creatures but a bear when startled."

I reflected that I had never seen a rabbit that resembled a bear in any way, startled or not. I suspected he was thinking of something else, though I was at a loss to think of what looked like a bear but wasn't a bear. It was a conundrum. Being charitable, I believe he meant rats or some other animal that is fierce when cornered but otherwise runs. His attempt to describe a unicorn was evidence enough that he was a casual zoologist at best.

"I'm also not partial to riding around on horses." My teacher continued. "I used to, you know, back when I was alive. Rode all over the place, charging here and there to do great and mighty deeds. Mostly revolving around some king or queen or something getting upset about something trivial. Ever since I settled down and got to grips with the real work, I feel that horses are for adventurous youth, and I am neither." He laughed. "Imagine me going about on some sort of *quest*. I'd look ridiculous! Besides, I'm the one who tells people to go charging about, now."

"Are you upset by something trivial often, sir?" I asked.

Xetic's eyes grew dimmer with suspicion. "There's that 'sir' again coming after a clear insult. If I were thirty years younger ..." He considered. "It wouldn't change anything except I'd be getting some quiet research done instead of trekking around trying to educate a boy who once considered owning two horses to be the height of wealth."

After a conversation with a terrified groom and sickly-looking coachman – he was quite healthy until he caught sight of Xetic –we were bouncing along the gravel path. It wasn't long before the path ran out, and then we were being thrown halfway out of our seats on the poorly maintained dirt road to the elves' meeting place. "Cripes, maybe we should have ridden after all!" Xetic complained. He rapped the top of the carriage, a sound made much more impressive by his bare knuckles. "Hey, are you trying to break an axle or are your eyes crossed! You're supposed to *avoid* the holes." He subsided into grumbles about how I probably didn't know how to ride a horse anyway, and would probably sit on the saddle backwards. Five minutes of stewing later, he seemed to cheer up.

"Since we've got a bit of time to ourselves, it occurs to me that I haven't yet told you how I got my name." He said, eyes sparkling merrily. I tried to interrupt and say that he had, but he bulled on through as if I hadn't said a word. "'Nal' is my personal name. It means 'quick-witted' in the language they spoke where I grew up. It was a city on the coast – the one I rule to this day in fact. It wasn't called Ydrasia back then. The name was prosaic like Fair Harbor or Friendly Port or something like that; I don't remember. Of course, that was in a different language; I digress. It was a *very* straightforward time, so our surname was the profession of whatever parent was the majority earner in the house, so in that case it was my mother, who was a cooper. I don't know why she wasn't also considered a silvermonger except nobody made that distinction for people who worked in copper. Giant of a woman, she was; muscles out to here. Once slipped with the hammer and it went sailing over the house. It's the most bizarre thing, you know, because 'Xetic' means 'baker' in that tongue. My father did all the errands, but when it came time to buy the bread, my mom always went and came back with this sort of thin lipped look on her face and the *worst* temper until she'd coppered someone's bottom. Sometimes she threatened to do that to my dad, which I guess would have at least kept the barnacles off. Oh, look, we're almost there."

I was getting thin lipped myself, and I welcomed the reprieve from the ramifications of that story. The coachman moved as if to help us out of the carriage, looked at Xetic's hand, and decided to remain where he was. "Remind me next time to tell you about how I grew up in a palace surrounded by servants who all tried to assassinate me by the time I was eleven." Xetic said brightly, deciding I hadn't given him enough of a reaction in the carriage. "It's a whale of a story. They weren't even paid to do it; they just didn't like me."

I ignored him, which was easy to do in our surroundings. We were entering through the only gap in a colossal outdoor chamber. The stories about the wonders of elven gardening have not been exaggerated. Nothing in the twenty-meter meeting hall looked to have been worked by tools, but had grown, fallen, or weathered away into a soaring arboreal hall. It was as if a cathedral or a wizard's entryway were to be transformed into plants and native stone. Grass, weeds, and flowers twined together, bound by still living vines into a solid wall of vegetation. Trees formed the pillars and spread their boughs thickly into a roof that let in weak, indirect sunlight. A flat stone ridge about ten meters long jutted from the center, a table that would be high even for me. There were no chairs, and the only carpet was one of of leaves and needles.

"It all looks like it spontaneously formed this way, doesn't it?" Xetic said. "No marks, no sign of magic, just growth and nature making a space for them. Do you know what happens when it rains? That roof doesn't look solid after all."

"No, sir, what happens?"

"I don't know. It *never rains* on days the elves have meetings with us. Think that over."

Lady Xenos was standing at one end and we joined her. "Remember our agreement." She said.

"You remember it too." Xetic's eyes danced. "You said Zunvect could talk. I'm sure his contributions will be most instructive for both sides."

"Whatever you're planning had better not damage our relations."

"On the contrary." Xetic said. "Oh, Zunvect, you can't find a chair because there aren't any. It's an elf thing; they like to sit on the floor."

I was going to comment that the table would come up to my shoulders when five elves came in and answered my question for me. I'd read that they were tall, but it was different seeing them in person. Most were more than two and a half meters, and some seemed almost three! It was the first time in years I'd felt short. I could only imagine how difficult it was for the one and a quarter meter Xenos and one-point-seven Xetic to cope with a species like that, if only because their surfaces meant having to stand while they sat. They had a bovine air as they looked around and placidly took in the three of us. Only after a few seconds did their wide eyes narrow slightly and some tension form around their jaws. Each held a stylus and paper, though of a quality and shape that suggested it was the leaf of a plant rather than a processed item. Their clothing was likewise rough and woven.

"Good morning to you, Lady Xenos." The lead elf said, arranging her skirts as she sat across from us, sparing a glance at Lady Xenos' staff and then deciding to ignore it. Her hair was short but remarkably clean and neat; the part of me that spoke with Xetic's cynicism said that she probably used magic or a chemically derived shampoo to do it. Her wide gray eyes took in myself and Xetic, her bony, narrow face accentuating the inhuman size of those eyes. If my village were humans scaled up, these elves were humans stretched out. And then given extra joints, big eyes, and prehensile feet. Not that it was obvious, but they also had smaller teeth with no canines. It was difficult to get a good look at an elf's teeth because they had to consciously decide to smile with them, which they usually only did around humans to add feigned civility to their arguments. "There are some," she said with the slow, musical way of elves, "that would say that bringing your overlord to this conclave is tantamount to an act of war."

"No elf would say that, proconsul." Xenos replied. "It has been a point made often and strongly that elves do not sanction war except for survival." I could *feel* Lord Xetic's desire to amend that, but only because I'd learned to read his posture and caught the brief blaze in his eyes.

"You are correct." The elf said. "War is an activity for the less enlightened. I seek only to register my dismay at his inclusion." The other elves were busily taking down notes and occasionally passing missives and documents to one another.

"Lord Xetic is here as a silent observer." Lady Xenos said. "You may feel free to continue to address all of your questions and concerns to me."

"I am gratified." The elf responded. "It is a rare pleasure to see your overlord and not be afflicted by his odious opinions." She smiled at me, which was a bit like seeing a cow wink. "I am the Proconsul Allaria Korgadden De Lenfes Dellou." She said. "It is a pleasure to meet one of the youth of your species."

"Zunvect," I said except not because I hadn't taken the name yet, "Stetza, Wizard-Lord-apprentice to Lord Xetic-Nal."

"You have the deepest sympathy of the elven people." She said, and then returned to Xenos. "Let us take up old business."

"Is there any other kind?"

The elf looked over at the collection of documents her assistants were sorting. "We'll find that out when we take up new business. Thaumic pollution has increased by six percent in the past five years. While any increase is regrettable, it is a significant decrease in the *rate* of increase, which we ascribe to your having one fewer active thaumocrat." Xetic-Nal, already grinding his teeth, clenched his fists at the word. "This being a temporary state, we remain deeply concerned by your continued reckless use of Uidranic power." Xetic's eyes were almost gone, they'd shrunk so much.

Lady Xenos spread her hands. "We cannot change if you cannot explain the difficulty in a way we understand. Magic maintains a quality of life we otherwise could never achieve. We will not abandon it without better proof than you have provided."

"Yes. That you do not understand the danger is a contributing factor to that same peril. We hope that you will realize how detrimental your magic is before it becomes apparent through the damage that is done."

"Let us move on to another question with the same answer. We again offer the same terms for an exchange of the Marbles, Manuscript, and Temple."

"We again reject it." The elf said. "Since your overlord is present, I will expand on our position for his benefit, though I am sure you have made it very clear yourself." She was always careful not to address comments to Lord Xetic since that would invite rebuttal. "Those artifacts belong to us. Your overlord's possession of them is an insurmountable barrier to establishing friendly diplomatic ties between our governments. There will be no trade, and we deplore the methods by which he is attempting to obtain intelligence by subterfuge on the nature of the Engine of Ry. None of our legacy is his to study, and we would destroy the Engine before we allowed him to get even a glimpse of it. There will be no *trade*, and we only forbear from declaring war because of our respect for the innocent lives that would be lost if we did so, and in memory of those who died last time. We do not wish to inflict such sorrow again."

The elf was looking with something like sympathy at Xetic, who seemed to have withdrawn into himself completely. I'd never seen such stillness, such intense concentration on not doing anything. I had seen this in the behavior of some of the men of my town. Their tempers were so explosive that when they got truly enraged, they had to stay completely still or else risk lashing out. It was a little harder to see in Xetic, who lacked muscles to clench, but his posture was unmistakable. He didn't just distrust or dislike elves, he hated them with passion.

I thought he couldn't get more agitated, but I was wrong.

"Let us then move on to new business." The elf said. "We would like to thank you for your continued forbearance. We understand your need to expand your empire given your unfortunate birth rate. We would urge you again to try to remedy this. Your expansion, however, has remained coastal, and so it is not our concern. On behalf of the elven government, we thank you for not moving further inland. Of course, this cannot last forever, so we again ask that you find a way to arrest the growing need for land that your government has expressed."

"It will be taken under advisement, but I fear that internal and cultural norms make this difficult." Xenos replied. "On the subject of thanks, your intervention with the draconic embassy …" The discussion moved into period geopolitics, which I'm sure is of no interest to you. Preparing for the four-species summit was tedious and dull, yet Lord Xetic showed no sign of relaxing.

Xetic was silent during the carriage ride back, even as Lady Xenos tried to make conversation. "Talks with them are the most boring; I apologize for him making you sit through that. Elves don't even set a decent table for their guests; it's because they're something like ruminants. They don't explain the biology, but they only ever eat plant matter and whatever they can find in the wild, as far as I know. Lord Xetic says that it's why they're so thin and slow witted. I guess I can see the first, but despite appearances elves can be quick when they want."

I tried to keep up my side, but my master's quiet fulmination was deeply distracting. I couldn't remember ever seeing him angry, much less speechless with fury. "You'll forgive me if I depart immediately." He said, barely slowing to hear Xenos' gratitude for not having to continue hosting us as he pulled me into the teleportoire and tore a hole open with a vicious gesture. I was grateful when he let go of me; he'd had me in an iron grip which isn't any fun when the fingers have no flesh. We'd arrived outside of the tower, and the reason became perfectly clear when Xetic-Nal rose into the air. His eyes were a conflagration, blood red flames wreathing his robed, skeletal body.

I felt the air around me start to crackle at the same time I saw spellcraft form around Xetic that was terrifying in its form, like serpentine stormclouds of arcane will. I had never seen anything like it; block manipulation is orderly, linear. Even when the spell is disorienting in its complexity, it's still only a tight knot of intersecting and undulating ribbons, each one straight and traceable – if sometimes repeating and turning in on themselves – if you can only discern the path they take. What Xetic was doing looked organic, angry, and decidedly *not* a linear set of instructions and conditionals.

There was no thought of dignity, dexterity, or how hard it was to walk, much less run, in the robes that were more sculpture than clothing. I ran. I hadn't yet learned the right spell blocks for wood, but long forgotten instincts and routine sprang to mind. Forms that I hadn't practiced in years, but which had been drilled into my muscles and mind came to the fore in my panic. For the first time since I began studying with Xetic-Nal, I reached out not with wizardry, but sorcery. The air around the doors solidified and strengthened to hurl the great steel bound oak doors open, me diving through and tripping over my robe in my hurry. From the floor, I got a glimpse of the inferno expanding outward and heard Xetic-Nal let out an ear-rending scream that sounded like he was calling his own name. Then I threw all the magic I could muster into closing the doors behind me.

The strength of a spell meant to be fueled with limited reserves cast with the full power of a wizard made the entryway echo with the thunderclap when the doors hit the jamb. It was painful, but effective; sorcery is designed to draw on internal magical stores, and while I could use a wizard's thaumaturgical form and pool to cast it, the spell still *tried* to pull internally at first, consuming a tiny part of my Fade-converted body before I could redirect the flow to external sources.

I was just in time. The tower itself shook, the wards ringing a great peal of panic and pain around me. The spells of stability and protection, locked for thousands of years into stone, layer upon layer built up by the most learned wizard of all time began to *move*. They tilted around me, making me dizzy at the sight of the magical shadow of the tower at an angle to the unmoving bricks. Flickers of dark red and midnight black ran along them, guided away from the functional lower parts of the tower and up, turning the tower into an enormous, evil torch. It was a storm of magic a thousand times greater than I'd ever imagined, a hurricane of destruction that bent the wards like a tree in a typhoon.

The silence was, if anything, worse than the rage. The stillness. I struggled to my feet, but then fell back to my hands and knees when the doors opened with a hollow boom that shook the floor beneath me again. Xetic entered, my master now ice cold, regarding me with a pinpoint gaze which seemed to find me wanting in every way. The gaze warmed as I continued to kneel before him, not daring to meet the flaming gaze which had almost consumed the tower and me with it. "Look outside." I struggled to my feet, not daring to answer. I staggered up to the door and almost fainted again at the sight that met me.

I had thought that my experiment with fire had been bad. This was beyond anything I could have conceived. There was nothing living within sight. No birdsong, no buzz of insects. The grass was ashen and already crumbling in a sterile wind, and the trees that ringed the tower, the *forest* was gone. Replaced with the dry, broken skeletons of trees, their leaves already falling to dust. I knew somehow that if I looked out from a greater height, it would be death all the way to the horizon.

"Take a long look and remember, Zunvect." Lord Xetic-Nal, First Wizard said. I jumped, my heart thumping in terror. "You see that? That is Gramayre. That is what the elves think is natural magic for a human." He looked at me gravely. "It's not all bad, of course. It's magic, and magic is a tool, but Gramayre is a poor and unreliable one. It does what you *want*, which is a very dangerous thing. There is no one-to-one cause and effect with Gramayre. It might do a hundred different things with the same emotions and desires. My teachers and theirs back a thousand years before the first tower was built learned to control Gramayre to an extent. There are even legends of what we would call an Autothaum, a true master of Gramayre who had perfect control and could effect their will with a thought. Gramayre is not magic for the powerful. You at the height of your strength one day could have a bad day and kill thousands, or lose all restraint and lay waste to millions.

"The eighty-odd living Wizard-Lords can end civilization even now, but if we still worked with Gramayre they could do it *by accident*. The elves are foolish to think that because it's natural, it is good. And they have much to answer for, not the least making me so angry that lashing out with the old power was the only way to restore my equanimity. That's the other great weakness, you see. To control it, you must control your emotions, but then it grows weaker. The balance was never an easy thing, and those that could not manage it either became impotent or had to be killed – excepting the mythical Authothaum who supposedly could use Gramayre the way we use UML. I ended the days of the evil, rage and hate fueled wizards in their dark demesnes. Now we only have to worry about one," he chuckled. "The last bastion of stubborn Gramayre is necromancy. Centuries of research and no answer as to how it's possible, so it cannot be integrated into wizardry. I am a creature of the old magic and yet I am the strongest bulwark against it." He gently closed the door. "Get angry and it can burn nations, fall in love and it enthralls a city. Get scared ... and all hells break loose. Come on. A new tea's been grown, and I think even your leather tongue will be able to appreciate its bouquet."

"Sir." I said, cursing myself, but unable to resist. There is an instinct, I think, to turn to humor after a traumatic event. Is it healing or denial? I don't know, but the adrenaline and shock had shaken loose an observation I'd intended to make earlier, and I couldn't help but frame it ... inappropriately.

Xetic laughed. "I've just demonstrated that I'm the last extant dark wizard by obliterating a forest. The impudent 'sir', Zunvect?"

"Bullshit."

Xetic was brought up short. "After *this*, you choose to refute me in so … earthy a way?"

"It's not about Gramayre, sir. Since you sound like you'll never teach it, I have no choice but to believe you about that. No, I'm both contradicting an argument Lady Xenos said you made, and pointing out the counterargument in a single word."

Xetic's eyes gleamed as his mind worked. Then he burst out in immoderate laughter, which was perhaps even more disturbing than his rage. An angry fire-eyed skeleton makes sense. One that has his head thrown back and is cackling in a way that sounds as if he can barely speak for the mirth always looks like he's mocking you. Provoking him to hilarity so soon after hearing a lecture about how strong emotion feeds unstable magic was perhaps the most idiotic thing I have ever done, and I regretted it the moment the ground began to shake to the beat of his laughter. "Bullshit! Such a concise argument." He chortled. "The marbling, yes. Oh, crimeny that's good. Mark this on your calendar, Zunvect, you've won an argument with Lord Xetic-Nal. Grazing animals *can* be fat. Trust a student of a veterinary sorcerer to catch that one and keep thinking about it even after witnessing a criminally irresponsible lack of control." He didn't stop laughing until he'd poured the tea and we were up in his study, though the tremors ceased long before.

I'd barely taken a sip of the somewhat oddly flavored drink when Aika appeared in the room, hands balled into fists and hair spread out behind her like a midnight cloak. "Has it finally happened?" She asked scathingly. "You're *laughing*, Lord Nal? Has your mind finally reached its limit and produced a post-mortem analogue of dementia? *Are you insane?*"

"An interesting question, Aika." Xetic said mildly. "Can I with any surety diagnose my own –"

"Don't turn this into an ontological discussion of whether a person can be aware that their mind is warped." Aika spat. "I felt that.

Given that he's pale as a specter, Zunvect felt that. I wouldn't be surprised if every wizard, sorcerer, magician, and *goat* felt that. I don't care if I'm being insubordinate in front of Zunvect," she said, correctly interpreting Xetic's censorious look. "People accuse *me* of being death's own handmaiden! You could have blown down the tower, you … you … foolish old buffer!" She slammed her fist on the desk and it actually shook with a thump. "If you want to commit suicide, there are more convenient ways to do it." She looked at me. "Good work with the doors." She disappeared.

"Excitable girl." Xetic mused. "Though there *will* be a reckoning about this. The Board of Governors will be very displeased." He seemed to notice me. "Forget I said anything about them." He continued to drink his tea and I decided to keep quiet for at least a day, until everything blew over. I had a lot to think about between elves and the ravages of irresponsible Gramayre.

It was a reminder that, though I had grown comfortable with Lord Xetic and Lord Aika after living with and learning from them, they were ancient and powerful people whose secrets could be deadly and their responsibilities grand. They had founded nations, defeated foes, and done things that I now realized were unimaginable to me. I never recaptured the original feelings of easy familiarity I'd had before that day, which was for the best. It *was* for the best, I reminded myself whenever I felt wistful about those days of simple scholasticism. I needed to remember that there was a world outside the tower and by being Lord Xetic-Nal's apprentice, I was to be thrust into the direst – and most dangerous – situations. All of a sudden, Aika's blood thirst and Xetic's offhanded remarks about killing gods didn't seem as fun and *clean* as they'd felt before.

I woke up the next day filled with dread. I'd been overwhelmed by lectures and visits and meeting elves on top of my first serious step into the world described in *Us* and *Them*. It hadn't sunk in that I'd watched and felt something out of a story book. I'd seen a wizard lay waste to kilometers of ground, kill hundreds of thousands of plants and animals. The air around me was still, silent, and not in the sleepy way of winter but in a way that told me even before I went to the window that I hadn't been dreaming, it hadn't been illusion. Lord Xetic had really lashed out in a fit of rage and obliterated a forest in the way an enraged man at home might have ripped up a fencepost or broken a mug.

The lesson was well learned; a wizard who lost control of their emotions was a common threat to us all, and Gramayre was the conduit of that danger. That was why all offenses adjudicated against a wizard were capital crimes. There were only eighty-four of us. We couldn't be imprisoned – that would take more than one Wizard-Lord to accomplish. Censure would only harm innocent subjects in the Wizard-Lord's territory. An unstable or corrupt Wizard-Lord had to be killed, I understood that now, and a stupid one was especially dangerous.

I turned away from the devastation outside my window. The meadow might recover in a few years, but the forest would take a century. Another lesson. Destruction was fast, but recovery was slow. No wizard could swiftly repair the damage that had been done, though I'd occasionally read about times when priests seemed able to grow plants quickly across entire fields. It had to be possible if they did it.

Aika didn't say anything about Xetic-Nal's angry outburst, or even about the meeting with the elves. She tried to help me through lessons on manipulating various solid objects, starting that day with igneous rock, but I wasn't in a good frame of mind to take in the differences between holding up one kind of stone or another, or even the larger differences of manipulating rock and wood.

The books went flying back to their places and Aika sat on the table. "You'll have to get used to it." She said quietly. "Pain, death, moving fast to stay alive. You *shouldn't* have to fear your master losing his mind and making you run for it or else have your soul torn to pieces, but that's life with Xetic." It was the first time I could remember her using his familiar name. "He can go decades without an episode, but having a living apprentice is reminding him of life. He … lived in a different time than we did. He grew up and became a wizard with rules that bear little resemblance to the ones he's put in place. He's never confided even in me, but I think he's done things that make my … excesses seem only on the severe side of moderate. Wizards these days, we don't really have to worry so much about Gramayre. Most of us only ever experience it by accident, or in highly controlled circumstances like Lord Jones. Lord Nal does an injustice to you by describing it as magic which reacts to emotion and desire. It's more than that, I think. The few times Lord Nal has used it in my presence, I think it *increased* what he put into it. As if the magic is a mental feedback loop with a control signal that is only as strong as the will of the magician. Once you use it, you have to fight to stop."

"Why did Lord Xetic make you immortal?" I asked. It wasn't the first time I'd approached the subject, but I'd never asked outright. Aika had always evaded the question in the past.

She looked at me for a long time and I felt ashamed. It was the wrong kind of question, the kind that pried and brought pain but didn't illuminate. What did it matter to me? Something in her eyes softened and she looked away. "You're old enough, you're learning magic. I hate it, but you may need to know this. It's because I deserved it. You're surprised; of course you are. You're in a place – you're of an age – where you think that everlasting existence is something awarded for doing something good, or succeeding above all expectations. That's not how Lord Nal views it. Ask him what he thinks of immortality and who ought to have it.

"In my case, I was terrified of dying. I didn't believe that the gods made afterlives for us, and yet … there was a nugget of worry there as I approached old age. I was becoming dimly aware that something was wrong with me. That perhaps being called 'bloody shoulder' and everyone falling on their faces as I passed by wasn't a compliment. I shook it off as best I could, but as I felt the Fade taking me, I panicked. In those final hours of life, I realized that everyone around me seemed so … relieved. I'd never seen them so relaxed, so free of fear and anxiety. I saw festivals in the streets outside my tower and it struck me that perhaps they weren't celebrating my life like I originally thought they were. I'd like to think that that's why I went to see Lord Nal, but I can't pretend that I wasn't also coming to the realization that I'd failed him. I wasn't going to be First Wizard and rule in his place for ten thousand years before finding my own successor. I was going to die, to succumb to the Fade, and be replaced. I was hours away from dying, and I finally saw what any sane wizard would have known for decades. *I wasn't the one.* I went to Lord Nal and pleaded for my life. He gave me that look, you know the one, and told me he'd give me a suspended sentence.

"I passed out and woke up in the library, a ghost. I must have cried for a year when I tried to open the door with telekinesis and couldn't. Losing my body was much less painful than waking up powerless. To be without magic was to lose the greater part of my *self*. If I was neither a wizard nor a ruler, then what was I? Over time, I changed my appearance. As I've told you, I didn't grow up in the islands, so my present ethnicity is an affectation, and even a wizard doesn't remain quite as youthful as I am now. From the moment I became their lord, I thought of myself as one of *my people,* so it's been natural that, as my projected body conformed to my self-image, I'd become more like them. I loved them in my own way, Zunvect. I was only trying to make them see sense, to correct their misbehavior."

She looked at me for the first time, eyes liquid with emotion, and with a shock I realized she was asking for *my* forgiveness. I kept my silence, unable to think of the right thing to say. She looked away again. "A part of me knows what's wrong, but I will never be able to accept it. That's why my sentence is suspended. I know I ought to feel remorse, but I cannot. Until I either give up hope or finally learn to feel bad for what I did, rather than for the fact that I don't, I serve Lord Nal as I am. Neither here nor there."

She laughed bitterly, but for all the appearance of emotion, she'd been careful to leave out a detail of her status as a ghost. One which was very important to us later, and which I learned from an unexpected source. "I exist because I hope that one of those choices will lead to him returning me to life and power. I know that if accepting what I've done brings me back, that I will only do it all over again, and if losing hope brings the reward of return, that I will probably never use magic again. I hope for life and I fear it, just as I hope for and fear being consigned to my final death."

She floated away, passing through the ceiling and leaving me feeling much worse than I had before. Being told a sad story was not how I'd hoped to be distracted from Lord Xetic's xenocidal outburst. I was beginning to worry that something about Lord Xetic-Nal brought out the killer in people. Aika was a genocide, Black Matthew, by all accounts, had been happy to fill the ranks of his zombie army with the corpses of his enemies, and Lord Xetic himself was obviously unhinged if he could blast down a forest in rage and then use it as a teachable moment. I'd never heard of him killing an apprentice but then again, would I? None of them ever talked about the first apprentice beyond saying she hadn't been up to his standards. Maybe she'd displeased him and had been killed for it.

Idalia 9:

Rights

Idalia stretched, arranging her skirts as she got up. She yawned widely. "I think I need a lunch break." She opened the door to the stone cell she'd been using as a containment chamber. "Since I doubt you'd enjoy the company of a Lupine, is there anything *edible* that you'd like me to bring back? They've got abysmal vegetable dishes, but the best meat I ever tasted."

"That's odd." Zunvect said. "I'd have thought they'd eat all of theirs raw – don't call me a racist!" He said abruptly as several runes on his staff shone out clearly.

"I didn't." Idalia stammered.

"I heard you thinking it." Zunvect retorted. "I'm getting better at being your god. Don't deny it; I am, even if you don't want me to be." He tapped the butt of the staff on the nearest containment sigil. "This is connecting you to me closely enough that I can begin to pick out your thoughts from the minds of the magi. Don't worry; it's only the loud ones."

"It is a bit inappropriate to assume that just because they're morphologically similar to wolves, that the Lupines wouldn't cook their food." Idalia told him.

"Don't get righteous with me, Idalia. Apart from it being totally backwards for anyone to claim righteousness above their own deity – to be fair we wizards did, but that's beside the point – your civilization hasn't got a leg to stand on when it comes to xenological egalitarianism."

"We have a better claim than you do." Idalia said.

330

Zunvect threw back his head and laughed raucously. "That's hilarious, Idalia. Do you want to go through the list right now?"

Idalia sniffed. "I'd rather eat first."

"I'll have whatever you're having, assuming you made provision for provisions crossing the boundary." He settled back, toying with his staff between his index and middle fingers as if it were a baton. Idalia swept out, closing the door with unnecessary force. She returned a few minutes later with two platters. The braised meat was not from an animal with a close analogue to those of her homeworld, but the Lupines had assured her that she could digest it. They'd even done a halfhearted attempt at grilled fruit and whatever vegetables were edible, though the mass of stalks and leaves didn't look appetizing. The meat was gamy, but delicious, and the braise seemed to be made from the stock of another animal. She'd politely declined to see what either of them looked like in life.

"Promise not to try to escape?" Idalia said, setting the two platters down.

"I promise," Zunvect said. She made the ward momentarily permeable and passed Zunvect one of the platters. They ate in silence. When the plates were clean, the argument began again.

"Let's begin with the elves, since I've been talking about them recently. In my time there were tensions but also open diplomatic relations. The issue of their allegations again Xetic-Nal were a sore spot that would never heal, but we respected their borders and they respected ours. They distrusted our magic and we did likewise. It was a chilly but peaceful relationship, and our expansion would only disturb them when we finally shared borders and the frisson of border skirmishes brought tensions to a boil. How are relations with elves now, Idalia?"

"We don't speak, and we haven't for over a thousand years." She admitted. "On the other hand, there is no difficulty with your imperialism, so border issues are nonexistent. Contact has been sporadic, but treaties exist."

"Treaties that you famously forgot about when you unearthed my staff and began to use it against the express terms of an agreement made four thousand years ago." Zunvect grinned. "And don't call us imperialists when we had political control of five percent of the land surface. You own ninety percent of the land *and* ocean surface, Idalia. We were expansionists, you reaped the benefits. In my time we had routine contact with dwarves and benefitted from mutually advantageous trade. They had their underground technocracy, and we never tried to take what was theirs – well, almost never."

"It's broadly the same now." Idalia said. She caught Zunvect's skeptical glint and sighed. "Except yes, we had a war and the dwarves now produce for us with terms set by the armistice treaty."

"They're a vassal state in all but name." Zunvect said. "*Given* their mines by your supposed generosity and protection, and not because they are a recognized equal and sovereign power. The Aqueous in my time were gone, living so deep below the surface of the ocean that we never had any contact with them."

"Our … difficulties are because they refuse to be reasonable." Idalia said.

"You've been at war for twenty-five *hundred* years, in conflicts that ranged from skirmishes to all out battles."

"We have never invaded their space. It has *always* been an Aqueous strike force that comes on land." Idalia said. "This wasn't our fault. Yes, there were pollution issues, but had they come to us in peace instead of destroying homes, businesses, and ships, it would have been different."

Zunvect snorted. "Knowing us, it would have been a pre-emptive strike, but I take your point. The war was, as many wars are, the fault of both sides."

He grinned broadly. "Ah, but that brings us to my favorite pair. How strange that they would share a fate. Dragons and unicorns. When I lived, the draconic lands were envied but deeply respected. Their power was unquestionably greater, and they were considered just but fair when someone entered their lands uninvited. If they crossed the border by mistake, humans were peacefully but firmly expelled, and if it was plain that they had ignored the warning signs, they were eaten. It was brutal, but the draconic nation made it clear that bodily consumption was the fate of trespassers, and they did occasionally trade some marvelous things to us for our own artifacts. They ruled the sky and we left them to it, confident that they would protect us as we did them on the rare occasions either side required it. Despite being arguably the least like us in form, we *understood* one another. As for unicorns, with some notable exceptions, neither humans nor unicorns paid the other any mind. The unicorns were exceptionally adept at remaining out of sight and unmolested. Until the magi figured out how to detect them, and *that* was the first step towards them and dragons ending up where, Idalia?"

"There are preserves and well protected grounds for them. We try to leave them to themselves when we can." Idalia said. "There aren't very many left of either."

"Which is why the majority of both can be found where?" Zunvect purred.

"In licensed and regularly inspected facilities, where the restoration and rehabilitation can be pursued in a manner that raises awareness and makes it possible to continue the effort of –"

"Zoological gardens, Idalia. You magi have them in zoos because there are so few of them. You *breed* sapient races, Idalia. You convince yourself it's for their own good, that you're making amends for hunting them to near extinction." He lay back in his bubble, smiling at her. "I know something you do not, and the joke's on you magi for not realizing it. Leaving aside the abomination that has taken the place of the draconic people – their culture has been all but destroyed by you, and most of you seem to actually *believe* that drivel about conservation – you haven't actually got any unicorns in captivity."

"What, they're all fake?" Idalia said, almost laughing herself.

"No, but they're playing the long game against you, and are by no means an endangered species. We'll reach unicorns eventually, Idalia. I ought to be getting back to my autobiography, now that we've established that you're no better than we were."

"You–"

"I was just about to tell you about my first encounter with the Peacemakers. A wonderfully direct, and some might say brutally exploitative, solution to the problem of keeping the oligarchy together. It's painful for me to talk about any of my meetings with poor Anya, but you need to know what it was like before I ruined everything.

Zunvect 20:

Peacemaker

Excerpt from *Us* by Lord Xetic-Nal, 74th ed. (3893 [XR]),
Chapter 5: Getting Along

This volume has covered, and will further illuminate later, the means and methods by which a Wizard-Lord may legally enter and sustain conflict with another Wizard-Lord.
This is the extreme, and while woefully common, is con-
strained so heavily because it is strongly discouraged. You
should be able to get along with your fellows in our grand
old oligarchy, and provisions have been made for settling
disputes that have not become so dire as to necessitate war,
duel, or assassination attempts. Is it worth throwing away
lives and cash just to settle who first published a thesis on
the most recent development in visual acuity in constructed
spellcraft? A surprisingly large quantity of wizards over the
years has answered that question in the affirmative, but let's
assume that the reader in these peaceful and reasonable
times has grasped that arguments over borrowed books and
small changes to border locations are not the basis for battles
and bloodshed.

For years, I was the arbitrator of arguments – mostly petty and pointless – between Wizard-Lords. However, I am
pleased to say that this is no longer the case. In the two
thousand seven hundred and twelfth year of my rule, I de-
volved that authority to Atreya Peacemaker, first of the lineage. Over the centuries, the Peacemakers have honed this

skill, and the associated empathic and telepathic spellcraft, to the degree that within two generations I had conferred upon them another unique property. They are the only Wizard-Lords licensed to use a Lineage Link. In case that was too subtle, let me be blunt. Don't try it yourself; I'm not even sure if it works on men, in fact I'm not even sure if it would work well on someone other than a Peacemaker. Don't take that as an invitation to experiment – I have no desire to see the empirical research on that particular spell.

There isn't much I can tell you about the old Peacemakers that you don't already know. The spells that made a Peacemaker who they were remain illegal even now. You'd experimented a little, but when I was alive, they were the only wizards who had – to our knowledge – even attempted to pass by lineage rather than by reference. Sorry, mind magic humor. The Peacemakers were probably the most respected of the official foundations, and in constant demand. I remember reading about calls to expand the Peacemaker family in the first journals I'd been allowed to peruse. Having more than one elder at a time was deemed difficult but not infeasible, if the lineages were kept separate. There was even talk of a new tower on Ismun for a new Peacemaker, who would take over the duties of being councilor to Ismun and the islands.

Of course, any plans that might have been underway ended with me. It's painful to talk about the Peacemakers. They were a monument to what the oligarchy had become and, in that sense, they were beautiful in their very concept. My deepest regret comes from what became of them, and though you know most of the story of how I turned them into the Peacebreakers, it is important to know exactly what they were, so you can see just how great a crime

I committed in destroying them. Murder looks like the least of crimes compared to the forging of Anya Peacebreaker.

I was done up in my usual immobile finery on the edge of Xetic's mosaic of arrival and departure. It was a banner day for me; I was to meet my first apprentice Wizard-Lord. It was a shame, I thought, that I'd be entertaining the younger Peacemaker rather than hearing the elder's report since, like Xenos, hers were far more salacious than the fathomless depths of specialized magic or the whinging of a wizard who'd lost out on an opportunity to look clever when another published ahead of them. The Peacemakers' arrival was strange, as they were the only wizards I've met who landed rather than appeared. Or I should say that they did both.

With a dainty click, the pair of them alighted on the mosaic, azure and jade robes rippling around them as they walked forward, as if they'd been walking already and had just descended from a small step before teleporting to the tower. Apart from matching gold belts, emerald earrings, and gold embroidery around their necklines and cuffs, their satin robes were all the finery they needed. Peacemakers flaunted their down to earth pragmatism, always ready to take a comfortable seat and attend to the personal needs of a planetary government. Yes, Idalia, we were pathetic. That's why I tore down the unstable oligarchy and replaced it with the thriving and corrupt technocracy you enjoy today. I'm telling my story, so we're not getting into the 'your civilization is worse than mine' game just now.

They were also two of the most beautiful women I've ever met. I often wondered if they used material manipulation on themselves to improve their appearance. Certainly Bella – the elder – had almost supernaturally clean, shiny, and smooth black hair to go with her milky complexion, and the combination of honey blonde waves with a suspiciously artificial tan on Anya – the younger – was enough to convince me that if they weren't using magic to make themselves pretty, they'd been breeding for it for a long time.

Please excuse me if I rhapsodize for a moment on their lovely curves and round bosoms. At that point in my life, I was a nineteen-year-old virgin who hadn't seen a woman within four centuries of my own age up close in years. It was almost overwhelming when Anya took a step towards me and touched my hand. A female! Possibly one who had the same number of digits in her age as I did! It would have been breathtaking even if she hadn't been a Peacemaker, and thus intentionally designed to be attractive to us poor, biddable male Wizard-Lords.

We exchanged greetings and Xetic took the lead. "Zunvect, you can show Anya the library and perhaps a few other places." He'd warned me already about keeping her from reading too much – I was not yet so advanced as to know what texts were for my eyes only.

"I've been there once or twice before." Anya smiled at me as we ascended, breaking away from Bella and Xetic as they continued up to his study. I was, for once, glad of my all-encompassing formal robe, which slowed us down but hid any embarrassing signs of my reaction to how close she was staying to me. I remember being excited by a scent she was wearing but not quite what it was. I was frustrated but also a little relieved that the robe also kept her from getting too close. It was hard enough having to conduct my first visiting apprentice, much less one who was young, female, and pretty. Luckily, she was a Peacemaker, and likely even then accustomed to Wizard-Lords who were only verbose in writing or in lecturing about their favorite topics. "You must have just started here. Mother Bella comes to see Lord Xetic at least every two years."

"Yes, I only started ..." I tried to work out the time dilation in my head. "Sometime last summer, maybe early autumn. I came from another part of the world, so the seasons don't quite match up."

"That can be difficult at first." Anya agreed. "Good morning, Lady Chimamire no Kata." She said to Aika, who had passed through a shelf to join us.

"To you as well, Anya." Aika replied. "That mode of address is outdated in three ways, but I thank you for your consideration in using my title as it would have been when I lived."

Anya inclined her head. "It is required of me to use the courtesy most familiar to any I meet."

"We are in some ways similar in that regard." Aika smiled. "As Zunvect appears to be entertaining you satisfactorily, I will withdraw. With him here, it is not my place to remain." Before I could protest, she vanished.

"She was more formal than I usually see her." I said.

"That's how they spoke and behaved when she was alive." Anya told me.

It was odd to me that with so few words she could have seemingly brought Aika back to her former self. Aika had even begun to look different as she spoke. I was also surprised that Anya would even have studied something so obscure as the correct way to speak two thousand years ago. It was a quintessentially Peacemaker thing to do, going to that much trouble to put someone at their ease. I regretted my next statement as soon as I made it. "Is it strange, being made into something different to fulfil a purpose?"

Anya smiled openly, sensing my distress – and likely seeing the creeping blush. This was a question she and her antecedents were asked often. "Is being purposefully made into something any worse than the unexpected changes that come from life and study? You're different now than you were a year ago when you came here, aren't you? It is like that with us. In fact, I find it soothing to know that my course of study, the enchantments used on me, and my very being are molded with purpose that goes back centuries. Most Wizard-Lords seek the thrill of breakthrough, of the chaos that can alter them from week to week as they stand at the forefront of progress. We tread a well-worn path, comfortable and predictable. It is rare for a Peacemaker to see or do something that is out of our experience in the same way most other Wizard-Lords do."

"I can understand that. I came from a very traditional village, and most would agree with you that being raised with purpose, learning the way of doing things that has worked for generations, has a kind of comfort to it." I still wasn't sure I'd enjoy being mentally and physically altered like the Peacemakers were for any reason, much less so I would become a counselor and friend of all wizards. What I'd heard about the molding process was disturbing, and yet I couldn't help but feel attracted to, and even a little protective of, the young woman sitting next to me.

"You must be much further into learning magic than I am." I said, trying to think of something that wouldn't get me into trouble. "I'm only just learning basic telekinesis."

"I won't need much of that." She said. "As a matter of fact, I'm not as far along as you might think." She colored. "I shouldn't tell you this, but you're Lord Xetic's apprentice, so I think you're an exception to most rules. Mother Bella didn't exactly plan on having me until later – though she says it's been a blessing to know she'll soon have an assistant that will last much longer than is usual. Since she'll live at least another seventy years, she's not in a hurry to teach me everything I'll need to know when it's time for her to pass the Lineage to me." She licked her lips. "Would it be all right if we went to your room?" She saw my surprise and laughed, high and tinkling. "Oh, nothing like that! I need a glass of water, Zunvect. It's rare for me to speak this much all at once, though Mother Bella makes sure I'm eloquent and pleasant to hear."

"It's about ten flights up." I said.

"I'm sure I'll be able to manage." She looked down at the trailing hem of my robe and grinned. "Perhaps better than you can."

"You and Lord Bella don't talk?" I asked as we made our way up.

She shook her head. "Not the way you do." She stopped and lightly placed her finger on my forehead. "Do you grant permission?"

"Yes." I said, somehow trusting her implicitly.

"It's like this," she continued, though now her voice was in my mind rather than out loud. "The most important thing a Peacemaker's apprentice needs to know is telepathy, so I almost never say a word except with company or when practicing my diction and tone. It can be embarrassing." She looked back shyly. "You haven't learned any telepathic skills at all, so your … assumption when I asked to go up to your room was audible even without your consent. Nothing against men, but you're more visual than verbal, so you tend to leak more." The panic in my mind set her to laughing out loud again. "I'll get bad habits from you." She chided before assuring me, "Don't worry about it. If you ever do learn to open your mind to others, try walking through a crowded tavern's common room and you'll understand that I can't take offense. It's not like you can control what you broadcast right now, and no man can completely control his reactions to a pretty girl." She allowed me to open the door for her. "I'm a Peacemaker. The effect I have on you is intentional. Oh, this is lovely!" She said, looking around at my sitting room. She sat on the sofa across from the fireplace. "I wasn't expecting anything so cozy and neat."

"Lord Xetic is responsible for the first. I'm used to putting things away." I replied. "I'll get that glass of water for you." I left for the kitchen, hoping to recover a little as I filled two cups, but her voice followed me, sounding as if she were at my arm.

"You'd be surprised how many Wizard-Lords are slovenly in their personal lives but fastidious in the laboratory. Oh? What was it like living in such a small community?" My thoughts weren't even formed into words before her replies came. "I couldn't imagine having so few people around. Aristeum is almost as large as Ydrasia. You've never been there? Oh, I'm sure Lord Xetic will take you there soon. It's his capital city, after all. He can't stay away forever." The last thought came with a hint of something amusing about it, but I didn't catch what. The staccato rhythm of Anya's responses to my half-formed thoughts was making me dizzy, and she giggled at my inner observation that I needed a glass of water now.

"It's overwhelming at first," she told me as I came back into the sitting room. "If you were a telepath as well, the conversation would be going by even faster." She'd tucked her feet under her robe and was half lying down on the sofa. "No, I'm perfectly warm. It's just ... you value honesty, so I'll admit I did it because I sensed that it was something you'd find attractive. I must need more practice because I can't find a reason why."

I tried to sit on an armchair with an easy line of sight to continue our one-and-a-half-sided conversation, but she patted the remaining sofa space insistently. "None of that. You'll be much more comfortable right here." She moved over a little to accommodate my large frame. "You're certainly the tallest apprentice I've ever met." She said. "And keeping fit." She tried to rest her head on my shoulder, then on my lap, and then sat up with a half annoyed, half amused laugh out loud while I tried to keep my breathing even and thanked Valya that she hadn't succeeded. There was no way she'd have missed that I was reacting to her in the way any healthy male might. "That dress robe of yours is ridiculous!" She said, speaking audibly in mock outrage. "Was Lord Xetic expecting you to be attacked or was he trying to make my job harder?"

"Job?" I asked.

She tossed her head. "Well, yes. Job might be a strong word for it." She took a deep breath and returned to telepathic speech. "Wizard-Lords are an unhealthy breed, Zunvect." She smiled at how her saying my name made my breath catch. "You're keeping physically fit, which is admirable. Most Wizard-Lords are real slugs and only stir themselves at mealtimes. You're in the same shape as they are mentally and socially, though. Isolated and focused. Even when a Wizard-Lord tries to relax, they usually take it too far and become like Vectreon and Mycontree." She put her hand on my chest. "You're feeling all the normal things an inexperienced youth should." She was carefully picking her way past the protrusions of my robe and her lips brushed my cheek. "Panic, worry that you're not attractive enough for me, so much excitement. Yet there's that part of your mind trained to be a wizard, the place where your magic lives. It's still analyzing the situation even as you become short of breath and you can barely think about anything else." She kissed me hard and then with a cry slipped on the leather frontpiece of my robe and hit the ground. "So much for seduction," she said, her tinkling laugh echoing in my head.

I sat stunned. "Are you all right?" I gasped.

"Fine," she said, standing and rubbing her bottom. "You've got a very soft carpet." She sat down next to me. "That wasn't the first question that entered your mind," she said playfully. "The first was 'will this disrupt her telepathic contact?' Ah, you're blushing even deeper than when I was pawing all over you. See? Normal humans aren't supposed to detach a part of their thought process to constantly ask questions like that. Oh, there are the odd inappropriate thoughts, but that's not what's happening with you. It's not intrusive, but continuous. No, I'm better trained than that. Yes, the empathic link does mean I feel some of what you feel when I kiss you. No, this isn't going any further … without consent." She said the last two words in a breathy whisper. "You gave it to start contact, but I need it again now, and I'll have to explain what's about to happen in more detail."

"You mean because I'd agree to anything right now?"

"I'd do it anyway, but yes, you're an attention starved teenager, so you'd say almost anything to get me to start again." She brushed her hair back with a smirk. That expression drove home the duality of her existence. Her maturity seemed to wax and wane as lack of experience mixed with her extensive training. Sometimes she'd act as innocent as ... well, me. Other times, it was like she had already taken the Lineage and had guided a hundred men along this path before. "It's nothing to be ashamed of. You're nineteen if I remember right, and so even if you'd had a normal life, I'd be hard to resist. Growing up somewhere with few romantic prospects – and leaving before even having the *chance* to engage in some hanky panky with the mayor's daughter for a life of chastity and loneliness – hasn't done you any favors. That's one of the things we Peacemakers help with. Wizards often lack a sense of ... I guess the best thing to call it is proportion. You study and study and research and get so deep that spending weeks with beakers and books and no one to say a word to seems normal. We help you refresh your perspective and regain some balance so that you can look at the world with fresh eyes and see all the important things you're forgetting to do because the latest puzzle has so intrigued you.

"Now, with most people that's not too hard," she continued, "but we wizards are trained to separate ourselves from our emotions, so that we don't use Gramayre, and to keep some of ourselves back all the time so that we can analyze everything that happens to us. Something a Peacekeeper learns is how to ... turn off that incessant voice asking questions and trying to find out how everything works as it's happening. You will, for a little while, stop feeling the compulsive need to study everything. You will instead find yourself living in the moment."

She held up a hand as she felt my panic building. "No, not like that. Nothing I do can be permanent; it's against my training and the binding magic that is already part of me. An hour from now, you'll be no different than you were an hour ago, except that there will be a discontinuity which will help you break any obsessions you might have developed. It's like a normal person taking a vacation and coming home to realize just how much there is to do around the house when seeing it with fresh eyes. I'll withdraw and let you consider." She slid over and seemed to become interested in the fireplace.

I thought about everything she'd said. In truth, there *was* a lot of sense in it. I'd almost missed congratulating my brother on my sister-in-law's pregnancy. I was going to be an uncle, and I'd dashed off a note before diving in to – what was I doing then? – making the lantern spell cycle through its colors, I think. I'd not gone outside or even opened the window since Xetic's outburst. I wasn't even testing some of the doors as I went upstairs, instead rushing back down as soon as I'd done the exercise Aika insisted on, so I could get back to learning how to move liquids around. I looked at Anya and knew that all this was secondary. It didn't matter if she was right. She was there, she was the most beautiful woman who had ever talked to me, and I would do just about anything to make it so that both my first and second ever kisses were from her. In the rush of hormones and desire, any I might have had at home in the village were forgotten. "I consent."

"I hoped you would." She said. "No, really. You're healthy, young, strong, and pretty good looking. This will be fun." She *very* carefully got close to me again and succeeded in maneuvering into a kiss that only required some neck craning. "No, really, it will be fun for me, Zunvect," she said as she felt my reticence. "I'm not quite as experienced a lover as you think I am. I'm twenty-two, and Mother Bella has not called on so many Wizard-Lords with apprentices that I've had … extensive experience. So, not as old as you thought, but thanks for the compliment. I can tell it was motivated by how I behave rather than how I look, so don't get too flustered; the Peacekeeper training regimen is very heavy on the therapeutic uses of telepathy and empathy, so I'm acting a little more mature than my age because this is something I have experience with. Contrary to popular opinion, Peacemaker Daughters are *not* trained courtesans. I'm doing this because you're a special case, isolated as you are. We Peacemakers usually find that apprentices find the time to go out and have fun with other people. It's the full Wizard-Lords who are starved of love and intimacy. Speaking of which, the process is helped if your curiosity is momentarily sated. I can force that instant of gratification to last for ten or fifteen minutes – Mother Bella is much more accomplished at that. She can also simulate romantic affection, which takes more practice and a subtler touch than I have yet."

She took a deep breath. "All right, I'm ready. Ask the most burning question uppermost in your mind. I'll answer and then you'll feel nothing at first except a lack of any follow-up questions, which may seem strange. Don't try to force yourself to find another question; just let go. Oh, I forgot, it also works better if you're already partly distracted by something else." She scrabbled at my robe, then her arms fell to her sides in resignation. "Your dress robe may be the most annoying thing I've ever had to deal with. Here, since it's as big as a tent I may as well use it like one."

Before I knew it, she was on the floor and then wriggling under the hem of my robe, sliding her way up my body. I wore nothing underneath – what would be the point? – so now I had a satin clad young lady grinding against me. To say I was mortified would be to understate the situation gravely. I was well beyond excited; I thought my heart was going to stop and my lungs explode with the effort of breathing normally. I felt her grab my bare chest and then she dragged herself the rest of the way, her head emerged from the neck of my robe and she rested her cheek against mine. "Much more comfortable, and I don't even have to be an empath to tell that you're extremely distracted now."

Oh, Idalia. If only I'd been older and wiser, or a tiny bit more considerate. If I'd been less *selfish*, less obsessed with her as a magical artifact and more interested in her as a living, thinking human being. No matter how well trained, she was still a person and had the same weaknesses and trials any of us must face. If only I'd asked the question which would have saved her, saved the Oligarchy if I'd asked it and somehow acted on that answer. I probably wouldn't have changed a thing, but maybe … maybe. The Peacemakers were a bulwark that held back the flood which had once made wizards like Aika, the soothing hand which had ensured a stable, wonderful peace rather than the dangerous and cold stalemate that Xetic-Nal had enforced before their foundation. The question I should have asked would have showed me the hole in that dam, the trickle of water that meant that sooner or later the flood would break through and engulf us all. I should have asked, "Who helps you?"

I'll give this to the magi, Idalia. You understand that a therapist needs their own person to talk to and work their problems out with. That it isn't a chain, but a ring of people who each help each other in turn until we circle back to the first, and that the larger that ring, the stabler the society it works with. The Peacemaker Lineage helped maintain their sanity in the face of eighty feuding, neurotic, needy wizards, but it didn't guarantee it.

Oh, sorry, things were getting steamy and I stopped the action right in the middle. Well, Anya was about to do the same anyway. What question did I ask? Anya's answer should reveal what was uppermost in my mind.

"Of course I want the Lineage! It's everything I was born and raised to become. When Mother Bella begins to get the Fade, she'll pass the Lineage to me, and I will become a *we*. The experience, knowledge, and *selves* of all the Peacemakers before me added to mine. Of course, this will kill Mother Bella, but that doesn't matter because she and all the others are contained in the Lineage. We'll be a single mind with a memory stretching back centuries. I'm not afraid at all. I won't be who I am now, but who is? I can hardly wait!"

I felt like I ought to have something else I wanted to know about that process, about what it was like to be a Peacemaker and how the Lineage worked. Just as I reached in that direction, began to try to scratch the itch of curiosity, Anya reached down and with a jolt I forgot everything except for the young, amorous woman in intimate contact with me. The last of my worries left me with her assurance, "Mother Bella always has plenty to report about," and all that remained was the tinkling laugh echoing in my mind and the building, transcendent pleasure as we fell to the rug and I made love for the first time. I'd brag about how much I impressed her, but that wouldn't be fair to Anya. It also wouldn't be true. Yes, I'd better not reminisce too much more about that, or else I might shock your modern sensibilities. I'll leave things with the comment that we had fun and I got better at it with practice, as most people do. Oh, what the hells! Yes, I know I'm a flaming egotist, Idalia, but I can't help but also mention that my enchanted physique might have surprised Anya a little, and that her surprise made me strut around for days.

From *Testimonies of Zunvect*, a manuscript of collected interviews and personal writings released in 8126 MR by Xetic-Nal, Chapter 3, Report 1 (Fragmentary Record of Initial Examination and Actions Taken with respect to [Name burned away, presumed from references to be Zunvect], recovered from the wreckage of Peacemaker Tower in Aristeum)

[introductory notes illegible or nonexistent, recovered portion begins] … life in isolated location under tutelage of non-vital personnel results in state usually seen in second century of life. Subject […] [rep]orts over a year since meaningful contact with … Daughter-Pe[acemaker] A[nya] … taken extreme action with respect to … in dire need of … no physical intimacy likely to result in … Recommend immediate relocation to Ydrasia and significant increase in lei[sure] … other living humans.

… lacking any contact with living human being in years.

Summary of actions taken: Sexual encounter required to perform emergency psycho-social fulfillment. Procedure stopgap measure, likely to relapse in no more than two …

… actions recommended: Increase in contact with humans of similar age (within same century of birth preferable), Ydrasia most preferable.

[Rest of record destroyed in demolition of Peacemaker Tower]

Idalia 10:

Lost Arts

"Well, that was a bit disgusting." Idalia said.

"What do you mean?" Zunvect asked. "I might have gotten carried away, but I was –"

"Yes, yes. You were a teenager, you're telling it from your evolving perspective. It's what you paid attention to." Idalia recited. "That argument is getting weak, Zunvect. You *were* nineteen. A bit more maturity, perhaps, and a little less bragging and describing every pretty female you meet?" Idalia stood and set aside her lap desk. "That wasn't what I was talking about, anyway. I meant what the Peacemakers did. Was it really their job to sleep with all eighty Wizard-Lords in rotation? Seems like you could have built automatons for that, and spared those poor women whatever mental and physical conditioning you used to make them do it."

"Of course it wasn't – oh my me!" Zunvect looked aghast. "Hold on a second!" His eyes unfocused, and the runes along the staff moved so quickly that they became vertical streaks. "Of all the – how did you – all right, this can't stand." Zunvect returned to himself. "I just had a flick through the minds of the Magi. I'd seen that you had fragmentary records, and so I thought you'd reconstructed what the Peacemakers were like."

"We have theories," Idalia said. "Most of the records–"

"Yes, they're in much worse shape than I'd surmised. You know about Anya *after* she became the Peace*breaker,* but worse than nothing about her and her ancestors." His mouth hung open as more information flowed through his connection to the Magi. "You … you … you filthy monsters! You made it sound like they were some kind of manipulative psychomantic cult! Oh, Idalia, they never used mental *or* emotional manipulation to subvert wizards into becoming their political allies. Sadly, it was almost the reverse of that. All right, I don't want to get bogged down, and you'd get the idea if I kept going to the next time I met the Peacemakers, but I need to make a few corrections now so that you don't wonder about it.

"First, Anya wasn't fully trained. She shouldn't have done what she did, but it was the only option open to her. If she'd had the full suite of skills and conditioning, she could have fixed me up just by talking to me. Instead, she used an emergency intervention that required my mind to be completely occupied by something, and the least harmful thing she knew how to do was use sexual release mixed with a psychomantic suggestion. Peacemakers weren't Wizard-Lord concubines, they were our *friends*."

Idalia sat down again to make notes. "She sure was friendly to you."

"An unfortunate early-stage outlier!" Zunvect insisted. "Oh, isn't it obvious? Think about it, Idalia. You've already noticed, I'm sure, that I was drifting away from my family and friends. It was organic, because I wasn't near them, but also part of a deep institutional bias. Wizard-Lords are lonely, Idalia. Lonely because they are constantly being told that they're different, that only another Wizard-Lord can really understand and appreciate them. Then they're told that all other Wizard-Lords are conniving crooks who want their secrets and would have killed them for their territory if Xetic-Nal hadn't been there. Maybe not quite that bad," Zunvect relented at Idalia's glance, "but there was a deep and repetitive strain of 'you are alone' in our work. The first book that we read is called *Us*. It states that we are responsible, no one else can help us, and then lists about a hundred ways to resolve our inevitable arguments.

"What does that leave us with? Eighty-odd men who are paranoid that all the others want to steal their valuable research or resources, and who feel so superior to non-wizards that they can't see them as equals. They're alone, friendless. Not all, of course. Some of us resisted that message in the end and made friends, either with non-wizards or fellows in the oligarchy. Most didn't. They were starved of friendship, love, companionship, things we need to stay sane. Once, these frustrations were taken out in the form of bloody and destructive war. Then the Peacemakers came. They would *talk* to us. Be our equals, our friends, and yes, the loves of our lives if we needed it. Most Wizard-Lords never took it that far. Not to be crass, but there were plenty of opportunities to find sexual release elsewhere, and most Wizard-Lords were suspicious even of the temporary love that they felt at the hands of a skilled Peacemaker, who could make them feel as if they'd had the passion and romance of a lifetime in a single afternoon."

"That still sounds horribly exploitative." Idalia said.

"Then you agree with me. I said much the same, and so did many. That's partly how I and a few of us ended up as friends. We wanted to prove that the need was over. That we could stop forcing young girls to be altered by specialized magic, forced to be everyone's friend. It took away some of their free will, you know. None of us would have let someone as accomplished in psychomancy anywhere near us without that. They *couldn't* hurt us, you see. It was programmed in. To that extent, I am relieved that your world is far more enlightened than ours. Use of those spells, and ones like them, are rightfully considered a capital crime. There's more, of course, but Aika explains some it better than I can, and the rest will be revealed as we go along."

Zunvect 21:

Departure

After the two Peacemakers departed, I went up to the library and sat down with what apparently was a very self-satisfied look on my face. "Looks like you had a very satisfactory session with Anya Peacemaker." Aika said. "I believe we were addressing imparting and removing motion from common aqueous solutions today. You've already learned how to manipulate the major salts, and since it's only about two percent by weight, this simulated sea water should be easy enough to move around. The trick is to get ahold of everything in the mixture at once, because if you just grab the water, the salt will mostly follow along but there are cases where it's best to be sure. Spells can be surprisingly adept at filtration when you're not careful, and this is good practice for when you're – for example – lifting a human being and you want to make sure they aren't suspended in the air by just their bones." Nothing in this was new. When I'd gone through moving solids, I'd had to practice the same things. It was interesting we were skipping to mixtures rather than staying with compounds; I hadn't even manipulated common liquids like vegetable oil or the liquid forms of metals I'd worked with like iron and copper. Something else was at the forefront of my mind, however.

"Thank you for not making a big deal out of it." I said.

"Aqueous solutions are a very – "

"I mean what happened with Anya."

"Oh, you mean the sexual intercourse part." She said. Aika shrugged. "Is it unusual? You had sex with a Peacekeeper; it's their job."

"Perhaps I'm still a dirt farmer at heart," I said, "but it seems wrong. If anyone else were born into a family that told her she'd have to have sex for the rest of her life as part of her job, we'd put them in jail."

"Anya could walk away." Aika said. "Not easily, true, but a Peacemaker has to want to be a Peacemaker or else they'd make a very poor one."

"Aika, she's been mentally conditioned. Is her consent valid?"

Aika floated silently in front of me, looking pensive. "You seem to have an aversion to psychomancy."

"It feels wrong. To alter someone's mind – even by choice – to become different. I … I don't know how to put it any way other than feeling like a mistake. I know there are good reasons for the Peacemakers. They serve a vital purpose – "

"I'm willing to go as far as to *wish* they'd been around when I ruled."

"Being necessary doesn't mean they're right. If the system needs someone to be altered with psychomancy and become intimate with all the other members in order to continue, then the system is fundamentally flawed and should be replaced."

Aika looked out into the distance. "The system is flawed and should be replaced. I remember when Matt said those words."

"He was wrong in some things but not others."

"As everyone is."

"Your defense of them is a bit faint," I said, realizing that she hadn't said a word to contradict me when I accused the Peacemakers of being no more than what you, Idalia, seemed to assume them to be just a few minutes ago. "Forgive me if I'm hearing something you didn't say, but everything you've argued is necessity, not humanity, and that … intimate relations are all that they do. They *are* people, even after the conditioning, and they do a little more than sleep around."

"Are they?" Aika asked in that challenging way she had when it was time for *her* style of thought experiment. I'll say this for Xetic-Nal: his discussions were challenging but rarely uncomfortable. Despite her protestations that she had no morals, she seemed to always be ready to challenge mine. "I guess I should be more charitable towards the Daughter. It would take longer, but you could probably brainwash someone using non-magical means to believe and act as she does, and her physical changes are not far out of the norm for Wizard-Lords who engage in those sorts of things. Bella, however, and all full Peacemakers, are another. In fact, it is more accurate to say *the* Peacemaker. There has only ever been one."

I thought about this, teasing out the meaning. "You're saying that the Lineage is an individual?"

"Yes, an individual *construct*. Like me, Zunvect. The living me could never have done my job. I am aware of the locations of every book and most of the other high value assets in this tower. I can quote at least a summary of each, and often the entire volume verbatim. I am immortal, possessed of memory and cognition beyond that of an unaugmented human, and I am bound to a single location until Lord Nal says otherwise. The Peacemaker – the Lineage – is bound to a family, has its own specialized knowledge and skill set, and has its loyalty to the oligarchy reinforced every time it passes. It is true that its new host influences it – if nothing else, it is vital that each host be imprinted with the baseline Peacemaker mental suite so that Lineage and Host are compatible."

"Anya acted like it was something that would complete her."

"It will. It will complete her change from a skilled, if inexperienced, therapeutic psychomancer into the single most accomplished practitioner of social stabilization there ever was or can be. The first Peacemaker was a genius in her own right, and centuries of experience has made her unparalleled in skill." Aika tapped her chin. "It's like this, Zunvect. The Lineage was once a person. A human being who made herself into something not quite human but still recognizably an individual with all the quirks and faults one might expect. Then she passed those memories, skills and proclivities on, and that person made improvements and did the same. Anya will be the ninth Peacemaker. When the Lineage passes to her, she will be about a hundred years old. She will, in an instant, become fifteen times older. All the previous Peacemakers' memories will be hers as if she'd lived them and experienced each event that the Lineage can recall. Can one individual be expected to survive having eight lifetimes of memories added to them? By the time the fourth Peacemaker took the Lineage, it was plain that the Lineage over-whelmed the Host. Anya will live on, her memories integrated into the Lineage. The Lineage was once like an ever-growing pitcher of water, difficult to drink but manageable with enough preparation. Now that pitcher has become a lake, making the Hosts part of *it* ra-ther than the other way around. So, no, I don't really see the Peacemakers as people. Their human part may still have some au-tonomy, but that decreases with each generation. I should count myself lucky. At least any growth I've made as a person has been entirely me. My immortality – my continuity of self – doesn't come at the cost of killing my own daughter's personality. Still, we're both circumscribed in our own ways, creations of the mind which can be influenced and modified if those who built us desire it. Back to the lesson."

I was relieved to get back to the less fraught topic of kinetic ma-nipulation. I thought about what Aika said, though, and decided that I wasn't convinced. Aika didn't act like she had no choice in what she did. She argued often enough with Xetic. The Peacemak-er, too, still had a choice, even if it was restricted in some actions like Aika was. While Aika couldn't leave the tower, she could still refuse to do something if she didn't feel it was right. The same went for the Peacemaker. It – she – wasn't allowed to harm or betray a Wizard-Lord, but she could still choose to stay in her tower rather than come out and socialize – or help us do the same. I think, Idalia, that there was a measure of jealousy to Aika's dismissal of the Lineage as an automaton that was becoming less of a person with each generation. After all, it was immortal like she was, it served a purpose as she did. Yet it could use magic, and she could not.

Despite my misgivings about the existence and provenance of the Peacemakers, I felt much better than I had before. Calmer, more open to what was around me. For the first time in what felt like weeks, I opened my window and looked outside, expecting to see the same crushing desolation. To my astonishment, that was only true for the meadow around the Tower. It was still as dead as ever, but the death ended in a stark, perfectly circular border. The forest, as far as I could see, had been replaced with saplings planted in mulch – probably the chopped up remains of the old trees. I was so amazed that I did something I'd never done before – I ran upstairs and knocked on Xetic-Nal's door.

There was no answer, so I knocked harder. I waited on the landing for a few minutes and then tentatively tried again. "If you're here to tell me how wonderful sex is," Xetic said from behind me, "I already know. I had more when I was alive than you ever will, back when I was a rugged stallion of a man with flowing locks and a –"

"The forest is back!" I said.

"Oh, so you're not here to trade salacious tales then." He said. "I was about to launch into a full account of my many centuries of sexual escapades back in the pioneering days of the early wizarding revolution. In that case, what's with the ruckus? I could hear you banging on my door from the laboratory on level nineteen."

"The forest is back." I repeated. "Someone's planted new trees."

"Have they? I wondered when the Board of Governors would take care of that. I do recall telling you that someone lived in there; you should listen more carefully." He turned and a hole in space opened. We stepped through and he surveyed the newly planted wood. "I'm sure I'll see the bill for this at the Conclave." He looked around, focusing on something distant. "I think you're responsible enough." He said. "Yes, you'll be able to handle it."

"What, sir?"

"Moving the Tower back to Ydrasia. Bella said I'd been away too long and she's right. I needed to make sure you wouldn't make a fool of yourself when confronted with a city, and you're halfway there. The move itself is an opportunity to fill in the other half." He turned to me. "I always did learn so much in my adventuring days, so here's a quest. Make your way from here to Ydrasia, and ring the Bell of Recall so I know you've made it."

"Through the forest, sir?"

"That will be the least important part." He said. "More important is that you see the world, or the hefty chunk that lies between here and the seat of global government. Strike south and make for the coast, then take a ship west until you're around the Horn. You should be able to catch a caravan, or another ship up the coast. I'd recommend the caravan since it will let you see more."

"It would go much easier if I could open holes in the air."

"I don't intend to give you that many weeks to practice." Xetic said. "Tunneling is far more dangerous than it looks. A branch of chronomancy, oddly enough, like teleportation and future sight.

The catch is that it can reach an arbitrary distance, and do you know what's that far away?"

"Nothing? The stars?"

"Both. Mostly nothing. No air, so you get sucked through. I think you may have read about those little accidents. I'm not going to teach you something that can result in having a whacking great stellar furnace blast you and the whole world to ashes. You're bad enough with pyromancy. Do some walking, and then you can get started on the truly dangerous material. You can learn Tunneling when you get to the Tower in Ydrasia. I'll give you time to finish up with kinetics, and that should be all the magic you'll need. Work quickly and you might be able to get started on illusion before I decide to kick you out."

"What about food? There's a lot of land to cross between here and the nearest human settlement."

"I'll make arrangements." Xetic said. "This wouldn't be much of a quest without a proper task, so have a discreet word with Wizard-Lord Neryk in the south before you take ship, and Mycontree when you arrive at the Horn. There's something fishy going on with those two and I want answers. Neryk's been avoiding reporting to me, and the rumor is that Mycontree ate his apprentice. I need to know more before I start throwing my weight around."

"*Ate* his –" I began.

"I'll give you the whole report on both before you go." He turned and there was another Tunnel behind us. "We've both got work to do. You leave in a month and a half. Should be enough to do all the major liquids and gasses. Aika will be annoyed that you won't be able to cover liquid tin or vaporized wood, but you can finish up when you get back. I strongly doubt you'll be coming across anything so exotic in a walking tour of southern Bomarie."

Aika was more than annoyed. "I sometimes wonder if the undead can have second childhoods because Lord Nal regresses to his swashbuckling days whenever he gets an apprentice." She grumbled. "There's no way in hells that I'm going to send you out with only kinetics and pyromancy, so we'll skip all the fun chemistry and cover basics on the other energy types. Starting with photomancy and then elemagnetics. Magnetics and kinetics have some very important overlaps, and it's vital that you learn..."

A month and a half went by in a blur. I was rushed through learning to move and concentrate all the common materials, as well as to how magnetism can work better than kinetics on certain materials. Despite her resolve, Aika didn't get a chance to even begin with electricity, and I had to promise that I'd read up on it while I was away. Making lightning did seem very tempting. I hadn't forgotten about the pyromancy incident, but I couldn't help but imagine the things I could do with that kind of power. Mainly blowing things up, which I could already do, I thought. Perhaps electricity wasn't very useful after all.

Photomancy was what Xetic-Nal called illusion, though Aika was always quick to point out that the 'I-word' was a truly ancient anachronism that Xetic insisted on using. It was somewhat inaccurate to call focusing, redirecting, and producing light illusion except in specialized cases which I sadly didn't learn. I always loved the magic puppet shows some people were so good at, but I was no artist. They were so full of wonder and delight; stories that made magic seem simple, just a wave of the hand and a quest for enchantments that would do exactly what you needed them to. I couldn't keep a crisp and consistent image in my head, which meant that making illusory things would have to be done in the painstakingly slow method of pure block manipulation, one feature or vector at a time. I never got a good feel for it, but I did enjoy the rest of photomancy immensely. It seemed so precise, so multifarious. I couldn't wait to get back to the tower after my trip to learn how to focus light like I had back when I was still an apprentice sorcerer. Big blasts were grand, but I could already see that being able to place a lot of power in a very small area would be much more useful overall.

It was a week before my journey was to start and I was getting nervous. I'd lie awake thinking about all the things I'd gotten used to in the tower. It was all well and good for Lord Xetic to extol the virtues of roughing it, and how travel was going to be more luxurious than when I'd been a dirt farmer. I was thinking about having to wipe my butt with a leaf for the first time in two and a half years. Sorry to get so lavatorial, Idalia, but I'd gotten accustomed to a standard of hygiene that would be impossible out in the wide world. Sleeping on the ground, drinking out of streams, walking through forests. It had all be fun when I was a boy and didn't know any better but even then, I'd never been far from home. I was about to strike out into a wilderness I had no experience with after a life of luxury and study. Then there was the question of provisions. What was I going to eat?

It's strange to look back and realize that some of my anxiety came from a source that I wasn't mature enough to be aware of at the time. I was afraid of how the journey would change me. I'd become comfortable as a student in Xetic's tower. There was something new every day, but it was the *same* new thing. Walking up and down the stairs, reading, experimenting in my lab, and talking to Aika. Occasionally a philosophical discussion with the governor or a field trip. I was content with who I was, and though I couldn't have articulated it at the time, I was afraid of becoming someone else. I'd return to the tower after my trip with a different perspective. I liked the one I had.

Aika had warned me that Xetic would ask me The Question again just before I left. He wanted to see if I answered differently after meeting some Wizard-Lords, whether the answer would change after my trip, and in what way. It was the first topic of my pre-departure meeting with him. "You've learned some magic, met some wizards. Does your design or plan change based on this? Better yet, do you believe now more than you did before that you would be a better agent of change than they are agents of the current government?"

"I do not consider myself the best person to implement or lead the new regime." I said. "My plan does change; it is obviously vital that the Peacemakers agree. With them on my side, the transition is much easier."

"The structure remains, though? You still believe that we can end expansion, form into governments with more than one wizard?" Xetic said, leaning forward.

Aika had warned me to stick to my ideals no matter what. "I do. We might need more wizards like the Peacemakers, but they hold us together. Help us work as one and settle our differences without violence. If one Peacemaker can keep eighty Wizard-Lords relatively harmonious, then increasing their numbers should help maintain a larger number of wizards working in a single polity."

Xetic sat back in his chair. "The distance that separates Wizard-Lords makes the Peacemaker's job easier. We all have our towers to retreat to, our polities to administer. Most of us have neighbors, but rarely more than three, and so there's a very limited amount of co-operation required. Increase our numbers and, even with more Peacemakers, you're going to see a significant increase in stress as the Wizard-Lords are forced into closer association."

"Perhaps, then, we should stop pretending that Wizard-Lords are cats, and instead think of ourselves as human beings with the mental capacity to act like mature adults." I said, growing heated at the implications of what he was saying. "I don't like the Peacemakers. I acknowledge that, right now, we appear to need them. At the risk of going off on a tangent about morality, I'm not convinced that necessity excuses the crime of willfully *designing people*. Call me biased, but I don't believe we would need them if there were more of us. Anya tells me that much of what preys on a Wizard-Lord's mind is isolation. Perhaps, instead of coddling our membership and letting them intentionally go without the company of their peers, they should be forced to socialize for their own good. Let that be the *last* mission of the Peacemakers. To convince the Wizard-Lords to increase their numbers and to help them learn to talk to each other, rather than endlessly competing and backstabbing."

Xetic paused. It was always difficult to read the subtler emotions from his lifeless body. I think he was impressed, but he might also have been surprised or confused. Something I'd said had hit home. Going by later events, I think I'd pointed something out that he'd not expected me to understand yet, and followed up by suggesting a course of action which he'd never considered. Yes, I think I might have provoked a tiny crisis of conscience. I'd momentarily left him with hope rather than resignation, and had I pushed harder, I might have changed his plans and made the world a much better place. Or driven humanity to extinction. That's the problem with idealistic plans; the successes are greater, but so are the failures. "Interesting reversal. Passing over several points I agree with, you suggest that you're not the best agent of change. I assume you mean that it would be better if – say – Bella led the transition with you as the architect but not the mover and shaker."

"She is the most qualified person to convince the Wizard-Lords to accept change."

"That's the point, she's an ambassador and councilor, not a leader or a politician. She may be a valuable ally, but she isn't a dynamic personality, a strong arm to guide the way. Still, you understand more than you did before." It was strange to me that he seemed far more interested in my role than in what I'd proposed to do.

He moved on to the next topic on our agenda. "Your trip may help your sense of perspective on this. Speaking of which, the two wizards I would like you to speak with are Mycontree and Neryk, in case your living brain has already forgotten their names. Mycontree's become corrupt. It's a common issue with older Wizard-Lords, and usually I turn a blind eye, but I've had reports that his gluttony is becoming severe. I doubt he ate an apprentice, but I can neither ignore the concerns being brought nor legitimize them by going there myself. Neryk is an even more worrying situation. He's always been a bit of a weasel, but I've gotten a report that he's *sold* the contents of NLAT. It would be laughable if I hadn't had confirmation from multiple sources. Find the truth and rectify both situations as needed. Here are the full reports."

He slid over a sheaf of papers, and then a sealed envelope that felt like it contained both the letter itself and a disc-shaped object. "I'm also sending you with a letter granting you pluripotent authority as a special investigator of the First Wizard. Don't use it unless there's no other way to get what you need, but don't hesitate to pull it out if you feel that there's a credible threat to your life from Mycontree or Neryk. If they get stroppy about the authenticity of the letter, show them the seal that came with it." His eyes sparkled. "It roots their tower, which means that you can remove their authority to command the tower's magic and grant it to yourself. Like I said, don't use it unless they try to get rid of you.

"Let's see, there's also the matter of provisions for when you're out and about. I've put together a pack which turned out to be far too bulky for you to carry without magical augmentation – which would take roughly a year to teach right. I shouldn't do this," he said confidentially, with that same merry glint, "but I expanded the internal dimensions of your traveling pack a little. Since the inside no longer occupies the physical frame of the outside one-to-one, you'll have no difficulty carrying everything. Do you know how to pitch a tent? I thought not; you probably just laid down under a tree or something. Not practical, so the tent will put itself up and break down with a keyword I wrote on this card.

He set out a chunky gold bracelet ringed with faceted gems. "It's also got all the commands and instructions for using this. I strongly suspect you won't need it, but please try a few of the tricks it can do. It's a bit of a prototype, so I wouldn't mind the real-world testing, and I'd be very interested to hear how it performs in a pinch."

I knew what that meant; don't rely on it. If I were threatened it *might* act on its own to help me, or it might just be a bracelet. The spells contained in the gems also might be particularly energetic if cast in a crisis, so I should stand well away if it started to glow, turn red-hot, or smoke.

"What else, what else? Money. I want you to make your own way, but a few coins in your pocket help get you started. You're used to roughing it, but just in case there's trouble, this cup can produce water or a nourishing bowl of boiled oats. If you want something that tastes better, you'll just have to find it yourself. Remember to pack your working clothes. I think that covers everything. South through the forest, then southwest through the dry parts until you hit the river Arrek. The city of Dariz is Neryk's capital in Andapar, and it's about a hundred kilometers upriver of the sea. You'll probably arrive by the same riverboat you'll leave in, and at the coast you'll find ships to everywhere else. Oh, and since we don't have the six months to be sure you'd use the deportation spell properly, try not to tangle with any Jinni or Genies while you're passing through the spatially unstable region."

I'd grown familiar with my teacher's love for the romantic past he came from. Wanting a little more information, I tried appealing to his sense of the classical. "Shouldn't you give me three pieces of sage advice before I go?" It was fifty-fifty whether he'd do it, and about ninety-ten that he'd tell a joke instead, but it couldn't hurt to try.

"Advice, yes!" Xetic enthused as if he'd thought of it. He settled down to think. "First," he said at length, "beware of cheap imitations." Another long pause. "Second, you may find in times of stress that emotions are leeching into otherwise normal UML spells. This is called Going Grammatic, and you are better off running away to recover your poise than trying to continue using magic. Bizarre and eldritch things can happen to a spell which has been infected with Gramayre." An even longer pause than the first two. "Third … third … I'm all out of sage advice. Let's see, maybe something practical. Never trust a man whose boots are too shiny when it rains, or a woman whose hair stays tidy in muggy weather. And if a man tips his hat to a horse, be sure to do the same. There, sage advice dispensed."

With that, I was dismissed to stuff as many robes as I felt I needed into a sack with two straps for my arms. Since they were so easy to wash, I didn't pack many; the concept of a desert wasn't one I had grasped yet. The bracelet weighed my right wrist down, but I decided I was best off getting used to it. I was resolved not to take it off until I was once again safe within the walls of Xetic-Nal's tower. The sack was – as promised – much larger inside, something which confused me at first. Not because it was unexpected, but because I couldn't quite make sense of how I was supposed to fish anything out without risking falling in. It was a bit like trying to shove my arm down a well. Of course, the answer was obvious: as Aika might have said, I'm a wizard. Cloth, metal, organics, just about everything felt different and had slightly different blocks so if I wanted something, I could just use kinetics. I was irrationally proud of thinking of it by myself. It felt like I was really starting to get used to being a wizard.

Saying goodbye to Aika took longer than I expected. She seemed to want to try to pack everything into a single conversation, dragging it out as if determined to keep me in the tower for as long as possible. She insisted I take books on electromancy, photomancy, spectromancy, and even the introductory text on fabrication and reorganization of matter. She was insistent that I continue my studies at as fast as pace as I could *safely* manage. "Don't try anything unwise," she cautioned me when she gave me the last book. "I *really shouldn't* give you this unsupervised, so don't let me down. When they tell you not to cast the spells written on the red pages, they really mean it."

With the ominous clue that I was to learn even more dangerous magic than I had so far, Aika at last let me go. It seemed so sudden to find myself standing on the bare earth in front of the tower, the sun above me and the trees in front. With the tower at my back, I made for the treeline and the gloom beneath the canopy. I felt light and a little dizzy, and not just because the saplings had changed to old growth in a matter of weeks. I was free to go where I pleased and do what I liked, as long as I made two stops and then ended up in Ydrasia. I'd packed the Letterbox. Maybe I'd visit my dad and the village. It was hundreds of kilometers out of the way, but Xetic hadn't told me I *couldn't* go. With that sense of freedom buoying me, I began the long hike through the wood. It would be months before I reached human habitation again, but solitude didn't bother me. With one last breath of the open air, I plunged into the forest and adventure.

Excerpt from *Faith in our Founder*, the definitive collection of the myths and legends of Zunvect the Sunlord, 60th ed, revised 7943 MR

Zunvect's First Adventure, the story of Zunvect's supposed first journey. Predominantly sourced from the *Sunlord's Canon* by Lorn Malthaum, this story is also influenced by local legends. Every community that could have possibly been in Zunvect's path according to the *Canon* appears to have its own story, though many are almost certainly apocryphal.

Excerpt of relevant passages:

And so many years passed and Zunvect grew into his manhood. Many dark and terrible secrets did he learn, and many hints at secrets far darker that awaited. Lord Xetic-Nal beheld Zunvect, and declared this part of his learning complete. "You must be tested," he said to Zunvect, "before you are worthy to delve into that which no man knows but I." Seven Tasks he gave to Zunvect, and seven Boons to aid him in this quest. So Zunvect was sent into the world with only the Boons, his magic, and the grand destiny that no man, not even Xetic-Nal, could gainsay.

The sun shone bright upon him as he began this great quest, for its lord walked the green hills and shaded forests again. Bright as the Sunlord's heart, for what Task could hinder his might? Bright were the words he bore upon his tongue, and bright were the days that were to come for all whom his path would cross.

Epilogue:

Excerpt from *Testimonies of Zunvect*, a manuscript of collected interviews and personal writings released in 8126 MR by Xetic-Nal, Chapter 2, Report 12: Notes on Beginning of First Walkabout of Apprentice [Name Redacted, assumed from description to be Zunvect's birth name]

Aika's been giving me the business about sending Zunvect into the forest alone. While it is true that the Board of Governors are number six in my list of eight greatest fears, she's overreacting as usual. The Board do not care at all about individual humans, especially ones that are no threat to the forest. Zunvect will have a lovely stroll through some beautiful landscapes and emerge on the other side of their land totally unaware that the Board of Governors is even there. Since she won't stop making a big deal out of how I should have teleported Zunvect to the opposite side, I'm logging her protest and including the transcript of my personal diary for the relevant period.

Log begins

5/24/2940: Entering forest to explore weird feeling I get that something I ought to know about is living there.

5/25: Approximately two hundred k inside. Feeling is stronger. There's thaumaturgic activity, but nothing I can clearly make out. Suspect visual hallucinations part of effect because I've begun seeing fairies. Sources indicate no such thing, so likely either illusion or previously undiscovered psychomantic effect.

6/1: Also seeing gnomes, small fire lizards, dryads, and the silhouette of a manticore. Something here likes ancient folk tales.

6/2-6/18: EXPUNGED

6/19: What what what what what!!!!!????? I didn't remove those days. Not from the log and certainly not from my *hellblasted bloody fireandbrimstone memory!* All right, calm down Xetic and stick to the facts. The facts…

1. My last clear memory is the night of the 1st of seeing green lights among the trees
a. Inference: I walked towards them to investigate and that caused whatever just happened
2. I just woke up (ie. I lost consciousness, which is a severely bad sign) in my own study
a. Inference: Whatever sent me here could do one or more of the following
i. Knock me out
ii. Remove memories
iii. Teleport me into my tower *through the wards* without disturbing any of them
iv. Leave absolutely no trace of same
b. Inference: Not the work of any known entity or aggregation other than the Uidrana, who are unlikely to be hiding out in a forest
3. Memory surfacing – name – Board of Governors. Impression – desire that I not return and that I pay a penalty for trespassing.
Interesting. I just found a note on my desk stating that if I require any further negotiation with them, that I can present my case to an interspecies conclave and they'll find out and reply. Not that they attend, just that they are aware. Whoever this Board of Governors is, I think I'll do as they ask. If

they're not going anywhere, it doesn't hurt much to cordon off the forest and leave them to it.

Log Ends

Now that I look at it, why on Ry-Kel *did* I just send my apprentice, and a viable Plan B candidate, into the den of a terrifying and mysterious hermit organization that hates trespassers? Inference: I was to make restitution for trespassing, and they made sure I would do so. Inference: They have very long sight. The Chronoculum didn't see Zunvect until less than fifty years ago, and only as a smudge on the canvas of time. Player two identified, and well played indeed. I've revised my estimate on that. I think there are at least five players here.

Identified:

Me – Obviously

The Board of Governors – I can see no other reason I would be so blasé about sending Zunvect in. I wonder if they planted any other suggestions in my mind. I may need to do some deep diving to see if I can find out. Appointment to be made with the Peacemaker to help.

Unsure:

Alok'derosh – So much for being deader than dead. Too many coincidences. It used to be a god of some type of horrible thing, but I forget the particulars. I'll need to look it up and find out what it's most likely to do.

Aika – She's been giving Zunvect some dodgy advice, but I'm flummoxed if I can work out what she's trying to accomplish.

Totally unknown – I sense another hand, someone pushing him in a direction totally at odds with the rest of us (except maybe ol' shadowfingers). Whoever it is knows my methods and is to some extent mimicking them. Is there another Chronoculum on Ry-Kel? Are the koan heads actually *doing* something? Extremely unlikely. Urgent note to self: Check the diary shelf before we make the shift over to Ydrasia. Matt may be stirring. Another urgent note: Remember to warn Zunvect when he gets back that if he uses magic to kill, be sure he finishes them off right then and there. Leaving an enemy to die of magic out of sight is a mistake I've made too often.

Companion:

A. Characters:
    a. Major
        i.   Zunvect Stetza – As of the modern era (8000 years after main narrative) the god of magi, real name unrecorded, noted for ending the period of rule by wizard-lord and the inspiration of Lorn the First to found the University system. Colors: Black and luminous white. Birthday: Spring festival of hometown.
            1. Starts out blue on first magical scale
            2. Reaches green on second by first journey (average wizard's output)
            3. Should end at least on yellow of fourth, perhaps somewhere in fifth scale
        ii.   Idalia Periscalitin – Demonologist who captured Zunvect and released the gods from the long sleep. Currently in exile offworld while the world governments debate the issue.
        iii.   Xetic-Nal – Formerly the First Wizard, having built and maintained the towers and system in which wizard-lords ruled. Noted for being the first human chronomancer and necromantically immortal. Dedicated to research and apparently motivated politically by a desire to improve humanity. Developed

UML and attempted to eradicate Gramayre.
Colors: Black and dark red

      1. Member of the Society for the Promotion of Rational Magic in the old days.

      2. Founded the League of Scientific Sorcerers

  iv. Aika Chimamire no Kata – Permanent librarian to Xetic-Nal, once his student, noted tyrant and genocide, nickname: Bloody Shoulders. Colors: Seafoam and black

  v. Silveria Chronomarien – Highly influential politician in Idalia's time. Archmage Huywer university, President of the Unity Senate, Lord of the Sun in the Solar Conclave. A Node, and the most politically powerful human being in four thousand years.

  vi. Anya Peacemaker – Final Peacemaker. Colors: Blue and white

  vii. Vektar – Noted colleague of Zunvect Stetza. Colors: Orange and black

  viii. Larirem – Noted Colleague of Zunvect Stetza Colors: Purple and Gray

  ix. Lorn Maltham – Self-proclaimed Acolyte of Zunvect

  x. Ivan Solinsky – A veterinary sorcerer, first teacher of Zunvect.

b. Minor

  i. Bella Peacemaker – Mother of Anya, last true Peacemaker. Referred to by her title as 'Mother' by Anya, denoting both her status as elder to Anya's 'Daughter' and the literal familiar tie.

ii.   Matthew D'Angkou aka Black Matthew – Former student of Xetic-Nal, eighth lord of Angkoura. Attempted to overthrow wizard-lord rule using necromantic army.

iii.   Neryk – Last administrator of NLAT, Lord of Andapar in the city of Dariz on the river Arrek.

iv.   Darrin Jones – Last administrator of G2UML-N

v.   Boris and Mikel Stetza – Respectively the father and brother of Zunvect

vi.   Vectreon – Deceased wizard-lord of Zunvect's territory.

vii.   Lady Xenos – Wizard-lord Ambassador to the Intendant Races, a rare case of lateral promotion as she was originally Wizard-Lord Terina, Lord of a territory in the Crescent.

viii. Golaran - Senator from Sularat, and leader of the opposition in the Senate

B. Glossary

a. Wizardry – Method of using magic using understanding of natural law and block manipulation.

b. Sorcery – Similar to wizardry, can only draw from internal stores of magic and highly limited by doing so. Sorcerers can hear music, wizards cannot. Sorcerers can use music to combine spells with one another.

c. Gramayre – Old form of magic, uses desire and intent rather than express understanding. Banned by Xetic-Nal

d. UML – Block manipulation language. Developed by Xetic-Nal and based on stolen Uidrana manuscripts (Uidrana Magical Logic)

e. Intendant Races – Elves, dwarves, dragons, aqueous. One for each place in the world; ruled the world as regents of Uidrana.

f. Uidrana – Ancient race, origins unknown. Disappeared during lifetime of Xetic-Nal. Believed capable of any and all magic which are mentioned or conceived by magicians of any period. Appeared as four-meter-high humanoids made of mist with spherical, featureless heads which glowed. Spoke as one entity and numbers unknown.

g. Teleportoire – Wizard-lord room to teleport into inside tower to prevent accidents and provide location to make final preparations for entering territory.

h. Territory – Land politically claimed by a wizard-lord. In practice, only areas near settlements of humanity and their roads are considered safe and truly claimed. Thus many territories are large on maps, but the wizard-lords who own them gratefully allow their territories to be split when another wizard-lord needs one since they never really ruled much of it anyway. There are eighty-six wizard-lord territories, three ruled by Xetic. Some are small, like Ydrasia which is a single city-state ruled by Xetic and others are impractically enormous, like those further west in Bomarie where there are few humans. The practice of claiming a political boundary that encompasses other species' land, leaving them alone for centuries, and then settling there claiming they've owned that land unchallenged for the intervening centuries is a major source of friction especially with elves and dragons.

i. Thaumic vs Thaumaturgical – Thaumic refers to phenomena related to magic, thaumaturgical refers to use of magic

j. Thaumine – Magical mineral that increases power of those who hold it

k. Obdurin – Extremely strong insulating metal

l. Ductin – Room temperature superconductor

m. Fade, the – Common name for thaumic saturation syndrome, in which a wizard's body is slowly replaced with magic until they are unable to remain stable and evaporate.

n. Demolition – When Zunvect destroyed the wizard-lords

o. Rebuilding – When Lorn founded the magi

p. Foundation – A tower provided with a Marque of Waiver to be the single point of study for spellcraft deemed too dangerous to be practiced by wizards generally.

C. Selected arcana

a. LetterBox – A small container which teleports objects placed inside to a corresponding container.

b. MAP – Magical Activity Perceptor. Means by which wizard-lords surveil Ry-Kel for unfamiliar, unexpected, or strategically interested thaumic emissions.

c. Anecho – The tailored Lineage Link which all Nodes experience.

D. Species of Ry-Kel

a. Confirmed

i. Humans

1. Magical capabilities highly variable, as of Zunvect's time they claim political control of most of the world, but effectively only have about

5% of the land area, mostly around the west and south coasts of Bomarie

  2. Sub-race in the era of the Magi: Node – The "children" of Zunvect, created by magic, and possessed of stupendous power. They pay for this with short lifespans and very low numbers.

ii. Elves

  1. Magical capabilities presumed great, but difficult to accurately estimate because they try never to use magic when other species might see. Confirmed to have complete control of the Bowl, conjectured to inhabit several other locations across Ismun and Bomarie

  2. Tribes/nations: Known Bowl civilization usually speaks for all Elves, but theorized that elves further afield often disagree. External elves are isolationist and have chosen to allow Bowl Elves to act as ambassadors rather than being forced to reveal themselves.

iii. Dwarves

  1. No magical capabilities, but also highly resistant. Effectively control all stable subterranean space. Mouths usually sealed in front of outsiders, forcing them to communicate exclusively in gestures and written word.

iv. Dragons

1.   Magical capabilities great, possibly greatest of all living races on Ry-Kel. Confirmed ownership of most of northern Ismun, with mixed ownership zones along central Ismun shared with Dwarf and Human polities. Believed to have significant numbers in upper altitudes of Bomarie with confirmed sightings in altitudes as low as the desert of Sul.

2.   Sub Races: Wizard-lords believe that the scale color and consistency denote either different subspecies, ethnicities, or social rank. Dragons don't divulge significance.

v.   Aqueous

1.   No longer active in any wizard-lord controlled area. Conjectured extinct in Zunvect's time.

vi.   Uidrana

1.   Magical capability orders of magnitude greater than any other species on Ry-Kel. Once controlled effectively 100% of planet. Arrived with minimal – but very official – warning and left on unknown mission and never returned.

vii. Unicorns

1.   Rarely seen. Would be considered mythical if not for reliable corroboration from Uidranic sources. Absolutely immortal, of unknown capability. Isolationist to degree that no

unicorn has allowed itself to be seen in the entire history of the Nal Oligarchy
  b. Apocryphal
    i. Forest Dragons – Believed relative of draconic race. Wingless, serpentine, spends most of its life levitating in purely magical flight. No confirmed sightings.
    ii. Variant humanoids – Comprise several nature, avocation, and morphologically organized races including gnomes, fairies, nixies, pixies, dryads, nyads, etc.
E. Geography
  a. Population – 760 million humans in the polities of the wizard-lords, all other figures unknown
    i. 2.5% can be wizards, so 19 million as of this point
      1. As of the modern era, there are 200 million Magi Firsts (wizard-equivalent) and almost 1 billion Seconds (sorcerer-equivalent) with some degree of training to confer on them the rank
  b. Landmasses and landmarks
    i. Ismun – Western continent, shaped a bit like a dumbbell oriented north-south with plains on the northern bell, a high tableland on the southern, very high mountains along the middle separating approximately equally land to either side. Home to nineteen territories.
      1. Sky Vision – Southern tableland dotted with caves inhabited by prophetic hermits who spend their lives looking into the future for mon-

ey. Sky Vision is the name of the polity – a council which rules on matters of commerce mainly – Skyland is the common name for the area, Plateau of Endless Sky is the proper name.

    2. Singing City – Home of the Symphonics, outcast sorcerers who combine their magic with music-based harmonization

ii.   Bomarie – Eastern continent, much larger east-west but about the same distance north-south as Ismun. Almost all older civilizations originated on Bomarie and in the furthest east (which is seen as almost west on maps) lies the Bowl. The western coast is an inward bowing arc called the Crescent enclosing a shallow bay-sea which opens up into the straits between Ismun and Bomarie. North of the Crescent is the Hook, a protrusion of land which arcs west and eventually back south. The center is tropical, with the southern coast being mostly arid and the northern along with the hook being rocky and cold.

    1. Crescent – Forty-three territories including one owned by Xetic

    2. The Crooklands – Nine territories, one by Xetic (modern name Huywer)

    3. Anchorage Horn – Southern end of Crescent

    4. South Coast – Six territories

    5. Elsewhere – Xenos and Xetic. Xenos is on the northeastern edge in

the foothills of the Bowl and Xetic's eastern tower is approximately 3000 km inland from the furthest inward bow of the Crescent, well outside of human occupied lands.

      6.   Internal – Temperate as far as Xetic's tower eastward. South of Xetic's tower is the Desert of Sul, and north is a rainforest. The rainforest spreads south and east so that traveling east of the tower one can also reach it, and it becomes a jungle further northeast of that. There are plains and a veldt southeast of the edge of the rainforest, and becomes temperate again near the Bowl.

   iii.   Islands – Archipelagoes to the north and south of the major continents, though the southern set are much larger. Central islands all ruled by Zile. Four additional territories amongst the southern islands and two in the north make seven.

   iv.   The Bowl – Only landmass never to be occupied or explored by humans. A ring of mountains surrounding totally unknown lands on the eastern edge of Bomarie. Held closely by elves.

  c.   Planet has several cordillera radiating from Bowl and one perpendicular along center of Ismun

  d.   Bodies of water

   i.   Halfin sea – A shallow, semicircular sea which separates the Crescent from Ismun. Warm throughout the year and uninteresting to the Aqueous, who prefer deeper oceans.

  ii. Droa Ocean – Ocean spanning entire northern latitudes of Ry-Kel

e. Named Territories

  i. Angkoura – Occupying the land at the base of the Crooklands and including lands on the Crescent, home of the last sanctioned Necromancer

  ii. Zile – Largest of an archipelago of islands in the southern ocean, south of both Ismun and Bomarie. Zile itself is south of Bomarie, while smaller islands extend to the east and west. Founded by Aika, now ruled by Katzuvect

  iii. Ydrasia – De facto capital of human civilization, the only populated territory/city ruled by Xetic-Nal

  iv. Andapar – Ruled by Neryk, south coast of Bomarie

  v. Aristeum – Peacemaker, Central Crescent

f. The Capitol Church Cities – "Halidoms"

  i. Mors Media – Drotaka, just south of the Horn

  ii. Panaceplis – Huruum, Crescent Bay north of Ydrasia

  iii. Multecopia – Nenya and Valya, Near Anchorage Horn

  iv. Indican – Garliem, Crescent Bay south of Ydrasia

  v. Unknown – Hylentor, Undisclosed

g. Modern geography

  i. Thirteen territories

1. Huywer – Modern Crook-
lands, represented by Senator Silveria
Chronomarien
2. Sularat – Encompassing much
of the southeastern coast of Bomarie –
represented by Golaran, a hard liner
and ranking member
3. The old Crescent (Including
Horn) – represented by Ezippio
Latore, aligned mostly with whoever
seems strongest and always worried
4. Southwestern Bomarie
5. Center Bomarie
6. Northwestern B
7. Northeastern B
8. Bowl (also representing interests of dragons, elves, and other non-
human sapience in the Senate)
9. Center Ismun - Centrism
10. Symphonic Collective (the only
Mage Second in the Senate)
11. Sky Flat
12. Glacier
13. South Islands - Southarch
14. North Islands – Meldich

ii.   Independent Autonomous Zones
1. Katzunvect – Also known as
The Nodehome, a small island in the
Halfin Sea.
a. The Curia – The building which houses the Solar
Conclave
b. The Solar Conclave –
The governing body of the

Nodes. Acts as a check on the power of the Magi.

2. Unified Human Cause capitol building – An orbital bubble which houses the gateways to the Senate and Parliament, respectively the upper and lower houses of the world government. "Unity" as it is known for short is the coalition government of all races on the planet, though the human Magi have ultimate power over most things in the Senate, and humans are the vast majority in Parliament.

F.   Divinities - Active

a.   Hylentor – Not believed local, more powerful than others, extremely unpredictable. Encompasses cosmic entropy, tricksterism, fortune, slapstick comedy. Can incarnate as almost anything and is believed to often do so. Adherents are insane and capable of any act or magic imaginable.

b.   Drotaka – Death god, female, usually somber. Known to grant her adherents long life and knowledge of the moments of people's deaths

i.   Ranks

1.   Capitalis – Leader of the church

a.   Merendi Kinarl

2.   Ianor – Stand between the worlds of the living and dead. High ranking guides, communicators, and channelers.

a.   Gierna

ii.   Demigods

1. Saint Munstable – Former mortal servant, died while destroying a key temple of one of gods that made use of undead
        iii.   Status as of Idalia's time – Male, named Drotank
c. Nenya– Growth and agriculture, female, twin of Valya. Usually cheerful, merry, but also wrathful side when crops won't grow. Adherents capable of creation and destruction.
        i.   Demigods – Plethoral
        ii.   Status as of Idalia's time – Merged with Valya, lost most of combined portfolio to other deities. Now a goddess of erotica named Nenyala.
d. Valya – Rebirth and reproduction, female, twin of Nenya. Almost always in a good mood. Grants her adherents supernatural skill and endurance, often used to teach or enlighten in some way.
        i.   Demigods – Nature spirits and some agriculturally related lesser deities
e. Huruum – Healing, nature, life in general, male. More carefree than might be thought at first. Adherents can heal mortal wounds, and in one very special case bring back the dead. Incarnates as a bald monk in a simple green habit.
        i.   Demigods – None
        ii.   Status as of Idalia's time – Broadly unchanged, lost sun component and is more focused on healing than all life
f. Garliem – Knowledge, learning, information, male. Has a permanent headache and a burning need to impart what he knows, which is everything all at once.

    i. Demigods – Hundreds of spirits, heroes, and lesser gods helping with the filing and paperwork

      1. Known demigods – Goddess of stationary, who keeps paperweights from moving and inkwells full

    ii. Status as of Idalia's time – Female named Garlimé

G. Divinities – Inactive

  a. Alok'derosh – The most intelligent and far-seeing. God of several things including assassins, particularly those who killed magicians.

  b. Nalagash

    i. May still have small cult following, unable to act in real world, gifted Alok with farsight.

  c. Zoroktelitan

    i. May still have small cult following, unable to act in real world, gifted Alok with necromancy.

  d. Uberiub

    i. May still have small cult following, unable to act in real world, gifted Alok with greater creativity.

H. Divinities – New

  a. Zunvect

    i. Demigods – Lorn, Idalia

    ii. Technically god of Nodes

  b. Wizard-lord Etiquette; Wizard-lords have a complex system of rules for interaction in various circumstances. Examples include:

    i. No wizard-lord visits another's territory without first sending word. Apprentices are given leeway since they do not always have the resources to do so, however the bare minimum of presenting themselves at the earliest possible moment is still required.

ii.   A wizard-lord teleporting into another's tower is to be given at least 5 minutes to ready themselves before being met. Xetic-Nal ignores this. The social inferior – usually the visitor – speaks first, unless the host has invited them to come for a specific reason.

iii.   Apprentices are an extension of a wizard-lord, and their actions can be accounted those of their masters.

iv.   If a visiting wizard-lord is harmed, their host is liable, and if they die, the host may be charged with their murder regardless of the cause. Guests may never be assaulted or assassinated.

68271833R00231

Made in the USA
Middletown, DE
15 September 2019